Praise for *Something Blue*

"Giffin's writing is warm and engaging; readers will find themselves cheering for Darcy as she proves people can change in this captivating tale." —*Booklist* (starred review)

"Witty and compelling, *Something Blue* reaffirms a lesson we all should have learned long ago: Love doesn't need a fairy tale, fancy wrapping or a big price tag. Often, it's better without." —*Charlotte Observer*

"Giffin's plotting and prose are so engaging that she quickly becomes a fun, friendly presence in your reading life." —*Chicago Sun Times*

"Highly entertaining . . . Despite a happy ending, Giffin raises thorny questions. A long friendship can (like marriage) turn claustrophobic or abusive. Is infidelity the solution? And why are pretty girls so easily taken in by scheming Plain Janes?" —*Boston Globe*

"Darcy is Scarlett O'Hara set in modern [day] . . . Giffin orchestrates her gradual change ingeniously and successfully answers any *Gone With the Wind* fan who wondered if, after Rhett Butler decided he didn't give a damn, Scarlett ever morphed into someone softer." —*Newark Star-Ledger*

"Smartly written. The dialogue is real with lightly rendered lessons about what really matters in life . . . Emily Giffin knows what she's doing." —*Winston-Salem Journal*

also by emily giffin

Something Borrowed
Baby Proof
Love the One You're With
Heart of the Matter

something blue

emily giffin

St. Martin's Paperbacks

This is a work of fiction. All of the characters, organizations, and events portrayed in this novel are either products of the author's imagination or are used fictitiously.

SOMETHING BLUE

Copyright © 2005 by Emily Giffin.
Excerpt from *Something Borrowed* copyright © 2004 by Emily Giffin.
Excerpt from *Baby Proof* copyright © 2006 by Emily Giffin.
Excerpt from *Love the One You're With* copyright © 2008 by Emily Giffin.

For information address St. Martin's Press, 175 Fifth Avenue, New York, NY 10010.

EAN: 978-0-312-54807-0

Printed in the United States of America

St. Martin's Press hardcover edition / June 2005
Griffin trade paperback edition / May 2006
St. Martin's Paperbacks edition / May 2011

St. Martin's Paperbacks are published by St. Martin's Press, 175 Fifth Avenue, New York, NY 10010.

10 9 8 7 6 5 4 3

For Buddy, always.

And for Edward and George.

acknowledgments

I would like to thank my family and friends for their love and support, especially my parents, who were a great source of strength to me over the past year. Thanks to my agent, Stephany Evans; my editor, Jennifer Enderlin; and my publicist, Stephen Lee, for being so professional, enthusiastic, and kind. Deep gratitude to my loyal triumvirate, Mary Ann Elgin, Sarah Giffin, and Nancy LeCroy Mohler, who read every draft of this book and offered so much valuable insight; thanks for always being there, in big ways and small. Thanks also to Doug Elgin and Brian Spainhour for joining the party late and offering their quality male perspective. To Allyson Wenig Jacoutot for being the best of confidantes. To Jennifer New for her enduring friendship. And to all the readers of *Something Borrowed*, who came to my signings, invited me to their book clubs, or took the time to share their very generous comments. Finally, my biggest and most heartfelt thanks go to my husband, Buddy Blaha, and our twin sons, Edward and George. I love being on your team.

prologue

I was born beautiful. A C-section baby, I started life out right by avoiding the misshapen head and battle scars that come with being forced through a birth canal. Instead, I emerged with a dainty nose, bow-shaped lips, and distinctive eyebrows. I had just the right amount of fuzz covering my crown in exactly the right places, promising a fine crop of hair and an exceptional hairline.

Sure enough, my hair grew in thick and silky, the color of coffee beans. Every morning I would sit cooperatively while my mother wrapped my hair around fat, hot rollers or twisted it into intricate braids. When I went to nursery school, the other little girls—many with unsightly bowl cuts—clamored to put their mat near mine during naptime, their fingers darting over to touch my ponytail. They happily shared their Play-Doh or surrendered their turn on the slide. Anything to be my friend. It was then I discovered that there is a pecking order in life, and appearances play a role in that hierarchy. In other words, I understood at the tender age of three that with beauty come perks and power.

This lesson was only reinforced as I grew older and continued my reign as the prettiest girl in increasingly larger pools of competition. The cream of the crop in junior high and then high school. But unlike the characters in my favorite John Hughes films, my popularity and beauty never made me mean. I ruled as a benevolent dictator, playing watchdog over other popular girls who tried to abuse their power. I defied cliques, remaining true to my brainy best friend, Rachel. I was popular enough to make my own rules.

Of course, I had my moments of uncertainty. I remember one such occasion in the sixth grade when Rachel and I were playing "psychiatrist," one of our favorite games. I'd usually play the role of patient, saying things like, "I am so scared of spiders, Doctor, that I can't leave my house all summer long."

"Well," Rachel would respond, pushing her glasses up on the bridge of her nose and scribbling notes on a tablet. "I recommend that you watch *Charlotte's Web*. . . . Or move to Siberia, where there are no spiders. And take these." She'd hand me two Flintstones vitamins and nod encouragingly.

That was the way it usually went. But on this particular afternoon, Rachel suggested that instead of being a pretend patient, I should be myself, come up with a problem of my own. So I thought of how my little brother, Jeremy, hogged the dinner conversation every night, spouting off original knock-knock jokes and obscure animal kingdom facts. I confided that my parents seemed to favor Jeremy—or at least they listened to him more than they listened to me.

Rachel cleared her throat, thought for a second, and then shared some theory about how little boys are encouraged to be smart and funny while little girls are praised for being cute. She called this a "dangerous trap" for girls and said it can lead to "empty women."

"Where'd you hear *that*?" I asked her, wondering exactly what she meant by *empty.*

"Nowhere. It's just what I think," Rachel said, proving that she was in no danger of falling into the pretty-little-girl trap. In fact, her theory applied perfectly to us. I was the beautiful one with average grades, Rachel was the smart one with average looks. I suddenly felt a surge of envy, wishing that I, too, were full of big ideas and important words.

But I quickly assessed the haphazard waves in Rachel's mousy brown hair and reassured myself that I had been dealt a good hand. I couldn't find countries like Pakistan or Peru on a map or convert fractions into percentages, but my beauty was going to catapult me into a world of Jaguars and big houses and dinners with three forks to the left of my bone-china plate. All I had to do was marry well, as my mother had. She was no genius and hadn't finished more than three semesters at a community college, but her pretty face, petite frame, and impeccable taste had won over my smart father, a dentist, and now she lived the good life. I thought her life was an excellent blueprint for my own.

So I cruised through my teenage years and entered Indiana University with a "just get by" mentality. I pledged the best sorority, dated the hottest guys, and was featured in the Hoosier Dream Girls calendar four years straight. After graduating with a 2.9, I followed Rachel, who was still my best friend, to New York City, where she was attending law school. While she slogged it out in the library and then went to work for a big firm, I continued my pursuit of glamour and good times, quickly learning that the finer things were even finer in Manhattan. I discovered the city's hippest clubs, best restaurants, and most eligible men. And I still had the best hair in town.

Throughout our twenties, as Rachel and I continued

along our different paths, she would often pose the judgmental question, "Aren't you worried about karma?" (Incidentally, she first mentioned karma in junior high after I had cheated on a math test. I remember trying to decipher the word's meaning using the song "Karma Chameleon," which, of course, didn't work.) Later, I understood her point: that hard work, honesty, and integrity always paid off in the end, while skating by on your looks was somehow an offense. And like that day playing psychiatrist, I occasionally worried that she was right.

But I told myself that I didn't have to be a nose-to-the-grindstone soup-kitchen volunteer to have good karma. I might not have followed a traditional route to success, but I had *earned* my glamorous PR job, my fabulous crowd of friends, and my amazing fiancé, Dex Thaler. I *deserved* my apartment with a terrace on Central Park West and the substantial, colorless diamond on my left hand.

That was back in the days when I thought I had it *all* figured out. I just didn't understand why people, particularly Rachel, insisted on making things so much more difficult than they had to be. She may have followed all the rules, but there she was, single and thirty, pulling all-nighters at a law firm she despised. Meanwhile, I was the happy one, just as I had been throughout our whole childhood. I remember trying to coach her, telling her to inject a little fun into her glum, disciplined life. I would say things like, "For starters, you should give your bland shoes to Goodwill and buy a few pairs of Blahniks. You'll feel better, for sure."

I know now how shallow that sounds. I realize that I made everything about appearances. But at the time, I honestly didn't think I was hurting anyone, not even myself. I didn't think much at all, in fact. Yes, I was gorgeous and lucky in love, but I truly believed that I was also a decent person who deserved her good fortune. And

I saw no reason why the rest of my life should be any less charmed than my first three decades.

Then, something happened that made me question everything I thought I knew about the world: Rachel, my plain, do-gooding maid of honor with frizzy hair the color of wheat germ, swooped in and stole my fiancé.

one

Sucker punch.

It was one of my little brother Jeremy's pet expressions when we were kids. He used it when regaling the scuffles that would break out at the bus stop or in the halls of our junior high, his voice high and excited, his lips shiny with spittle: *WHAM! POW! Total sucker punch, man!* He'd then eagerly sock one fist into his other cupped palm, exceedingly pleased with himself. But that was years ago. Jeremy was a dentist now, in practice with my father, and I'm sure he hadn't witnessed, received, or rehashed a sucker punch in over a decade.

I hadn't thought of those words in just as long—until that memorable cab ride. I had just left Rachel's place and was telling my driver about my horrifying discovery.

"Wow," he said in a heavy Queens accent. "Your girlfriend really *sucker punched* you good, huh?"

"Yes," I cried, all but licking my wounds. "She certainly did."

Loyal, reliable Rachel, my best friend of twenty-five years, who always had my interests ahead of, or at least tied

with, her own, had—*WHAM! POW!*—sucker punched me.
Blindsided me. The surprise element of her betrayal was
what burned me the most. The fact that I never saw it coming. It was as unexpected as a seeing-eye dog willfully
leading his blind, trusting owner into the path of a Mack
truck.

Truth be told, things weren't quite as simple as I made
them out to be to my cab driver. But I didn't want him
to lose sight of the main issue—the issue of what Rachel
had done to me. I had made some mistakes, but I hadn't
betrayed our friendship.

It was the week before what would have been my wedding day, and I had gone over to Rachel's to tell her that
my wedding was called off. My fiancé, Dex, had been the
first to say the difficult words—that perhaps we shouldn't
get married—but I had quickly agreed because I'd been
having an affair with Marcus, one of Dexter's friends. One
thing had led to another, and after one particular steamy
night, I had become pregnant. It was all hugely difficult to
absorb, and I knew the hardest part would be confessing
everything to Rachel, who, at the start of the summer, had
been mildly interested in Marcus. The two had gone on
a few dates, but the romance had petered out when, unbe-
knownst to her, my relationship with Marcus began. I felt
terrible the entire time—for cheating on Dex, but even *more*
for lying to Rachel. Still, I was ready to come clean to my
best friend. I was sure that she would understand. She always did.

So I stoically arrived at Rachel's apartment on the Upper East Side.

"What's the matter?" she asked as she answered the
door.

I felt a wave of comfort as I thought to myself how

soothing and familiar those words were. Rachel was a maternal best friend, more maternal than my own mother. I thought of all the times my friend had asked me this question over the years: such as the time I left my father's sunroof down during a thunderstorm, or the day I got my period all over my white Guess jeans. She was always there with her "What's the matter?" followed by her "It's going to be all right," delivered in a competent tone that made me feel sure that she was right. Rachel could fix anything. Make me feel better when nobody else could. Even at that moment, when she might have felt disappointed that Marcus had chosen me over her, I was sure she'd rise to the occasion and reassure me that I had chosen the right path, that things happened for a reason, that I wasn't a villain, that I was right to follow my heart, that she completely understood, and that eventually Dex would too.

I took a deep breath and glided into her orderly studio apartment as she rattled on about the wedding, how she was at my service, ready to help with any last-minute details.

"There isn't going to be a wedding," I blurted out.

"What?" she asked. Her lips blended right in with the rest of her pale face. I watched her turn and sit on her bed. Then she asked me who called it off.

I had a flashback to high school. After a breakup, which was always a very public happening in high school, guys and girls alike would ask, "Who did it?" Everyone wanted to know who was the dumper and who the dumpee so that they could properly assign blame and dole out pity.

I said what I could never say in high school because, to be frank, I was never the dumpee. "It was mutual. . . . Well, technically Dexter was the one. He told me this morning that he couldn't go through with it. He doesn't think that he loves me." I rolled my eyes. At that point, I didn't believe that such a thing was possible. I thought the only reason Dex wanted out was because he could sense my growing indifference. The drifting that comes when you fall for someone else.

"You're kidding me. This is crazy. How do you feel?"

I studied my pink-striped jeweled Prada sandals and matching pink toenail polish and took a deep breath. Then I confessed that I had been having an affair with Marcus, dismissing a pang of guilt. Sure, Rachel had had a small summer crush on Marcus, but she had never slept with him, and it had been weeks since she had even kissed him. She just couldn't be *that* upset by the news.

"So you slept with him?" Rachel asked in a loud, strange voice. Her cheeks flushed pink—a sure sign that she was angry—but I plowed on, divulging full details, telling her how our affair had begun, how we tried to stop but couldn't overcome the crazy pull toward each other. Then I took a deep breath and told her that I was pregnant with Marcus's baby and that we planned on getting married. I braced myself for a few tears, but Rachel remained composed. She asked a few questions, which I answered honestly. Then I thanked her for not hating me, feeling incredibly relieved that despite the upheaval in my life, I still had my anchor, my best friend.

"Yeah . . . I don't hate you," Rachel said, sweeping a strand of hair behind her ear.

"I hope Dex takes it as well. At least as far as Marcus goes. He's going to hate him for a while. But Dex is rational. Nobody did this on purpose to hurt him. It just happened."

And then, just as I was about to ask her if she would still be my maid of honor when I married Marcus, my whole world collapsed around me. I knew that nothing would ever be the same again, nor had things ever been as I thought they were. That was the moment I saw Dexter's watch on my best friend's nightstand. An unmistakable vintage Rolex.

"Why is Dexter's watch on your nightstand?" I asked, silently praying that she would offer a logical and benign explanation.

But instead, she shrugged and stammered that she didn't know. Then she said that it was actually *her* watch, that she had one just like his. Which was not plausible because I had searched for months to find that watch and then bought a new crocodile band for it, making it a true original. Besides, even had it been a predictable, spanking-new Rolex Oyster Perpetual, her voice was shaking, her face even paler than usual. Rachel can do many things well, but lying isn't one of them. So I knew. I knew that my best friend in the world had committed an unspeakable act of betrayal.

The rest unfolded in slow motion. I could practically hear the sound effects that accompanied *The Bionic Woman,* one of my favorite shows. One of *our* favorite shows— I had watched every episode with Rachel. I stood up, grabbed the watch from her nightstand, flipped it over, and read the inscription aloud. "All my love, Darcy." My words felt thick and heavy in my throat as I remembered the day I had his watch engraved. I had called Rachel on my cell and asked her about the wording. "All my love" had been her suggestion.

I stared at her, waiting, but she still said nothing. Just stared at me with those big, brown eyes, her always ungroomed brows furrowed above them.

"What the fuck?" I said evenly. Then I screamed the question again as I realized that Dex was likely lurking in the apartment, hiding somewhere. I shoved past her into the bathroom, whipping open the shower curtain. Nothing. I darted forward to check the closet.

"Darcy, don't," she said, blocking the door with her back.

"Move!" I screamed. "I know he's in there!"

So she moved and I opened the door. And sure enough,

there he was, crouched in the corner in his striped navy boxers. Another gift from me.

"You liar!" I shouted at him, feeling myself begin to hyperventilate. I was accustomed to drama. I *thrived* on drama. But not this kind. Not the kind of drama that I didn't control from the outset.

Dex stood and dressed calmly, putting one foot and then the other into his jeans, zipping defiantly. There wasn't a trace of guilt on his face. It was as if I had only accused him of stealing the covers or eating my Ben & Jerry's Cherry Garcia ice cream.

"You lied to me!" I shouted again, louder this time.

"You have got to be kidding me," he said, his voice low. "Fuck you, Darcy."

In all my years with Dex, he had never said this to me. Those were my words of last resort. Not his.

I tried again. "You said there was nobody else in the picture! And you're *fucking* my best friend!" I shouted, unsure of whom to confront first. Overwhelmed by the double betrayal.

I wanted him to say, yes, this looks bad, but there had been no fornicating. Yet no denial came my way. Instead he said, "Isn't that a bit of the pot calling the kettle black, Darce? You and Marcus, huh? Having a baby? I guess congratulations are in order."

I had nothing to say to that, so I just turned the tables right back on him and said, "I knew it all along."

This was a total lie. I never in a million years could have foreseen this moment. The shock was too much to bear. But that's the thing about the sucker punch; the sucker element hurts worse than the punch. They had socked it to me, but I wasn't going to be their fool too.

"I hate you both. I always will," I said, realizing that my words sounded weak and juvenile, like the time when I was five years old and told my father that I loved the devil more than I loved him. I wanted to shock and horrify, but he had only chuckled at my creative put-down. Dex, too, seemed merely amused by my proclamation, which enraged me to the brink of tears. I told myself that I had to escape Rachel's apartment before I started bawling. On my way to the door, I heard Dex say, "Oh, Darcy?"

I turned to face him again. *"What?"* I spat out, praying that he was going to say it was all a joke, a big mix-up. Maybe they were going to laugh and ask how I could think such a thing. Maybe we'd even share a group hug.

But all he said was, "May I have my watch back, please?"

I swallowed hard and then hurled the watch at him, aiming for his face. Instead it hit a wall, skittered across her hardwood floor, and stopped just short of Dexter's bare feet. My eyes lifted from the watch to Rachel's face. "And you," I said to her. "I never want to see you again. You are dead to me."

two

Somehow I managed to make it downstairs (where I gave Rachel's doorman the gruesome highlights), into a cab (where I again shared the tale), and over to Marcus's place. I burst into his sloppy studio, where he sat cross-legged on the floor, playing a melody on his guitar that sounded vaguely like the refrain in "Fire and Rain."

He looked up at me, his expression a blend of annoyance and bemusement. "What's wrong *now*?" he said.

I resented his use of the word *now*, implying that I am always having a crisis. I couldn't help what had just happened to me. I told him the whole story, sparing no detail. I wanted outrage from my new beau. Or at least shock. But no matter how much I tried to whip him into my same frenzied state, he'd fire back with these two points: *How can you be mad when we did the same thing to them?* And, *Don't we want our friends to be as happy as we are?*

I told him that our guilt was beside the point and, *HELL NO, WE DON'T WANT THEM TO BE HAPPY!*

Marcus kept strumming his guitar and smirking.

"What's so funny?" I asked, exasperated. "Nothing is funny about this situation!"

"Well maybe not *ha-ha* funny, but ironic funny."

"There is nothing even *remotely* funny about this, Marcus! And stop playing that thing!"

Marcus ran his thumb across the strings one final time before putting his guitar in its case. Then he sat cross-legged, gripping the toes of his dirty sneakers, as he said again, "I just don't see how you can be so outraged when we did the same thing—"

"It's not the same thing at all!" I said, dropping to the cool floor. "See, I may have cheated on *Dex* with you. But I didn't do anything to Rachel."

"Well," he said. "She and I did date for a minute. We had potential before you came along."

"You went on a few lousy dates whereas I was *engaged* to Dex. What kind of person hooks up with her friend's fiancé?"

He crossed his arms and gave me a knowing look. "Darcy."

"What?"

"You're looking at one. Remember? I was one of Dexter's groomsmen? Ring a bell?"

I sniffed. True, Marcus and Dex had been college buddies, friends for years. But it just wasn't a comparable situation. "It's not the same. Female friendships are more sacred; my relationship with Rachel has been lifelong. She was my very best friend in the world, and you were, like, the very last one stuck in the groomsman lineup. Dex probably wouldn't even have picked you except that he needed a fifth person to go with my five girls."

"Gee. I'm touched."

I ignored his sarcasm, and said, "Besides, you never painted yourself as a saint like she did."

"You're right about that. I'm no saint."

"You just don't go there with your best girlfriend's fiancé. Or ex-fiancé. Period. Ever. Even if a gazillion years elapsed, you still can't go there. And you certainly don't hop in bed with him one day after the breakup." Then I hurled more questions his way: *Did he think it was a one-time thing? Were they beginning a relationship? Could they actually fall in love? Would they ever last?*

To which Marcus shrugged and answered with some variation of: *I don't know and I don't care.*

To which I yelled: *Guess! Care! Soothe me!*

Finally, he caved, patting my arm and responding satisfyingly to my leading questions. He agreed that it was likely a one-time thing with Rachel and Dex. That Dex went over to Rachel's because he was upset. That being with Rachel was the closest thing to me. And as for Rachel, she just wanted to throw a bone to a broken man.

"Okay. So what do you think I should do now?" I asked.

"Nothing you can do," Marcus said, reaching over to open a pizza box resting near his guitar case. "It's cold, but help yourself."

"As if I could eat now!" I exhaled dramatically and did a spread eagle on the floor. "The way I see it is, I have two options: murder and/or suicide. . . . It would be pretty easy to kill them, you know?"

I wanted him to gasp at my suggestion, but much to my constant disappointment, he was never too shocked by my words. He simply pulled a slice of pizza from the box, folded it in half, and crammed it in his mouth. He chewed for a moment, and with his mouth still full, he pointed out that I would be the prime and only suspect. "You'd wind up at a female corrections facility in upstate New York. With a mullet. I can see you now slopping out gruel with your mullet flapping in the prison yard breeze."

I thought about this and decided that I'd vastly prefer

my own death to a mullet. Which brought me to the suicide option. "Fine. So murder is out. I'll just kill myself
instead. They'd be really sorry if I killed myself, wouldn't
they?" I asked, more for shock value than because I was
really considering my own death.

I wanted Marcus to tell me that he couldn't live without me. But he didn't take the bait in the suicide game as
Rachel had when we were in junior high, and she'd promise that she'd override my mother's classical music selections and see to it that Pink Floyd's "On the Turning Away"
was cranked up at my funeral.

"They'd be so sorry if I killed myself," I said to Marcus. "Think they'd come to my funeral? Would they apologize to my parents?"

"Yeah. Probably so. But people move on fast. In fact,
sometimes they even forget about you *at* the funeral, depending on how good the food is."

"But what about their guilt?" I asked. "How could they
live with themselves?"

He assured me that the initial guilt could be assuaged by
any good therapist. So after a few weeknights on a leather
couch, the person, once racked with *what ifs,* would come
to understand that only a very troubled soul would take her
own life, and that one, albeit significant, act of betrayal
doesn't cause a healthy person to jump in front of the number 6 train.

I knew that Marcus was right, remembering that when
Rachel and I were sophomores in high school, one of our
classmates, Ben Murray, shot himself in the head with his
father's revolver in his bedroom while his parents watched
television downstairs. The stories varied—but, bottom line,
we all knew that it had something to do with a fight he'd
had with his girlfriend, Amber Lucetti, who had dumped
him for a college guy she met while visiting her sister at
Illinois State. None of us could forget the moment when a

guidance counselor ushered Amber out of speech class to give her the horrific news. Nor could we forget the sound of Amber's wails echoing in the halls. We all imagined that she'd lose it altogether and end up in a mental ward somewhere.

Yet within a few days, Amber was back in class, giving a speech on the recent stock market crash. I had just given my speech on why grocery-store makeup was the way to go—over more expensive makeup—as it all comes from the same big vats of oils and powder. I marveled at Amber's ability to give such a substantive speech, barely glancing at her index cards, when her ex-boyfriend was in a coffin under the frozen ground. And her competent speech was nothing compared to the spectacle she created when making out with Alan Hysack at the Spring Dance, fewer than three months after Ben's funeral.

So if I were striving to destroy Rachel and Dex's world, suicide might not be the answer, either. Which left me with one option: stay on course with my charmed, perfect life. Don't they say that happiness is the best revenge? I'd marry Marcus, have his baby, and ride off into the sunset, never looking back.

"Hey. Give me a slice after all," I said to Marcus. "I'm eating for two now."

That night I called my parents and broke the news. My father answered and I told him to put Mom on the other extension. "Mom, Dad, the wedding is off. I'm so sorry," I said stoically, perhaps too stoically because they instantly assumed that I was solely to blame for the breakup. Dear ol' Dex would never cancel a wedding the week before it was to take place. My mother turned on her sob switch, wailing about how much she loved Dexter, while my father shouted over her in his "Now, Darcy. Don't be rash" tone. At which point, I dropped the closet-story bomb on them. A rare hush fell over the phone. They were so silent that I thought for a second that we had been disconnected. My father finally said there must be some mistake because Rachel would never do such a thing. I told them I never would have believed it either. But I saw it with my own two eyes—Dex in his boxers in Rachel's closet. Needless to say, I said nothing about Marcus or the baby to my parents. I wanted to have their full emotional and financial support. I wanted them to cast the blame on Rachel, the neighborhood girl who had duped them just as she had duped me. Perfect, trustworthy, good-hearted, loyal, reliable, predictable Rachel.

"What are we going to do, Hugh?" my mother asked my father in her little-girl tone.

"I'll take care of it," he said. "Everything will be fine. Darcy, don't you worry about a thing. We have the guest list. We'll call the family. We'll contact The Carlyle, the photographer. Everyone. You sit tight. Do you want us to come out on our same flight on Thursday or do you want a ticket to come home? You say the word, honey."

My father was in full-on crisis mode, the way he got during a tornado watch or a snowstorm or anytime our declawed, half-blind indoor cat would escape out the back door and dart out into the street, while my mother and I freaked out, secretly delighting in the drama.

"I don't know, Daddy. I just can't even think straight right now."

My dad sighed and then said, "Do you want me to call Dex? Talk some sense into him?"

"No, Daddy. It won't do any good. It's over. Please don't. I have some pride."

"That *bastard*," my mother chimed in. "And Rachel! I just can't believe that little tramp."

"Dee, that's not helping," my father said.

"Well, I know," my mother said. "But I just can't believe that Rachel would do such a thing. And how in the world could Dex *want* to be with *her*?"

"I know!" I said. "There's no way that they're *actually* together, right? He couldn't *really* like her?"

"No. No way," my mother said.

"I'm sure Rachel is sorry," my dad said. "It was a very inappropriate thing to do."

"*Inappropriate* isn't the word for it," my mother said.

My father tried again. "Treacherous? Opportunistic?"

My mother agreed with this assessment. "She probably wanted him the whole time you were with him."

"I know," I said, feeling a fleeting sense of regret that I had let Dex go. Everyone viewed him as such a prize. I looked at Marcus to reassure myself I had done the right thing, but he was eyeing his PlayStation.

"Has Rachel called to explain or apologize?" my dad continued.

"Not yet," I said.

"She will," my mom said. "And in the meantime, you stay strong, honey. Everything will be fine. You're a beautiful girl. You will find someone else. Someone better. Tell her, Hugh."

"You're the most beautiful girl in the world," he said. "Everything's going to be just fine. I promise you."

three

Ironically, it was Rachel who had introduced Dex and me. They were both first-year law students at NYU, and because Rachel insisted that she wasn't in school to date, but rather to learn, she passed her friend Dex, the most eligible man on campus, along to me.

I remember the moment well. Rachel and I were at a bar in the Village, waiting for Dex to arrive. When he walked in, I instantly knew that he was special. He belonged in a Ralph Lauren ad—the man in the glossy ads squinting into the sunlight on a sailboat or bending thoughtfully over a chessboard with a fire roaring in the background. I was sure that he didn't get sloppy, fall-down drunk, that he would never swear in front of his mother, that he used expensive aftershave products—and perhaps a straight-edge razor on special occasions. I just knew that he could enjoy the opera, that he could solve any *Times* crossword, and that he ordered fine port after dinner. I swear I saw all of this in one glance. Saw that he was my ideal—the sophisticated East Coaster I needed in order to create a Manhattan version of my mother's life.

Dex and I had a nice conversation that evening, but it took him a few weeks to call and ask me out—which only made me want him more. As soon as he called, I dumped the guy I was seeing at the time, because I was *that* sure that something great was about to be launched. I was right. Dex and I fast became a couple, and things were perfect. *He* was perfect. So perfect that I felt a tiny bit unworthy of him. I knew I was gorgeous, but I sometimes worried that I wasn't quite smart enough or interesting enough for someone like Dex, and that once he discovered the truth about me, he might not want me anymore.

Rachel didn't help matters, because as usual, she seemed to have a way of highlighting my shortcomings, underscoring my apathy, my indifference to topics that she and Dex cared so much about: what was happening in third world countries, the economy, who stood for what in Congress. I mean, the two of them listened to NPR, for God's sake. Enough said. Even the sound of the voices on that station makes my eyes glaze over big time. Never mind the content. So after a few months of exhaustively feigning interest in stuff I cared little about, I decided to come clean with the real me. So one night, as Dex was engrossed in a documentary on some political happening in Chile, I grabbed the remote and switched the channel to a *Gidget* rerun on Nickelodeon.

"Hey! I was watching that!" Dex said.

"I'm so tired of poor people," I said, tucking the remote between my legs.

Dex chuckled fondly. "I know, Darce. They can be so annoying, can't they?"

I suddenly realized that for as much substance as Dex had, he didn't seem to mind my somewhat shallow outlook on the world. Nor did he mind my unapologetic zeal for pursuing quality goods and a good time. Instead, I think he admired my candor, my honesty about where I stood. I might not have been the deepest of gals, but I was no phony.

Bottom line, Dex and I had our differences, but I made him happy. And for the most part, I was a good and loyal girlfriend. Only twice, before Marcus, did my appreciation for the opposite sex spill over into something slightly more—which I think is a pretty admirable record for seven years.

The first minor slip happened a few years ago with Jack, a fresh-faced twenty-two-year-old I met at Lemon Bar one night while having a few drinks with Rachel and Claire, who was my best friend from work, former roommate, and the most well-connected girl on the East Coast. Rachel and Claire were as different as Laura Ingalls and Paris Hilton, but they were both my friends and both single, so we often went out together. Anyway, the three of us were standing at the bar chatting when Jack and his friends clumsily hit on us. Jack was the most outgoing of the group, full of boyish exuberance and charm, talking about his water polo tales from his very recent Princeton days. I had just turned twenty-seven and was feeling a bit tired and old, so I was flattered by young Jack's obvious interest in me. I humored him as the other guys (less cute versions of Jack) worked on Claire and Rachel.

We sipped cocktails and flirted, and as the evening wore on, Jack and his crew wanted to find a livelier venue (proving my theory that the number of times you change bars is inversely proportional to your age). So we all piled into cabs to find some party in SoHo. But, also in youthful fashion, Jack and his boys turned out to have the wrong address and then the wrong cell phone number of the friend of the friend having the party. They did the whole inept routine where they blame each other: *Dude! I can't believe you lost the shit,* etc. We ended up standing on Prince Street, in the cold, ready to call it a night. Rachel and Claire left first, sharing a cab to the Upper East Side. Jack's friends took off next, determined to find their party. So there Jack and I were alone on the street. I was buzzed, and Jack looked so smitten that I threw him a few harmless kisses. It was no big deal. It really wasn't. At least it wasn't to me.

Of course, eager little Jack called me repeatedly the next day, leaving a multitude of messages on my cell. Eventually, I phoned him back and confessed that I had a serious boyfriend, and that he couldn't call me again. I told him I was sorry.

"I understand," he said, sounding crushed. "Your boyfriend is a lucky guy. . . . If you ever break up with him, give me a call."

He gave me his work, home, and cell number, and I absentmindedly scribbled them on the back of a Chinese take-out menu that I ended up tossing later that night.

"Okay. Great. Thanks, Jack. And sorry again."

As I hung up, I felt a twinge of guilt and wondered why I had kissed Jack in the first place. There hadn't been much of a point. Even in my buzzed state, I had no delusions of real interest. The only thing that went into the calculation was, "Do I want to, at this moment, kiss this boy or not?" and because the answer was yes, I did it. I don't know. Maybe I was bored. Maybe I just missed the early days when Dex seemed to be crazy about me. I fleetingly worried that the thing with Jack was evidence of a problem in our relationship, but then I figured that a kiss was just a kiss. No big deal. I didn't even bother telling Rachel about Jack. It was over—there was no point in watching her mount her high horse as she had done when I cheated on my high school and college boyfriends.

After Jack, I was the portrait of the ideal girlfriend for

a long stretch, close to a year. But then I met Lair at a launch party thrown by our PR firm for a new line of hip sportswear called Emmeline. Lair was a gorgeous model from South Africa with caramel-colored skin and eyes so blue they nearly matched the aqua sweatsuit he was wearing.

After he smiled at me twice, I approached him. "So, I have to know," I shouted over the music, "are those fake?"

"What?"

"Your eyes. Are you wearing blue lenses?"

He laughed a melodic South African laugh. "Jeepers, no. They're mine."

"Did you just say *jeepers*?"

He nodded and smiled.

"How quaint." I studied the edges of his corneas just to be sure he was telling the truth. Sure enough, no telltale contact lens lines. He laughed, exposing gorgeous white teeth. Then he extended his hand. "I'm Lair."

"Leah?" I said, sliding my hand into his strong, warm one.

"Lair," he said again, still sounding like *Leah*. "You know, *liar* with the *a* and *i* inverted, right?"

"Oh, Lair. What a cozy name," I said, picturing us both curled up in a little hideaway together. "I'm Darcy."

"Pleasure, Darcy," he said, and then glanced around the party that I had been planning for months. "This is quite an event."

"Thanks," I said proudly. Then I threw out some PR jargon. Something about what a challenge it is to make a client a real standout in today's competitive marketplace.

He nodded then bobbed his head to the bass.

"But . . ." I laughed, giving my long, dark hair a seductive toss. "It's a lot of fun too. I get to meet great people like you."

We kept talking, interrupted at regular intervals by my colleagues and other guests. Fellow model Kimmy, who was wearing pink fleece sweatpants with a navy *69* across her butt and a matching *69* jog bra, sought out Lair repeatedly and snapped pictures of him with her digital camera.

"Smile, honey," she'd say, as I did my best to squeeze into her photos. But despite Kimmy's overtures, Lair never diverted his attention, and our flirting evolved into more serious conversation. We talked about his home in South Africa. I admitted that I knew nothing about his country except that it used to have apartheid before Nelson Mandela was released from prison. As Lair explained more about South African politics, the problem with crime in his hometown of Johannesburg, and the amazing beauty of Kruger National Park, I realized that he was more than just a pretty face. He told me that he was only modeling to pay for school, even tossing out the word *sartorial*.

After the party, Lair and I hopped in a cab together. My intentions were basically pure—I wanted only a kiss on the street, Jack-style. But then Lair whispered in my ear, "Darcy, would you possibly consider joining me back at my hotel?" And I just couldn't help myself. So I went to The Palace with him, convinced that we would only engage in some heavy-duty making out.

And that is pretty much all we did. Then around three in the morning, I stood, dressed, and told him that I really needed to get home. Technically, I could have stayed, as Dex was out of town on a business trip, but somehow falling asleep with a guy made it seem like real cheating. And to that point, I felt that I wasn't a full-fledged cheater. Although in truth I think the threshold test of whether you have cheated is rather clear: if your partner could see a video of the event, would he or she think you had cheated? An alternative test is: if you could see a video of your partner in the identical situation, would you think he or she had cheated? On both counts, I clearly failed. But I had not crossed that bright sex line, and this fact made me proud.

I left a pining Lair that night, and after a few weeks of hot and heavy e-mailing, we gradually stopped talking and then lost touch altogether. The evening started to fade in my mind—and I nearly forgot those incredible eyes until I spotted him, in white boxer shorts, smiling down at me from a billboard in the middle of Times Square. I conjured the details of our tryst, wondering what would have happened if I had broken up with Dex for Lair. I pictured us living in Johannesburg amid elephants and carjackers, and decided, once again, that our relationship was best left at The Palace.

Dex and I got engaged a few months later, and I vowed to myself that I would be true to him forever. So we didn't have a ton in common, and he didn't thrill me every minute. He was still an amazing catch and a good guy to boot. I was going to marry him and live happily ever after on the Upper West Side. Okay, maybe we'd eventually move to Fifth Avenue, but other than such minor tweaking, my life was scripted.

I just hadn't planned on Marcus.

four

For years, I knew Marcus only as Dexter's slacker freshman roommate from George-town. While Marcus finished next to last in the class and got stoned all the time, Dex graduated summa and had never tried an illegal drug. But the freshman-roommate experience can be a powerful one, so the two stayed close throughout college and afterward, even though they lived on opposite coasts.

Of course, I never gave his college pal much thought until Dex and I got engaged and his name was thrown out as a groomsman candidate. Dex only had four clear-cut picks, but I had five bridesmaids (including Rachel as maid of honor), and symmetry in the wedding party lineup wasn't a negotiable point. So Dex phoned Marcus and bestowed the honor upon him. After the two yucked it up for a while, Marcus asked to speak to me, which I thought was good form, especially given the fact that we had never met face-to-face. He gave me the standard congratulations with some other remark about promising not to get the groom loaded the night before the wedding. I laughed and told him that I was holding him to that, never imagining that what he should have been promising was not to sleep with me before our wedding.

In fact, I didn't expect to see him at all before the wedding, but a few weeks later he took a new job in Manhattan. To celebrate, I made reservations at Aureole, despite Dexter's insistence that Marcus wasn't a fancy guy.

Dex and I arrived at the restaurant first and waited at the bar for Marcus. He finally walked in sporting baggy jeans, a wrinkled shirt, and at least two days' growth of beard. In short, he wasn't the kind of guy I usually look at twice.

"Dex-*ter*!" Marcus shouted as he approached us and then gave Dex a hearty, man-style hug, clapping him on the back. "Good to see you, man," Marcus said.

"You too," Dex said, gesturing at me with a gentlemanly sweep of his hand. "This is Darcy."

I stood slowly and leaned in to kiss the fifth groomsman on his whiskered cheek.

Marcus grinned. "The infamous Darcy."

I liked being called "infamous"—despite its negative connotations—so I laughed, put my hand to my chest, and said, "None of it's true."

"Too bad," Marcus said under his breath, and then pointed to the statuesque redhead hovering beside him."Oh. This is my friend Stacy. We used to work together."

I had seen the woman come in at the same time as Marcus, but hadn't thought they were together. Nothing about them matched. Stacy was a total fashion plate, wearing a cropped teal leather jacket and a sweet pair of lizard pumps. As we were led to our table, I shot Dex a dirty look, irritated at him for suggesting that I might want to "tone it down" when I had busted out with my Louis Vuitton white cape and red tartan taffeta bustier. So now I was stuck in an understated black-and-white tweed jacket next to splashy Stacy. I assessed her again, wondering if she was prettier than I was. I quickly decided that I was more beautiful, but she was taller, which annoyed me. I liked being both. Incidentally, I had always believed that every woman wanted to be the most attractive in any group, but once when I admitted my feelings to Rachel, she gave me this blank stare followed by a diplomatic nod. At which point I backtracked somewhat and said, "Well, unless I'm friends with her and then I don't compare."

Fortunately, Stacy's personality wasn't nearly as scintillating as her wardrobe, and I succeeded handily in outshining her. Marcus was extremely entertaining, too, and kept our table in stitches. He wasn't an outright jokester, but was full of wry observations about the restaurant, the fancy food, and the people around us. I noticed that whenever Stacy laughed at him, she'd touch his arm in a familiar way, which made me fairly certain that if they weren't dating, they had at least hooked up. By the end of the night, I reevaluated Marcus's looks, upgrading him several notches. It was a combination of Stacy's obvious interest in him, his sense of humor, and something else. Something was just sexy about him: a gleam in his brown eyes and the cleft in his chin, which made me think of Danny Zuko in *Grease* (that first beach scene in the movie was my idea of romance for years).

After dinner, as Dex and I were cabbing back to the Upper West, I said, "I like Marcus. He's really funny and has surprising sex appeal."

Dex had grown accustomed to my candid commentary on other men, so it no longer fazed him. He just said, "Yeah. He's a character, all right."

I waited for him to say that he could tell Marcus approved of me as well, and when he didn't, I prompted, "What did Marcus say to you at the end of the night when you were getting our coats? Did he say something about me?"

Stacy and I had been chatting a few feet away and I had figured that Marcus was saying something like "You got yourself a hell of a woman" or "She's way hotter than your college girlfriend" or even a nice, straightforward "I really like Darcy—she's great."

But after I pressed Dex at length, he told me that what Marcus had shared was that he and Stacy had been dating, and despite the fact that she gave "bombass blow jobs," he was ending things because she was too demanding. Needless to say, the fact that Marcus garnered blow jobs from a girl like Stacy made him rise even more notches in my book of judgments.

And the more Dex and I hung out with Marcus, the more I liked him. But I still didn't think of him as anything other than Dexter's friend and a groomsman in our wedding until a few months later, the night of Rachel's thirtieth birthday, when I threw a surprise party for her at Prohibition, our favorite bar on the Upper West Side. I remember sometime that evening sidling up to Marcus and telling him that he may have been the party boy back in college, but that I could drink him under the table now.

He smirked and slapped the bar and said, "Oh, yeah? Bring it, big talker."

We proceeded to do Jägermeister shots. It was quite a bonding experience, not only because we were drinking together but because we hid the shots from Dex, who hates it when I get wasted. *It's unbecoming. It's immature. It's unhealthy. It's dangerous,* he would lecture. Not that it ever stopped me, especially not on that night. At one point, before our final round of shots, Dex found us at the bar and looked at me suspiciously. "Are you doing shots?" he asked, glancing at the empty shot glasses on the bar in front of us.

"That wasn't mine," I said. "Those were Marcus's. He did two."

"Yeah, man. Those were mine," Marcus said, twinkly eyed. ·

As Dex walked away, with raised eyebrows, Marcus winked at me. I laughed. "He can be so uptight. Thanks for the cover."

"No problem," Marcus said.

As of that moment, we had a secret, and having a secret—even a little one—creates a bond between two people. I remember thinking to myself how much more fun he was than Dex, who never lost control. On top of the fun factor, Marcus was looking hot that evening. He was wearing a navy polo shirt—nothing special—but for once it wasn't totally baggy so I could tell he had a pretty nice body. As I sipped a martini, I asked him if he worked out, which is a flirtatious question at best, downright cheesy at worst, but I didn't care. I wanted to go there.

"Once or twice," he said.

"C'mon. You have a great body. Do you lift? Run?"

He said only if he's being chased. He then proceeded to tell me that he had gone running with a girl the other day, despite his better judgment. "I never should have gone," he said, rubbing his thighs. "I'm still paying for it. And the date went nowhere."

"Was this with Stacy?"

"Who?"

"Stacy. You know, the redhead that you brought to Aureole?"

"Oh! *That* Stacy. Ancient history."

"Good," I said. "I wasn't a big fan. She was a bore."

Marcus laughed. "She wasn't your brightest bulb."

"So then, who was your jogger girl?" I asked.

"Just this chick."

"Does this chick have a name?"

"Let's call her Wanda."

"Okay. Wanda. . . . So did Wanda give you blow jobs as good as Stacy's?" I asked, proud of my outrageousness.

He smirked, poised for a comeback, but at this point, Dex and Rachel both joined us and I never got my answer, only a sexy little wink. I remember thinking that I wished I could show him my talents in that arena. Not that I really wanted to go down on a groomsman in my wedding party—it was just one of those fleeting thoughts of alcohol-induced attraction.

Sometime after that, my memories of the night end, except for a vague recollection of Dex ushering me out of the bar and an even vaguer memory of puking in a paper bag beside our bed.

I didn't think of Marcus for a couple of days after that, until he called to talk to Dex. I told him Dex was still at work, feeling happy for the opportunity to talk to Marcus.

"He works too much," Marcus said.

"Tell me about it. . . So how's it going? What's new? Think you stayed out late enough the other night?" I asked. After taking me home, Dex had gone back out with Marcus and they had ended up staying out that night until nearly seven in the morning.

"Oh. Yeah. Sorry about that," he said.

"Did you stay out of trouble?"

"Yeah."

"So you didn't talk to any girls?" I asked.

He laughed. "You know I always talk to the ladies."

I recalled that moment at the bar, my unmistakable attraction to him. "Oh. I *know*," I said flirtatiously. "So how is Wanda anyway?"

"Wanda?"

"You know. Wanda. The jogger."

"Oh, *that* Wanda! Right. It didn't work out with Wanda. . . . But I was wondering . . ."

"Wondering what?" I asked coyly, sensing that he was poised to flirt back with me.

But instead he asked, "What is the deal with Rachel?"

I was stunned to hear him say her name. "What do you mean?"

"Is she dating anyone?"

"No. Why?" I asked, feeling irrationally territorial and a little bit jealous that Marcus was interested in my friend. Perhaps, on some level, I even wished that he were pining after me. It was selfish, given the fact that Rachel was single and I was engaged. But you can't help your feelings.

Marcus continued, "She's pretty hot in that studious way of hers."

"Yeah, she's a cute girl," I said, thinking it was weird to hear her described as hot, although I had recently noticed that she seemed to be improving from our school days and early twenties. I think it was her skin. She didn't have as many lines around her eyes as other girls our age. And on a good day, when she put a little effort into her appearance, you might even call her pretty. But hot was going too far. "Well, if you want to go out with my friend, you have to go through me," I said jokingly, but actually meaning it. I was going to play gatekeeper on this one for sure.

"Fine. . . . Tell her I'm gonna ask her out. And tell her she'd better say yes. Or else."

"Or else what?"

"Or else it will be the biggest mistake of her life."

"You're *that* good?"

"Yeah," he said. "Actually, I am *that* good."

And then I got that wistful pang again. That feeling that it was just too bad that I couldn't sample Marcus before marrying Dex. Even beyond any minor feelings I felt for Marcus, I thought about what a shame it was that I would never experience another first kiss. That I'd never fall in love again. I think most guys experience such feelings in a relationship, typically right before they break down and buy the engagement ring. But from what I can tell, most women aren't like this—at least they don't admit to having such feelings. They find a good man, and that's it. They seem relieved that the search is over. They are content, committed, totally in it for the long haul. I guess I was more like a guy in this regard.

Still, despite my occasionally chilly feet, I knew that nothing could happen with Marcus. So I set about doing the noble thing: I encouraged Rachel to go out with Marcus and took an active interest in their potential relationship. And when they actually did go out, I was happy for them.

But then both he and Rachel flatly refused to include me in any postdate gossip, and that irritated me as I was better friends with each of them than they could have become with each other on one stupid date. Rachel gave me nothing, wouldn't even tell me if they had kissed—which left me wondering if they had done much more than that. The more I pried, the more private they became, and the more intrigued with Marcus I became. It was a vicious cycle. Consequently, over the next few weeks, whenever Marcus called to talk to Dex, I made it my goal to keep him on the phone for as long as possible. Occasionally, I'd even call him to talk at work, under the pretext of asking about our Hamptons share or something related to the wedding. I'd hang up and follow up with a clever e-mail. He'd shoot one back at the speed of light, and we'd have a playful repartee that would last throughout the day. Harmless stuff.

Then over the July Fourth weekend, Dex and Rachel both stayed in the city to work rather than joining the rest of us in the Hamptons. Mostly I was annoyed and disappointed that my best friend and my fiancé were staying behind, but part of me was excited at the idea of spending unchaperoned time with Marcus. Not that I wanted anything to happen. I just wanted a little intrigue.

Sure enough, the intrigue bubbled up at The Talkhouse over part two of our little shot game, only this time it was without the Dexter safety net. I had a few too many, but managed not to get sick, black out, or become completely stupid. Still, I was unquestionably drunk. So was Marcus. We danced until two in the morning, when he, Claire, and I returned home. Claire put on her Lilly Pulitzer pajamas and went straight to bed, but Marcus and I kept partying, first in the den and then in the backyard.

It was all good fun—the teasing and the laughing. But then the boisterous put-downs gave way to playful slapping, which led to some wrestling around in the damp, cool grass. I remember yelling at Marcus to stop after he had tackled me under a tree. I told him that I was going to get stains all over my Chaiken white halter sundress. But I really didn't want him to stop, and I think he knew this because he didn't. Instead he pinned my arm behind my back, which I have to say is a huge turn-on. At least it was with Marcus. I could tell that he was turned on, too, because I felt him there on top of me. Which of course only turned me on more.

At some point, it started to rain, but neither of us made a move for the house. Instead we stayed glued on top of each other, almost frozen in place. Then the laughing stopped. We weren't even smiling, just staring at each other, our faces so close that our noses touched. After a long time like that, in sexual limbo, I tilted my head to the side and brushed my lips against his. Back and forth one time, lightly, innocently. I wanted him to kiss me first, but I had waited long enough. The brief seconds of contact were tellingly delicious. I could tell he thought so, too, but he pulled away and asked, "What's going on here?"

I found his lips again. This time it was a real kiss. I remember feeling completely alert, all my senses buzzing. "I'm kissing you," I said.

"Should you be doing that?" he asked, still on top of me, pressing slightly harder.

"Probably not," I said. "But here we are anyway."

I kissed him again, and this time he kissed me back. We made out for a long time with warm rain falling on us and thunder rumbling in the distance. I knew we were both thinking that we couldn't, shouldn't, do more than kiss, but we were both stalling to be sure. Calling the other's bluff. He said stuff like *We gotta stop,* and *This is nuts,* and *We can't do this,* and *What if Claire busts us out here?* but neither of us changed course or even braked.

Instead, I took firm hold of his hand and moved it up under my sundress. And he sure knew what to do after that. If there had been any doubt in my mind before as to Marcus's expertise, I had no doubt anymore. He was just one of those guys. Dex might be handsome, I remember thinking, but he can't do this. Not like this. And even if he did, it wouldn't feel like this. And the thought that I'd never have with Dex what Marcus was offering me, made me whisper into his ear, "I wanna be with you."

"We can't go there," Marcus said, his hand still working between my legs.

"Why not?"

"You know why."

"But I *want* to."

"No, you don't."

"I do. I'm sure I do," I said.

"Hell, no. We can't."

But by then I was wriggling out of my thong and unfastening his jeans, reaching down into the warmth of his boxers, determined to make him breathe as hard as I was. We went through the whole high school charade of inching forward step by step, only delaying the inevitable. But the inevitable finally came. Right there under that tree in the pouring July rain.

I'd like to say that I was thinking big, important thoughts—about what I was doing, what it meant in the scheme of my life, the impact it would have on my engagement, my relationship. But no, it was more like, *Am I better than his other girls? Will Dex ever find out? Will Marcus ever go out with Rachel again? Why does this feel so damn good?*

We lasted a long time together, perhaps because of all that we had had to drink, but I decided that it had more to do with perfect chemistry and with Marcus's sexual prowess. Afterward, we rolled onto our backs, catching our breath, our eyes mostly closed. The rain came to a sudden stop, but we were both soaking wet.

"Wow," he said, moving a stick from under his back and flinging it several feet away from us. "Fuck."

I could tell I had made an impression, so I smiled to myself.

"We shouldn't have done that," he said.

"Too late," I said, intertwining my fingers with his.

He squeezed my hand. "Way too late. . . . *Ffffuck.*"

"You're not gonna tell Dex, are you?" I asked.

"Are you fuckin' nuts? No way. Nobody. You're not either," he said, looking slightly panicked.

"Of course not. Nobody," I said. Rachel flashed through my mind—her expression changing from shock to hurt to piousness. Especially not Rachel.

Marcus ran his hand over my wet thigh. "We should go in. Shower."

"Together?"

"No." He let out a nervous laugh. "Not together. I think we've done enough damage tonight."

I wanted to ask him what would happen from here. I wanted to know what it had meant to him, how he was feeling, whether it was a one-time thing or whether we'd have a repeat performance. But I was starting to feel groggy, confused, and a little bit worried. We went inside, kissed good night, and took separate showers. I couldn't quite believe what had happened—and although I didn't regret it, I still cried a little under the hot water when I looked at my beautiful diamond engagement ring and thought about Dexter asleep in our bed on the Upper West Side.

After my shower, I tried to rub the grass stains out of my dress with some Woolite that I found under the sink, but it was hopeless, and I knew bleach would only ruin the delicate fabric. So I wrung out the dress, crept down to the kitchen, and stuffed it into the bottom of the plastic trash bag under a banana peel and an empty box of Trix. I wasn't about to crash and burn over a dress like some kind of Monica Lewinsky.

five

The next day I awoke with a dry tequila mouth and a searing headache. I checked my watch; it was nearly noon. The night before seemed like a blurry dream. A blurry, *good* dream. I couldn't wait to see Marcus again. I got up, brushed my teeth, swept my hair up in a ponytail, added a hint of pink blush to my cheeks, put on a Juicy Couture lime-green skirt and a white tank, and sauntered out to find him.

He was in the den alone, watching television.

"Hiya," I said, taking a seat next to him on the couch.

He glanced over at me, squinted, and let out a hoarse, "Morning. Or afternoon, I guess." Then his eyes returned to the TV.

"Where is everyone?" I asked.

He told me that Claire went to brunch and that Hillary, our other housemate, hadn't returned home the night before.

"Maybe she got some action too," I said to break the ice.

"Yeah," he said. "Maybe."

I tried again. "So how do you feel?"

"Like ass," he said, changing the channel and still avoiding eye contact. "Those shots weren't such a hot idea."

"Ahh. I get it," I said. "We're blaming what happened on the alcohol, are we?"

He shook his head and struggled not to smile. "Always knew you were trouble, Darcy Rhone."

I liked that that was his impression, but at the same time I didn't want him to think that I was a slut, or that I often cheated on Dexter, so I set the record straight, told him that nothing like that had ever happened before. It was, in a technical sense, the truth.

"Yeah. Well. It won't happen again. Back to reality," Marcus said.

It hurt my feelings and bruised my ego that he was treating me with no particular gentleness. We had, after all, shared a night of passion. Passion that I hadn't experienced in years. Maybe not ever. I like to think of myself as a woman of the world, and I certainly had had sex in my share of interesting spots—including, but not limited to, a church parking lot, a cornfield, and the waiting room of my father's dentist office. But the thunderstorm hookup was a first, and I was annoyed that Marcus wasn't giving our liaison its proper due.

"So you're sorry it happened?" I asked.

"Of *course* I am."

I sighed and tried another angle. "So you . . . didn't enjoy it?"

He finally cracked, looked up at me, and grinned. "Totally beside the point, Rhone."

"Don't call me Rhone," I said. "You weren't calling me Rhone last night."

"Last night," he said, shaking his head, "was fucked up. I think it's best we drop the whole thing."

"No," I said.

He looked at me. "No?"

"No. I can't drop it," I said. "It happened. We can't take it back."

"I know we can't take it back, but we gotta forget it," he said. "It was a shitty thing to do. You're engaged . . . and Dex is my boy . . . It's done."

"Right," I said, giving him a suggestive once-over.

He looked away, then crossed his legs, man-style. "It was fucked up."

It made me mad that he was worrying about Dex, instead of me. "Marcus," I said.

"What?"

"I think we should talk about what happened. I think we should talk about *why* it happened." I wanted to test the waters, determine how much he liked me and whether I could have him again if I wanted him. Which I sort of did. Maybe once or twice more. I mean, once you cheat, is it *that* much worse to cheat two or three times?

"It happened because we drank too much."

"That's not *why* it happened. There was more to it than that. You weren't out there with Claire."

He cleared his throat, but said nothing.

"What if I'm not *supposed* to be with Dex?"

"Then you better call off the wedding."

"You want me to do that?" I asked.

"No. I didn't say that. You should marry Dex." His voice was just cold enough to make me want to break him.

"What if I'm supposed to be with you?" I asked, staring purposefully into his eyes.

He looked away. "Ain't gonna happen."

"Why not?"

"Can't happen."

"Why?"

"Because." He got up and shuffled into the kitchen,

returning with a bottle of orange Gatorade. "It was a mistake. One of those things."

"You have no feelings for me whatsoever?" I asked. It was a trap. He couldn't deny any feelings or he would be an asshole for sleeping with me. But if he admitted that he had feelings for me, then the door wouldn't be completely closed.

He thought for a second and skillfully replied, "Sure I like you, Darcy. We're friends."

"So you always do that with your friends?" I snapped back.

He turned the volume down one notch, crossed his arms, and looked at me. "Darce. I thoroughly . . . *enjoyed* last night. . . . But it was a dick move. And I regret it. . . . It was a mistake."

"A *mistake*?" I said, looking highly offended.

"Yeah," he said calmly. "A mistake. An alcohol-related *incident*."

"But it did mean *something* to you?"

"Yeah." He yawned, stretched, and smiled slightly. "Like I said, I enjoyed it. But it's done. Over."

"Okay. Fine," I said. "But you're not going to go out with Rachel again, are you?"

"I dunno. Maybe. Probably. Why?"

"You *are*?" I asked indignantly.

He just looked at me, took a swig of Gatorade. "Why not?"

"Don't you think that's sort of weird now?" I asked. "Like a conflict of interest or something?"

He shrugged, showing me that he saw no problem with it whatsoever.

"You aren't going to sleep with her, are you?" I asked, assuming, based on Rachel's track record, that he hadn't already.

He laughed and said, "Can't rule it out."

"Are you serious?" I asked, horrified. "That's just too weird. We're best friends."

He shrugged.

"Okay. Look. I gotta ask you this. One question . . . If I were single, who would you choose? Rachel or me?" I asked. I was pretty sure I knew the answer but wanted to hear him say it.

He laughed. "You're too much."

"C'mon. Answer me."

"Okay. Here's the truth," he said somberly. I anticipated his first soft words since our encounter. "I'd try to hook up with both of you at once."

I punched his arm and said, "Be serious."

He laughed. "You guys have never done that before?"

"No, we've never done that before! You're gross," I said. "I'm game for a lot, but I like my love one on one. . . . So c'mon, you have to pick. Rachel or me?"

He shrugged. "Close call."

"Close because of Dex, right? But you're more attracted to me?" I asked, looking for affirmation. It wasn't so much that I wanted to beat Rachel. It was more that she had her turf—the intelligent-lawyer thing—while being hot and desired by men was my domain, my main source of self-esteem. And I wanted—and needed—the lines to stay clear.

But Marcus wouldn't grant me any satisfaction. "You're pretty in different ways," he said as he turned the volume back up on the television to show me that our conversation was over. "Now. Let's watch some Wimbledon, what do you say? How about that Agassi?"

For the rest of the weekend, as Marcus did his best to avoid being alone with me, I found myself obsessing over him. And when we all returned to the city, my preoccupation only grew stronger. I didn't necessarily want to have an affair with him, but I wanted him to want me.

But that clearly wasn't happening. Despite a barrage of e-mails and phone calls, Marcus pretty much ignored me. So about a week later, I took drastic measures and showed up at his apartment with a six-pack of beer and *Pulp Fiction*, a movie all men love. Marcus buzzed me up to his apartment and was standing in his open door with his arms crossed. He was wearing gray sweats with a hole in the knee and a faded, stained T-shirt. Still, he looked hot, as one can only look after you've just had forbidden sex with them in the pouring rain.

"Well? Can I come in? I brought treats," I said, holding up the beer and the video.

"Nope," he said, still smiling.

"Please?" I said sweetly.

He shook his head and laughed, but didn't budge.

"C'mon? Can we please just hang out tonight?" I asked. "I just want to spend time with you. As friends. Strictly friends. Is that so wrong?"

He made an exasperated sound and moved over just enough to let me squeeze by him. "You're a trip."

"I just want to see you again. As friends. I promise," I said, surveying his stereotypically messy bachelor pad. Clothes and newspapers were strewn everywhere. A Stouffer's frozen lasagna sat thawing on his coffee table. His bed was unmade, the bottom sheet straining to cover a ratty blue mattress. And a large fish tank, badly needing a good scrub, sat next to a plasma screen television and dozens of video games. He saw me take it all in.

"Wasn't expecting company."

"I know. I know. But you wouldn't return my calls. I needed to take drastic measures."

"I know about you and your drastic measures," he said,

pointing at a futon opposite his leather sectional. "Have a seat."

"Come on, Marcus. I think we can handle sitting on the couch together. I swear, nothing's going to happen."

It was a lie, and we both knew it.

So halfway through the movie, after a few smooth moves by me, Marcus and I were making our second big "mistake." And, I have to say, I liked him even better on a dry, soft couch.

six

After that night on the couch, Marcus stopped resisting and stopped referring to us as a mistake. Although he seldom initiated contact, he was always available when I asked to see him—whether during lunch in the middle of the day or at night whenever Dex worked late. All my free time involved Marcus. And when I wasn't with Marcus, I was thinking about him, fantasizing about him. The sex was ridiculous, over-the-top stuff I thought only existed in movies like *9½ Weeks*. I couldn't get enough of Marcus, and he clearly was just as obsessed with me. He tried to play it cool, but every now and then, I'd get a clue about his feelings by the sound of his voice when I'd call or the way he'd look at me after sex when I'd lounge naked in his apartment.

But despite our escalating romance, Marcus never so much as hinted that I should call off the wedding. Not once. Not even when I pressed him on it, asking him point-blank if I should go through with it. He'd just say, "That's up to you, Darce." Or, even more frustrating, he'd say that I should marry Dex. I know it was just his guilt talking, but I hated it anyway. Although I had no intention of canceling my wedding and should have been enjoying the freedom that came with a demand-free love affair, I still wanted Marcus to tell me that he *had* to be with me, that if I didn't tell Dex the truth about us, he would. Such measures would have matched the passionate idea of us— that unstoppable, unnameable force drawing us together. But that wasn't Marcus's style. Although he overcame the guy's guy hurdle by sleeping with a friend's fiancée, he wasn't willing to go the whole way and actually sabotage the wedding.

And so my engagement to Dex stayed on course, the partition between fiancé and lover firm. I'd leave Marcus's apartment and return to my own, completely switching gears, picking up my wedding files and ordering three hundred wedding favors without batting an eye. As into Marcus as I was, I still thought of myself as part of the golden couple and believed that nobody was better for me in the long run than Dex. At least on paper. Dex had it all over Marcus on paper. For one, he was better looking. If you polled a hundred women, Dex would get every vote. Marcus wasn't as tall, his hair wasn't as thick, and his features weren't as chiseled. And in other categories, too, Marcus came up short: he wasn't as neat, he had a terrible work ethic, he didn't make as much money, he didn't come from as good a family, his taste wasn't as refined, he had cheated on past girlfriends, and was capable of lying to a friend.

Marcus only prevailed in that fuzzy, intangible way that either matters a lot or not much at all, depending on whom you ask. We were all about all the stuff you can't really articulate. The lust, passion, the physical connection. He was irresistible, imperfections and all, and I couldn't stop going back for more. Not that I really tried. I breezed along, making wedding plans, returning home to Dex after having sweaty, intense sex with his groomsman. I reassured myself that I'd get my fix before the wedding, and that from that day forward, I'd be a loyal wife. I was just having a final fling. Just getting things out of my system. Plenty of guys did it. Why couldn't I?

Of course, I didn't tell a soul about my affair. Not my mother, with whom I usually shared all. Not Claire, who wouldn't even begin to understand why I would cheat on someone with Dexter's pedigree and jeopardize my future. And certainly not Rachel. Because she's so judgmental and because I knew she had a small crush on Marcus.

Only once did I come close to divulging the full truth. It was after I misplaced my ring in Marcus's apartment and accused his maid of stealing it. I was in a panic, worried about getting a replacement before the wedding, worried about telling Dex that the ring was missing, and suddenly worried about whether I should marry Dex at all. So in desperation, I turned to Rachel for guidance. She had always been my decision maker on even the most trivial matters, like whether to buy the chocolate or tan raw leather Gucci boots (although at the time, that didn't feel very trivial), so I knew she'd rise to the occasion in my hour of need. I confessed my affair, but downplayed its importance, telling her that it had only happened once. I also told her that I had slept with a guy from work—rather than Marcus. I just wanted to spare her feelings because at that point I didn't think the full truth would ever emerge.

As always, Rachel gave sound advice. Over Chinese delivery, she convinced me that the affair was simply a manifestation of cold feet, the cold feet that only a man— or a woman with endless options—can understand. She made me see that although the initial passion of an intense affair is hard to pass up, what I had with Dex was better, more enduring. I believed her, and decided that I was going to marry Dex.

Then, one night in August, about three weeks before my wedding, something happened that made me question my decision. I had a client dinner that was canceled at the last minute, so I showed up at Marcus's apartment to surprise him. He wasn't yet home, but I convinced his doorman to give me his spare key so I could wait inside for him. Then I went upstairs, got undressed except for a pair of leopard-print heels, and sprawled out on his couch, anxious for him to come find me.

About an hour passed, and just as I was dozing, I heard unmistakable female giggling in the hallway and Marcus's low voice, obviously cracking up his companion. I scrambled to get dressed, but couldn't do so before Marcus and a blonde—who vaguely reminded me of Stacy from Aureole—walked inside. She had a pretty face but was pear-shaped, and worse, wearing Nine West footwear from about three seasons ago. The three of us stood there, mere feet apart. I was still completely naked but for my Blahniks.

"Darcy—you scared the shit out of me," Marcus said, looking not nearly scared enough as far as I was concerned. "My doorman didn't tell me you were up here."

I managed to throw on one of Marcus's dirty T-shirts that was draped over the back of his couch, but not before I caught the girl giving me an envious once-over. "I guess he forgot," I hissed.

"I'll leave," the blonde said, backing up like a trapped doe.

"You do that," I said, pointing at the door.

Marcus said, "Bye, Angie, I'll—"

"He'll call you tomorrow, Angie," I spit out caustically. "Toodle-oo."

As soon as the door closed, I tried to hit him, while screaming at him: *You bastard, you liar, you tainted my engagement, you ruined my life.*

I knew deep down that I had no right to be so enraged, that I was only a few weeks away from marrying somebody else. And yet, at the same time, I felt that I had every right. So I kept delivering inept blows while he effortlessly blocked each one with his hands or forearms just as my personal trainer does during a kickboxing session.

This battery went on for some time, until finally Marcus got angry. He grabbed my wrists, shook me a little, and shouted, "What did you think was going to happen, Darcy?"

"With Angie?" I said, hoping that he was about to tell me that he and Angie were strictly friends, that *nothing* was going to happen.

"No," he said with disgust. "What did you think was going to happen after you got married? Have you even stopped to think about that?"

Of course I had, I told him, suddenly on the defensive. I hadn't expected this line of questioning.

"And?"

"I don't even know if I am getting married," I said. Of course, I had every intention of getting married but thought I had a greater right to be indignant if my nuptials were up in the air.

"Well, assuming you do," Marcus said. "Did you think we'd keep seeing each other?"

"No," I snapped back self-righteously.

"I mean, Jesus Christ, Darcy," he shouted. "It's bad enough that I've been seeing my friend's fiancée for almost two fucking months. But, you know, I draw the line there. I'm not gonna sleep with his wife in case that's what you had in mind."

"I did *not* have that in mind," I said. If he was going to take the high ground, then so would I—although the high ground was eroding quickly.

"So what then? Did you think I was going to be celibate

after you got married? Pine away after you for the rest of my life? Hang out with you and Dex all the while thinking, 'Gee whiz, what a lucky guy he is. How I wish I could be him.'?"

"No," I said, although I did like the whole star-crossed lovers theme. Who doesn't? I mean, there is a reason why *Romeo and Juliet* is such a beloved tale.

"Then Christ, Darcy, what do you want from me?" he shouted louder, now pacing back and forth across his apartment.

I considered this for a moment and then said, in a pitiful, small voice with my dying-calf-in-a-hailstorm expression, "I want you to love me."

He made a *puh* sound and looked at me, disgusted. Everything was backfiring. Why was I suddenly the bad guy?

I sat down, pulling his T-shirt over my knees. Tears streamed down my cheeks. Crying always worked with Dex. But Marcus didn't fold. "Oh, *stop* crying!" he said. "Stop it *now*!"

"Well, *do you* love me?" I pressed, hopeful.

He shook his head. "I'm not playing your manipulative little games, Darce."

"I'm not manipulating you. . . . Why won't you answer the question?" I was suddenly on a singular quest.

"Why don't you answer *my* question? Okay? You tell me what the hell difference it would make if I did love you? Tell me that. Huh?" His face was turning red and his hands were moving all over the place. Unless it involved a sporting event or gambling, I had never seen him agitated, let alone angry or upset.

For a second, I was enchanted by the intensity of his reaction, as well as the word *love* coming from him. It was the closest he had ever come to telling me that he had real feelings for me. But then I pictured Angie and I was straight back to being furious. "Well, if you do love me, then what about *Angie*?" I pointed at the door, where my weak competition had exited. "Why was she here? Who is she, anyway?"

"She's nobody," he said.

"If she's such a nobody," I asked, "then why were you going to have sex with her?"

I expected a denial, but instead he looked at me defiantly.

"*Were* you going to have sex with her?" I asked.

He waited several beats, and then said, "Yup. Matter of fact, that was the plan."

I delivered a solid punch to his shoulder. My hand hurt, but he didn't flinch.

"You're such an asshole," I said. "I hate you *so much*!"

He gave me a blank stare and said, "Just go, Darcy. Leave now. This is over. We're done. I'll see you at your wedding."

I could tell he meant it. I was stunned, simply couldn't believe it would all end like this. "Is that what you really want?"

He spit out a disdainful laugh. "Has this ever been about anything other than what *you* want?"

"Oh, puh-*lease*," I said. "As if you haven't been enjoying every second of it."

"Sure. It's been fun," he said flippantly.

"That's it? *Fun?*"

"Yeah. Fun. A blast. A real joyride. The time of my life," Marcus said. "What do you want me to say? What do you want from me?"

I considered the question and answered it honestly. "I want you to want me. For more than just fun. For more than just great sex. I want you to want me for real."

He sighed, laughed, and shook his head. "Okay, Darce, I want you. I *want* you. I want you all to myself. Are you happy now?"

Before I could answer, he turned the corner into the bathroom, slamming the door behind him. I waited a minute before I followed him, finding the door unlocked. He was leaning against his sink in the dark. From the light in the hall, I could see his face in the mirror. He looked sad, and that both surprised and softened me.

"Yes," I said quietly.

"Yes what?"

"Yes to your question. I am happy that you want me," I said. "And I love you too."

He gave me a disarmed look. I had my answer. Marcus loved me. I felt a rush of joy—a feeling of triumph and passion. "I'm calling off the wedding," I finally said.

More silence.

"Did you hear what I said?"

"I heard you."

"What do you think of that?"

"Are you sure you wanna do that?"

"Yes. I'm sure."

In truth, I wasn't at all sure, but it was the first moment I could actually picture doing it—cutting the long, safe cord with Dex and starting a new life. Maybe it took seeing Marcus with someone else and realizing that we were over in a matter of days if I didn't make a choice. Maybe it was watching him lean against his bathroom sink with those sad brown eyes. Maybe it was hearing him use the word *love*. And maybe it was the fact that the emotional ante had been so raised, I had nowhere else to go but there. It would have been anticlimactic to say anything else.

Moments later, Marcus and I were having intense, condomless sex.

"I'm going to come," Marcus finally breathed, after I had twice.

"Two more seconds," I said, crouching over him.

"Move now. I mean it."

So I moved harder, right down on him, not caring that I was in the middle of my cycle, probably at the most perilous millisecond of the month.

"What are you doing?" he shouted, his eyes wide and scared. "You wanna get pregnant?"

At that instant, it seemed like a great idea—the perfect romantic solution. "Why not?"

He gave me a half-smile and told me I was crazy.

"Crazy for you," I said.

"Don't *ever* do that again," he said. "I mean it."

"Okay, Daddy," I said, although I really didn't think we had hit the jackpot with our effort. There had been plenty of times in my life—especially in college—when I forgot to take my pill or hadn't been careful enough. But I had never gotten pregnant. In fact, part of me believed that I couldn't get pregnant. Which suited me just fine. When the time came, I would just hop on a plane and pick up a baby in China or Cambodia. Like Nicole Kidman or Angelina Jolie. And *presto,* I'd become a glam mom with my perfect body intact.

"That's not funny," Marcus said, smiling. "Go do something. Wash up or pee or something, would you?"

"No way," I said, tucking my legs underneath me, the technique my high school friend Annalise described using while she and her husband were trying to have a baby. "Swim, you little spermies, swim!"

Marcus laughed and kissed my nose. "You freak."

"Yes, but you love me," I said. "Say it again."

"Again? I never said it the first time."

"Pretty much you did. Say it again."

He exhaled and looked at me fondly. "I kinda love you, you freak."

I smiled, thinking that I had finally succeeded. Marcus

was broken. He was mine if I wanted him. In the days that followed, I floundered, looking for a sign, any sign. Should I choose Dex or Marcus? Marriage or sex? Security or fun?

Then, one day in early September, a week before my wedding, I finally got my final answer in the form of two parallel pink lines on a plastic, urine-soaked stick.

seven

"What's it say?" Marcus asked, as I emerged from the bathroom with the plastic stick in hand. He was waiting for me on his couch while flipping through a *Sports Illustrated*.

"It says . . . 'Congratulations, Daddy.' "

"No way."

"Yes way."

"You're shitting me."

"Nope. I'm pregnant."

Marcus leaned back on his couch and closed his magazine. I sat next to him, took his hands, and waited for more. Perhaps an embrace, a gentle touch, a few tears.

"And . . . you're sure . . . that it's mine?"

"Yes," I said. "That question is insulting and hurtful. I haven't had sex with Dex since—well, since forever. And you know it."

"You're sure about that? Not even one time this month? It isn't the time to exaggerate, Darce."

"Yes, I'm sure," I said firmly. It was the truth, thank goodness.

I thought of my high school friend Ethan, who is fair and blue-eyed and how he had married his pregnant girl-friend, Brandi, also a blonde. Months later she gave birth to a dark-skinned baby with eyes the color of Oreos. Rachel and I felt so sorry for Ethan—for the heartache and humiliation he had to endure during his divorce. But I actually felt almost as bad for Brandi. For some reason, I identified with her in a kindred, fellow-rule-breaker way. I knew she must have suffered incredibly for nine months, hoping and praying that the baby would come out looking like her husband and not the Native Alaskan she was melt-ing igloos with on the side. The waiting must have been agonizing. Just thinking about it made my stomach turn. So it was a very lucky thing that I hadn't had sex with Dex in at least a month. I was sure the baby was Marcus's.

I put the stick on his coffee table and stared at the two pink lines. "Wow," I said, feeling giddy. "A positive test. I've never seen one of those . . . and I've taken plenty."

"Should we do another test? Just to double-check?" Marcus asked, pulling another box of tests from the Duane Reade bag. "I got two brands."

"I don't think you get many false positives with preg-nancy tests," I said. "It only works the other way."

"Humor me," Marcus said as he tore the plastic wrap-per off another test.

I sighed loudly as I retrieved the mug full of my pee from his bathroom.

Marcus's face fell. "You peed in my Broncos mug?"

"Yeah. So?"

"That's my favorite mug," he said, cringing.

"Oh, for heaven's sake, just wash it," I said. "And anyway, haven't you ever heard that urine is completely sterile?"

Marcus made a face.

"Since when are you a stickler for germs?" I asked, looking around his sty of an apartment.

"I'll never be able to drink out of that mug again," he grumbled.

I rolled my eyes and stuck a fresh stick into his precious mug. Then I slowly counted to five aloud, before withdrawing it and placing it on the coffee table next to the first test.

Marcus studied the second hand on his watch until I said, "A cross! That means positive!"

"Lemme see," he said, looking stunned and wide-eyed as he examined the stick, comparing it to the diagram on the back of the box. "It looks kind of faint compared to the picture."

"A faint cross still counts," I said. "It's the whole 'you can't be a little bit pregnant' concept. Here. Read the directions."

Marcus scanned the page of fine print, obviously hoping to find a disclaimer—a section on false positives. A flash of fear crossed his face as he put the directions down. "So what now?"

"Well, for starters, we're having a baby in about nine months," I said jubilantly.

"You can't be serious." His voice had a hard edge.

I gave him a look that told him I was totally serious. Then I took his hands in mine.

Marcus stiffened. "Are you sure that's what you want? 'Cause we have other options."

The implication was clear. I raised my chin and said, "I don't believe in abortion."

I'm not sure why I said it, because I am actually as pro-choice as they come. Furthermore, I didn't particularly want to be a mother at this stage of my life. I had none of the biological cravings that so many of my friends had been experiencing lately as we reached our thirtieth year. And I certainly didn't want to gain a bunch of pounds. Or have all of that responsibility, and those restrictions on my freedom and night life.

But at that moment, I was inexplicably happy with my positive pregnancy tests. Perhaps because I was so wrapped up in Marcus that the idea of having his baby seemed thrilling. The ultimate romantic endeavor. Or maybe I liked the feeling of reeling him in just a little bit more. Not that I questioned his commitment to me. I could tell he was crazy about me in his own peculiar way. But he was one of those guys you could never quite control, and being pregnant with his child tightened my grip. Not that I consciously got myself pregnant. Not really. I thought back to our make-up sex. Clearly, it was just meant to be.

And even clearer to me at that moment was this: a positive pregnancy test meant that my wedding was off. The fact that my relief was so palpable meant that I had my true answer: I didn't want to marry Dex. In one instant, I felt over Dex and our fairy-tale wedding, only thrilled to be a part of an even greater drama.

"I'll tell Dex today," I said with an aplomb that surprised even me.

"That you're pregnant?" Marcus asked, aghast.

"No. Just that the wedding is off."

"Are you sure you wanna do that? Are you sure you wanna have a baby?" he asked, looking panicked.

"Positive." I looked over at the sticks. "*Positive*. Get it?"

Marcus just sat there, looking shell-shocked and a little bit pissed.

"Aren't you at *all* happy?" I asked him.

"Yeah," he said glumly. "But—but I think we need to slow down and discuss our . . . options."

I let him stumble on. "I could have sworn you said you were pro-choice?"

"Okay. So I *am* pro-choice," I said with an exaggerated nod. "And I *choose* to have this baby. *Our* baby."

"Well, take your time thinking it all over . . ."

"You're hurting my feelings," I said.

"Why?"

"Because I *want* to have this baby," I said, getting upset. "And I wish you felt the same. . . . I can't believe you haven't even hugged me yet."

Marcus sighed and put his arms loosely around me.

"Tell me you're happy. A little bit happy," I whispered in his ear.

Marcus looked at me again and said unconvincingly, "I'm happy. I'm just saying that maybe we want to slow down and think things through. Maybe you should talk to someone."

I gave him a scornful gaze. "You mean a shrink?"

"Something like that."

"That's ridiculous. People go to therapists when they are filled with despair. But I'm *thrilled*," I said.

"Still, you might have some issues around this thing," Marcus said. He always talked in generalities about our relationship—*some issues, this thing, our deal, the situation*—and sometimes with just a quick flourish of his hand. It always irritated me that he thought a hand motion could capture our essence. We were so much more than that. Especially now. We were going to be parents.

"I have no issues. I'm in love with you. I want to keep our baby. And that is that." Even as I said it, I knew that *that* was never just *that* in my world. *That* was *maybe that* or *some of that* or *that along with a dose of this*. But I kept going, resolute. "Now, if you'll excuse me, I have a wedding to cancel."

And that's exactly what I did. I marched right back over to the Upper West Side to break the news to my fiancé. I found Dex putting away his dry cleaning, stripping off the plastic coverings and separating his blue shirts from the white. For one moment, I couldn't do it, couldn't imagine telling Dex that after years of being together, we were finished. But then I thought about Marcus and drew confidence from him.

"We need to talk," I said, all business.

"All right," Dex said slowly. And I could tell he knew exactly what was coming. He had appeared clueless for weeks, but his expression at that moment told me that even men have intuition.

Mere sentences later our wedding was officially canceled. A seven-year relationship over. It was bizarre how fast and easy it was. Technically, Dex was the one to pull the cord, saying that it would be a mistake to get married. Hearing him use the word *mistake* in relation to me made me backtrack for a second, but then I convinced myself that he was simply acknowledging a reality I had created. He was reacting to my emotional and physical withdrawal from him. I watched him, with all that balled, dry-cleaning plastic at his feet, and felt sorry for him.

I kissed his clean-shaven cheek and said what people always say when they dump someone under amicable circumstances. I told him that I wished the best for him and hoped that he would find happiness. And I meant it on one level. After all, I certainly didn't want Dex to die alone. But if I'm completely honest, I'd say that I *did* want him to grieve for a good long while before seeking out his next girlfriend, a girlfriend I hoped would never quite measure up to me. Little did I know that he would be looking for that runner-up in my best friend's apartment.

eight

The morning after the great closet fiasco I awoke in Marcus's bed, momentarily disoriented. I had only spent the night with him once before, when Dex had gone on a business trip to Dallas, but I had left very early the next morning while it was still dark. So that really didn't count as a full-fledged sleepover.

This morning felt different. Everything felt different. I looked around, noticing how bright the morning sun was in his apartment. It was almost as if I were seeing it for the first time, seeing Marcus for the first time. I studied his profile and his receding (but still sexy) hairline as it hit me that the end of our saga had finally come. Marcus and I were a done deal with a baby on the way. There was no more Dex to creep back to. I felt a rush of adrenaline as I anticipated breaking the news to my friends, coworkers, and acquaintances. I wondered what explanation Dex would offer to his friends and family. I thought of all the celebrity breakups, wishing that I had a spokesperson to contact his spokesperson, to agree on one unified statement. Still, after seven years you know a person pretty well, and I was almost positive that Dex would keep the indelicate details to himself. So I could spin things pretty much my way. I considered my options. I could tell the whole truth, confess my relationship with Marcus. Or I could say nothing about Marcus and shift the blame to Dex and Rachel. Or I could maintain an aura of mystery.

It was tempting to divulge the closet tale and turn people against Rachel and Dex, but I certainly didn't want to look like some kind of tossed-aside loser. I had to safeguard my reputation in the city as a diva. After all, divas don't get played. So I decided that I would tell everyone that I broke up with Dex, simply announce that I was very sad to end our relationship, but it was for the best because we just weren't meant to be together. I would go for a somber, "I will survive" tone. It would elicit a certain degree of sympathy, but also inspire awe that I was the strong sort of woman who could voluntarily break free of a tall, dark, and handsome man. I'd omit the Marcus part of the equation for the time being. And of course I'd leave out my pregnancy. I was all for appearing to be a woman in charge, but not a full-on hussy. My public would know the truth at some point, but that was a worry for later.

In the meantime, I'd just cross my fingers and hope that nobody would find out about Dex and Rachel. I mean, *surely* they wouldn't keep seeing each other. It was an absolute impossibility. She wasn't his type. He was only using her in his moment of extreme sadness. He was a lost soul, she a familiar, comforting friend. As for Rachel, she had just succumbed to the most attractive man ever to cross her radar. A girl like Rachel only has such an opportunity once in her life. But she would come to her senses and return to the average Joes. She would never date such a significant ex of mine. It's a cardinal rule—and Rachel was all about rules. I was sure she was already racked with guilt for her fleeting weakness. Any day now she was going to come crawling back to me, eloquently detailing exactly how sorry she was. And if she begged long enough, talked of our friendship with enough passion, I might eventually let her back into the fold. But it would take a long, long time for her to win back the accolade of best friend.

I turned to look at Marcus again, now sleeping with one hand tucked behind his head, the other hanging off the bed. His brow was furrowed as if he were doing long division in his sleep. Then his lips curled into a sexy pout, accentuating the cleft in his chin. Suddenly his face morphed into Dexter's, like the faces at the end of Michael Jackson's "Black or White" video.

"Marcus, wake up," I said, shaking his arm. "I'm starting to freak out."

He kept snoring. I leaned over and kissed him. He made a low, throaty noise, opened one eye, and mumbled, "Mornin', Darce."

"Do you think they're together right now?" I asked.

"I told you already," he said. I guess he was referring to the *no* that he'd given a dozen times the night before.

"Tell me again."

"Nah . . . I highly doubt it. I'm sure you ruined the mood, and he probably left."

I decided to believe him. "Okay . . . But even so, I don't think I can go to work today. I'm too distracted. You wanna call in sick with me?"

In the seven years I had dated Dex he had never once called in sick unless he truly was extremely ill. Things were going to be different with Marcus. Our life was going to be so much more spontaneous and fun.

Sure enough, Marcus said, "All right, you twisted my arm. I'll sleep in."

I felt a fleeting sense of victory, but then realized that in

some twisted way, I was actually looking forward to the
wave I was about to create at work, so I said with a martyr's sigh, "I guess I *should* go in and get it over with."

"Get what over with?"

"You know . . . telling everyone that the wedding is off."

"Hmm-mmm."

"What exactly should I say?"

No response.

"Marcus!"

"You don't have to tell anyone anything," Marcus said,
rolling over toward me. "It's nobody's business."

"Of course I have to tell them. They think I'm getting
married on Saturday. Some of them are invited."

I admired Marcus's laid-back approach to life, but this
was a perfect example of him underestimating the requi-
site effort something would take. It might even prove to
be problematic later, if he underestimated my desire to
have nice things on my birthday, Christmas, Valentine's,
and randomly throughout the year. Dex knew the drill:
flowers arrived like clockwork every other month, which
meant a standing order rather than a rush of emotion, but
that was fine with me. Attention was attention. Nice things
were nice things.

But Marcus could be trained, I was sure of it. Every
man can be trained. I welcomed the challenge of molding my new boyfriend into a responsible—but still sexy
and spontaneous—husband and father. For now, I had to
make him understand that breaking the news to my colleagues was going to be a huge, emotional ordeal and that
I would need his support—i.e., phone calls and e-mails
during my trying day. Maybe even a luxury good waiting
for me upon my return to his apartment. I imagined him
coming through the door with an orange Hermès box
and a doting smile.

"I know you have to tell the people you invited," Marcus

said. "I just think it's unnecessary to explain the whole thing in detail. Just send a mass e-mail and be done with it."

"But they're going to ask what happened," I said, thinking that I'd be disappointed if they didn't. "People want details."

"I know you would, you little information hound, but not everyone is like you."

"Everyone is like me in the world of public relations. Trust me. It's our business to gather, hoard, and disperse juicy details. And this is big-time juicy."

"Well, I'm just sayin' that it's your prerogative to tell people to mind their own fuckin' business," Marcus said.

I told him that wasn't my style. Then I got up quickly, resisting the urge to have sex. After all, I had a lot to accomplish in a day. I showered, put on my makeup, and then checked Marcus's closet, which was full of my clothes that I had brought over the night before. I opted for an Escada pencil skirt, a green Versace V-neck, and a pair of Ferragamo slingbacks. Then, I leaned into the bathroom to say good-bye to Marcus, who was singing "Purple Rain" at the top of his lungs, and, impressively, in tune.

"See you tonight, hon!" I called into the bathroom.

He stopped singing and poked his head around the shower curtain. "Sounds good. . . . C'mere and give me a quick kiss."

"Can't. The steam will ruin my hair," I said, blowing him a kiss from the doorway. Then I maneuvered through the busy city streets to the subway as I considered my strategy for how to break the news. I could tell Claire, coworker and new best friend effective immediately, that she was free to spread the word. Then I remembered that she had an out-of-office meeting with a potential new client this morning, and I couldn't stand the thought of waiting for her return. So I would send a mass e-mail as Marcus suggested, adopting just the right tone.

When I got to my office, I settled into my chair in front of my computer and quickly typed out my breaking news:

> *Good morning, everyone. I just wanted to let you all know that my wedding will not be taking place this Saturday. It was a difficult decision, but I think I'm doing the right thing. I know it's a bit odd to send out a group e-mail regarding such a personal matter, but I thought this was the easiest way.*

Perfect. It was strong but emotional. And most important, it clearly signaled that I had done the dumping. I reread it, thinking that something was missing. I added an ellipsis at the end. Yes. Perfect touch. Those three little dots would conjure the sound of my voice trailing away mysteriously. Now for a subject line. Should it say "Wedding" or "Canceled" or "News"? None seemed right, so I kept the subject line blank. Then, as I selected my personal e-mail group and prepared to send the shocking nugget via cyberspace, my phone rang.

"Darcy," my boss, Cal, said in his breathy, effeminate voice. "How are ya?"

"Not so good, Cal," I said in my "I can't deal with taking instructions" voice. One that he knew well. It was the beauty of working for Cal. He was a complete pushover.

"Well, may I please see you in Conference Room C?"

"For what?"

"We need to talk about the Celebrity Golf Challenge."

"Right *now*?"

"Yes, if you could. Please?"

I sighed as loudly as possible. "Okay," I said. "I'll be there when I can."

Damn. Had I arrived a few minutes earlier, he'd be opening my e-mail and contacting someone else about the golf tournament. I was sure that once I told him the news, he'd pass the project elsewhere, especially if I could work up a few tears. In fact, I could probably squeeze a few leisurely weeks out of my purported hardship. Maybe Marcus and I could even take a vacation together. I minimized my e-mail, deciding that I'd give it a final tweaking and a spell-check before sending, and then made my way downstairs to the conference room. I pushed open the heavy door with a hangdog expression.

And there before me was the entire staff of Carolyn Morgan and Associates, all packed into the room, yelling *"Surprise!"* and hurling their heartiest congratulations at me from all directions. A gigantic blue box from Tiffany perched on one end of the lacquered table. An ivory-frosted cake with pink gel writing sat temptingly at the other. My heart raced. Talk about your audiences! Talk about your drama!

"We knew you'd expect your party later in the week!" Claire squealed. "Gotcha! And you believed I had that meeting!"

She was right. They had, indeed, gotten me. But I was about to get them right back. Top their surprise. I smiled hesitantly, and said, "You shouldn't have."

"Of course we should have," Claire said.

"No. You *really* shouldn't have," I said.

Cal stepped toward me and put his arm around me. "Speech," he said.

"I'm speechless," I said. "I'm literally without speech."

"Impossible," Cal said. "I've known you for years and never seen it happen yet."

Laughter rippled through the room, affirming that, indeed, I had the biggest mouth in the place. I cleared my throat again and took a step forward, smiling demurely. "Well. Thank you all so very much . . . but . . . there isn't going to *be* a wedding. I'm not getting married."

Cal and some others laughed again. "Yeah. Yeah. You're going down like the rest of us poor, married fools," he said.

I smiled bravely and said, "No. Actually, I called the wedding off this weekend."

Like a Red Cross volunteer during a fire at an orphanage, Claire sprang into action. *"Omigod! No! Way!"* She pressed one hand to her temple and whisked me out of the conference room back up to my office, her arm around my waist as if I might, at any moment, faint. "What in the *world* is going on?" she asked when we were alone.

"It's over." I sniffed.

"Why? You and Dex are perfect together! What happened?"

"It's a long story," I said, my eyes filling with tears as I thought about Dex in Rachel's closet. Despite all my plans to the contrary, I just couldn't resist telling her. I needed her sympathy and full support. I needed her to tell me that Dex could not possibly be interested in boring old Rachel. So I dropped the bomb on her. "We broke up this weekend, and then, yesterday afternoon, I caught Dex and Rachel together."

"What?" Claire's mouth fell open.

I nodded. "You're telling me."

"What do you mean 'together'? Are you sure?"

"Yes. I went over to talk to Rachel about this whole situation and Dex was there, in his boxers, all crouched down, hiding in her closet."

"No!"

"Yes," I said.

"Oh. My. God." Claire covered her mouth with both hands and shook her head. "I—I don't even know what to say. I just can't . . . what in the world was he thinking? What was *she* thinking? How *could they?"*

"Please don't tell anyone," I said. "It's all so humiliating. I mean, my maid of honor!"

"Of course not. Cross my heart," Claire said, making a big X over her bubble-gum-pink twin set. She gave me a few seconds of respectful silence before launching into Q&A mode. "Was it a one-time thing?" she asked.

"It *had* to be a one-time thing, don't you think?"

"Oh. I'm sure. Dex would *never* like her," she said.

"I know. I just can't see it. There's no way, right?"

"No way. He just couldn't go from you to her. She's just so plain, and . . . I don't know. . . . I know she's your best friend so I don't want to say anything bad—"

"What? She is *so* not my best friend anymore. I despise her."

"I don't blame you," Claire said solemnly, ready to step up and fill Rachel's bland shoes.

I threw her the bone she so craved. "You're my best friend now."

Claire clasped her hands together and looked at me as though she might cry. Ever since our roomie days together, Claire had jockeyed for position as my most favored friend. At times, she was downright obsequious. But it was what I needed at that moment, and she delivered. "Oh, Darce. I'm *totally* here for you."

"Thanks," I said. "I appreciate that."

"We're going to have the *best* time hanging out as single girls again," she said. "What are you doing tonight? Henry Fabuss is throwing a big bash at Lotus this evening—for his thirtieth. We should totally go. He's such a hoot—and he's so totally dialed in, you know? Everyone's going to be there. It would really get your mind off this."

"Not tonight," I said. "I think I just need some alone time. In fact, I think I'm going home now. I can't stand being here—and I don't want anyone to see me crying."

"Want me to come with you? I'm sure Cal would let me leave with you," she said. "We could go shopping. Retail therapy."

"No, thanks. I think I want to be alone," I said, even though I was actually planning to be with Marcus.

"Okay," she said, obviously disappointed. "I understand."

"I just need to get this e-mail out before I leave. Can you read it and see what you think?"

Proofing my e-mails used to be Rachel's role. She had been so good at it. I vowed to banish her from my thoughts. She was persona non grata until her apology came forth in skywriting. Meanwhile, Claire took her job seriously, leaning in close to my monitor, and reading the e-mail twice. She finally looked up, gave me a brisk nod, and said it was fine, just fine. So I hit send and sashayed down the hall, relishing the stares and whispers from my colleagues along the way.

nine

Marcus agreed to leave work early and meet me back at his apartment, where we had fantastic sex. Afterward, I rested my head on his chest and told him my conference room tale.

"I'm surprised you didn't jet with the Tiffany box," he said after I had finished the story.

"I wanted to," I said. "I bet it was something good. . . . Oh, well. We'll get a replacement when you and I get married."

No response.

"Do you want to talk about that?" I probed, stroking his arm.

"Talk about what?"

"Us getting married."

"Um—okay. What exactly do you want to talk about?"

"Well, don't you want to do it before the baby's born?" I asked, thinking that I couldn't even focus on my pregnancy until the details of our relationship were squared away. Besides, I was already in full-on wedding mode. There was no reason to let my preparations lapse. I even planned on keeping my dress, knowing that I couldn't find a better gown. "I think we should talk about it. Don't you?"

"I guess so," he said reluctantly.

I chose to ignore his tone and pressed on. "Okay—so when do you think we should do it?"

"I don't know. In six months?"

"When I'm totally showing? No, thanks."

"Five months?"

"Marcus!"

"Four?"

"No. Too long. I think we should do it right away. Or as soon as we can get some plans together."

"I thought you said that we were going to just get a justice of the peace?"

I had, in fact, said something like that somewhere along the line. But that was back when I actually worried about Dexter's feelings. Back when I wasn't even sure that Marcus and I were going to end up together. Now I wanted to have a big wedding just to spite Dex and Rachel and invite all of our mutual friends. I'd invite Rachel's parents too, and then they could report back to her how beautiful I looked, how thrilled I was in my new relationship, how moving Claire's toast was.

"Well, I was actually thinking that we could have a little ceremony. Just something small. Like fifty people or so." My count was more like one hundred, one twenty-five, but I would ease him into the idea.

"Fifty, huh? So pretty much immediate family?" he asked as he scratched the back of his neck.

"Yeah, pretty much. And our closest friends."

He smirked. "Like Dex and Rachel?"

I gave him a look.

"No?" he asked, grinning. "Not Dex and Rachel?"

"Be serious! What do you think about having a real wedding?"

He shrugged and then said, "I'm not sure about all that. That's not really my thing. I'm still kind of thinking that the justice of the peace is the way to go. Or we could elope. I don't know. Do we have to talk about this right now?"

"Okay, fine." I sighed, resigning myself to the fact that he probably wasn't going to be satisfying about a wedding. But what guy really is? Other than those repulsive, girly types on TLC's *A Wedding Story* who blubber their way through the ceremony. And who wants a guy like that?

Later that evening, after Marcus and I came back from dinner, I checked my messages. I had twenty-two at work, fourteen at home. Thirty-six messages in eight hours. And only two were work related. Which meant thirty-four personal messages. Likely an all-time personal record. I sat at Marcus's table, listening to the words of support as I took notes on a pad. When I got to the very last message, the third one from Claire, I looked up at Marcus. "They didn't call," I said, shocked. "Neither one of them."

"Did you think they would?" Marcus asked.

"Yes. They *owe* me a call. Especially Rachel."

"But didn't you say that you never wanted to speak to her again?"

I shot him a look of annoyance. "She should still *try* to call and apologize . . ."

Marcus shrugged.

"And as for Dex, I *have* to talk to him. About logistics. The wedding stuff," I said. "I just can't believe neither one of them called."

Marcus shrugged again. "I don't know what to tell you."

"Okay. For the record, I *abhor* that statement."

"What statement?"

" 'I don't know what to tell you.' "

"Well, I *don't* know what to tell you."

" 'I don't know what to tell you,' " I mimicked again. "It's what repairmen say when they can't fix what's broken. 'But I just bought this car/computer/dryer last month!' you say, at their mercy, and they shoot back with an 'I don't know what to tell you.' Translation: 'It's not my problem and I *really* don't give a shit.' "

Marcus smiled. "Sorry. I won't say it again."

"Thank you," I said, still clutching the phone. "So do you think I should call Dex?"

"Do you want to call him?" Marcus asked as he inspected the bottom of his foot and picked at a callus.

"It's not a question of *want*. It's a question of *need*. We have logistics to work out," I said, slapping his hand away from his foot. "Like canceling the photographer and caterer and band. And reaching everyone on our invite list. Like the honeymoon tickets. Like his moving out."

"So call him."

"But he should call me."

"So wait for him to call you."

"Look, mister. You better start taking a more active interest in these details. In case you forgot, you're an integral part of this whole saga, and you better start having an opinion on all related matters."

Marcus made a face as if to say, *I don't know what to tell you.*

The next few days, leading up to what would have been my wedding day, were jam-packed with nonstop drama. More phone calls, e-mails, and long drawn-out conversations with Claire about why in the world Dex would want to hook up with Rachel, even longer sessions with my mother, who still cried often and could not seem to accept that Dex and I were not going to reunite.

But there was still no word from Dex or Rachel. It infuriated me that they weren't calling. As much as I didn't want to be the one to phone first, I finally broke down and dialed Dexter's work number. We only discussed logistics—the money he owed me, the number of days he had to come remove his belongings from my apartment, that sort of thing. After I had given him my orders, I paused, waiting for him to tell me that the thing with Rachel was a fluke, and that he was only using her to get back at me. When he didn't, I reasoned that he was still so pissed about Marcus that he actually wanted me to think the worst. So I certainly wasn't going to give him the satisfaction of asking about her. Nor would I ask him where he was staying. Never one to impose on a friend, he had likely checked into a hotel. I pictured him ordering a club sandwich from room service and stirring whiskey from the minibar into a glass of Coke as he clicked his way through the Pay-Per-View selections.

"Well. Good bye, Dex," I said as emphatically as possible. This was it. He had one more chance to tell me something, issue a final statement, plead his case. Maybe even tell me that he was sorry or that he missed me.

"All right, then. Bye, Darce," he said without the slightest trace of emotion. I told myself that it just hadn't hit him yet, the finality of it all. When it did, there was going to be some serious depression going on, some serious minibar bingeing happening somewhere in this city.

On what would have been my wedding night, Marcus and I hunkered down in his apartment, ordered Chinese, and had sex twice. Throughout the evening I kept announcing how happy I was not to be making "the biggest mistake of my life." In truth, I felt a bit wistful. Not because I wanted to be marrying Dex. Not because I missed Rachel. I had way too much indignation brewing to be nostalgic about either of them. It was more about the wedding, the party-that-almost-was. It would have been the event of the year, I told Marcus.

"I hear ya," Marcus said. "I could be hanging with my college buddies right now, drinking for free."

I punched him in the arm and told him to take it back. He obliged as he tilted back his third Miller Lite. "Besides, I wasn't in the mood to get dressed up. I hate wearing a tux."

I would have been miffed at the emotionless spin he was putting on our momentous evening together, but I could tell that deep down, he was really happy to have won the grand Darcy prize. I was in the heart of a "boy steals girl away from other boy" love-triangle thriller. Marcus was the victor, and Dex was so crushed that he was driven to hook up—or nearly hook up—with Rachel, a consolation prize if there ever was one. At least that's the way I saw things in those sweet early days.

ten

I don't think my pregnancy truly sank in until the following week, when I had my first prenatal doctor's appointment. Marcus came with me, but only after I guilt-tripped him into it. As we sat together in the waiting room, I filled out insurance forms while he flipped through a *Time* magazine, looking like he'd rather be anywhere else in the world. When the receptionist called my name, I stood up. Marcus stayed put. "Well, come *on*," I said impatiently.

"Can't I wait here?"

I caught a very pregnant woman, sitting with her husband, glance disdainfully at Marcus.

"Get up *now*," I hissed at him.

He did so, but with a loud sigh. More like a groan.

We followed a nurse to the corridor behind the waiting room, where she asked me to step on the scale.

"With all my clothes on?" I asked. I make it a firm policy only to weigh myself naked and first thing in the morning. Or after a long sweat at the gym.

"Yes," the nurse said impatiently.

I slipped off my Tod's, handed my heavy silver cuff bracelet to Marcus, and instructed him to turn around. He did, but not before he rolled his eyes.

The nurse skillfully adjusted the scale with several quick sweeps of her fingertips until it finally steadied at 126½.

"127," she said out loud.

I glared at her. Why did she think I'd wanted Marcus to turn around? "Looked like 126½ to me," I said.

She ignored me, recording 127 on my chart.

Still, this was good news. I was 127, which meant 124 or 125 without clothes. No weight gain yet.

"How tall are you?" the nurse asked.

"Five nine and a half."

She recorded this on my chart and led us to a small, chilly examining room. "The doctor will be with you shortly."

I got up on the table, while Marcus glanced at another magazine rack. Upon discovering that his only offerings were *Parents* and *American Baby,* he chose to read nothing. Minutes later a young, petite blond woman who looked no older than twenty-five bounced into the room. She wore her thick blond hair in a short, pixie cut that showcased huge, brilliant-cut diamond studs. Black leather knee-high boots met the edge of her crisp white doctor's coat.

"Hi. I'm Jan Stein. Sorry I'm running a little behind today." She beamed, reminding me of Tammy Baxter, our head cheerleader in high school—who always got to top the pyramid while I was stuck steadying her heel.

"Darcy Rhone," I said, sitting up straighter, noticing that she had an unusually large chest for such a small frame. Surely a doctor wouldn't get a boob job, though. So they had to be natural. As a relatively flat-chested woman, that is the one combination that has always irked me. Fine, give a gal her big chest if it comes with a cellulite-covered ass. But Jan's assets just weren't fair. Maybe Marcus wouldn't notice, I thought, as I introduced him as "the father."

"It's nice to meet you both." She beamed at Marcus as I noted with satisfaction that she had a slight smear of crimson lipstick on her right front tooth.

Marcus smiled broadly back. I wanted to kick myself for requesting a female doctor.

"Should I take my clothes off?" I asked impatiently, before Jan could engage Marcus further.

"No, I think we'll just chat for a bit first. I want to go through your medical history and answer your questions. I'm sure you have plenty."

"Sounds good," I said, although I actually had none except whether it was okay to have an occasional cup of coffee or glass of wine.

Jan took a seat across from us, rolled her chair closer, and pressed my chart into an old-school wooden clipboard and said, "So. First off. Can you tell me the first date of your last menstrual period?"

"Yes. I can," I said, proud that I'd thought to check the date on my calendar that morning. "August eighth."

She made a note on her chart as I studied the enormous emerald-cut rock on her finger. She had to have been wearing at least a hundred thousand dollars' worth of diamonds. I bet she was engaged to an older, gray-haired surgeon. I had a sudden pang for my engagement ring, which I planned to sell, but reassured myself that it was hip to be at a prenatal appointment with your partner, rather than your husband. I was like a celebrity. Plenty of them skipped the marriage and went right to having babies.

"So when is the baby due?" I asked. I knew she was due around early May, but I was eager to hear an exact date.

Jan pulled out a paper wheel, spun it, and squinted as she checked the dates. "Okay. Your estimated date of delivery, or EDD as you may hear me refer to it, is May second."

The second of May would be Dexter's thirty-fifth

birthday. I looked at Marcus, who was clueless as to the implications of the due date. It's amazing to me how few guys know their friends' birthdays. So I announced to Jan and Marcus, "I hope I'm late—or early—because that's my ex-fiancé's birthday."

Marcus rolled his eyes and shook his head while Dr. Stein laughed and then reassured me that only about 10 percent of babies are born on their actual due date.

"Why's that?" I asked.

Jan looked stumped for a second—not a good sign if such an easy question threw her—and then said, "The due date is only a useful guide."

"Oh," I said, thinking that an older doctor would be able to come up with a better answer than that one. Or even a younger doctor who was less attractive. Ugly girls had more time to study in medical school. I bet Jan finished at the bottom of her class. I bet she wouldn't even be sitting here today but for her surgeon boyfriend. "I see."

"So," Jan said briskly. "I'd like to run through your medical history, ask you some questions."

"Sure," I said, catching Marcus examining Jan's toned left thigh.

I glared at him as Jan launched into her Q&A. She asked me my age (I was glad to say twenty-nine and not thirty), all about my medical history, what medications I was taking, and a bunch of questions about my lifestyle: how often I drank, exercised, whether I smoked, all about my diet, etc. After she had my life story fully recorded, she looked up, a smile plastered on her heavily made-up face.

"So, how have you been feeling?" Jan asked. "Any symptoms? Nausea?"

"My breasts are a little sore," I said.

Marcus looked embarrassed, so I added a gratuitous, "When he touches them."

Jan nodded earnestly. Marcus cringed.

I kept going. "And they're a little bigger, fuller . . . And the areolae are darker. . . . But other than that, I feel exactly the same. And my weight is the same," I said proudly.

"Well, you're only about five and a half weeks pregnant, so it would be a little early for weight gain," Jan said. "Although you might notice an increase in your appetite if you haven't already."

"Nope," I said proudly. "And I don't plan on being one of those chowhound pregnant women. I'm sure you see plenty of those."

Jan nodded again, making a note on my chart. Then she announced that we were ready for the physical examination.

"Should I go?" Marcus asked.

"You're fine to stay," Jan said.

"Told ya," I said to him. And then to Jan, "He feels all awkward."

"Well, he shouldn't. It's great that he's so involved."

"Yeah—we're not married yet," I said. "But he's still very into it."

Jan smiled and told me to change into the gown on the table, she'd be right back. As soon as she left, I asked Marcus if he thought our doctor was pretty.

"She's all right," he said. "Cute, I guess."

"How old would you say she is?"

"Twenty-eight?" he asked.

"Am I prettier?"

"Yes, Darce. You're prettier."

"Will I still be prettier when I'm twenty pounds heavier?"

"Yes," he said, but without much conviction.

Jan returned right as I was getting settled on the table. She took my blood pressure and then examined my heart, breasts, and lungs. "Now I'm going to examine your cervix."

"Does that confirm the pregnancy?"

"Well, we're going to give you a blood and urine test for that, but yes, this will give us further information about the approximate age of the pregnancy, as well as help us assess the size and shape of your pelvis."

I nodded.

"Now, just relax," Jan said.

I let my knees fall apart. "No problem," I said, looking past her at Marcus, who was clearly pretending that he was somewhere else.

After the physical examination was complete, I dressed, went to the bathroom, and peed into a cup, got my blood drawn in a small lab, and returned to the exam room, where Jan told me she'd be in touch with the results of my blood work.

"In the meantime, Darcy, I'm going to give you a prescription for prenatal vitamins. They contain folic acid. It is extremely important for your baby's spinal cord development. You're going to want to take them on a full stomach." She wrote out the prescription in uncharacteristically neat handwriting for a doctor (another bad sign—real doctors should be messy) and handed it to me. "So congratulations to both of you. We'll see you in another four weeks for your first ultrasound."

Marcus and I shook Jan's hand and then headed off to Duane Reade to fill my prescription. For some reason, I remember that five-block walk well. It was a brilliant fall day—brisk but sunny, the sky bright blue and filled with cotton-candy clouds. I remember cinching my blue suede trench coat around my still tiny waist and skipping a few steps, feeling little-girl happy. As we waited at a crosswalk, Marcus took my hand without being prompted and smiled at me. That smile of his is frozen in my mind. It was warm and generous and sincere. It was the kind of smile a man gives you when he's happy to be with you, happy to be marrying you, happy that you are pregnant with his child.

eleven

My apartment's contents hadn't been too depleted when Dex moved out, but he had taken our kitchen table, two lamps, and a dresser. I was thrilled to see them all go, especially the rustic pine table that looked as if it belonged in an Amish home. I planned on going for a sleeker, more contemporary look that would complement the slick high-rise apartment with a view that Marcus and I would purchase together. Good riddance to Dexter's traditional taste, his insistence on prewar buildings long on charm and short on closet space.

So about two weeks after what would have been my wedding day, I dragged Marcus on a furniture-shopping expedition. We took the subway uptown to Fifty-ninth and Lex and walked over to Crate and Barrel on Madison Avenue. As we pushed open the glass doors, I felt a surprising wave of sadness, remembering my last visit to the store, when Dex and I had registered for wedding gifts. I shared the memory with Marcus, who had developed a pat response to such recollections.

"Ahh. The good ol' days," he said, as he followed me to

the second floor. At the top of the stairs, I admired an ob-
long cherry table with tapered legs. It was exactly what I
had in mind for our table, but never imagined I would find
it so easily. I swept my hand across the smooth surface.
"This is perfect. Do you like it? What do you think? Picture it with upholstered chairs. Something in lime green,
perhaps?"

Marcus shrugged. "Sure. Sounds good." He was staring at something behind me. "Um, Darcy . . . Rachel and
Dex are here," he said in a tone that made me know it was
not a joke.

"What?" I froze, and my heart stopped for several
seconds. Then it began to race, beating faster than it does
after a spinning class. "Where?" I whispered.

"At your nine o'clock. Over by that brown couch."

I turned around slowly, cautiously. Sure enough, there
to my left, less than thirty feet away, was the enemy, scru-
tinizing a chenille couch the color of baby poo. They both
had the whole casual Saturday look going—jeans and tennis shoes. Dex had his standard Saturday gray Georgetown
sweatshirt, and Rachel was wearing a navy blue BCBG
sweater that I helped her pick out at Bloomingdale's last
year. The weekend before Dex had proposed, to be exact.
A lifetime ago.

"Oh *shit*! How do I look?" I fumbled for the compact tucked into the side pocket of my Prada bag, and
remembered that at the last minute I had removed it to
add more blush and left it on Marcus's coffee table. I
had no mirror. Instead I had to rely on Marcus. "How's
my face?"

"You look fine," Marcus said. His eyes darted back to
Rachel and Dex.

"What do we do? Should we get out of here?" I said.
My knees felt weak as I leaned on my prospective table.
"I think I'm gonna be sick."

"Maybe we should go have a chat," Marcus deadpanned. "It'd be the well-adjusted, mature thing to do."

"Are you crazy? I don't want to have a *chat*!"

Marcus shrugged. Dex had called Marcus a couple of days earlier to say "no hard feelings and congratulations on the baby." They had both glossed over the details, neither of them uttering my name or Rachel's. Marcus said the conversation was awkward, but had lasted fewer than three minutes. He said there was a tacit understanding that the friendship was over; even for guys, our situation was too much to get past.

"Okay, Darce. Let's get outta here," Marcus said. "I'm not in the mood for a reunion either." He pointed behind me at the staircase leading to the ground floor. We had an easy escape route. Clearly, we hadn't been spotted yet. Dex and Rachel were cheerfully chatting away, completely oblivious to the furniture-shopping coincidence of the century.

I wanted to turn and walk down the stairs, but I couldn't make myself go. It was like watching a gruesome scene in a scary movie. You don't want to see the girl get decapitated, but somehow, you always part your fingers to sneak a peek. I hid behind a bookcase and pulled Marcus down next to me. We watched Rachel and Dex stand and wander over to another couch, slightly closer to us. This one was boxier than the first, and as far as I was concerned, the better choice. Dex studied it and then made a face. It was too modern for him. I translated what had just transpired for Marcus. "See, he doesn't like clean lines. See?"

"Darcy, I don't give a shit about the couch they buy."

"*They buy?* You mean you think it's a *joint purchase*?"

"They buy. He buys. She buys," Marcus said, as if conjugating a verb in French class.

"Does she look good? Do they look happy?"

"Come on, Darce. Let's just go," he said.

I kept staring at them, my insides churning.

"Tell me," I demanded. "Does she look prettier than usual? Thinner maybe?" We watched Rachel and Dex return to their boring, brown couch. She sat and reclined smugly. Then she looked up at Dex and said something. His back was to us, but I could see him nod, run his fingers along the back of the couch. Then he stooped to flip through a book of color swatches on a coffee table next to the couch.

"Do you think they're moving in together?" I asked.

"How the hell should I know?"

"Did he say anything about that when you talked?"

He sighed. "I told you ten times every word of that conversation."

"He's just replacing our couch then, right? She's just helping him, right?"

He sighed harder this time. "I don't know, Darcy. Probably. Who cares?"

"Look. Don't lose your patience with me, mister," I said. "This is *major*." I thrust a finger toward them and then studied Dex and Rachel more, taking in every little detail. Three weeks ago, they were the people that I knew the best. My best friend and my fiancé. Now they seemed like strangers or estranged loved ones whom I hadn't heard from in years. As Rachel turned her head, I noticed that her hair was layered a bit at the bottom, a radical departure from her usual blunt ends.

"Do you like her hair like that?" I asked Marcus.

"Sure. It's great," he said dismissively.

I gave him a look that said, *Wrong answer.*

"Okay. It sucks. It's hideous."

"Come on. Look at it! Tell me your honest opinion!" I was feeling frantic, wishing that Claire were with me. She'd find *something* to criticize. Sneakers. Hair. Something.

Marcus thrust his hands in his pockets and glanced over at Rachel. "She looks the same to me."

I shook my head. "No. They both look better than usual," I said. "What is it? Is it just that some time has passed?"

Then, just as Dex sat down beside Rachel, it hit me. Dex was tanned. Even Rachel didn't have her usual white glow. The realization slashed through my heart. They had gone to Hawaii together! I gasped. "Omigod. They're tan. She went on *my* trip to Hawaii! She went on my honeymoon! Omigod. Omigod. I'm going to confront them!" You hear people say that rage can be blinding, and I learned at that moment that it was true. My vision became blurry as I took one step toward them.

Marcus grabbed my arm. "Darce—do *not* go over there. Let's just leave. *Now.*"

"He told me he was going to eat those tickets! How *dare* she go on my honeymoon!" I was crying. A couple standing near our bookcase bunker looked at me, then over at Dex and Rachel.

"You told me he offered them to you," Marcus said.

"That is totally beside the point! I wouldn't have taken you to Hawaii!"

Marcus raised his eyebrows as if to consider this. "Yeah—that is kind of fucked up," he conceded. "You have a point."

"She went on my honeymoon! What kind of a psycho bitch goes on her friend's honeymoon?" My voice was louder now.

"I'm leaving. Now." He took the stairs, two at a time, and as I turned to follow him, I got one more sickening visual: Dex leaning down to kiss Rachel. On her lips. Tan, happy, smitten, kissing couch consumers.

My eyes filled with tears as I rushed down the stairs, past Marcus, past the barware, out the door to Madison Avenue.

"I know, honey," Marcus said, when he caught up to me. For the first time, he seemed to have genuine empathy for my ordeal. "This has gotta be hard for you."

His kindness made me sob harder. "I can't *believe* she'd go to Hawaii," I said, hyperventilating. "What kind of person does that? I hate her! I want her to die!"

"You don't mean that," Marcus said.

"Fine. Maybe not death. But I want her to get a bad case of cystic acne that Accutane won't cure," I said, thinking that incurable acne would actually be worse than death.

Marcus put his arm around me as we jaywalked across Sixtieth Street, narrowly escaping a delivery guy on a bike. "Just forget about them, Darce. What does it matter what they do?"

"It *matters*!" I sobbed, thinking that there was no way around it: Dex and Rachel were a couple. I couldn't pretend otherwise. A wave of buyer's remorse washed over me. For the first time, I started to wonder if I should have stayed with Dex—if only to keep this from happening with Rachel. When my affair with Marcus began, the grass seemed so much greener with him. But after watching my former fiancé furniture-shop, Dexter's pastures seemed blissfully bucolic.

Marcus hailed a cab, and then helped me inside. I cried the whole way down Park Avenue, picturing Rachel and Dex in all of the scenes that I had studied from our honeymoon brochures: the two of them in a Jacuzzi sipping champagne . . . at a luau grinning over a roasted pig amid native dancers twirling flames . . . frolicking in turquoise water . . . having sex under a coconut tree.

I remembered saying to Dex that we were a better-looking couple than any of the featured honeymooners in those brochures. Dex had laughed and asked me how I got to be so modest.

"Can we go to Hawaii on our honeymoon?" I asked Marcus when we arrived back at his apartment.

"Whatever you want," he said, sprawling on his bed. He motioned for me to join him.

"We should go somewhere even more exotic," I said. "Dex picked Hawaii, and if you ask me, Hawaii is a trite choice."

"Yeah," he said, wearing his "I want sex" expression. "Everyone goes to Hawaii. Now c'mere."

"Where will we go, then?" I asked Marcus as I reluctantly lay down next to him.

"Turkey. Greece. Bali. Fiji. Wherever you want."

"You promise?"

"Yeah," he said, pulling me on top of him.

"And can we get a new, big apartment?" I asked, looking around at his stark white walls, his overflowing closet, and his hulking stereo equipment belching wires all over the scratched parquet floors.

"Sure."

I smiled a sad but hopeful smile.

"But in the meantime," he said, "I know how to make you feel better."

"Just one sec," I said, as I picked up the cordless phone next to his bed.

Marcus sighed and gave me an exasperated look. "Who are you calling? Don't you call them!"

"I'm *not* calling them. I'm over them," I lied. "I'm calling Crate and Barrel. I want that table."

Rachel may have stolen Dex and my trip to Hawaii, but I was sure as hell going to have a nicer table.

But even the table (which was in stock) and sex with Marcus (which was incredible) did nothing to repair my mood. I just couldn't believe that Rachel and Dex were actually together—that their relationship was real. Real enough to go shopping for couches together. Real enough to go to Hawaii.

And from that day forward, I was totally obsessed with Rachel and Dex. They were two people cut entirely from my life, yet from my perspective, the three of us had never been so inextricably and permanently bound together.

twelve

Things only got worse when I turned thirty. I woke up on the morning of my birthday to my first dose of morning sickness. I was in bed with Marcus, on the side farthest from the bathroom, and barely made it over him to the toilet before I puked up the fajitas I had eaten for dinner the night before at Rosa Mexicano. I flushed, rinsed my mouth with Listerine, and brushed my teeth. Another wave overcame me and more red and yellow bits of pepper descended. I flushed, rinsed, brushed again. Then I collapsed onto the floor and moaned loudly, hoping that Marcus would wake up and come to my rescue. He didn't.

I thought to myself that Dex would have heard me puking. He was a very light sleeper, but at the moment, I chalked it up to him having greater compassion. Maybe Marcus wasn't nurturing enough for me. I moaned again, louder this time. When Marcus still didn't stir, I picked myself up from the cold tile and returned to bed, whimpering, "Hold me."

Marcus snored in response.

I nestled into the crevice between his arm and body and made some more needy sounds as I surveyed his clock. Seven thirty-three. The alarm was set for seven forty-five. I had twelve minutes before he officially wished me a happy birthday. I closed my eyes and wondered what Rachel and Dex were doing at that moment—and more important, what they were going to do about my birthday. This was their *last chance,* I had ranted to my mother and Marcus the night before. I wasn't quite sure what I expected or wanted them to do—but a phone call or e-mail seemed a step in the right direction.

Surely Rachel and Dex had discussed the issue in recent days. My guess was that Dex voted to leave me alone, Rachel to call. "I've been celebrating her birthday for over twenty-five years," she would say to Dex. "I just can't blow this day off. I have to call her." I could hear Dex saying back, "It's for the best. I know it's hard, but no good can come of it." How long had they debated the point? Perhaps it had escalated into an argument, maybe even a permanent rift. Unfortunately, neither Dex nor Rachel was particularly stubborn or argumentative. Since they were both pleasers by nature, I was sure that they had a calm, reasoned conversation and came to a unanimous conclusion about how to approach the anniversary of my birth.

One thing I did know for sure was this: if Dex and Rachel did not wish me a happy birthday in some form, there would be no redemption. Ever. My hatred for them was growing faster than the fruit flies had multiplied in our peanut butter jars in biology class sophomore year. I tried to remember what that experiment sought to prove, vaguely recalling something about eye color. Red eyes versus green eyes. I forgot the details. With Rachel as a lab partner, I hadn't needed to pay too much attention. She had done all the work. I suddenly wondered what color eyes my baby would have. I hoped for blue, or at least green like mine. Everyone knows blue eyes are prettier, at least on a girl, which is why there were so many songs about brown-eyed girls, to make them feel better. I listened to Marcus snore as I played with a tuft of hair on his chest. He had just the right amount.

"Hmm," he said, pulling me on top of him.

Having just puked fajitas, I wasn't in the mood for sex, but I caved. It seemed as good a way as any to begin my thirtieth birthday. So after a quick, perfunctory round, I waited for him to open his eyes and wish me a happy birthday. Tell me that he loved me. Reassure me that thirty wasn't old and that I had at least six good years left before I would need to think about plastic surgery. Ten, fifteen, twenty seconds passed with still no words from my boyfriend.

"Did you fall back asleep?" I demanded.

"No. I'm awake . . ." he mumbled, his eyelids fluttering.

The alarm clock sounded in a series of increasingly louder, high-pitched beeps. Marcus reached over and silenced his clock with a slap. I waited, feeling like Molly Ringwald in *Sixteen Candles* when her whole family forgot her birthday. Sure, it had only been a few minutes, whereas Molly's character had to endure a whole day of neglect, but after all I'd been through in recent weeks, all of the trauma and pain, those minutes felt like hours. It was bad enough that I had to turn thirty on a Monday and that I had to puke twice. But now the father of my child couldn't even muster a tiny, heartfelt "happy birthday" on the heels of gratuitous sex.

"I'm sick," I said, trying another angle for attention. "Morning sickness. I threw up twice."

He rolled over, his back toward me. "You feel better now?" he asked, his voice muffled under his comforter.

"No," I said. "Worse."

"Mmmmmm. I'm sorry, sweetheart," he said.

I sighed loudly and said in my most sardonic tone, "Happy birthday to me."

I expected his eyes to snap open, an immediate apology to spring from his lips. But he only mumbled again, still facedown in his pillow, "Happy birthday, Darce. I was getting to that."

"The hell you were. You *totally* forgot!"

"I didn't forget . . . I just gave you your present," he said. I couldn't see his face but knew he was smirking.

I told him I wasn't amused and then announced that I was going to take a shower. "By all means," I said, "you just stay in bed and relax."

Marcus tried to redeem himself after I had showered, but he didn't have much ammunition. It was clear he had not yet bought me a card or a present. Nor had he purchased my Pillsbury sticky cinnamon buns and pink candles even though I had told him that this was my family tradition, a tradition that Dex had continued over the past seven years. Instead, Marcus only offered me a few *sweeties* and *babies,* along with a pack of saltines from his delivery from the diner the night before. "Here," he said. "In case you start to feel morning sickness again. I heard once that these do the trick."

I wondered where he had heard that before. Had he ever gotten another girl pregnant? I decided to broach the topic later and snatched the crackers from his outstretched hand, saying, "You're way too good to me. Really, Marcus, you have to tone this down. I can't handle all the over-the-top gestures."

"Oh, relax. I got you covered, Darce. You'll get your present tonight," Marcus said as he sauntered naked toward the bathroom. "Now go play nice with the other kids."

"Buh-*bye*," I said, as I slipped on my favorite Marc Jacobs pumps and walked toward the door. "Have fun shopping for my gift!"

"What makes you think I don't have it already?" he said.

"Because I know you, Mr. Last Minute . . . and I mean it, Marcus. I want something good. Think Fifty-seventh Street!"

When I got to work, Claire was waiting in my office with yellow roses and what appeared to be a professionally wrapped gift. "Happy birthday, hon!" she trilled.

"You remembered!" I said. "What gorgeous roses!"

"Of course I remembered, silly," she said, placing the fishbowl vase of flowers on my desk. "So how do you feel today?"

I looked at her, worried that she could tell I had morning sickness. "Fine. Why?"

"Just wondering if it feels any different being thirty?" she whispered. Claire was still twenty-eight for another few weeks, in the safety zone, buffered by twenty-nine.

"A little," I said. "Not too bad, though."

"Well, when you look as good as you do, what's a little thing called age?" Claire said. She had been full of compliments since my breakup with Dex. I enjoyed them, of course, but sometimes I had the sense that they verged on pity remarks. She continued, "You could easily still pass for twenty-seven."

"Thanks," I said, wanting to believe her.

Claire smiled sweetly as she handed me my gift. "Here! Open! Open!"

"I thought you were going to make me wait until lunch!" I said, eagerly eyeing the present. Claire had excellent taste and never skimped in the gifting department.

I ripped open the paper and saw a satisfying, red Baccarat box. I lifted the hinged lid and peered down at the chunky green crystal heart threaded with a black silk cord.

"Claire! I love it! I love it!"

"You do? Really? I have a gift receipt if you want to get a different color. The purple one was really pretty, too, but I thought this one would look nice with your eyes . . ."

"No way! This is perfect!" I said, thinking that Rachel probably would have picked some boring limited edition book. "You're the best." I hugged her, silently taking back every mean thing I had ever thought about her, every petty criticism. Like how annoying and clingy she got after too many drinks, always needing to accompany me to the bathroom at bars. How she bragged about her hometown of Greenwich and her debutante days. And how she stayed so hopelessly lumpy despite daily visits to the gym. What was she doing, I used to ask Rachel, eating Ho Hos in the locker room?

"The green matches your eyes," Claire said again, beaming.

"I *love* it," I said, as I admired the necklace from my compact mirror. The heart fell at just the right spot, accentuating my thin collarbone.

Claire took me to lunch later that day. I kept my cell phone on, just in case Dex or Rachel decided that lunchtime was the appropriate time to phone, apologize profusely, beg for my forgiveness, and wish me a happy birthday. It rang five different times, and every time I'd say to Claire, "Do you mind?" and she'd wave her hand and say, "Of course not. Go on."

All of the calls (except Bliss Spa reminding me of my five o'clock facial) were from birthday well-wishers. But no Rachel or Dex.

I know it was on Claire's mind, too, as she mouthed, "Who?" each time I answered.

After the fifth call, she asked, "Have you heard from Rachel today?"

"No," I said.

"Dex?"

"Nope."

"How rude not to call on your birthday and try to make up."

"I know!"

"Any sightings since Crate and Barrel?" she asked.

"No. Have you seen them?"

"No. *Nobody* has seen them," Claire said—which was saying something as her network was expansive. The next best thing to hiring a private investigator (and believe me, I had considered it) was having Claire as my new best friend.

"Maybe they broke up," I said.

"Probably so," she said. "Out of guilt if nothing else."

"Or maybe they just went on another exotic trip together," I said.

She patted my arm sympathetically and ordered me a second glass of chardonnay. I knew I shouldn't be drinking—but Dr. Jan had specifically said that I could drink on special occasions. Besides, plenty of French babies were born undamaged, and I was sure their mothers kept up with their daily intake of wine.

"I do have a little nugget for you, though," I said, inhaling deeply, excited to drop the Marcus news on her. Minus the pregnancy, of course.

"Oh, really?" Her bangle bracelets clinked together as she crossed her arms and leaned toward me.

"I'm seeing someone," I said proudly.

"Who?" she asked, wide-eyed. I detected a hint of jealousy. Claire, bless her heart, was a fast and furious matchmaker, but she never seemed to make much progress in her own right.

I smiled mysteriously, took a sip of water, and wiped the lipstick off my glass with my thumb. "Marcus," I said proudly.

"Marcus?" she asked with bewilderment. "You mean, *Marcus* Marcus?"

I nodded.

"Really?" she asked.

"Uh-huh. Isn't that crazy?"

Something flashed across her face that I wasn't sure how to read. Was it jealousy that I had someone new so fast on the heels of a broken engagement? Did she, too, find him sexy in an unorthodox way? Or was it disapproval? My heart fluttered over the possibility of the latter. I desperately needed affirmation that Marcus was acceptable to a member of the Manhattan elite. I needed to be with someone whom everyone else wanted.

"When did this come about?" she asked.

"Oh, recently . . ." I said vaguely.

"I'm . . . I guess I'm a little bit surprised."

"I know," I said, thinking that she would have been less surprised if she hadn't been such a sound sleeper that night over our July Fourth weekend. "Who would have thunk it? . . . But I *really* like him."

"Really?" This time I definitely pegged her expression as disapproving.

"Why are you so surprised?"

"It's just . . . I don't know. I just didn't think Marcus was your type."

"You mean his looks?" I asked. "You mean the fact that I'm better looking than he is?"

"Well, that," Claire said, struggling for tactful wording. "And, I don't know, just everything. He's a nice, fun guy—don't get me wrong . . ." She trailed off.

"You don't think he's sexy?" I said. "I think he's *so* sexy."

Claire looked at me blankly. Her answer was clear. She did not find Marcus sexy. Not in the least.

"Well, I think he is," I said again, feeling highly offended.

"That's all that matters, then," Claire said, patting my hand condescendingly.

"Right," I said, knowing that that was *not* all that mattered. "I can't believe you don't think he's cute."

"I guess," she said. "In a . . . I don't know . . . 'guy's guy' kind of way."

"Well, he's great in bed," I said, trying to convince Claire—and myself—that this single fact could make up for all of his shortcomings.

By five o'clock, I had received a dozen or more birthday e-mails and phone calls, and a stream of chipper office visits from colleagues. Still nothing from Rachel or Dex. There was one last possibility: maybe they had sent a card, note, or gift to my apartment, which I hadn't returned to in several days. So after my facial, I cabbed it across the park to my apartment, anticipating the apologies that were surely awaiting me.

Minutes later I grabbed my mail from the lobby, unlocked my door, and surveyed my stash. I had cards from the usual lineup: my parents; my brother, Jeremy; my still-smitten high school boyfriend, Blaine; my grandmother; and my second-oldest friend from home, Annalise. The final one had no return address. It had to be from Rachel or Dex! I ripped open the envelope to find a picture of wriggling golden retriever puppies piled into a white wicker basket. A "Happy Birthday" banner stretched over the basket, each letter written in a different shade of pink. My heart sank, as I realized that the card was likely from my aunt Clarice, who still treated me as if I were ten. Unless

Rachel was playing on the whole "friends since childhood" theme. I slowly opened the card, feeling hopeful until I saw the telltale ten-dollar bill taped inside and Aunt Clarice's wobbly signature below the greeting "Hope your day is a basket of fun!"

And that was that. There was no getting around it—Rachel and Dex had blown off my thirtieth birthday, a day we had talked about for at least the past five years. I started to cry, undermining the treatment for puffy eyes that I had added to my regular facial. I called Marcus's cell to garner some sympathy.

"Where are you?" I asked.

"That's for me to know—and you to find out," he said, the noise of heavy traffic in the background. I pictured him tripping down Fifth Avenue, his arms filled with packages.

"They didn't call. Neither of them. No calls, e-mails, cards. Nothing."

He knew who I meant. "The *nerve* of some ex-boyfriends," Marcus joked.

"It's not funny!" I said. "Can you believe them?"

"Darcy, didn't you tell them that you never wanted to speak to them again? That they were—what were your words?—'dead to you'?"

I gave him credit for recalling my precise wording. "Yes—but they could at least try to *redeem* themselves. They didn't even try. It's my thirtieth birthday!"

"I know, babe. And we're gonna celebrate. So bring your skinny ass down here."

He was right, my ass *was* still skinny. This observation cheered me up a drop. "Am I going to be a basketball girl?"

"What's a basketball girl?"

"One of those girls who looks as if she has only a basketball under her shirt. You know, with thin limbs and a still-pretty face? And then the ball falls out and she is, *voilà,* perfect again?"

"Sure you will. Now get down here!"

He hung up before I could ask him where we were going for dinner, how dressed up I needed to be. Well, there's no such thing as being overdressed, I told myself, as I selected my slinkiest black dress, highest Jimmy Choo stilettos, and gauziest wrap out of my closet, lining the ensemble up on my bed. Then I showered, blew my hair out straight, applied makeup to my glowing skin, opting for neutral lips and dramatic, smoky eyes.

"Thirty and ab-so-lute-ly stunning," I said aloud to the mirror, trying not to look at the tiny crow's feet around my eyes. Or worry about the fact that I was no longer in my twenties, and therefore on the road to losing my two most valuable assets: beauty and youth. I was filled with an unfamiliar sense of self-doubt that I pushed aside as I grabbed Aunt Clarice's ten for cab fare and headed out the door.

Fifteen minutes later I sauntered into Marcus's apartment, catwalk-style.

He whistled. "You look great."

"Thanks." I smiled as I noticed that he was wearing old brown cords, a pilled gray sweater, and scuffed shoes. I pictured Claire's disapproving frown when I told her about Marcus. Maybe this was part of the reason why. He was sloppy. But not *couture* sloppy—you know, the whole low-hanging Dolce & Gabbana jeans with a cool Hanes wifebeater. Just *bad* sloppy.

"No offense, but you do not look so great," I said, remembering that Rachel once told me that anytime I had to preface a statement with "no offense" I was probably saying something I shouldn't be saying.

"No offense taken," Marcus said.

"Please change and kick it up a notch. And FYI, brown and gray don't generally go together . . . although somehow Matt Lauer manages to pull it off."

"I'm not changing," he said stubbornly.

"C'mon, Marcus. Couldn't you at least put on some khakis and a sweater purchased within the last six years?"

"I'm wearing this," Marcus said.

We argued for a few seconds, and I finally gave in. Nobody was going to be looking at Marcus anyway. Not with me on his arm. On our way out the door, I heard a clap of thunder. I asked Marcus for an umbrella.

"I don't have one," he said, sounding curiously proud of himself. "Haven't for years."

I told him that I truly didn't get how one can not own an umbrella. Fine, people lose umbrellas all the time, leave them in shops or cabs when the rain has cleared, not realizing it until the next rainy day. But how could you simply not own one?

"What am I supposed to use to keep dry?" I asked.

He handed me a plastic Duane Reade bag. "Take this."

"Really classy," I said, snatching it from him.

The evening wasn't off to a roaring start.

It only got worse as we stood on the corner struggling to find a cab, which is close to impossible when it's raining. Nothing frustrates me more about living in Manhattan than being stranded on the sidewalk in inclement weather and very high heels. When I expressed this to Marcus, he suggested we make a run for the subway.

I scowled and told him that I couldn't run in heels. And besides, Jimmy Choos shouldn't tread the underworld. Then, when a cab finally arrived, my left shoe got stuck in a gutter, wedged in so tightly that I had to remove my foot from the shoe, bend down, and yank. As I examined the scratched heel, the Duane Reade bag flew up and rain splattered across my forehead.

Marcus chuckled and said, "The shoes would have been better off in the underworld, eh?"

I glared at him as he slid in the cab ahead of me and told the driver the address. I couldn't determine the restaurant from the address but thought to myself that it had better be a good choice, appropriate for a thirtieth birthday. An all-caps Zagat entry I had forgotten about.

But minutes later, I discovered that Marcus's idea of an appropriate thirtieth-birthday dinner was my idea of an appropriate twenty-sixth birthday dinner if the guy is near broke and/or not that into the girl. He had picked an Italian restaurant I had never heard of on a street in the Village I had never bothered to walk down. Needless to say, I was the only one wearing Jimmy Choos in the joint. Then, the food was awful. I'm talking stale, recycled bread plopped onto the table in a red plastic basket with a waxed-paper liner, followed by overcooked pasta. The only reason I braved it and ordered dessert was to see if Marcus had at least thought to request a candle in my cake, do something ceremonious or special. Of course, my tiramisu arrived sans accoutrement. No drizzle of raspberry, no presentation whatsoever. As I picked at it with my fork, Marcus asked if I wanted my gift. "Sure," I said, shrugging.

He handed me a Tiffany box, and for a moment, I was excited. But like his choice of venue, he had bombed in the gift department. Elsa Peretti bean earrings in silver. Not even platinum or white gold. Sure, they came from Tiffany, but those bean earrings were mass-produced, suburban Tiffany. Again, appropriate for a twenty-sixth birthday, but not a thirtieth. Claire had done better. At least her gift was shaped in a heart rather than a gas-causing vegetable.

As Marcus signed the check, I resisted making a snide remark on the off chance that the bean-earring stunt was designed to throw me off the scent of the diamond ring, hidden in the pocket of his leather jacket. Instead, I graciously thanked him for the earrings, replacing them in the box.

"Aren't you going to wear them?" Marcus asked.

"Not tonight," I said. I wasn't about to switch out of my diamond studs, which, ironically, were given to me by Dex on my twenty-sixth birthday.

After dinner Marcus and I had a drink at the Plaza (my idea) and then returned to his apartment and had sex (his idea). For the very first time with Marcus, I didn't have an orgasm. Not even a tiny hiccup of one. What was worse, he didn't seem to notice, not even when I furrowed my brow and sighed, the portrait of a frustrated woman. Instead, his breathing grew deep and steady. He was falling asleep. My day was beginning and ending in the same frustrating way.

"Well, I guess this means no engagement ring," I said loudly.

He didn't respond, so I shot him another pointed barb, something about winning some and losing some.

Marcus sat up, sighed, and said, "What's your beef now, Darcy?"

And that was that. We were on our way to a full-on fight. I called him insensitive; he called me demanding. I called him mean; he called me spoiled. I told him that the bean earrings were not acceptable. He said he'd gladly return them. And then I think I said that I wished I were still with Dex. And that maybe we shouldn't get married. He said nothing back. Just gave me a cold stare. It wasn't the reaction I was after. I thought about what Rachel always said: *The opposite of love isn't hate; it's indifference.* Marcus's expression was the embodiment of utter indifference.

"You want to be off the hook!" I shouted. I turned away from him and sobbed quietly into my pillow.

After a long while, Marcus broke and put his arm around me. "Let's not fight anymore, Darce. I'm sorry." His tone was unconvincing, but at least he was apologizing.

I told him that I was sorry for the mean things I had

said, especially the part about Dex. I told him I loved him. He told me, for only the second time, that he loved me too. But as Marcus fell asleep again, his arm still around me, I knew that our relationship wasn't quite right. Moreover, I think I knew that it had never really been right in the first place. Sure, we had shared some passion under a tree in East Hampton. And we had had a few good times after that, but what else did we have together? I reminded myself that Marcus was the father of my baby, and I vowed to make things work between us. I tried to come up with names for our daughter. Annabel Francesca, Lydia Brooke, Sabrina Rose, Paloma Grace. I envisioned our life together, pictured the pages of the scrapbook: rosy snapshots on creamy, linen pages.

But in the final seconds before I drifted off to sleep, in that time of semiconsciousness when what you think dictates what you dream, I thought of Claire's disapproving stare and my own feelings of dissatisfaction. Then my mind was elsewhere, rooted in the past. Fixed on Dex and Rachel and what would never be again.

thirteen

In the following weeks, my relationship with Marcus disintegrated further. Even the sex—the cornerstone of our relationship—was starting to feel routine. I tried to tell myself that it was only the stress caused by the life changes hurtling our way: the apartment we had yet to look for, the wedding we had yet to plan, and our baby on the way.

When I asked Marcus why he thought we were fighting so much, he blamed it all on my "fixation" with Rachel and Dex. He said he had grown weary of my endless Q&A, that he didn't think it was healthy to spend so much time speculating over what they were doing, and that I should focus on my own life instead. I vowed to talk less about them, believing that in a matter of weeks, I would no longer care what they were doing. But a worry tugged at my heart that it wasn't that simple, that despite my efforts to make things work with Marcus, we were on the brink of a breakup.

What nagged at me even more than any relationship woes was the accompanying regret about the baby. I talked a big game, but deep down, I wasn't so sure I wanted a baby. Since I had been a teenager, my identity was about being thin and beautiful and fun and carefree. A baby threatened all of that. I didn't know who I was going to become. And I certainly didn't feel like anyone's mother.

My own mother called me every other hour in those transitional weeks, just to check on me, her voice filled with pity and worry. Being without a man was a fate worse than death to her, so I finally put her out of her misery and told her that I had a new boyfriend.

I was at Marcus's apartment, talking on his phone while he ate a slice of pizza. I was skipping dinner, as I had far surpassed my carb and fat allocation for the day.

When I told her the good news, she said, "That was fast," with not a hint of disapproval. Only pride that I was back on my horse. "What's his name?"

"Marcus," I said, hoping that she wouldn't remember that there had been a groomsman named Marcus. I wanted to ease her into that part of the story. Of course, I had no intention of breaking the baby news anytime soon.

"Is he black? Marcus sounds like a black name."

"No. He's white," I said.

"Does he go by Mark?"

"No. Just Marcus," I said, looking up at him and smiling.

"Marcus what?"

"Marcus Peter Lawson," I said proudly.

"I *like* the full name. *A lot.* I was never too keen on the name Dexter. Were you?"

"Not really," I said, even though I actually loved the name Dex. It had panache. But the name Marcus did too.

"What does he look like? Tell me all about him. How did you meet?"

"Well, Mother, how about you just meet him yourself? We're coming home this weekend. I got flights today."

Marcus's head jerked up to look at me. This was news to him. I hadn't quite gotten around to telling him about our travel plans.

"Fantastic news!" she shouted.

I heard my father ask in the background if I was getting back with Dex. My mother covered the phone, but I could still hear her say, "No, Hugh. Darcy has a *new* boyfriend."

Marcus frantically whispered something. I held up my hand and shushed him. He took an imaginary golf swing and mumbled that he had plans.

I shook my head and mouthed, "Cancel."

"Well, just give me a short prelude," my mom said. "What does he look like?"

"He's handsome," I said. "You'll love him. And as a matter of fact, he's here right now. So I better run."

"Oh! Let me say hello to him," she said.

"No, Mom. You'll meet him soon enough!"

"I can't wait," she said.

"You'll like him way more than Dex," I said, winking at Marcus. "I know you will."

"Dex?" My mother giggled. "Dex who?"

I smiled as I hung up the phone.

"What's the big idea?" Marcus demanded.

"I forgot to tell you," I said breezily. "I booked us flights to Indy."

He threw his slice of pizza back into the greasy box and said, "I'm not goin' to Indy this weekend."

"I asked you if you had plans. Remember? You said you didn't."

"You asked about Friday or Saturday nights. I'm golfing Saturday afternoon."

"With whom? Dex?"

Marcus rolled his eyes. "I have other friends in this town, ya know."

Very few, I thought. Another problem in our relation-ship. When I was with Dex, we traveled in a pack, a big group of friends. But Marcus and I spent all of our time alone, most of it holed up in his apartment. I knew I needed to stage our coming-out party, but I wasn't quite ready for my discerning crowd to sit in judgment of my new boy-friend. And in any event, I needed to buy him some new clothes first.

Marcus continued, "Darcy, you just can't book a trip like that without telling me. That's not cool."

"C'mon, Marcus. This is *really important*. Just play ball on this one," I said, using one of his many sports ex-pressions.

He shook his head.

I smiled and said in my sweetest voice, "You need to meet your in-laws. We need to get this show on the road."

He sighed wearily and said, "In the future, don't go signing me up for shit without asking me. But this time, I'll do it."

As if you ever had a choice, I thought.

For the first time in my long dating history, I could tell my parents actually wanted to like the boy I was bringing home. Their instinct in the past was always to judge and disapprove. My father would follow the script of the living room interrogator, the staunch enforcer of curfews, the guardian of my virtue. Although I'm sure he really did have some protective instincts, I always had the feeling that it was mostly for show. I could tell my mother loved the routine by the way she would rehash it all later. "Did you see the way your father put Blaine back on his heels?" she would ask me the morning after a date. I think it reminded her of her own teenage years, when she was the big prize in her sleepy Midwestern town and my grandfather had to chase away her suitors.

While my father was a tough customer on the outside, my mother was harsh in private, after being all sugar and spice to the boy's face. She had high standards for me. Specifically, any man of mine had to be as handsome as I was pretty. He had to be mainstream handsome at that. No quirky good looks would do. He also had to be smart, although she would let this one slide if he had money. And he had to have a certain well-mannered slickness. I called this "show quality"—the "impress the neighbors" factor. Dex had this one in spades. He passed with flying colors in every category.

Marcus, on the other hand, was far from perfect, but he had one significant thing going for him: my parents had a strong *need* to like him. What was their alternative? Have their daughter thirty and alone? I knew the thought made both of them shudder. Well, it made my mother shudder, and therefore it became my father's problem too. My mother loved that I had a glamorous job and made good money, but she made it perfectly clear that she thought I should get married, have babies, and live a life of leisure. She wasn't going to hear an argument from me over that game plan. My job could be fun, but not as much fun as a massage at Bliss, shopping at Bendel's, and lunch at Bolo.

So that Friday, Marcus and I flew to Indianapolis for the big introduction. We found my father waiting at baggage claim, all smiles. My father is what you would call polished. Full head of dark hair always in place, polo shirts and sweaters with pressed khakis, loafers with tassels. Glow-in-the-dark teeth befitting the best dentist in town.

"Daddy!" I squealed as we approached him.

"Hi, baby," he said, opening his arms wide to embrace me. I inhaled his aftershave and could tell that he had just showered before his drive over.

"It's so good to see you," I said in my "daddy's little girl," borderline baby-talk voice.

"You too, sweetie pie."

My father and I didn't know any other way to interact. When we were alone for any length of time, we'd fall silent and awkward. But on the surface, in front of an audience, we fulfilled our conspicuously traditional roles—roles that made us both feel comfortable. I don't think I would have even noticed this dynamic but for watching Rachel with her own father. They talked like real friends, equals.

My dad and I separated as I turned to Marcus, who was shifting from foot to foot and looking most uncomfortable. "Daddy, this is Marcus."

My dad squared his shoulders, stepped forward, and gave Marcus's hand a hearty pump. "Hello, Marcus. Hugh Rhone. Welcome to Indianapolis. It's a pleasure to meet you," he boomed in his chipper dentist's-office voice.

Marcus nodded and mumbled that it was nice to meet him too. I gave him a look, widening my eyes as if to say "Is that the best you can do?" Had he ignored my lecture during the flight, my tireless explaining that my parents were all about image? "First impressions are last impressions" was one of my father's favorite expressions. I had told Marcus this.

I waited for Marcus to say something more, but instead he averted his eyes to the luggage belt. "Is that your bag?" he asked me.

"Yes," I said, spotting my Louis Vuitton suitcase. "Grab it for me, please."

Marcus leaned down and heaved it from the belt. *"Sheesh,"* he said under his breath, the fourth comment he had made about my overpacking since we had left the city.

"Oh, Marcus, let me," my dad said, reaching for my bag. Marcus shrugged and gave it to him. "If you insist."

I cringed, wishing he had protested at least once.

"So that's it, Daddy. Marcus just has his carry-on bag," I said, glancing at his nasty pea-green satchel with a frayed strap and some defunct Internet logo emblazoned on the side. I saw my father take it in too.

"Okeydokey. We're off," my dad bellowed, rubbing his hands together vigorously. Then, as we found his BMW in the parking garage, he told us of his speeding ticket on the way over. "Was only going seven over."

"Daddy, was it really just seven?" I asked.

"Cross my heart. Seven over. Marcus, the cops in this town are relentless."

"That's what I told you in high school!" I said, hitting his arm. "A lot of good *that* excuse ever did me."

"Drinking vodka in the Burger King parking lot at sixteen? That is hardly what I'd characterize as overzealous police work." My dad chuckled. "Marcus, I have a lot of stories to tell you about our girl here."

Our girl. It was a big concession. That combined with his chipper mood on the heels of a ticket was only further proof of his determination to like my new boyfriend.

"I can only imagine," Marcus said from the back seat, his voice detached, bored. Was he missing my dad's cues, or was he simply unwilling to go along with the jovial routine?

I glanced back at him, but his face was in shadow and I couldn't read his expression. For the rest of the ride home, Marcus said virtually nothing despite plenty of effort from my father.

As we pulled into our cul-de-sac, I pointed out Rachel's house to Marcus. He made an acknowledging sound.

"Are the Whites away?" I asked my father, noticing that all of their lights were out.

He reached over and squeezed my knee with one hand

and then clicked our garage door opener with the other. "No. They're around, I think."

"Maybe they knew I was coming home and couldn't bear to face me," I said.

"Just remember, it's not their fault," my dad said. "It's Rachel's."

"I know," I said. "But they *did* raise a traitor."

My dad made a face as if to say, "Fair point."

"Think Mom will mind if we go in through the back way?" he asked me. My mother believes that visitors should always be brought through the front door—not that Marcus would ever notice the difference.

Sure enough, my mom peered into the garage and whispered, as if Marcus and I couldn't hear her, "Hugh, the *front* door."

"The kids have bags," he said.

My mother forced a smile and said in her turbo-charged, company voice, "Well then, come in! Come in!" As always, she was in full makeup—she put her "face" on even to go to the grocery store. Her hair was swept up in a jeweled clip I had bought for her at Barneys, and she was dressed in ivory from head to toe. She looked beautiful, and I was proud for Marcus to see her. If he subscribed to the whole "a daughter will end up looking like her mother" notion, he had to be exceedingly pleased.

Marcus and my father fumbled with our bags, maneuvering them between our car and the lawnmower as my mom lectured my father about pulling the car in too far to the left.

"Dee, I'm perfectly centered," he said, agitation creeping into his voice. My parents bickered constantly, more with every passing year, but I knew that they would stay together for the long haul. Maybe not for love, but because they both liked the image of the proper home—the good, intact family. "I'm perfectly centered," he said again.

My mom resisted a retort, and opened the door wide for us. As she kissed me, my nose filled with her heavier-than-usual application of Chanel No. 5. She then turned to Marcus, putting one hand on each of his cheeks and planting a big kiss just to the right of his mouth. "Marcus! Welcome! It's so nice to meet you."

"Nice to meet you too," Marcus mumbled back.

My mother hates mumblers. I silently hoped that the shame of greeting a guest between our dark garage and laundry room would distract her from noticing my boyfriend's poor enunciation. She quickly ushered us into the kitchen. A spread of cheese, olives, and her famous shrimp puffs was laid out on the counter.

My brother, Jeremy, and his girlfriend, Lauren, suddenly bounded around the corner like two overeager house pets. Neither of them was ever in a bad mood. My father once said that the pair had two modes: chipper or asleep. True to form, Lauren wasted no time postintroduction and launched into an inane tale about one of our neighbors. I have known Lauren since she was a baby—she lived down the street from us and Rachel occasionally babysat her—so I knew that she was the kind of girl who could dominate a conversation by saying absolutely nothing in the sort of way you expect from an old lady in church, not a twenty-five-year-old. The weather, the big sale at JoAnn Fabrics, or the latest winner of bingo at Good Haven, the nursing home where she worked.

As Lauren concluded her story, my father offered Marcus a drink.

"A beer would be great," he said.

"Get him a chilled glass, Hugh," my mother said, as my dad flicked off the top of a Budweiser.

"Oh, I don't need a glass. Thanks, though," Marcus said, taking the bottle from my father.

I gave him a look to indicate that he should have taken the glass as we all followed my mother to the living room. Lauren sat close to my brother on the couch, clutching his arm in a death grip. My brother is a bit of a dork, too, but as I studied his girlfriend's sweatshirt with the Good Haven logo, acid-washed, cropped jeans, Keds with no socks (a look I couldn't even stomach during its brief acceptable stint in high school), I determined for the hundredth time that he could do better. Marcus and I took a seat on the opposite couch, and my parents took the two armchairs.

"So," my mother said, crossing her ankles. I assumed she was ready to interrogate Marcus. I felt nervous, but also excited, hopeful that he would rise to the occasion and make me proud. But instead of focusing on Marcus, my mother said, "Lauren and Jeremy have some news!"

Lauren giggled and threw out her left hand, revealing what appeared from my seat on the opposite couch to be a princess-cut diamond ring set in white gold or platinum. "Surprise!"

I looked at my brother. I was surprised, all right. Surprised that it wasn't a marquis cut set in yellow gold.

"We're getting married," Jeremy confirmed.

Marcus spoke before I could. "Congrats." He raised his beer.

Jeremy returned the gesture with his glass of Coke. "Thanks, man."

Jeremy shouldn't say *man*. He just can't pull it off. He hasn't a cool bone in his body.

"Congratulations," I said, but my voice sounded stilted, unnatural. I stood to survey the goods, quickly determining that although the diamond was a decent size, it was slightly yellowish. I pegged it as a J in color.

"Very nice," I said, returning Lauren's hand to my brother's knee.

My mother started to gush about a May wedding in Indy and a reception at our country club.

I told them how happy I was for them, my mouth stretched into a fake smile as I tried to suppress a stab of envy. I wondered how I could possibly be jealous of my dorky little brother and this girl with bad bangs and thick thighs shoved into acid-washed jeans. Yet incredibly, I was. I was bothered by my mother's enthusiasm. Bothered that Lauren was replacing me as the bride-to-be, my mother's focal point. And what annoyed me the very most was that their spring wedding was going to shift the focus from my baby and me.

"Should I ask her now?" Lauren looked eagerly at Jeremy.

"Go ahead." Jeremy beamed.

"Ask me what?"

"We want you to be a bridesmaid," Lauren chirped. "Because you've always been like a big sister to me." She looked at Marcus and explained further, "Darcy used to babysit for me."

"I never babysat for you. Rachel did," I said.

"Well, true," Lauren said, her smile fading slightly. Mention of Rachel sombered up the room. I liked the effect—liked reminding everyone of my suffering. But the result was short-lived. Lauren's grin quickly returned in full force. "But you were always there helping her. You were *so* fun."

"Thanks," I said. "I try."

"So will you?"

"Will I what?" I asked, pretending to be puzzled.

"Be a bridesmaid?"

"Oh. Yeah. Sure thing."

Lauren clapped and squealed. "Goody! And I want your help. I *need* your help."

She could say that again, I thought. And sure enough,

she did. "I need you to help because you're so good at this stuff."

"Why? Because I'm the wedding expert now that I just spent almost a year planning one?" Another reminder of my pain.

Lauren flinched, but then recovered. "No. Not that. Just because you have the most excellent taste." She turned to Marcus again. "Incredible taste. Nobody has taste like Darcy."

This much was true.

Marcus nodded and then took another swallow of beer.

"So I need your help," she continued excitedly.

Okay. Let's start with those jeans. And the Keds. And your bangs.

I looked at my mother, hoping she was thinking the same thing. She was usually right on board with the Lauren criticism, recently ranting about her application of blush: two round circles of pink missing her cheekbones altogether. Not that Lauren had much in the way of cheekbones. She wasn't bringing the best genes to the table. But clearly my mother was not in her usual critical mode; she was hypnotized by the rosy glow of a new wedding to plan. She looked at Jeremy and Lauren adoringly. "Lauren has been dying to call you. But Jeremy and I convinced her to wait to tell you in person."

"I'm so glad you did," I said flatly.

"You were right, Mom," Lauren said.

Mom? Had I heard that right? I looked at Lauren. "So you're calling her 'Mom' now?" Pretty soon she was going to lay claim to my mother's jewelry and china.

Lauren giggled, pressed Jeremy's hand to her cheek in a nauseating display of affection. It looked like a bad Kodak commercial, the kind that's supposed to make you cry. "Yeah. I've felt that way about her for a long time, but now it feels right to call her that."

"I see," I said, with what I hoped was maximum disapproval. Then I glanced over at Marcus, who was finishing his beer.

"You want another?" I asked, standing for the kitchen.

"Sure," he said.

I gave him a look. "Come with me."

Marcus followed me into the kitchen, where I went off on my family. "How could they go on and on about this wedding after what I just went through? Can you believe how insensitive they're all being? I wanted to tell them about *us* getting married. Now it just doesn't feel right. Probably because I don't even have a ring," I said. I shouldn't have shifted the blame to Marcus like that, but I couldn't help it. Casting the blame net wide is just my natural instinct when I'm upset.

Marcus just looked at me, and then said, "Can I get another beer?"

I opened the refrigerator with such force that a bottle of Heinz ketchup flew from the side shelf onto the floor.

"Everything all right in there?" my mother asked from the living room.

"Just dandy!" I said, as Marcus replaced the ketchup and grabbed another beer.

I took a deep breath, and we returned to the living room, where my mother and Lauren were talking about the guest list.

"Two hundred seems just about right," Lauren said.

"I think you're going to realize that two hundred is the bare minimum. It adds up fast. If your parents invite twenty couples, and we invite twenty couples, that's eighty guests right there," my mother said.

"True," Lauren said. "And I'm going to want to invite a lot of people from Good Haven."

"Well, that should cut down on the liquor bill," Marcus joked.

Lauren shook her head and tittered. "You'd be surprised how much they can put away. Every year at the Christmas party, they get lousy drunk."

"Sounds like a wild and crazy time," I said.

"Do they ever . . . you know . . . hook up?" Marcus asked. His first substantive contribution to the conversation was about geriatric sex. Lovely.

Lauren giggled and then launched into a story about Walter and Myrtle and their recent escapades in Myrtle's room. After she exhausted the nursing-home romance tales, my mother finally turned to my boyfriend and said, "So, Marcus. Tell us a little about yourself."

"What would you like to know?" he asked. Dex would have posed the same question, but with a completely different tone.

"Anything. Everything. We want to get to know you."

"Well. I'm from Montana. I went to Georgetown. Now I work at a pointless marketing job. That's about it."

My mom raised her eyebrows and recrossed her ankles. "Marketing? How interesting."

"Not really," Marcus said. "But it pays the bills. Barely."

"I've never been to Montana," Jeremy remarked.

"Neither have I," Lauren said.

"Have you ever been out of the state?" I muttered under my breath. Then, before she could tell us about her childhood trip to the Grand Canyon, I said, "So what's for dinner?"

"Lasagna. Mom and I made it together," Lauren said.

"You and Mom, huh?"

Lauren was unfazed. "Yeah! And you'll be my sister! Like the sister I never had! It's just too, too wonderful."

"Uh-huh," I said.

"So Marcus, do you have brothers and sisters?" my mother asked.

"Yeah," he said. "One brother."

"Older or younger?"

"Four years older."

"How nice."

Marcus gave her a stiff smile, took another sip of beer. I suddenly remembered how much I wanted to kiss him the night of Rachel's birthday as I watched him drinking a beer at the bar. Where had those feelings gone?

The cocktail hour mercifully ended, and the six of us made our way into my mom's Ethan Allen dining room. Her china cabinet was polished to a high gloss and filled with her Lenox china and crystal.

"Take your seats, everyone. Marcus, you may sit there." She pointed at Dexter's old chair. I saw a pained look flash in my mother's eyes. She missed Dex. Then another look crossed her face—one of determination.

But despite her efforts, dinner was painful. There were stilted questions from my parents and terse answers coupled with more beer-guzzling from Marcus. Then he made the comment that will go down in history.

It started with Jeremy talking about one of his patients, an older man who had just left his wife for a much younger woman. Thirty-one years his junior.

"What a shame," Lauren clucked.

"Shocking," my mother added.

Even my father, whom I sometimes suspected of committing his own indiscretions, shook his head with apparent disgust.

But for some reason, Marcus couldn't just get on board and disapprove along with the rest of the group. Or simply say nothing at all, which he had mastered up until that point. Instead he chose to open his mouth and say, "Thirty-one years, huh? Guess that means that my second wife hasn't even been born yet."

My father and Jeremy exchanged glances, wearing identical raised-brow expressions. My mother deflated as she stroked the stem of her wine glass. Lauren laughed nervously and said, "That's really funny, Marcus. Good one!"

Marcus smiled halfheartedly, realizing that his joke had not gone over.

Suddenly, I was in no mood to salvage the night or my new boyfriend's image. I stood and carried my dishes into the kitchen, my posture ramrod erect. I heard my mother excuse herself and click after me in her heels.

"Sweetheart, he was only trying to be funny," my mother said under her breath when we were alone in the kitchen. "Or perhaps he's just nervous, meeting your parents for the first time. Your father can be intimidating."

But I could tell that she didn't believe her words. She thought Marcus was crass, subpar, nowhere close to Dexter's caliber.

"He's not usually like this," I said. "He's just as charming as Dex when he wants to be."

But as I tried to convince my mother, I realized that I knew that Marcus was absolutely nothing like Dex. Nothing. The last remaining drops of coffee dripped into the pot in time with my one and only thought: *I. Picked. Wrong.*

We returned to the dining room, where everyone pretended to enjoy a strawberry cream pie from Crawford's Bakery. My mother apologized twice for not baking one herself.

"I love pies from Crawford's! They taste homemade," Lauren said.

My father whistled the theme from *The Andy Griffith Show* between bites until my mother glared at him to stop. After another few painful moments I said, "I'm not in the mood for pie. I'm going to bed. Good night."

Marcus stood, drummed his fingers on the edge of the table, and said he was "bushed" too. He thanked my mother for dinner and followed me silently, leaving his plate at the table.

I walked up the stairs ahead of him, then down the hall, stopping abruptly at our guest room. "Here's your room. Good night." I was too exhausted to gear myself up for a big fight.

Marcus massaged my shoulder. "C'mon, Darce."

"Are you proud of yourself?"

He smirked—which only further riled me.

"How could you embarrass me like that?"

"It was a joke."

"It *wasn't* funny."

"I'm sorry."

"No you're not."

"I *am* sorry."

"How am I supposed to tell them that we're getting married and that I'm pregnant with your baby?" I whispered. "The man who plans to leave me in thirty years for another woman?" I felt a stab of vulnerability, something I had never felt before I got pregnant. It was an awful feeling.

"You know it was a joke."

"Good night, Marcus."

I went to my room, hoping he would follow me. He didn't. So I sat and stared at my lavender walls covered with photos from happier days. Photos that were yellowing and curling at the edges, reminding me of how much time had passed, how far removed I was from high school. I studied one picture of Rachel, Annalise, and me after a football game. I was in my cheerleading uniform, and they were both wearing Naperville High sweatshirts. Our cheeks were painted with little orange paw prints. I remembered that Blaine had just caught a long touchdown pass to win the game and advance our team to the state quarterfinals. I remember how he took off his helmet, his hair and face drenched with sweat like the sexy star of a Gatorade commercial. Then, as the crowd roared, he beamed up at me from the sidelines and pointed, as if to say, "That one was for you, sweetie!" It seemed as though everyone in that stadium followed his finger right to me.

Life was good then, I thought, as I started to cry. Not so much because I missed the good times, although I did. It was more that I knew I was turning into one of those girls who, upon looking at high school photos, feels wistful.

fourteen

The next morning I heard a light rapping at the door and my mother's voice. "Darcy, are you awake?" Her soothing tone—an unnatural one for her—made me feel even worse.

"Come in," I said, as I felt a wave of morning sickness.

She opened the door, crossed my room, and sat on the foot of my bed. "Sweetheart. Don't be so upset," she said, patting my legs through the covers.

"I can't help it. I know you hate him."

"I like Marcus," she said unconvincingly.

"No you don't. You couldn't possibly after last night. He barely said anything—except to announce that he plans to leave me someday."

She gave me a puzzled look. "Leave you?"

"The 'second wife' comment," I said, rearranging my head on my pillow.

"Well, you don't have plans to marry *this boy* anyway, do you?" she whispered.

The way she said "this boy" told the full story.

"Maybe," I whimpered.

My mother looked anxious and continued to whisper. "Marcus is probably just your *rebound* boyfriend."

I sniffed, stared back at her, wondering if I should tell her the big news. *You are months away from being a grandmother.* Instead I said, "He's just going through a difficult stage."

"Well, if he doesn't straighten up, just dump him and start over," she said, snapping her fingers. "You can get anybody you want."

If only it were that easy. If only I could go back to the drawing board and fix my mistake. The realization that I couldn't, that I was stuck with Marcus, made me feel even more nauseated. I told my mother I wasn't feeling so well, and that I thought I should get a few more hours of sleep.

"Sure, dear. You get your rest . . . I'll just get your laundry."

Our housekeeper always did the laundry, so my mother's offer was further confirmation of how much she pitied my current state of affairs.

"My dirty stuff is all in that turquoise mesh bag," I instructed as I closed my eyes. "And please don't put my La Perla bras in the dryer. They're very delicate."

"Okay, honey," she said.

I heard her unzip my suitcase and pull my clothes from it. Then I heard her gasp. My mother's gasp is one of her trademarks. A dramatic inhalation with more noise than you'd ever imagine possible. For a moment I thought she was making a point about my volume of dirty clothes. And then I remembered what I had popped last minute into my luggage: *What to Expect When You're Expecting.*

"What in the world is *this*?"

I had no choice but to fess up. I opened my eyes, sat up, and said, "Mom. I'm pregnant."

She gasped again, pressing her hands to her temples. "No." She shook her head. "No, you're *not*."

"Yes I am," I said.

"Dex?" she asked hopefully. She wanted desperately for me to tell her that Dex was the father. She wanted to believe that I could reconcile with the ideal man. Get my charmed life back.

I shook my head. "No. Marcus."

My mother collapsed onto the bed, dug her fists into my mattress, and wept. It wasn't exactly the "Mom, I'm pregnant" moment I had imagined.

"Mother, puh-*lease*! You're supposed to be happy for me!"

Her expression changed from mournful to angry. "How could you ruin your life like this? That boy is *awful*."

"He is *not* awful. He can be charming and *really* funny," I said, realizing that he hadn't been charming or even a little bit funny in a very long time. "And I'm marrying him, Mother. End of story."

"No. No. *No!* You can't do that, Darcy!"

"Yes, I can."

"You're throwing your life away. He's not good enough for you. Not even close," she said, her eyes filling with fresh tears.

"Because of *one* comment?"

"Because of a lot of things. Because you are not right for each other. Because of his behavior last night. Dex would never behave in such a deplorable—"

"Stop bringing up Dex! I'm with Marcus now!" I shouted at her, not caring who overheard me.

"You're ruining your life!" she yelled back at me. "And your father and I are not going to stand by and watch you do it!"

"I'm not ruining my life, Mother. I love Marcus and we're going to get married and have this baby. And you better just get used to it. Or else you're going to be one of those women on *Oprah* talking about how she's never met her grandchildren," I said, roughly pushing aside the covers and marching over to the guest room, into the arms of my husband-to-be.

After all, there is nothing like a mother telling you that you're making a bad decision to convince you that what you are doing is the absolute best course of action.

Minutes later, Marcus and I had packed our bags and were standing on the corner of the cul-de-sac waiting for the cab I had called. Nobody—not even my chipper little brother—tried to stop us from leaving. The cab dropped us off at the Holiday Inn next to the airport, where Marcus at least pretended to be contrite. I accepted his apology, and we spent the remainder of the weekend having sex and watching television in a darkened room that smelled of bleach and cigarette smoke. The whole scene was undeniably depressing, but strangely romantic and unifying. Marcus and I rehashed my fight with my mother, both of us agreeing that she was a heartless, shallow bitch.

And when we returned home, things continued to be good between us—or at least not altogether bad. But the peace was short-lived, and within a few weeks, we were at it again. Fighting about everything and anything. My chief complaints were his far-too-frequent poker nights with his newly acquired friends from the underbelly of Manhattan, his shabby wardrobe, and his unwillingness ever to make the trip up to my apartment. His chief complaints were my sudden lack of interest in giving him blow jobs, my keeping the thermostat too low in his apartment, and my obsession with Dex and Rachel.

Then one Saturday morning, after a doozy about baby names (he deigned to suggest the name Julie, when I knew that he had lost his virginity to a girl named Julie), Marcus kicked me out of his apartment, saying that he needed some time alone. So I left his place and went to Barneys, chalking it up to yet another lover's quarrel. Later that night, I expected him to call and apologize. But that didn't happen. In fact, he didn't call at all. Instead, I called him. Over and over. I left him angry messages. Then I left him threatening messages. And then I resorted to hysterical, pathetic, begging messages. When Marcus finally called me back, my venom and tears were gone. I only felt a cold uncertainty.

"Where have you been all weekend?" I asked, feeling pitiful.

"Thinking," he said.

"About us?"

"Yup."

"What exactly were you thinking?" I asked. "Whether you want to be with me?"

"More or less . . ."

At that moment, I knew that Marcus had all of the power. Every drop of it. I thought of all the times I had dumped guys, particularly remembering my breakup speech with my high school boyfriend Blaine. I remember how he had asked, "I want to stay together and you want to break up? How come you get your way?"

"Because, Blaine," I had said. "That's just how it works. The person who wants out of the relationship always gets her way. It's definitional."

The sad truth of the statement hit me in the gut now. If Marcus wanted out, there was absolutely nothing I could do to stop him.

I tried anyway, my voice shaking. "Marcus, please! Don't do this!"

"Look. We should talk face-to-face. I'll be over soon," he said.

"Are you going to break up with me? Just tell me now. Please!" I had waited for him all weekend, but the thought of waiting another twenty minutes was too much to bear.

"I'll be there soon," he said. His voice was flat, emotionless.

He arrived an hour later, wearing a Hooters T-shirt.

"You're dumping me, aren't you?" I asked, before he could even sit down.

He twisted the cap off a plastic bottle of Sprite, took a swig, and nodded twice.

"Omigod. I just can't believe this is happening. How can you dump me? I am pregnant with your baby! How can you do this?"

"I'm sorry, Darcy . . . but I just don't want to be with you."

It was the most surprising sentence I had ever heard. It was even more shocking than when Dex came out of the closet, so to speak. Perhaps because it was so utterly one-sided. I wanted Marcus. He did not want me. End of story.

"Why?" I asked. "Because of one fight?"

He shook his head. "You know it's not about any one fight."

"Then why?"

"Because I just can't ever see marrying you."

"Fine. We don't have to get married. We'll be like Goldie Hawn and what's his name?"

He shook his head again. "No."

"But I'm pregnant with your baby!"

"I know. And that's a problem." He raised his eyebrows and looked at me. "A problem with several different solutions."

"I've told you a million times, I'm *not* getting an abortion!"

"That's your decision, Darcy. Just like getting pregnant was *your* unilateral decision. Remember that?" he said angrily. "And now, here we are . . . and I just want you to have all the facts about the future—"

I interrupted him. "What does *that* mean?"

"It means I don't want to be with you, and I certainly don't want a kid. I'll help support it financially if you insist on having it, but I don't want to be . . . involved," he said, looking relieved. "At all."

"I don't believe what I'm hearing!"

"I'm sorry," he said, looking anything but sorry.

I begged. I cried. I pleaded. I promised that I would try harder.

Then he gave me the ultimate insult—"I'm just not that into you anymore"—before leaving my apartment.

It was Dex all over again. Only this time, I had no backup. No suitor waiting in the wings. I was, for the very first time in my life, completely on my own.

fifteen

The next day I caved and did the unthinkable. I phoned Dex. It was a pathetic and desperate move, but there was no denying it, I had become pathetic and desperate.

"Hi, Dex," I said when he answered his work line at Goldman Sachs.

He made a sound that was either a laugh or a cough, followed by silence.

"It's Darcy," I said.

"I know who it is."

"How are you?" I asked, keeping my voice steady.

"I'm fine. You?" he said.

"I'm . . . okay," I said. "I was just wondering . . . can you talk? Is this an okay time?"

"Um . . . Well, I actually have to run—"

"Well, how about later? Can you meet me after work?"

"I don't think so," he answered quickly.

"Please. I really need to talk to you about something," I said.

As I said the words, I realized that Dex likely no

longer cared about my needs. Sure enough, he said again,
"I don't think so."

"Why not?"

"I just don't think it's a good idea."

"Because of Rachel?"

"Darcy," he said, annoyed. "What do you want?"

"I just need to see you. Can't you just see me? Please?
I just want to talk to you. I'm sure she'd understand," I
said, wanting him to tell me that he wasn't seeing Rachel
anymore. That they had broken up. I was hungry to hear
the words.

But instead he said, "Rachel would be fine with me
seeing you."

The statement wasn't clarifying. It could mean she was
secure in their relationship. It could mean there was no
relationship. I decided not to press. For now. "Well, then,
why won't you see me?" I asked.

"Darcy, you need to move on."

"I *have* moved on," I said. "I just need to talk to you
about something."

He sighed and then folded. "Fine. Whatever."

I brightened. My plan was going to work. He gave in
because he secretly wanted to see me too. "So let's meet
back at our place at eight," I said.

"*Our* place?"

"You know what I mean," I said.

"No. I'm not going there. Pick somewhere else."

"Like where?" I asked, wondering if he had a nice restaurant in mind. "You choose."

"How about Session 73?"

The fact that the bar was mere blocks away from Rachel's apartment was not lost on me. "Why there?" I asked
snidely. "Is that your new Upper East hangout?"

"Darcy. You're on thin ice," he said. It was something

he always used to say to me in jest. I felt a wave of nostalgia and wondered if he felt it too.

"Why can't we meet at the apartment?"

"Don't press your luck."

"But I have some stuff to give you."

"What stuff? I got it all."

"Just a box of stuff you left. Stuff from the filing cabinet."

"Like what?"

"Maps, instruction booklets, a few letters . . ."

"You can toss that stuff."

"Can't you just meet me back at the apartment? We can talk for ten minutes. I'll give you your stuff and you can go."

"No. Bring it to Session 73."

"It's too heavy," I said. "I can't lift it, let alone carry it all that way—"

"Oh. Right. You're pregnant," he said bitterly. It was a good sign; he wouldn't be bitter if he didn't still care.

"So I'll swing by your place at eight," he said. "Please have the stuff ready."

"Okay," I said. "See you tonight, Dex."

Later that afternoon, I left work and zipped over to Bendel's, where I picked up a fabulous sea-foam-green cashmere sweater that plunged in the back. Dexter was a huge fan of my back. He always told me that I had the best back and that he loved how strong it was and the way I had no fat around my bra strap. Rachel definitely had her share of back fat, I thought, as I raced across Fifth Avenue to my hair appointment at Louis Licari. After a fabulous blowout, I changed into my new sweater in the salon bathroom. In case Dex made it back to my place before I did, I wanted to be ready.

Sure enough, when I returned home, there he was, sitting

on our front stoop, leafing through a document. He looked gorgeous. My heart raced just as it had when I first saw him walk into that bar in the Village so many years before. His tan had faded somewhat, but his skin still glowed. He had olive skin that would make any woman jealous. A perfect, even color, never a blemish. His sideburns were longer than usual—which gave him a sexy edge. I liked the subtle change. But with or without the sideburns, Dex was gorgeous. I had to get him back.

"Hello, Dex," I said, smiling a slow smile. "You're early."

Dex grimaced and tossed his document into his briefcase. Then he snapped it closed, stood up, and looked me straight in the eye. "Hi, Darcy."

"Come on up," I said, walking as enticingly as possible up the stairs to our third-floor apartment. Dex used to hate when I took the elevator three floors up, so I would show him that people could change. He followed me silently and then stood waiting with a grim expression as I unlocked the door. I walked inside, but he waited just outside the doorway.

"Well? Aren't you going to come in?" I asked, making my way over to the couch.

"Where's my stuff?" he asked, refusing to take another step.

I rolled my eyes. "Can't you please just come in and sit down? I want to talk to you for one second."

"I have plans at nine," he said.

"Well, it's only eight."

He glanced around nervously. Then he sighed, walked toward me, and perched on the very edge of the couch, placing his briefcase between his feet. I thought of all the times he had plopped down on that exact spot, kicked off his shoes, and reclined. We had eaten countless dinners on that couch, watched hundreds of movies and television shows there, even made love a few times in the early days. Now he looked out of place and stiff. It was weird.

I smiled at him, trying to alter the mood.

"Let's get this show on the road, Darcy. I gotta get going."

"Where are you going?"

"That is none of your business."

"Are you going out with Rachel? How are things going with her?" I asked, hoping to hear that their ill-advised romance—one based on hurt feelings and confusion— had fizzled, destroying their friendship along the way.

Dex said, "Let's not go through the charade of inquiring about each other's lives as if we're friends."

"What's that supposed to mean?" I asked.

"What part didn't you get?" he said.

"The part about us not being friends?"

"We're *not* friends," he said.

"We date for seven years and now we're not even *friends*? Just like that?" I asked.

He didn't flinch. "That's right. Just like that."

"Well. Regardless of whether we're friends, why can't you tell me if you're still with Rachel? What's the big deal?" I paused, praying that he would say, *Don't be ridiculous. Rachel and I don't have a relationship. That afternoon was just something that happened . . .* or even better . . . *almost happened.* Maybe I had even imagined their tans in Crate and Barrel.

"It's not a big deal," he said. "I just think it's best if we don't discuss our personal lives." He gripped the handle on his briefcase, pushing it from side to side.

"Why? I can handle it. You can't?"

He exhaled hard, shook his head, and said, "Fine. If you insist. Things with Rachel are very good. Great, in fact."

"So you're *actually* dating?"

"See? That's exactly why I don't want to discuss my life with you," Dex said, rubbing his hand along his jaw.

"Fine." I sniffed. "Let's just get your things. They're in the bedroom. You remember where that is, don't you?"

"You get them. I'll wait here."

"Dex, please," I said. "Just come with me."

"No," he said. "I'm not going back there."

I sighed, striding toward our bedroom, where I had planned on seducing him after a glass or two of wine. That clearly wasn't going to happen. So I grabbed a shoebox, dumped a pair of Jimmy Choos on my bed, and rummaged through my desk until I found a few instruction booklets. One for a fancy calculator he had bought for his home office. Another for our stereo. And a few maps of the D.C. area where his father lived. I put the papers in the shoebox. Then, just to add some heft, I threw in our studio engagement picture, expensive sterling silver frame and all. I knew it was one of Dexter's favorites of me, so it had surprised me when he took other pictures of us and left that one behind. I waltzed back into the living room, thrust the box toward him, and said, "Here."

"That's the heavy box you couldn't carry?" he asked, disgusted. He stood, poised to leave.

That's when it all sank in and I started to cry. Dex was serious with Rachel. He was leaving me to go meet her. Through tears, I begged. "Don't go. Please don't go," I said, wondering how many times I'd say those words.

"*Darcy,*" he said, as he sat back down. "Why are you doing this?"

"I can't help it," I said as I blew my nose. "I'm so sad."

He sighed loudly. "You act as if I did this thing to you."

"You *did* do this thing to me."

"You did it too. Remember?" He pointed at my stomach.

"Okay. Fine. I did it too. But . . ." I struggled to think of some way to keep him with me a bit longer. "But I need some answers before I can move on. I need closure. Please, Dex."

He stared at me blankly. His eyes said: "You don't have a choice about moving on. I'm outta here."

I asked my question anyway. "When exactly did you start dating? On the very day we broke up?"

"Darcy, that is entirely immaterial at this point."

"Tell me. Were you looking to be consoled? Is that why you went to Rachel's?"

"Darcy, just stop it. I want you to be happy. I want you and Marcus to be happy. Can't you want the same for me?"

"Marcus and I broke up," I blurted. All pride was out the window now.

Dex raised his eyebrows, his mouth forming the beginning of a question—*when* or maybe *why*. But he changed his response to, "Oh. I'm sorry to hear that."

"I miss you, Dex," I said. "I want us to be together again. Isn't there any way?"

He shook his head. "No."

"But I still love you." I linked my arm around his. "And I think that we still have something—"

"Darcy." He pulled roughly away, his features rearranging in a preachy expression. I knew this face well. It was his "my patience has expired" face. The face he got after I posed the same question a dozen times. "I'm with Rachel now. I'm sorry. There's no chance of us ever getting back together. Zero."

"Why are you being so *cruel*?"

"I'm not trying to be cruel. You just need to know that."

I put my face in my hands and sobbed harder. Then, suddenly, I had an idea. It was an awful, low thing to do, but I decided that I had no choice. I stopped crying, cast him a sideways glance, and said, "The baby is yours."

Dex was unfazed. "Darcy. Don't even start with that Montel Williams DNA-testing crap. That baby is *not* mine, and we both know it. I heard what you told Rachel. I know when we last had sex."

"The pregnancy is further along than I thought. It's yours. Why do you think Marcus and I broke up?"

"Darcy," Dex said, raising his voice. "Do *not* do this."

"Dex. The baby is yours. My doctor did an ultrasound to confirm the fetus's age. It happened earlier than I thought. It's yours," I said, shocking even myself with the disgraceful tactic. I told myself that I would come clean later. I just needed to buy some time with Dex. I could get him back if I just had time to work my magic. He wouldn't be able to resist me as Marcus had. After all, Marcus was impossible, weird about commitment. But Dex had been mine forever. There had to be some lingering feelings.

"If you're lying about this, it is unforgivable." His voice was almost shaking, and his eyes were wide. "I want the truth. Now."

I sucked in my breath, exhaled slowly, and maintained eye contact while I lied again. "It's yours," I said, feeling ashamed.

"You know I'm going to want proof."

I licked my lips, stayed calm. "Yes. Absolutely. I want you to take a blood test. You'll see that it's yours."

"Darcy."

"What?"

Dex put his head in his hands and then ran them through his thick, dark hair. "Darcy . . . Even if it *is* mine, I want you to understand that this baby won't change a thing between us. Not a thing. You got that?"

"What does that mean exactly?" I asked, even though it was pretty clear what he was driving at. After all, Marcus had just made the same point to me the night before. I had the concept down.

"We're over. Finished. It's never going to happen again with you and me. Baby or no baby. I'm with Rachel now."

I stared at him, feeling outrage well up inside of me. It was all so unbelievable! So utterly inconceivable! How could he be with Rachel? I stood and paced over to the window, trying to catch my breath.

"So tell me the truth right now. Is it mine?" he asked.

I turned and looked at him. He wasn't going to fold. You come to know a person well in seven years—and I knew that once Dex made up his mind, there was absolutely nothing that I could say to change it. His jaw was clenched. There was no opening for me. Besides, as brazen as I could be, I knew I could never actually go through with a ploy like this one, even as a temporary measure. It was just too awful, and I only felt worse for having tried it.

"Fine," I said, throwing up my hands. "It's Marcus's baby. Are you happy?"

"Actually yes, Darcy. I am happy. No, *ecstatic* is more the word." He stood and pointed angrily at me. "And the fact that you could lie about such a thing confirms to me—"

"I'm sorry," I said before he could finish his sentence. I was crying again. "I know it was *really* low . . . I just don't know what to do. Everything is falling apart for me. And—and—you're with Rachel. You took her on our honeymoon! How could you take her on our honeymoon? How could you do that?"

Dex said nothing.

"You did, didn't you? You went to Hawaii with her?"

"The tickets were nonrefundable, Darcy. Even the hotel was already paid for," he said, looking guilty.

"How could you do that? How? And then I see you two in Crate and Barrel, shopping for couches. That's how I knew about Hawaii. You were all tan. Shopping for couches . . . All tan and happy and buying couches." I was babbling now, a total mess. "Are you moving in together?"

"Not yet . . ."

"Not *yet*?" I said. "So you are eventually? Are you *serious*?"

"Darcy, please. Stop this. Rachel and I didn't do this to hurt you. Just like you didn't get pregnant to hurt me. Right?" he asked in his "please be reasonable" tone.

I looked out the window again at a pile of trash on the curb. Then I returned my gaze to Dex. "Please be with me again," I said softly. "Please. Give me another chance. We had seven good years together. Things were good. We'll forgive each other and move on." I walked back over to him and tried to hug him. He stiffened and recoiled like a puppy resisting the grasp of an overzealous child.

"Dex? Please?"

"No, Darcy. We don't belong together. We aren't right for each other."

"Do you love her?" I asked under my breath, truly expecting him to say no or that he didn't know or that he wouldn't answer the question.

But instead he said, "Yes. I love her." I could see in his eyes that he wasn't saying it to be mean; he was saying it out of a sense of loyalty to her. It was that committed, resolute look of his. It was Dex being a good person, being true to his new girlfriend. I marveled at how fast old loyalties, ones that took years to build, could be ripped apart and replaced. I knew I had lost him, but I felt desperate to recruit a small piece of his heart back to me. Make him feel even a sliver of what he used to feel for me. "More than you ever loved me?" I asked, looking for one small scrap.

"Don't do this, Darcy."

"I need to know, Dex. I really need to know the answer to that," I said, thinking that he couldn't possibly love her more in a few weeks than he had loved me when he had proposed after years together. It just wasn't possible.

"Why do you need to know, Darce?"

"I just do. Tell me."

He stared down at the coffee table for a long minute in that dazed way of his where he doesn't blink. Then he looked around the apartment, his eyes resting on an oil painting of a dilapidated, pillared house surrounded by terraced fields and a solitary oak. We had purchased the painting together in New Orleans right at the beginning of our relationship. We had spent nearly eight hundred dollars on it, which seemed like a huge sum of money at the time, as Dex was in law school and I had just begun to work. It was our first big purchase as a couple—an implicit acknowledgment of our commitment to each other. Sort of like buying a dog together. I remember standing in that gallery, admiring our painting, as Dex told me that he loved the way the early evening shadows fell across the front porch. I remember him saying that dusk was his favorite time of day. I remember we grinned at each other as the clerk bubble-wrapped our painting. Then we returned to the hotel, where we made love and ordered a banana split from the room service menu. Had he forgotten all of that?

I guess I had forgotten such moments when my affair began with Marcus. But I remembered every such occasion now. Regret surged through me. What I would have given to have a big ol' redo, take back everything with Marcus. I looked at Dex and asked the question again. "Do you love her more than you ever loved me?"

I waited.

Then he nodded and said so softly that it was nearly a whisper, "Yes. I do. I'm really sorry, Darcy."

I stared at him incredulously, trying to process what he was saying, how it could be possible that he could love Rachel so much. She wasn't that pretty. She wasn't that fun. What did she have that I didn't have besides a few measly IQ points?

Dex spoke again. "I can tell you're in a bad place right now, Darcy. Part of me would like to help you, but it just won't work. I can't be that person for you. You have friends and family you need to turn to. . . . I really have to go now." His voice was distant, his gaze detached. In a few seconds, he would walk out, hail a cab, and cross the park to see Rachel. She would greet him at her door, her brown eyes sympathetic, probing for details about our meeting. I could hear her asking, "How did it go?" and stroking Dexter's hair as he told her everything. How I had lied about the baby, then begged, then cried. She would feel both pity and disdain for me.

"Fine. Get out. I don't want to talk to you or her ever again," I said, realizing that I had said pretty much the same thing in Rachel's apartment. This time, my words had a watered-down, weak effect.

Dex bit his lower lip. "Please be well," he said, gathering up his briefcase and the shoebox of junk he didn't want any more than he wanted me. Then he stood and walked out of his old apartment, leaving me for good.

sixteen

It was incomprehensible. In my entire lifetime—throughout high school, college, and my twenties—I had never been dissed by a guy. Not dumped. Not stood up. Not even slighted. And there I was—a two-time loser all in a week's time. I was completely alone, didn't even have a prospect in sight.

I also didn't have Rachel, my steadfast source of comfort when other things, unrelated to romance, had unraveled in my life. Nor did I have my own mother—whom I refused to call back and hear some variation of "I told you so." That left Claire, who came to my apartment after I had called in sick to work for three straight days. I was surprised that it took her so long to rush to my aid, but I guess she had no way of suspecting my depth of despair. Up to that point in my life, my definition of down-and-out was a bad case of PMS.

"What has gotten into you?" Claire asked, glancing around my messier-than-usual apartment. "I've been so worried about you. Why haven't you returned any of my calls?"

"Marcus dumped me," I said mournfully. I had sunk too low to try to put a triumphant spin on the facts.

She raised the blinds in my living room. "*Marcus broke up with you?*" she asked, appropriately shocked.

I sniffed and nodded.

"That's ridiculous! Has he taken a look in the mirror? What was he thinking?"

"I don't know," I said. "He just doesn't want to be with me."

"Well, the whole world's gone mad. First Dex and Rachel and now *this*! I mean—come on! This is *nuts*. I just don't get it. It's like an episode of *The Twilight Zone*."

I felt a tear roll down my cheek.

Claire rushed over to give me a hug and a "buck up, little camper" smile. Then she said briskly, "Well, it's a blessing in disguise. Marcus was so *bush league*. You're better off without him. And Rachel and Dex are dullsville." She headed for my kitchen, holding up a plastic bag filled with all the fixings for margaritas. "And believe me, this whole situation is nothing that a few drinks won't cure . . . Besides, I have a much finer man all cued up for you."

I blew my nose and looked at her hopefully. "Who?"

"You remember Josh Levine?"

I shook my head.

"Well, I have two words for you. Hot and loaded," she said, rubbing her thumb against her fingers. "His nose is rather large, but not offensively so. Your daughter might need a minor nose job, but that's the only issue," she said brightly. She rolled up her sleeves and set about rinsing my dishes covered with day-old Kraft macaroni and cheese residue. "You briefly met him at that house in the Hamptons with the eighteen-person hot tub? Remember? He's friends with Eric Kiefer and that whole crowd?"

"Oh, yeah," I said, conjuring a well-dressed, thirtysomething banker with wavy brown hair and big, square teeth. "Doesn't he have a girlfriend who is a model or actress or something?"

"He *did* have a girlfriend. Amanda something or other. And yes, she's a model . . . but the low-rent catalog kind. I think she wore some pleated cords in Chadwick's of Boston or something. But Josh dumped her two days ago." Claire looked up smugly. "How's that for hot off the presses?"

Claire loved being the first to get a scoop.

"Why'd they break up?" I asked. "Did Josh catch his best friend hiding in Amanda's closet?"

Claire chuckled. "No. Word is she was just too dumb for him. She is as vapid as they come. Get a load of *this one* . . . I heard that she actually thought *paparazzi* was the last name of one particular Italian photographer. Apparently she said something like, 'Who is this Paparazzi guy and why didn't they arrest him years ago after he killed Princess Diana?'"

I laughed for the first time in weeks.

"So anyway, Josh is *a-vail-a-ble*," Claire sang and spun around ballerina-style.

I became momentarily suspicious. "Why don't you want him?"

"You know my uptight Episcopalian parents would never let me go down the Jewish-guy road or I would have claimed him for myself. . . . But you better act fast because the girls in this city are ready to *pounce*."

"Yeah. Don't let Jocelyn catch wind of this," I said.

Jocelyn Silver worked with Claire and me, and although I liked her in small doses, she was a total alpha female, way too competitive for me ever to trust. She also bore a strong resemblance to Uma Thurman, and if I had to watch her pretend to be annoyed when one more stranger approached her to ask if she was Uma, I was going to puke. Which, incidentally, was what Jocelyn did after every meal.

"No kidding . . . I haven't mentioned anything about the breakup to her. Even if I did, Josh would *totally* go for you over her."

I smiled with false modesty.

She continued, "So how about this? I'll make sure Josh comes to our club opening next week—the one Jocelyn's going to miss for her cousin's wedding . . ." She winked at me. "So stop this sniveling over Marcus. I mean, Christ, what was the deal there anyway? He could be fun, but he's certainly not worthy of macaroni-and-cheese-level grief."

"You're right," I said. I could feel myself cheering up as I thought of how Jewish men were supposed make great husbands. "Josh sounds divine. I'm sure I could convince him to have a Christmas tree, don't you think?"

"You can convince anyone to do anything," Claire said.

I beamed. That theory had been proven wrong a few times in recent days, but surely I was going to get back on track with my charmed life.

"And I had another thought on my way over . . ." Claire smiled mysteriously, poised to reveal another terrific surprise.

"What's that?"

"Well," she said as she uncorked the bottle of Patrón, our favorite brand of tequila. "What do you say we move in together again? My lease is up, and you have a spare bedroom. We could save a ton on rent and have a blast together. What do you say?"

"That's a fantastic idea," I said, remembering fondly our roomie days before I had moved in with Dex. Claire and I had shared the same shoe size, the same taste in music, and the same love of fruity mixed drinks that we consumed in quantity as we primped for our big nights out. Besides, it would be great to have her around when the baby arrived. I was sure she wouldn't mind getting up occasionally for nighttime feedings. I watched as she sliced a lime and hung perfect twists on our glasses. She had a nice touch when it came to entertaining, another perk of living with her. "Let's do it!"

"Excellent!" she squealed. "My lease expires next month."

"There's just one thing I should tell you," I said as she crossed the living room over to my couch, drinks in hand.

"What's that?"

I swallowed, reassuring myself that although Claire could be snobbish and judgmental, she had only demonstrated a sense of absolute loyalty to me over the years. I had to believe that she would be there for me in my hour of need. So as she handed me a temptingly perfect margarita on the rocks, salt lined evenly along the rim of the glass (an engagement present from Dexter's Aunt Suzy), I blurted out my big secret. "I'm pregnant with Marcus's baby." Then I took one tiny sip of my drink, inhaling the sweet smell of tequila, licking the salt from my lips.

"Get outta here," she said, her crystal drop earrings swinging as she plopped down next to me and curled her legs up under her ample bottom. "Oh—we didn't do a toast. Here's to being roomies again!"

She clearly thought I was joking. I clinked my glass against hers, took another tiny sip, and said, "No. It's true. I *am* pregnant. So I probably shouldn't drink this. Although a few more sips couldn't hurt. It's not that strong, is it?"

She looked at me sideways and said, "You're kidding, right?"

I shook my head.

"Darcy!" She froze, a fearful smile plastered on her face.

"I'm not joking."

"Swear."

"I swear."

It went on like that for some time before I could convince her that I wasn't putting her on, that I was, indeed, pregnant with the child of a man whom she had deemed woefully inadequate. As she listened to me ramble about my morning sickness, my due date, the problems with my mother, she gulped her margarita—which was highly unusual for Claire. She had finishing-school manners even when wasted. She never forgot to cross her legs on a bar stool or keep her elbows off a table, and she never gulped. But at that moment, she was rattled.

"So what do you think?" I asked her.

She took another swallow, then coughed and sputtered, "Whoa! Excuse me! I think it went down the wrong pipe."

I waited for her to say something more, but she only stared back at me with a plastered smile, as if she were no longer quite sure who it was she was having a drink with. I guess I expected her to be surprised, but I wanted the *giddy* brand of surprised, not the *freaked-out* version. I reassured myself that I had just caught her off guard. She needed a minute to digest the news. In the meantime, I gave a short, noble speech about how I never once considered having an abortion or giving the baby up for adoption. In truth, I had given some consideration to both options in the past forty-eight hours, but something made me stay on track. I'd like to say it was strength of character and good morals, but it also had a lot to do with stubborn pride.

"Congratulations. That's fantastic news," Claire finally said, in the tinny, insincere voice of a game show host informing the losing contestant that they weren't going to walk away completely empty-handed, but rather with a gift certificate for Omaha Steaks. "I know you'll do a great job with this . . . And I will be here for you to help in any way I can."

I could tell she added the last sentence as an afterthought, its generality smacking of obligation rather than any earnest desire to be involved in my baby's life. Or even mine, for that matter.

"Thank you," I said, my mind spinning to analyze the moment. Was I being too critical of her? Too paranoid? What exactly did I want her to say? Ideally, she could ask to be the baby's godmother or offer to throw me a big shower. At the very least, I wanted her to mention moving in with me again, or say something about Josh, how we needed to act fast while my body was still spectacular. Claire only laughed nervously and said, "This is all so . . . *so* exciting."

"Yes," I said defensively. "It really *is*. And I see no reason why I can't still date."

"Of course you will date," she said, pumping one fist in the air. But no further mention of my Jewish Prince Charming.

"Do you think Josh will mind?" I asked.

More nervous laughter. "Mind that you're pregnant?"

"Yeah. Mind that I'm pregnant?"

"Well, I . . . I'm not sure . . . I don't know him *that* well."

It was perfectly clear that she was quite sure that Josh would mind very much indeed. About as much as she would mind living with me and a newborn. She downed the rest of her margarita, chattering about how excited the girls in our office would be. Could she tell them? Was it public knowledge yet?

I said no, not yet, I wasn't quite ready for the world to know.

"I understand. Mum's the word," Claire said, pinching her lips between thumb and index finger. She giggled. "No pun intended."

I insisted that I wasn't ashamed of my pregnancy. It wasn't that at all. I babbled about how I would maintain my sense of self, referencing Rachel on *Friends* and Miranda on *Sex and the City*. Both women had managed to keep their lives and looks intact while embracing single motherhood. I saw no reason why I couldn't do the same.

"Oh, I know," Claire said in a condescending tone. "There's no reason you can't do it all, have it all. Be a modern woman!"

As I studied her big, fake smile, the exact contours of our shallow friendship came into focus. Sure, Claire liked me, but she liked me because I was fun to go out with and because I was a guy magnet, even when I had worn my engagement ring from Dex. She liked me because I was an invaluable asset. With her pedigree and my looks and personality, we had been unstoppable. The glamorous PR duo everyone either knew or wanted to know.

But in the time it took to down a margarita, my stock had plummeted in her eyes. I had been transformed into nothing but a struggling single mother. I might as well have had curlers in my hair and a welfare check in my callused hand. I was of no use to her anymore.

As she finished her drink, she eyed mine. "Well? May I?" she asked.

"Go ahead," I said.

She took a few sips from my glass and then glanced at her watch. "Oh, shoot. Look at the time!"

"Did you have to be somewhere?" I asked. Usually it was impossible to shake Claire.

"Yes," she said. "I told Jocelyn I'd give her a call. She wants to go out tonight. Didn't I mention that?"

"No," I said. "You didn't mention that."

Claire smiled tightly and said, "Yeah. Dinner and a few drinks. Of course, you can come if you want. Even though you can't drink. We'd love your company."

Claire was offering me, Darcy Rhone, a charity invite. I was tempted to go, to prove that I could still be fun. But I was too indignant to accept the invitation so easily. So I told her no, that I had some phone calls to return. I waited for a little coaxing, but she just stood, carried her glass over to the sink, swung her Prada bag over her shoulder, and said with all the cheeriness in the world, "All righty then, hon. . . . Congratulations again. Have a great night. You take good care of yourself, okay?"

Needless to say the next week passed and Claire never mentioned moving in with me again. Instead, I heard from another girl in our office that Claire and Jocelyn were apartment-hunting in the Village. I also heard from Jocelyn herself, in the office restroom after her postlunch-time purge, that she had met a great guy—Josh Levine— did I know him? It was the final straw, the salt in my open, bleeding, infected wound. Even dependent and doting Claire had joined the ranks and betrayed me. I hurried back to my office, stunned and teary, my mind racing about what to do next. Without even fully thinking it through, I found myself propelled down the hall to Cal's office, where I informed my boss that I needed to take a leave of absence, effective immediately. I told him I was having some personal issues. He asked if there were anything he could do. I said no, I just needed some time away. He told me they were overstaffed these days, anyway, and the economy was socking the PR business right in the gut, so I could take as much time as I needed and could come back whenever I was ready. Then he gave my midsection an unmistakable once-over. He knew my secret.

Claire, the biggest gossip hound in Manhattan, had added me to her inside scoop. So I added her to my ever-growing list of enemies—of people who would be sorry to have crossed me.

seventeen

FOR the next few days I cranked up "I Will Survive," Ace of Base's "I Saw the Sign," and other inspiring songs as I racked my brain, trying to come up with a plan, a way to escape the shame of so much rejection. I needed a fresh start, a change of venue, a new cast of characters. I scoured my list of contacts in the city, but everyone was somehow linked to Dex or to Claire or to my firm. I seemed to be without options. And then, just as true despair set in, a call from Indianapolis showed up on my caller ID. It was Annalise, my last girlfriend standing.

"Hi, Annalise!" I answered, feeling guilty for all the times in the past that I had dismissed her as boring, neglected to call her back, even scoffed at her suburban, kindergarten-teaching existence. I felt especially bad for not meeting her new baby, Hannah, when I was back in Indy.

"I'm so glad you called!" I told her. "How are you? How is Hannah?"

I listened patiently as Annalise gushed about her baby

and complained about the lack of sleep. Then she asked how I was doing, her tone implying that she already knew my tale of woe. Just in case she was missing some details, I filled her in on everything. "My life is falling apart, and I don't know what to do," I cried into the phone.

"Oh, wow, Darce," Annalise said in her heavy Midwestern accent. "I don't know what to say. I'm just . . . really worried about you."

"Well, you *should* be worried," I said. "I'm at the absolute end of my rope. And this is all Rachel's fault, you know."

I was yearning for one derogatory comment about Rachel, her other best friend. Just a tiny dig would have felt like a cooling salve. But Annalise was not one to be mean, so she only made a concerned clucking noise into the phone and then said, "Can't you and Rach just try to work things out? This is just too sad."

"Hell, no!"

Annalise made another remark about forgiveness, one of those annoying religious comments that had become her trademark after marrying Greg, a Bible beater from Kentucky.

"Never," I said. "I'll never forgive her."

Annalise sighed as Hannah Jane fussed in the background, making an annoying, and escalating, *ehh, ehhh, ehhhhhh* sound that wasn't exactly igniting my mothering instinct.

"So, anyway, I just think I need a change of scenery, you know? I thought about the Peace Corps or some outdoorsy type of adventure, but that's not really my scene. I like my creature comforts. Especially now that I'm pregnant . . ."

That's when Annalise suggested that I return home for a few months, live with my parents, and have the baby in

Indianapolis. "It'd be so fun to have you here," she said. "I'm in this amazing playgroup at church. You'd love it. It might be really grounding for you."

"I don't need to be grounded. I need the opposite. I need an *escape*. Besides, I can't go back to Indy. It just feels like such a downgrade. You know, like I'm selling out, settling, cashing in my chips, admitting defeat."

"Okay!" Annalise giggled good-naturedly. "I get the picture. We know we're small potatoes, don't we, Hannah?"

Hannah howled in response.

"You know what I mean. You like it there, and that's great for you. But I'm just not a small-town kind of girl . . ."

"You're far from small-town," Annalise said.

"And besides, I'm not speaking to my mother," I said, explaining what a bitch she had been upon hearing my news.

"Why don't you go to London and stay with Ethan?" she said, referring to Ethan Ainsley, our high school friend who was in London, writing some book.

The second she said it, I knew it was the answer. It was so obvious, I marveled that I hadn't thought of it first. I would sublease my apartment and head off to jolly ol' England.

"Annalise, that's a marvelous idea," I said, imagining everyone catching wind of my transatlantic move. Claire, who fancied herself such a world traveler, would eat her heart out. Marcus, who had yet to call and check on me, would be filled with guilt and second-guessing when he discovered that his baby was going to be born thousands of miles away. Rachel, who had always been closer to Ethan than I, would be jealous of my intense bonding with her dear childhood pal. Dex would wonder how he could have ever let such an independent, adventurous, gutsy woman go.

It was an idea whose time had come. I only had to convince Ethan to let me stay with him.

I had known Ethan since the fourth grade, when he moved to our town in the middle of the school year. There was always a flurry of intrigue when a new kid arrived, with everyone excited at the thought of fresh blood. I remembered Ethan's first day well. I could still see our teacher, Mrs. Billone, resting her hand on his scrawny shoulder and announcing, "This is Ethan Ainsley. He comes to us from Long Island. Please join me in welcoming him."

As we all muttered, "Welcome, Ethan," I found myself wondering where this island of his was located—in the Atlantic or Pacific?—and how a boy from the tropics could have such fair skin and light hair. I pictured Ethan running around half-naked, shimmying up trees to collect coconuts for all of his meals. Had he been rescued by a search team? Sent to foster parents in Indiana? Perhaps this was his first day in proper clothes. I suspected that it was torture for him to feel so restricted.

At recess that day, Ethan sat alone on the curb near the monkey bars, writing in the dirt with a twig as we all cast curious glances his way. Everyone else was too shy to talk to him, but I summoned Rachel and Annalise and the three of us approached him. "Hi, Ethan. I'm Darcy. This is Rachel, and this is Annalise," I said boldly, pointing to my timid sidekicks.

"Hi," Ethan said, squinting up at us over his oversized, round glasses.

"So how far away is your homeland?" I asked him, cutting right to the chase. I wanted the full scoop on his exotic childhood.

"New York is about eight hundred miles from here." He

enunciated every word, making him sound very smart. It wasn't the voice I expected from a native islander.

"New York?" I was confused. "But Mrs. Billone said you're from an island?"

He and Rachel exchanged an amused glance—their first of many superior moments.

"What's so funny?" I asked indignantly. "She did so say you're from an island. Didn't she, Annalise?"

Annalise nodded somberly.

"*Long* Island," Ethan and Rachel said in unison, with matching smirks.

So it was a *long* island as opposed to a short one? That didn't clear anything up.

"Long Island is part of New York," Rachel said in her know-it-all voice.

"Oh. Yeah. Right. I knew that. I just didn't hear her say *long,*" I lied. "Did you, Annalise?"

"No," Annalise said, "I didn't hear that part either."

Annalise never made you feel dumb. It was one of her best qualities. That and the fact that she was always willing to share anything. In fact, I was wearing her pale pink Jellies on that very day.

"Long Island is the eastern part of New York State," Ethan continued. His condescending tutorial made it clear that he didn't believe me about not hearing the word *long.* That really got my fur up, and I instantly regretted any attempt to be nice to the new kid.

"So why'd you move here?" I asked abruptly, thinking that he should have stayed back on his faux island.

He reported that his parents had just divorced, and that his mother, originally from Indiana, moved back to be closer to her parents, his grandparents. It was hardly a glamorous tale. Annalise, whose own parents were divorced, asked him if his father still lived in New York.

"Yes. He does," Ethan said, his eyes returning to his

dirt doodling. "I'll see him on alternating holidays and during the summers."

I would have felt sorry for him—divorce seemed just about the worst thing that could happen to a kid—right up there with having to wear a wig after leukemia radiation treatments. But it's hard to feel sorry for someone who makes you feel stupid for not knowing some insignificant geographical fact.

Rachel changed the subject from divorce and asked Ethan questions about New York, as if it were her idea to talk to him in the first place. The two rattled on about the Empire State Building and the Metropolitan Museum of Art and the World Trade Center, all places Ethan had visited and Rachel had read about.

"We have big buildings and museums in Indianapolis too," I said defensively, pegging Ethan as one of those annoying people who always say, "Back where I come from." Then I steered Annalise away from their big-shot conversation over to a game of four square.

After that day, I didn't give Ethan much thought until he and Rachel were placed in the academically gifted program called "T.G." for "talented and gifted" at the start of the following school year. I hated the T.G. program, hated the feeling of being excluded, of not making the cut. I couldn't stand the smugness of the T.G.ers, and resented them with a burning in my chest every time they trotted merrily down the hall to their mystery room and then returned, buzzing about their dumb experiments—like constructing clay boats in an attempt to hold the maximum number of tacks. Incidentally, Ethan won that contest, engineering a vessel that held nineteen tacks before sinking. "Big deal," I remember telling Rachel. "I stopped playing with Play-Doh and clay when I was four." I always sought to burst her bubble, insisted that T.G. really stood for "totally geeky." And just in case it looked like sour grapes,

I reminded Rachel often that I had only missed the T.G. test score cutoff by one point and that was only because I had strep throat the day of the test and couldn't concentrate on anything other than my inability to swallow. (The part about strep throat was the truth; the part about one point was probably not—although I never knew for sure how far I had missed the mark, because my mother had told me that it wasn't important what my score was, that I didn't need the T.G. program to be special.)

So in light of my irritation over Ethan's superiority, it was surprising when he turned out to be my first real boyfriend. It was also surprising because Rachel had had a crush on him since the day he arrived, while I was firmly in the Doug Jackson camp. Doug was the most popular boy in our class, and I was sure that he and I were going to become a hot-and-heavy item, until he taped a picture of Heather Locklear to his Trapper Keeper, announcing that he preferred blondes to brunettes. The sentiment put me in a huff and I decided to look for another candidate, perhaps even a sixth-grader. Skinny, pale Ethan was the farthest thing from my mind.

But one day, as I watched him search the card catalogue for Peru, I suddenly saw in Ethan what Rachel was always carrying on about. He was pretty cute. So I waltzed over and bumped into him on purpose under the pretense of trying to find a card on Paraguay, one drawer over. He gave me a funny look, smiled, and flashed his dimples. I decided right then and there that I would like Ethan.

When I delivered the news to Rachel later that week, I assumed she'd be pleased, happy that I was finally agreeing with her and that we'd have one more thing in common. After all, best friends should agree on all topics, certainly ones as major as who to have a crush on. But Rachel was not happy at all. In fact, she was furious, becoming strangely territorial, like she *owned* Ethan. Annalise pointed out that she and I had shared our crush on Doug for months, but Rachel wasn't persuaded. She just kept saying that Doug was somehow a different case, and she stayed huffy and self-righteous, muttering about how she had liked Ethan first.

That was true enough; she did like Ethan first. But the way I saw it was this—if she liked him so darn much, she should have done something about it. Taken some real action. And by action, I didn't mean writing his initials in the condensation on her mother's car window. But Rachel was never one for action. That was my department.

So a few days later, I wrote Ethan a note, asking if he wanted to go out with me, with instructions to check a box next to *yes, no,* or *maybe.* To be fair, I included Rachel's name as a fourth option. But at the last minute, I tore off that part of the note, reasoning that she shouldn't be the benefactor of my get-up-and-go. Besides, I didn't want to lose to Rachel when she was already beating me in so many other arenas. She was in T.G. after all. So I passed the note, and Ethan said yes, and just like that we were a couple. We talked on the phone and flirted during recess and it was all a tingly thrill for a few weeks.

But then Doug changed his mind, announcing that he liked brunettes better than blondes after all. So I dumped Ethan and put myself back on the fifth-grade market. Luckily, our breakup coincided with Ethan's Loch Ness Monster obsession; it was all he talked about for weeks, even planning a summer trip to Scotland or Switzerland or wherever the thing supposedly lived. So he had another focus and got over me relatively quickly. A short time later, Rachel got over Ethan too. She said she was no longer interested in boys, a convenient decision because she wasn't exactly being pursued by any.

So we all forged our way into junior high and high school. Annalise, Ethan, Rachel, and I formed a little clique (although I ran in more popular circles too) and none of us ever mentioned the fifth-grade love-triangle saga again. After high school graduation, I continued to keep in touch with Ethan, but mostly I did so through Rachel. Those two stayed very close, particularly during his divorce. Ethan came to New York often during his crisis, so much so that I wondered if he and Rachel might get together. But Rachel insisted that there was nothing romantic between them.

"Do you think he could be gay?" I'd ask her, referencing his close female friendships, his sensitivity, and his love of classical music. She'd say that she was sure he was straight, simply explaining that they were strictly friends.

So as I dialed up Ethan in London, I worried that he'd turn me down out of loyalty to Rachel, a sense that he had to take her side. Annalise loved us both equally, but Ethan clearly favored Rachel. Sure enough, when he finally called me back more than a week later, after I had left him two phone messages and sent him a well-crafted, slightly desperate e-mail, his hello was tight and tentative.

I worked up a stirring preemptive strike. "Ethan, I can't take it if you're going to shoot me down. I just can't take it. You gotta help me out. I know you're better friends with Rachel—I know you're on her side . . ." I hesitated, waiting for him to say he wasn't on anyone's side. When he didn't, I kept going. "But I'm begging you, Ethan. I have to get away from here. I'm pregnant. My boyfriend dumped me. I took a leave of absence from work. I can't go home, Ethan. It would be way too humiliating. Way." I said it all, knowing the risk—that he would call Rachel and tell her what a loser I was. But it was a chance I had to take. I said one final *please* and then waited.

"Darce, it has nothing to do with Rachel. It's just that I like living alone. I don't want a roommate."

"Ethan, please. Just for a few weeks. Just for a visit. I have nowhere else to go."

"What about Indy? You could stay with your folks."

"You know I can't do that. Could you have crawled back to Indy after you divorced Brandi?"

He sighed, but I could tell that I had hit an empathetic chord. "A few weeks? Like how many?"

"Three? Four? Six tops?" I said and held my breath, waiting.

"All right, Darce," he finally said. "You can stay here. But only temporarily. My place is really small . . . and as I said, I really relish solitude."

"Oh, thank you. Thank you. Thank you!" I said, feeling like my old victorious self. I just knew that my problems were solved and that his saying yes was the equivalent of bestowing me with a chance to fix my life, infuse it with European glamour. "You won't be sorry, Ethan. I'll be the perfect guest," I said.

"Just remember—a *short* visit."

"A short visit," I echoed. "I got it."

I hung up and envisioned my new life . . .

Strolling around cobblestone streets in Notting Hill, through the mist and fog, my basketball of a stomach peeking out between a cropped, cowl-neck sweater and chic, low-slung pants. A plaid Burberry cap is perched on my head, cocked slightly to the side. Beautifully tousled hair with chestnut highlights, compliments of the finest London salon, spills down around my shoulders. I stop by a charming patisserie, where I carefully select a pumpkin mousse tart. As I pay at the counter, I spot my future beau. As he glances up at me from his paper, his face lights up in a sexy smile. He is outlandishly handsome, with Dexter's strong features and Lair's light eyes and cute body. (His father is from Northern Italy—hence the blue eyes; his mother, British—hence the impeccable grooming, fine manners, and Oxford education.) His name is Alistair, and he is wickedly smart and sophisticated and ultra-wealthy. He might even be a duke or earl. He will top Dex in all categories. And he'll be sexier than Marcus. Of course, he'll fall madly in love with me at first sight. My pregnancy won't deter him in the slightest. In fact, it will turn him on—as I have heard is the case with some highly evolved men. Within weeks of our first meeting, Alistair will ask for my hand in marriage. I will move out of Ethan's charming flat into Alistair's enormous and perfectly appointed home, complete with a maid, cook, butler, the works.

And then, one night in late April, when spring has come to London, as we sleep naked in his canopied, carved-wood bed handed down through four generations, on his eleven-hundred-thread-count sheets, I will feel the first gentle stirrings of labor. "I think it's time," I will whisper, gently jostling Alistair. He will bolt out of bed, help me dress in my cashmere pajamas, run a silver brush through my hair, and summon his driver before we whisk off into the London night. Then he will hover by my hospital bed, stroking my brow and planting tiny kisses along my hairline, while murmuring, "Push, dahling. Push, my treasure."

It will be love at first sight all over again when he sees my daughter, who will look exactly like me. The daughter he will want to adopt. "Our daughter," he will tell people. By the time her first tooth appears, we will have both forgotten that a boorish American is the biological father. And by that time, I surely will have forgotten all about Rachel and Dex. I will be too caught up in my happily-ever-after to give them even a cursory thought.

eighteen

For the next two weeks, I was all about preparation and action, single-minded in my quest to shut down my New York affairs and get myself to London. I placed a classified ad and found a young couple to sublet my apartment. Then I sold my tainted engagement ring in the diamond district and my wedding gown on eBay. When I combined the proceeds with the balance in my checking account, I calculated that I had enough money to get through my pregnancy in London without a day's work.

Finally, I was all ready, my bags packed full of my finest belongings, on the way to JFK for my red-eye flight to London. As I boarded the plane, I felt a sense of absolute satisfaction, knowing that I was leaving the city without a word to the people who had betrayed me. I hunkered down in my business class seat, slipped on a pair of cashmere slippers, and fell into a deep and peaceful sleep.

Seven hours later, I awoke as the plane hovered over green meadows and a winding ribbon of blue that had to be the Thames. My heart galloped with the realization that my new life had begun. I only grew more excited as I made my way through passport control (fibbing about the length of my stay just as I had to Ethan), withdrew British money from an ATM machine, and took a black cab from Heathrow to Ethan's apartment.

I was invigorated on our drive into London, feeling more worldly already. I sat up straighter, speaking properly to my cabbie, and injecting plenty of niceties into our chitchat, instead of barking my usual yellow-cab orders. This was a civilized land, and in it I was going to find the good life. A more cultured existence. People like Madonna and Gwyneth Paltrow, who could live anywhere in the world, chose to live in London, instead of tired old New York City and Los Angeles. I had some significant things in common with these women. Style. Beauty. A certain je ne sais quoi. Maybe I'd even befriend Madge and Gwynnie. Along with Kate Moss, Hugh Grant, and Ralph Fiennes.

Forty minutes of polite conversation later, I arrived on Ethan's street. My cabbie got out of the car, came around to the passenger side, and helped me with my bags, lining my Louis Vuitton luggage up on the curb. I handed him two purple twenties and a pretty green five—all oversized, colorful bills adorned with a young Queen Elizabeth. Even the money was more interesting and lovely in England. "Here you go, sir. Please keep the change. Thank you kindly for your help," I said, curtsying ever so slightly. It seemed a very British thing to do.

My cabbie smiled and winked at me.

I was off to a good start. I took a deep breath and exhaled, watching my breath fog up in the chilly November morning. Then I marched up the six weathered marble steps to Ethan's building, located his flat number, and pushed the bronze button next to it. I heard an anemic buzzer followed by a "Yes?" over the intercom.

"Ethan! I'm here! Hurry! I'm freezing!"

Seconds later Ethan grinned at me through the beveled pane in the front door. He swung the door open and gave me a big hug. "Darcy! How are you?"

"Wonderful!" I said, doling out a double Euro-kiss, planting one on each of his pink cheeks. I ran my hand through his honey-colored hair. It was longer than usual, his curls loopy like a lion's mane. "Love the 'do, Ethan."

He thanked me, said he hadn't had time for a cut. Then he smiled and said in what seemed to be a sincere tone, "It's good to see you, Darce."

"It's *great* to see you, Ethan."

"How do you feel?" His hand moved in a comforting circle on my back.

I told him I'd be fine as soon as I got in out of the cold and cleaned my pores. "You know how flights wreak havoc on your skin. All of that nasty, recirculated air," I said. "But at least I wasn't stuck back in the cattle car. It's disgusting back there with the common folk."

"You're far from a common folk," he said, his smile fading as he looked beyond me and spotted my bags on the curb. "You gotta be kidding me. All of that for a few weeks?"

I had yet to tell him that my plan far exceeded a few weeks, and that I was thinking more along the lines of a few months, perhaps a permanent change. I'd ease him into that, though. By the time I told him the truth, our friendship would have supplanted his bond with Rachel. Besides, I'd be finding my Alistair in no time.

Ethan rolled his eyes. Then he heaved my two largest suitcases up his front steps. "Damn, Darce. You have a body in this bag?"

"Yes. Rachel is in this one," I said proudly, pointing to one bag. "And Dex is in that one."

He shook his head and gave me a look of warning, as if

to tell me that he wasn't going to bash his precious Rachel. "Seriously. What is all of this crap?"

"Just clothes, shoes. A lot of toiletries, perfumes, that sort of thing," I said, scooping up my lighter bags, explaining that pregnant women shouldn't lift anything heavier than twenty pounds.

"Gotcha," Ethan said, struggling his way through the front door. Four trips later, he had all of my bags inside the building. I followed him into the dark, mothball-smelling lobby complete with seventies-green carpeting. I must have made a face, because Ethan asked me if something was wrong.

"Mothballs," I said, wrinkling my nose.

"Better than moths," Ethan said. "Wouldn't want them to ruin your expensive jumpers."

"Jumpers?"

"Sweaters."

"My jumpers. Right," I said, feeling excited to adopt British slang for everything. Maybe even pick up an English accent.

Ethan led me to the back of the dark, cold hall and then, to my disappointment, down a flight of stairs. I couldn't stand basement apartments. They made me claustrophobic. They also translated to inadequate light and no terrace or view. Maybe the inside would compensate, I thought, as Ethan pushed open his door. "So this is it. Home sweet home," he said.

I looked around, trying to mask my disappointment.

"I told you it was small," he said, giving me a nonchalant tour. Everything was clean and neat and well decorated, but nothing struck me as particularly European except for some decent crown molding around fairly high ceilings. The kitchen was nondescript and the bathroom downright grim—with wall-to-wall carpeting (bizarre in a bathroom, but not uncommon according to Ethan) and an absolutely miniature toilet.

"Cute flat," I said with false cheer. "Where's my room?"

"Patience, my dear. I was getting to that," Ethan said, leading me to a room off the kitchen. It was smaller than a maid's room in a New York apartment, and its sole window was too narrow to squeeze through, yet it was still covered with a row of corroded iron bars. There was one white dresser in the corner that somehow clashed with the white walls, each making the other look sickly gray. Against the adjacent wall was a small bookshelf, also painted white, but peeling, exposing a mint-green underbelly. Its shelves were empty save for a few paperbacks and a huge pink conch shell. There is something about seashells displaced from the beach that has always depressed me. I hate the hollow, lonely sound they make when you press them to your ear, although I am always compelled to listen. Sure enough, when I picked up the shell and heard the dull echo, I felt a wave of sadness. I put it back on the shelf, then walked over to the window, peering up to the street level. Nothing about my view indicated that I was in London. I could just as easily have been in Cleveland.

Ethan must have read my reaction because he said, "Look, Darce. If you don't like your room, there are plenty of hotels . . ."

"What?" I asked innocently. "I didn't say a word!"

"I know you."

"Well, then you should know that I'm endlessly grateful and thrilled beyond belief to be here. I love my cozy little cell." I laughed. "I mean, room."

Ethan raised his eyebrows and shot me a look over the top of his tortoiseshell glasses.

"It was a joke! It's not a cell," I said, thinking that John Hinckley Jr. probably had better accommodations.

He shook his head, turned, and dragged my bags into the room. By the time he was finished, there was barely room left to stand, let alone sleep.

"Where will I sleep?" I asked him, horrified.

Ethan opened a closet door and pointed to an air mattress. "I bought this for you yesterday. Luxury blowup. For a luxury girl."

I smiled. At least my reputation was intact.

"Get organized. Shower if you want."

"Of course I want. I'm *soo* gross."

"Okay. Shower up and then we'll get a bite to eat."

"Perfect!" I said, thinking that perhaps his flat wasn't what I hoped it would be, but everything else would surpass my expectations. The London scene would more than make up for the mothball odor and my cramped quarters.

I took a shower, disapproving of the water pressure and the way a draft in the bathroom blew the plastic curtain against my legs. At least Ethan had a nice array of unisex bath products. Plenty of Kiehl's goodies, including a pineapple facial scrub that I have always enjoyed. I used it, careful to replace it on the tub exactly as it was so as not to give myself away. Nobody likes a houseguest who saps their best toiletries.

"Is there something wrong with your water?" I asked Ethan as I emerged from the bathroom in my finest pink silk robe, finger-combing my wet hair. "My hair feels gross. Stripped."

"The water here is very hard. You'll get used to it. . . . Only annoying thing is that it leaves stains on your clothes."

"Are you serious?" I asked, thinking that I'd have to dry-clean everything if that was the case. "Can't you get a water softener?"

"Never looked into it. But you're welcome to undertake the project."

I sighed. "And I assume you don't have a hair dryer?"

"Good assumption," he said.

"Well. Guess I'll have to go with the natural look. We're not hanging out with other people today, are we? I want to look my best when you introduce me to your crowd."

Ethan busied himself with a stack of bills on his dining room table, his back to me. "I don't really have a crowd. Just a few friends. And I haven't planned anything."

"*Phew*. I want to make a good first impression. You know what they say—first impressions are last impressions!"

"Uh-huh."

"So I'll pick up a hair dryer at Harrods today," I said.

"I wouldn't go to Harrods for a hair dryer. There's a drugstore up on the corner. Boots."

"Boots! How sweet!"

"Just your standard drugstore."

"Well, I better go dress then."

"Okay," Ethan said without looking up.

After I had changed into my warmest sweater and my hair had dried somewhat, Ethan took me to lunch at a pub near his house. It was charming on the outside: a small, ancient-looking brick building covered with ivy. Copper pots filled with tiny red flowers framed the doorway. But like Ethan's flat, the inside was a different story. The place was dingy and reeked of smoke, and it was filled with undesirable workman types with grungy boots and even grungier fingernails. This observation was especially noteworthy because I had read a sign on the front door that said: CLEAN WORKING CLOTHES REQUIRED. I also noticed a small placard near the bar that read: PLEASE REPORT ANY SUSPICIOUS BAGS OR PACKAGES TO THE PROPRIETOR.

"What's up with that?" I asked Ethan, pointing to the sign.

"The IRA," Ethan said.

"The who?"

"Irish Republican Army?" Ethan said. "Ring a bell?"

"Oh, that," I said, vaguely recalling some incidents of terrorism in years past. "Sure."

As we sat down, Ethan suggested that I order fish and chips.

"I'm feeling sort of queasy. Either from being pregnant or from the trip. I think I need something more bland. A grilled cheese, perhaps?"

"You're in luck," he said. "They have great croque monsieurs."

"Croque misters?" I said. "What's that?"

"Fancy French name for ham and cheese."

"Sounds like a delight," I said, thinking that I should brush up on my high school French. It would come in handy when Alistair and I took our weekend jaunts to Paris.

Ethan ordered our food at the bar, which he said was standard practice at English pubs, while I perused a newspaper someone had left on our table. Victoria and David Beckham, or, as the Brits called them, "Posh and Becks," were plastered across the front page. I knew David Beckham was a big deal in England, but I just didn't get it. He wasn't that cute. Sunken cheeks, stringy hair. And I hated the earrings in both ears. I made my observations to Ethan, who pinched his lips, as if David were a personal friend of his.

"Have you ever seen him play soccer?" Ethan asked me.

"No. Who watches soccer?"

"The whole world watches soccer. It happens to be the biggest sport in every country but America."

"Well, as far as I'm concerned this David guy," I said, tapping his picture, "is no George Clooney. That's all I'm sayin'."

Ethan rolled his eyes just as an ill-kempt waitress brought our food to the table and handed us each a set of cutlery wrapped in a paper napkin. She briefly chatted with Ethan about his writing. Obviously he ate here often. I noticed that she had dreadful, crooked, yellow teeth. As she walked away, I couldn't refrain from commenting. "So it's true what they say about the dental work over here?"

Ethan salted his fish and chips and a pile of green mashed potatoes. "Kiley is really nice," he said.

"Didn't say she wasn't. Just said that her teeth are bad. *Sheesh,*" I said, wondering if he was going to be so touchy about everything. "And what's with the green mashed potatoes?"

"They're peas. Mushy peas, they're called."

"Gross."

Ethan didn't respond. I took a tiny bite of my croque monsieur. As I chewed, I found myself bursting to say Rachel's name, get the full scoop from Ethan, find out everything he knew about her relationship with Dex. But I knew I had to tread carefully. If I launched into a tirade, Ethan would shut down. So after a few minutes of silent strategizing, I brought her up under the pretense of a shared high school memory, one that involved the three of us going to a Cubs game the summer after we graduated from high school. Then I cocked my head and said, very nonchalantly, "How is Rachel anyway?"

Ethan didn't take the bait. He looked up from his mushy peas and said, "She's fine."

"Just fine?"

"Darcy," he said, not fooled at all by my look of wide-eyed innocence. It was hard to pull one over on Ethan.

"What?" I asked.

"I'm not going to do this with you," he said.

"Do what?"

"Discuss Rachel."

"Why not? I don't get it," I said, dropping my sandwich onto the plate.

"Rachel is my friend."

"You're friends with me, too, you know."

He poured some vinegar on his fish and said, "I know that."

"Annalise is friends with both of us, and she'll talk to me about . . . what happened," I said, choosing my words carefully. "Why won't you tell me what you think? I won't be offended. I mean, clearly you're on her side." Reverse psychology was always worth a try, even with someone as smart as Ethan.

"Look, Darcy, I just don't feel comfortable with this whole topic. Don't you have anything else to talk about besides Rachel?"

"Trust me. Plenty," I said, as if my world were as chock full of glamorous intrigue as it had always been before tough times had befallen me.

"Well, then . . . stop trying to get me to bash her."

"I'm doing no such thing. I just wanted to talk to you, my childhood friend, about our other childhood friend and . . . the current state of affairs. Is that so wrong?"

He gave me a long look, and then finished his lunch in silence. When he was finished, he lit a cigarette, took a long drag, and exhaled in my general direction.

"Hey! Watch it! I'm with child!" I squawked.

"Sorry," he said, turning his chair and exhaling in the other direction. "You're going to have a rough time in this country, though. Everybody smokes."

"I can see that," I said, looking around. "It stinks in here."

He shrugged.

"So. Can I just ask a few questions?"

"Not if they're about Rachel."

"C'mon, Ethan, they are perfectly harmless questions. Please?"

He didn't respond so I asked my first question. "Have you talked to her recently?"

"Fairly recently."

"Does she know I'm here?"

He nodded.

"And she's okay with that?" I asked, hoping that she was decidedly *not* okay with it. I wanted her to be jealous that I was here in London with her precious Ethan. I wanted her to feel territorial stabs. I couldn't wait for Ethan to send her postcards from our trips together—jaunts to Vienna, Amsterdam, Barcelona. Perhaps I'd scratch out a haphazard PS on the occasional card. "Wish you were here," I'd write. To show her that I was *so* over the whole Dex thing. That I had moved on big time.

"She's fine with it. Yes."

I made a snorting sound to indicate that I highly doubted that that was the case.

Ethan shrugged.

"So what's new with her?"

"Not much."

"Is she still with Dex?"

"Darcy. No more. I mean it."

"What? Just tell me! I don't care if they're together. I'm just curious, is all . . ."

"I *really* mean it," he said. "No Dex questions."

"Fine. Fine. I think it's bullshit that we—two friends— can't talk frankly. But whatever. Your issues."

"Right. My issues," Ethan said, looking drained.

After lunch I unpacked while Ethan retreated to his bedroom to write. I made several trips to his room to request more hangers, and every time I'd pop in, he would glance up from his laptop with an annoyed expression, as if one little hanger request somehow threw him off his whole train of thought.

By midafternoon, my room was as organized as it could be considering the lack of space. I had stuffed my closet full of clothes, lined my favorite shoes in two rows along the bottom, and had set up all of my makeup, toiletries, and lingerie on the bookcase. It wasn't pretty, but it was functional enough. Just as I was in the mood to call it quits for the day and round up Ethan for some fun, I caught him in the living room stuffing papers and a pack of cigarettes into a messenger bag.

"Are you going somewhere?" I asked him.

"Yeah."

"Where?"

"Out. To write."

"What exactly are you writing again?"

"A chapter in a book on London architecture. And I recently started writing a novel. And I have a ton of freelance articles due. You know, stuff to pay the rent."

"What's your novel about?" I asked, thinking that my life would make for an excellent read. I was sure I could provide him with some good material.

"It's about a guy who loses his whole family in a carbon monoxide accident and goes to live in the woods alone to heal."

"Sounds cheery."

"It's ultimately uplifting."

"If you say so. . . . But do you have to work on my first day?"

"Yes. I do," he said unapologetically.

I frowned, asked him why he couldn't stay at home and write. I told him I'd be extra quiet. "Like a church mouse," I whispered.

He smiled. "You? A church mouse?"

"C'mon, Ethan. Please," I said. "I'll be lonely here."

He shook his head. "I can't think here."

No wonder. It's a cramped little shit hole, I thought to myself. Instead I just threw up my hands and said, "Fine. Fine. But just so you know . . . glasses and caps don't go together. Pick one or the other. It's like . . . overaccessorizing or something. Edit your look."

He shook his head as I followed him to the door.

"Where do I find you if I need you?" I asked.

"You don't," he said.

"Seriously, Ethan! Where will you be?"

"I don't know. I just wander around until I find a café with a good vibe. Nothing too quiet. Nothing too clamorous. Just a nice dull din. I left my mobile number on that pad," he said, pointing to a tablet on the hall table. "Call only if absolutely necessary."

"Can't I come with you?"

"No."

I sighed. "What am I supposed to do for the rest of the day without you? I didn't think I'd be all alone on my first day here."

He shifted his bag to the opposite shoulder and looked at me, poised to lecture.

"Okay. Okay. Sorry . . . I'll make do."

He handed me a set of keys and a spiral book with a map on the front. "The small key works the front door. The brass one goes in the top lock. Skull key for the bottom. All turn to the left. And take this *A to Zed*. Your bible to the London streets."

"I hate maps," I said, flipping through the book. "And this one looks impossible. There are too many pages."

"*You're* impossible," Ethan said.

"Just tell me where I should go to shop," I said.

"There's an index in the back of the *A to Zed*. Look up

Knightsbridge. You have plenty of shopping in that general area. Harrods. And Harvey Nichols, which is more your bag."

"How so?" I asked, anticipating a compliment.

"More fashionably elite."

I smiled. I was nothing if not fashionably elite. "How far away is Knightsbridge?"

"A long walk. Or short cab ride. I'll explain the tube another day. No time now."

"Thanks, Ethan," I said, kissing his cheek. "I'll see you tonight. And in the meantime, I'm going to find some cute clothes!"

"Sounds like a swell plan," he said with a supportive smile. It was as if Ethan understood that if I were going to start a new life, I needed a whole new wardrobe too.

nineteen

As it turned out, Ethan was right. Harvey Nichols was *exactly* my bag. I started out at Harrods, but it was too large and packed with touristy riffraff in much the same way Macy's is at home. Harvey Nics, as I overheard one British girl call it right outside the Sloane Street entrance, was more upscale and boutiquey, reminding me of Henri Bendel or Barneys in New York. I was in heaven, going from rack to rack, gathering various gems by Stella McCartney, Dolce & Gabbana, Alexander McQueen, Jean Paul Gaultier, and Marc Jacobs. Then I threw some new names into the mix, finding splendid, wintery garments from designers I had never heard of.

My only bad moment of the afternoon came when I discovered that I could no longer squeeze into a size six. I was seventeen weeks pregnant, and my initial few pounds of pregnancy weight had already propelled me up from my usual size four, but when even the sixes didn't fit, I panicked. I examined my ass and thighs in the dressing room mirror, and then simulated the old pencil test, where you stand with your feet together, place a pencil between your legs, and see if it stays put between your thighs or drops to the ground. I was relieved to see that there was still adequate space—a pencil would definitely fall to the ground. So how could it be that my size had changed so significantly, seemingly overnight? I poked my head out of the dressing room and summoned a striking salesgirl wearing a funky leather skirt and orange vinyl boots.

"Excuse me, but are the sizes a bit off in Dries Van Noten?" I asked her.

She gave me a melodious laugh. "American?"

I nodded.

"The sizes run different here, love. Are you a four at home?"

"Yes," I said proudly. "I am normally. But lately I take a six at home."

"That's a ten here typically."

"Oh, what a relief!" I said.

"Would you like me to get you some new sizes?"

I nodded gratefully, handed her my stash, and asked her if she would add a skirt like hers to my pile. Then I waited, half naked, in the dressing room, studying the small bump protruding from my stomach. It had popped out seemingly overnight, but my body was otherwise still trim and well toned. I had fallen off my rigorous, prewedding workout schedule, but I reasoned that as long as I was careful with my diet, I could maintain my figure for at least a few more months.

When the salesgirl finally returned, she squealed, "Oh, my, you're pregnant! How far along are you?"

"Four months and change," I said, running my hand down along my bump.

"You look *smashing* for four months," she purred in her chic accent.

I thanked her as I moved aside to let her hang my size

tens in the dressing room. An hour later, I was buying five amazing outfits that would have made Claire drool. As I forked over my Visa, I remembered that my spree added up to many more dollars than pounds, but I told myself not to bother with the conversion. I would just pretend to be spending dollars. And anyway, what was a few thousand dollars in the scheme of things? Nothing. Not when I thought of it as a kick start to my new life. It was an investment.

And as long as I was investing in myself, I figured that I might as well throw in a couple pairs of Jimmy Choos, which after all had great practicality as I could wear them throughout my pregnancy, maybe even tapping home in them from the hospital with Alistair by my side.

I left Harvey Nics and found my way back out to glorious Sloane Street, visiting my old friends—Christian Dior, Valentino, Hermès, Prada, and Gucci—discovering with delight that each store had slightly different inventory than what the New York stores carried. So I treated myself to a gorgeous Gucci tan leather hobo bag with the most satisfying brass hardware.

After my final purchase, I hailed a cab and returned to Ethan's flat, exhausted but thrilled with my purchases, anxious to show him what I had discovered, conquered, and made my own. Ethan wasn't yet back at the flat so I helped myself to a cup of raspberry sherbet and turned on the television. I discovered that Ethan only had five channels, and I ended up watching a string of remarkably unfunny British sitcoms and a reality television show based in a hair salon. Ethan finally walked in the door just after ten o'clock.

"Where have you been?" I asked, hands on my hips.

He glanced at me as he tossed his bag on the floor. "Writing," he said.

"This whole time?"

"Yes."

"Are you sure? You smell like a bar," I said, burrowing my nose in his jacket. "Don't discount my ability to party just because I'm pregnant."

He jerked his arm away, his blue eyes narrowing. "I wasn't partying, Darce. I work in cafés. Smoky cafés. I told you that."

"If you say so . . . but I'll have you know I've been bored stiff here. And I'm famished. I only had some sherbet all night. I really shouldn't be skipping meals like this when I'm pregnant."

"You could have eaten without me," he said. "I have stuff here—and there are plenty of places to eat up on the High Street. For future reference, there's a good Lebanese joint called Al Dar. . . . They don't deliver but you can call ahead for takeout."

I was a little annoyed that he wasn't being more nurturing, but I decided not to pout. Instead, I embarked on a mini fashion show, showing Ethan all my purchases, twirling and posing while he watched the news. I got a lot of cursory compliments, but mostly he seemed disinterested in my goods. During one clip on a suicide bomber in Jerusalem, he even shushed me, holding up the palm of his hand inches from my face. At that point, I let the dream of a bonding session die and retired to my room to blow up my air mattress. Sometime later, Ethan appeared in the doorway with a sheet, blanket, and small, flat pillow. "So you figured that thing out?" he asked, pointing down at my mattress.

"Yeah," I said, sitting on the edge and bouncing slightly. "It had a little pump. Much easier than blowing."

"Told you it was luxury."

I smiled, yawned, and politely requested a good-night kiss. Ethan leaned down and planted one on my forehead. "'Night, Darcy."

"Good night, Ethan."

After he closed the door, I turned off the light and struggled to get comfortable on my mattress, arranging and rearranging my pillow and blanket. But I couldn't fall asleep despite how tired and jet-lagged I was. After an hour of tossing, I took my blanket and pillow and shuffled into the living room, hoping that Ethan's couch would be more comfortable. It wasn't. It was too short by several inches, which gave me that desperate feeling of needing to straighten my knees. I tried to drape my feet over the edge of the couch, but the arms were slightly too high and after several minutes with elevated legs, I felt as if all my blood were rushing to my head. I sat up, whimpered, and stared into the still, dark room.

Only one option remained. Still swaddled in my blanket, I tiptoed down the hall toward Ethan's room, pressing my ear against his door. I could hear his radio and realized that the quiet in my room might be part of the problem. I was used to the lulling sound of New York City traffic. I knocked softly, hoping he was still awake and willing to talk for a few minutes. Nothing. I knocked again, more loudly. Still nothing. So I tried the doorknob. It was unlocked. I pushed the door open and whispered Ethan's name. No response. I walked over to the bed and peered down at him. His mouth was slightly open, his hands tucked under one cherubic cheek.

I hesitated and then said in a normal tone, "Ethan?"

When he still didn't stir, I walked around to the other side of the bed. There was plenty of room for me so I got in bed next to him, on top of the covers, still wrapped in my own blanket. Although I would have preferred a long conversation, I instantly felt less lonely just being close to a familiar friend from home. Just as I was drifting off, I sensed movement. When I opened my eyes, Ethan was squinting over at me.

"What are you doing in my bed?"

"Please let me stay," I said. "It's too lonely sleeping in that room with bars on the windows. And I think the air mattress is bad for my back. Take pity on a pregnant girl. Please?"

He made an exasperated sound but didn't protest. So of course I pressed my luck. *Quit while you're ahead* is advice I've never been able to follow. "Can I get under the covers with you, please? I need a human touch. I'm dying inside."

"Don't be so dramatic." Ethan grunted wearily, but then shifted slightly, lifting the covers for me.

I shed my blanket and crawled in beside him, nestling against his slender, wiry frame.

"No funny business," he mumbled.

"No funny business," I said cheerfully, thinking how nice it was to have a good male friend. I felt grateful that we had never hooked up—so it didn't feel at all weird to be in the same bed together. In fact, unless you count elementary school, we had only had one close call over the years. We were at a party following our ten-year reunion. I was a little tipsy and something came over me—perhaps it was the realization that Ethan, although slightly nerdy in high school, had become the most popular guy in our class. Everyone was clamoring to talk to him. The adulation made me appreciate him on a whole new level. So I guess I got a little carried away for a few seconds and thought it might be fun to make out with him. The details are blurry, but I remember running my hands through his curly hair and suggesting that he give me a lift home. Luckily, Ethan showed superhuman restraint in the name of our friendship. Or maybe he really *was* gay. Either way, the lines of our friendship were clear now—which was a good thing.

"I'm glad I'm here," I whispered happily.

"Yeah. Me too," he said unconvincingly. "Now go to sleep."

I was quiet for a few minutes but then realized that I had to pee. I tried to ignore it, but then kept myself up debating whether to get up. So I finally got up, and tripped over a pile of books next to Ethan's bed.

"Darcy!"

"I'm sorry. I can't help it that I *have* to pee. I'm pregnant. Remember?"

"You might be pregnant, but I have insomnia," he said. "And I better be able to fall back asleep after all your shenanigans. I have a *lot* to do tomorrow."

"I'm sorry. I promise I'll be quiet when I get back," I said. Then I scurried down the hall to the bathroom, peed, and returned to his bed. Ethan lifted the covers again for me, his eyes still shut. "Now be quiet. Or it's back to your cell. I mean it."

"Okay. I'll be quiet," I said, cuddling next to him again. "Thanks, Ethan. I needed this. I really needed this."

For the next couple of weeks, my routine stayed the same. I shopped all day, discovering a wide array of fashion boutiques: Amanda Wakeley and Betty Jackson on Fulham Road, Browns on South Molton Street, Caroline Charles on Beauchamp Place, Joseph on Old Bond Street, and Nicole Farhi on New Bond Street. I bought fabulous designer pieces: playful scarves, beautiful jumpers, chic skirts, unusual handbags, and sexy shoes. Then I sought out the bargain spots on Oxford Street—Next, River Island, Top Shop, Selfridges, and Marks & Spencer—because I've always maintained that it is totally effective to work such low-end pieces into an otherwise couture wardrobe. Even overt knockoffs, if paired with high-end pieces and worn with confidence, can look positively fabulous.

Every night I would return home with my purchases, and wait for Ethan to finish his day of work. Then we would eat takeaway together, or he would whip us up a meal, followed by a little bit of television and conversation. When it was time for bed, I always retired to my room first, pretending to give my air mattress a good-faith try before transferring to his bed. Ethan would act exasperated, but I could tell he secretly enjoyed my company.

On my third Wednesday in town, after much nagging on my part, Ethan finally promised to take the following day off and hang out with me.

"Awesome! What's the special occasion?" I asked.

"Um. Thanksgiving? Remember that holiday? Or have you been in England too long?"

"Omigod. I totally forgot about Thanksgiving," I said, realizing that it had been days since I had consulted a calendar or talked to anyone from home. I had yet to call my parents or brother and notify them that I had left New York, and I felt satisfied knowing that I would be a topic of conversation at the dinner table the following day.

"What would you like to do?" Ethan asked me.

"Well, the stores will all be open, right?" I asked. "Since it's not a holiday here?"

He made a face. "You want to shop more?"

"We could shop for you," I said, trying to entice him. "I love men's clothing." I thought of all the times I had shopped for Dex—how gorgeous he had looked in the outfits I had assembled. Now with only Rachel to help him, I was sure he was sporting Banana Republic clothing. His wardrobe was definitely going to take a hit without me.

"I was thinking more along the lines of a nice, long walk along the Thames. Or a stroll around Regent's Park. Have you been there yet?"

"No," I said. "But it's freezing out there. You really want to spend the day outside?"

"Okay. Then how about a museum? Have you been to the National Gallery?"

"Yes," I fibbed, in part because I didn't want to be dragged there. Museums make me weary, and the dim lighting depresses me. But I also lied because I didn't want any attitude about the number of days I had spent in stores in lieu of museums. If he called me out on it, I had a rationale ready—the museums and cathedrals weren't going anywhere, whereas fashion was changing by the second.

"Oh, really? You didn't mention you'd been there," he said, with a hint of suspicion. "What did you think of the Sainsbury Wing?"

"Oh. I *loved* it. Why? What do you think of it?" Deflection is always a good technique when you're in mid-fib.

"I love it . . . I wrote an article about it."

I struck a thoughtful pose. "What was the article about?"

"Oh, I wrote about how the modernists criticize it because they prefer a streamlined simplicity in architecture. You know, 'less is more' . . . whereas the postmodernists, including Robert Venturi, the American who designed it, believe that a structure should be in sync with its surroundings . . . so the rooms in that wing reflect the cultural context of the Renaissance works housed within it." Ethan spoke excitedly despite the dull topic.

He continued, "Thus you have this grand interior with all sorts of things going on, like this perspective illusion where these aligned arches get smaller in the distance, just as they do in the Scala Regia, at the Vatican Palace . . . because in Venturi's words, 'Less is a bore.' "

"Hmmm," I said, nodding. "Less *is* a bore. I'd have to agree with Venturi on that point."

Ethan adjusted his glasses and said, "So would Prince Charles. Upon seeing the initial design plans for a much more simple design by modernists, he made the comment that the wing would be 'a monstrous carbuncle on the face of a much-loved friend.' "

I laughed. "I don't know what a carbuncle is, but it doesn't sound pleasant. I wish one upon Rachel's nose."

Ethan ignored the remark and asked me what were my favorite paintings in the National Gallery.

"Oh, I couldn't begin to choose just one."

"Did you see *The Supper at Emmaus*?"

"Yes. Brilliant."

"And how about Jan van Eyck's Arnolfini Portrait?"

"Oh, I loved that one too," I said.

"Did you notice the inscription on the back wall in the painting?" he asked.

"Refresh my memory?"

"The inscription over the mirror . . . Its English translation is 'Jan van Eyck was present' and sure enough you can see his reflection in the mirror, along with the couple getting married and another guest. I've always wondered why Jan van Eyck wanted to include his own image in that painting. What do you suppose he was trying to say?"

I had the sudden feeling that I was back in college, being put on the spot by an art history professor. "Hmm. I dunno."

"I don't either . . . but it does make you think . . . And don't you just love how huge that painting is? Just dominating the room?"

"Uh-huh," I said. "It's huge, all right."

Ethan shook his head and laughed. "You're full of shit, Darce. That painting is tiny. You've never been to the National Gallery, have you?"

I tossed my hair off my face and smiled sheepishly. "Okay. No. You got me. You know I don't like museums, Ethan! I'd rather live life than walk around some dark rooms with a bunch of dorky American tourists." It sounded like a good excuse. Sort of like people who say they don't read the newspaper because the news is too depressing. I had subscribed to that one in the past too.

"I'd agree that when you go to a new city, you shouldn't spend every moment in a museum, but you'll miss a lot if you blow off *all* museums. . . . In any event, I'd like to show you something of London. Something other than Harrods and Harvey Nichols. What do you say?"

I thought to myself that what I really wanted was to return to Joseph for a leather jacket I had resisted the day before. It was over four hundred pounds but classic enough to last forever, the kind of purchase you never regret. I was sure it would be gone if I didn't get back there tomorrow. But I relished the idea of having daytime companionship, so if Ethan wanted London culture, I'd oblige.

The next day Ethan woke me up at eight, chirping excitedly about the full day he had planned for us. We showered and dressed quickly, and by nine, we were making our way up to Kensington High Street. It was a frigid, gray day, and as I slid on my aubergine leather gloves trimmed with rabbit fur, I asked Ethan why London always felt so much colder than the actual temperature.

"It's the dampness in the air," he said. "Permeates every layer of clothing."

"Yeah," I said, shivering. "It's downright bone-chilling. Glad I wore my boots."

Ethan made an acknowledging sound as we walked at a faster clip to keep warm. Moments later we were at the entrance of Holland Park, both of us slightly out of breath.

"Of all the parks in London, this is my favorite," Ethan said, beaming. "It has such an intimate, romantic aura."

"Are you trying to tell me something, Ethan?" I joked, as I linked my arm around his.

He smiled, rolled his eyes, and shook me off. "Yeah. I'm about to propose. How'd you know?"

"I hope you have an emerald-cut diamond in your pocket. I'm so over brilliant cuts," I told him as we walked along a wooded path that curved around a big, open field.

"Brilliant cuts are the round ones?" he asked.

"Yeah."

"Damn. I bought you a fat, round diamond. Guess we'll have to stay friends then."

I giggled. "Guess so."

"So anyway, this," he said pointing to the field, "is called the Cricket Lawn."

"People play cricket here?"

"Historically, yes. And I've seen the occasional cricket game here, but more often it's football—soccer. And in the summer, it's a giant lounging ground. People spread out everywhere on blankets. It only takes about sixty degrees before the Brits will be out here sunning. . . . My spot is right there," he said, pointing to a shady area on the outskirts of the field. "I've had many delicious naps under that tree."

I pictured Ethan with his various notebooks, trying to write, but succumbing to sleep. I thought how nice it would be to come here with him in the summer with my baby and a picnic lunch. As we circled the top of the field next to an outdoor theater, I thought about how contented I was to be hanging with Ethan. Then I thought of Rachel, and wished that she could see a snapshot of us together, strolling around a London park on Thanksgiving morning. I wondered what she and Dex were doing, whether they had gone back to Indianapolis for the holiday. Perhaps they were in Rachel's kitchen now, sitting by her bay window with a cup of coffee and a view of my house.

I told myself not to corrupt my good mood and turned my attention back to Ethan, who was spouting off all kinds of facts, as he often does. He told me that the park comprised the former grounds of Holland House, which used to be a social and political hot spot in the city. He explained that it was bombed and damaged during World War II. He said that it currently provided shelter for several peacocks that we were bound to see.

"Oh, I *love* peacocks."

He looked at me sideways and snickered. "You sort of remind me of one."

I told him that I'd take that as a compliment.

"I figured you would," he said, and then pointed out a restaurant called the Belvedere. He told me they had the most elegant brunch, and that if I were good, he might take me there.

Beyond the restaurant was a beautiful, formal garden, which Ethan told me was planted in 1790 by Lady Holland with the first English dahlias. I asked him how he could remember so many names and dates and facts, and if his mind didn't ever feel cluttered with useless information.

He told me that history wasn't clutter. "Clutter is knowing all of the things that you absorb through your fashion magazines. Clutter is knowing which celebrities broke up with whom and why."

I started to explain that today's celebrities would be tomorrow's historical figures, but Ethan interrupted me. "Check it out. A peacock!"

Sure enough, a gorgeous bird in brilliant blues and greens was strutting around a fenced-in grassy area, his feathers splayed just like the NBC mascot. "Wow. So pretty," I said. "I wouldn't mind having a coat in those colors."

"I'll keep that in mind when I'm Christmas-shopping for you," Ethan said. Although I knew he was joking, it made me happy to hear him reference Christmas. I hoped that I could extend my stay at least that long. If I could make it until then, I was home free until my baby arrived. He surely wouldn't banish me as I approached my third trimester. "Okay. This is my favorite part of the park coming up. The Kyoto Garden, built during the Japan festival."

We climbed a few steps and passed a placard on our way to the garden.

"Isn't it lovely?" Ethan asked, pausing at the entrance of the garden.

I nodded. It was. The tiny garden was a tranquil enclave with a pond, bonsai-like trees, wooden walkways, and waterfalls. I told Ethan that the whole scene reminded me of Mr. Miyagi's garden in *Karate Kid*. Ethan laughed as he led me across one footbridge. He stopped on the other side and sat on a wooden bench. Then he closed his eyes, propped his hands behind his head, and said, "This is the most peaceful spot in London. Nobody ever comes here. Even in warm weather, I always seem to have it all to myself."

I sat down next to Ethan and looked at him as he inhaled deeply, his eyes still closed. His cheeks were pink and his hair was curled up around the edges of his navy wool hat, and suddenly, out of nowhere, I felt a flicker of attraction to him. It wasn't the sort of physical attraction I had felt toward Marcus, nor was it the objective admiration I had felt for Dexter. It was more a welling of fondness for one of my only remaining friends in the world. Ethan was both a tie to my past and a bridge to my new life, and if gratitude can make you want to kiss a person, at that moment I had an unmistakable urge to plant one on him. Of course I resisted, telling myself to stop being crazy. Ethan wasn't my type, and besides, the last thing I wanted to do was disrupt our living (and sleeping) arrangement.

A moment later, Ethan stood abruptly. "You hungry?"

I told him that I was, so we walked back to Kensington High Street, past his flat, and over to a tea shop on Wright's Lane called the Muffin Man. The inside was shabby but cozy, filled with little tables and chairs and waitresses wearing floral aprons. We took a table by the window and ordered toasted sandwiches, tea, and scones. As we waited for our treats, we talked about my pregnancy. Ethan asked me about my last trip to the doctor. I told him it was right before I came to live with him and that I was due for another one soon.

Ethan caught my slip and raised his eyebrows. "To *live* with me?"

"I mean to visit," I said, and then quickly changed the subject before he could inquire about my departure and discover that I had bought a one-way ticket. "So at my next appointment, I'll find out the gender of the baby. . . . But I just *know* that it's a girl."

"Why's that?" Ethan asked, as the waitress arrived with our treats.

"It's just a very strong feeling. God, I hope it's a girl. I'm not a big fan of men these days. Except for you, of course. And gay men."

He laughed.

"You're not gay, are you?" I asked. It seemed like as good a time as any to broach the subject.

"No." He smiled and shook his head. "Did you think I was?"

"Well, you don't have a girlfriend," I said. *And you've never hit on me,* I thought.

He laughed. "I don't have a boyfriend either."

"Good point . . . I don't know. You have good taste, you know so much about artsy things. I guess I thought maybe Brandi would have turned you off women."

"She didn't turn me off *all* women."

I studied his face, but couldn't read his expression. "Did I offend you?"

"Not at all," Ethan said, as he buttered a scone.

"Oh, thank goodness," I said. "I'd hate to offend my best friend in the world."

I wanted him to be flattered, maybe even reciprocate by saying "Why, you're my best friend too." But he just smiled and took a bite of his scone. After our tea break, Ethan led us back to Kensington High Street over to the tube stop.

"We're taking the tube?" I asked. "Why not a cab?" I wasn't a big fan of the subway in New York, always favoring cabs, and I had not changed the practice in London.

"Suck it up, Darce," Ethan told me, as he handed me a pink ticket. "And don't lose your ticket. You'll need it to exit on the other side."

I told him that I didn't think that was a particularly good system. "Seems to me an awful lot of people would misplace their ticket during their journey and be stuck floundering on the other end."

Ethan stuck his ticket in a slot, went through a turnstile and down some stairs. I followed him and found myself on the very cold, outdoor platform. "It's freezing," I said, rubbing my gloves together. "Why don't they have enclosed platforms?"

"No more complaining, Darce."

"I'm not complaining. I'm simply commenting that it's a very chilly day."

Ethan zipped his fleece jacket up around his chin and looked down the tracks. "Circle Line train coming now," he said.

Moments later we were seated on the train, a woman's voice announcing the next stop in a very civilized British accent.

"When are they going to say 'mind the gap'?" I asked. "Or do they not really say that?"

Ethan smiled and explained that they only give that caution at certain stops where there is a substantial gap between the train and the platform.

I looked up at the tube map over us and asked him where exactly we were going.

"Charing Cross Station," he said. "We're off to cover some basics, including the National Gallery. I know you aren't a big fan of museums, but tough. It's a must. You're going to see some Turners, Seurats, and Botticellis whether you like it or not."

"I like it," I said, meaning it. "Please enlighten me."

So that afternoon, we hit some more London highlights. We lingered by Nelson's Column, in the middle of Trafalgar Square amid all the people and pigeons, as I got a lesson about Lord Horatio Nelson's naval victory over the French. (Ethan was astonished when I admitted that I had no idea that the French and British were ever at odds.) We visited Ethan's favorite church, St. Martin-in-the-Fields, which he said was famous for its social activism. Then we had another tea break in the Café-in-the-Crypt, located in the basement of the church. Afterward, we made our way over to the National Gallery. Ethan showed me a smattering of his favorite works, and I have to admit, I enjoyed myself. His commentary made the paintings almost interesting. It was as if I were seeing things through his eyes, noticing details of color and shape that otherwise would have been lost on me.

We returned home just after dark, and prepared our untraditional Thanksgiving dinner of salmon, asparagus, and couscous. After we ate, I crawled in bed next to Ethan and thanked him for my tour of London.

He rolled over to face me and gave me a strange, serious look. "You're welcome, Darcy."

"It was my best Thanksgiving ever," I said, surprised to feel my heart beating faster. Our eyes remained locked, and my thoughts returned to that moment on the park bench. I wondered if Ethan occasionally felt a vague attraction to me too. If he did right now.

But as he turned away abruptly, leaning up to switch off his lamp, and repositioning himself farther away from me, I told myself that I was being crazy. It was likely just my pregnancy hormones making me imagine things.

After several minutes, Ethan said quietly, his voice muffled against his pillow, "I had a nice time, too, Darce."

I smiled to myself. It may not have been Ethan's best Thanksgiving ever, but I was pretty sure that the day would buy me some more weeks in London. He wasn't going to send me packing just yet.

twenty

One morning the following week I told Ethan I was desperate for a night out on the town and a little social interaction. I insisted that he take me somewhere other than his pub and introduce me to his friends.

"After all," I said, "a pregnant girl shouldn't be forced to go to a bar alone, should she?"

"I suppose not," he said, and then reluctantly promised that he'd invite a few people out to dinner on Saturday night.

"Let's go somewhere *fabulous*!"

"I don't generally do fabulous. Would you settle for a slightly upscale gastropub?" he asked, as he gathered up his cigarettes and lighter and headed outside for a smoke.

I wasn't a big fan of pubs, gastro or otherwise, but I'd take what I could get, so I lightheartedly called after him, "Whatever you want. Just invite your coolest friends. Preferably male!"

* * *

So on Saturday night, I got all decked out in my favorite
Seven jeans (which I could still button right under my
belly), an ivory silk brocade coat, a new pair of Moschino
leather pumps, and the perfect tourmaline drop earrings.

"How do I look?" I asked.

He gave me a cursory glance and said, "Nice."

"Can you tell I'm pregnant?" I asked, following him
into the hall outside his flat. "Or does this jacket sort of
hide my stomach?"

He looked at me again. "I don't know. I know you're
pregnant, so I see it, I guess. Why? Are you trying to hide
it?"

"Well, naturally," I said. "I don't want to scare off all
the eligible men before they get to know me."

I caught Ethan rolling his eyes before he ran to the
corner to hail a passing cab. I took my time catching up to
him, deciding to let his eye-roll slide. Instead I told him
that he looked very nice too. "I really like your Levi's," I
said.

"Thanks. They're so old."

I nodded and then said, "Guys fall into two camps, you
know."

"How's that?" he asked with a bemused expression.

"Those who wear good jeans and those who don't. . . .
And it's not about the brand *per se*. It's more about the fit,
the wash, the length. All those subtleties. And you, my
friend, have the art of the blue jean mastered." I kissed
my thumb and index finger and made an okay sign in the
air.

Ethan laughed and ran the back of his hand along his
forehead. "I was worried."

I smiled, squeezed his thigh, and said, "This is fun . . .
Where are we going again?"

"The Admiral Codrington. In Chelsea."

I was worried when I heard the stodgy name of the restaurant, but there was an excellent vibe when we walked inside. It was nothing like Ethan's nasty local pub. The bar area was packed with a smartly dressed, professional crowd, and I instantly spotted two prospects, one leaning on the bar, smoking, the other telling a story. I smiled at the guy talking. He winked at me, still talking to his smoking friend. The smoking friend then turned to see who was winkworthy, spotted me, and raised his eyebrows as if to second his friend's judgment. I gave him a smile too. Equal opportunity for all Brits.

"Either one of those guys your friend Martin?" I asked, pointing at the cute pair.

"No," Ethan said, giving them a quick look. "My friends are out of their teens."

"Those guys are not teenagers!" I said, but upon second glance, I saw that they were probably in their early twenties. That is one of the problems with getting older. There is a distinct lag time between how you see others and how you view yourself. I still thought of myself as looking about twenty-four. "So," I asked Ethan, "where are Martin and Phoebe?"

"Probably seated already," Ethan said, glancing at his watch. "We're late."

Ethan hated being late, and I could tell he was annoyed that I had taken a bit too long getting ready for our outing. As we made our way to the back of the restaurant, I remembered one night in the tenth grade, just after Ethan got his driver's license, when he took Rachel, Annalise, and me for his inaugural spin to the movie theater. Like tonight, I guess I had taken a bit too long primping, so the whole way to the theater, Ethan kept ranting, saying things like, "By God, Darcy, we better not be stuck seeing some inane chick flick because everything else is

sold out!" Finally, I had had enough of his verbal abuse
and told him to stop the car immediately and let me out,
never mind that we were cruising down Ogden Avenue, a
busy street with very little shoulder. Rachel and Annalise
tried to smooth things over from the back seat, but Ethan
and I were both too fired up. Then, in our escalating battle, Ethan ran a red light, nearly smashing into a minivan.
The driver looked like a prim, well-coiffed soccer mom,
but that didn't stop her from leaning on her horn with one
hand and flipping Ethan the bird with the other just as a
cop pulled Ethan over to issue him his first ticket. Despite
the incident, we *still* made it to the theater in time to see
Ethan's first choice of movies, but he brought the night up
often anyway, saying that it was "emblematic of my in-
considerate nature."

I remembered the night with a mixture of nostalgia
and sheepishness as Ethan spotted his friends. "That's
Martin and Phoebe," he said, pointing to his two closest
friends in London. My heart sank as I studied them because, to be frank, I judge books by their covers, and
neither of them was impressive. Martin was a thin, bald-
ing guy, with a prominent Adam's apple. He was wearing
a lackluster corduroy jacket with dark patches at the elbow, and cuffed jeans (which, incidentally, placed him in
the bad-jean camp). Phoebe was a large, ruddy woman with
man hands and hair like Julia Roberts in *Pretty Woman*
(before she becomes refined).

My face must have registered disappointment because
Ethan made a disgusted sound, shook his head, and walked
past me toward his unpolished pals. I followed him, smiling brightly, deciding to make the most of the evening.
Maybe one of them had a hot, single brother.

"Martin, Phoebe, this is Darcy," Ethan said when we
reached the table.

"Darcy. Pleasure," Martin said, standing slightly to shake

my hand. I tried not to look at his Adam's apple as I gave him a demure smile and said, "Likewise" in the Jackie O, finishing-school voice I had mastered from Claire.

Meanwhile, Phoebe's face was frozen into a knowing little smirk that made me instantly, and intensely, dislike her.

"Darcy. We've heard *so* much about you," she said, her voice loaded with sarcasm and innuendo.

My mind raced. What had Ethan told them that would cause Phoebe to smirk? I considered the possibilities: *Pregnant and alone?* No. That didn't warrant a smirk, especially from a hulking woman with orange hair whose best hope of offspring sat in a Petri dish at a sperm bank. *Mooching roommate?* No. I hadn't been in the country long enough to achieve that status. Besides, I was still (barely) self-sufficient. *Shallow New Yorker?* Perhaps that was it, but I wasn't about to feel ashamed for being well-groomed and wearing fine clothes.

Then it hit me. Phoebe was smirking about Rachel and Dex. Ethan must have told them the whole story. Sure enough, as I talked about how much I was enjoying my visit to London, Phoebe's smile evolved into a full-on jackal grin, and I became convinced that she was amused by my plight, amused that my former best friend was shagging my former fiancé.

"What's so funny here? Am I missing something?" I finally asked, glancing around the table.

Martin muttered that nothing was funny. Ethan shrugged, looking flustered and guilty. Phoebe hid her smile with her pint of frothy Guinness, a fitting drink for a beast of a woman. *At least I don't have fat sausage limbs. At least I'm pretty and not wearing a nappy puce turtleneck.* How could she not see that I had it all over her? As I watched Phoebe guffaw at her own bad jokes and order pint after pint to wash down her pork chops covered with thick, oniony sauce, I marveled at her abundance of misplaced confidence. To make my displeasure known to Ethan, I remained mostly silent.

Then, as we waited for our bill, Phoebe confirmed my hunch as she turned to me and slurred, "I met your friend Rachel a few months back. She was lovely."

I inhaled sharply and held her gaze, struggling to remain calm. "Oh, you met Rachel? That *is* lovely. . . . Ethan didn't mention that." I glared at Ethan as he flinched, recrossed his arms, and averted his eyes to a nearby raucous table.

"Yeah," he said. "Martin and Phoebe met Rachel when she visited me . . ."

My heart pounded with indignation, and I could feel my face tighten and contort in an attempt not to cry. How dare Ethan bring me out with these people after introducing Rachel to them—and not give me any warning? And worse, from the way Phoebe was acting, I just knew that Rachel had had feelings for Dex during her visit to London, and that she had shared her thoughts with Ethan and his friends. Before tonight, I was sure that Rachel had not confessed much to Ethan. At least not anything too incriminating. I had assumed this because when we were kids Rachel once told me that she didn't divulge anything embarrassing or controversial even in her own diary because she feared an early demise from a fluke accident—something undignified like dropping her hair dryer in the bathtub or choking on a hot dog. And upon her death, she couldn't bear the thought of her parents reading an entry that might make them think less of her. "But you'd be dead," I remember saying to her. "Even worse," she'd say. "Because if I were dead, I wouldn't be able to change my parents' opinion of me. That would be their final impression."

So, because of Rachel's heretofore unflagging morality, coupled with her anxiety over what people might think of her character, I had assumed that if she had had feelings for Dex prior to our breakup, she surely hadn't shared them with anyone. I think I also wanted to believe that Ethan, although closer to Rachel, was my friend, too, and that he therefore wasn't holding out on me in any significant way. It was sickening to realize that not only did he likely know much more than he had let on—but that total strangers in London knew everything too. I felt like a fool—and feeling foolish is one of the all-time worst emotions. Suddenly I was burning up, fanning at my face with my small Chanel purse, panicking that perhaps Rachel and Dex had hooked up even before the day I caught them together.

In an attempt to ferret out the truth, I looked Phoebe straight in the eye and asked in a volume way louder than necessary, even in a noisy restaurant filled with a bunch of drunken Brits, "When you met my friend Rachel, did she happen to mention that she wanted to fuck my fiancé? Or had she already fucked him at that point?"

Martin looked pained as he intently studied our bill. Ethan shook his head. Phoebe let out a gleeful chortle.

"I'm glad that somebody here is amused," I said, standing angrily from the table. My heel caught on the edge of my chair, causing it to crash to the ground. Everyone— including the two cute twenty-something guys who were now joined by two cute twenty-something girls—turned to stare, looking embarrassed for me. I fumbled in my purse for money, realizing that I had left my wallet on the floor next to my air mattress. This was unfortunate, because it would have been a way stronger statement to throw down a wad of bills before exiting. Instead I had to mumble to Ethan that I'd pay him back later. Then I stomped off, wondering if I could find my way home, and how much my feet were going to ache walking all that way in my new shoes. As I spilled onto the dark street, I realized that I had no idea where I was. I walked in one direction, then turned in the other, and was hugely relieved when Ethan appeared from the door of the restaurant.

"Darcy, just wait here. I have to pay our part of the bill," he said, as if he were the one who had the right to be annoyed.

"You owe me an apology!" I shouted.

"Just wait here. I'll be right back. Okay?"

I crossed my arms, glared at him, and said fine, I'd wait. As if I had much of a choice. A minute later Ethan was back on the street, his lips set in an angry line. He hailed us a cab and opened the door roughly. How dare he be mad at me! I was the wronged party here. My instinct was to unleash, but I bit my lip, literally, waiting for him to talk first. He said nothing for several minutes and then spoke in a wry tone. "So you and Phoebe got along brilliantly."

"She's such a miserable cow, Ethan!"

"Calm down."

"Don't tell me to calm down!" I shouted. "How dare you bring me out with them when they know everything about me! You should have told me they had already met Rachel! I can't believe you all had a good laugh at my expense! I thought you were my friend!"

"I *am* your friend," he said.

"Then tell me what you told them, Ethan! And while you're at it, tell me *everything* you know about Dex and Rachel!"

His neck muscles twitched. "We'll talk about it at home, okay?"

"No. We'll talk about it *now*!" I shouted, but Ethan looked resolute, and I was afraid of pressing my luck. I wanted the truth too much to jeopardize pissing him off. It took all of my resolve, but I managed to keep my mouth shut the rest of the way home.

When Ethan and I arrived back at his flat, he disappeared to his bedroom, possibly to call Rachel and seek permission to divulge her dirty little secrets. I paced in the living room, wondering what he was going to tell me. How bad the truth was. After a few minutes, he returned to the living room and began rummaging through his CDs. I took off my jacket and heels and sat cross-legged on the floor, keeping my face placid, as I waited for the truth. The *whole* truth. Ethan calmly selected a Coldplay CD, turned the volume higher than I thought appropriate, and sank into his couch. He gave me a steely gaze. "Okay. Look," he said over the music. "I'm really tired of this shit, Darcy. I am *really, really* sick of it."

"So am I," I said, reaching over to turn down his stereo.

He held up his hand as if to warn me that interrupting was not an option.

"So we're going to discuss this tonight and then never again, okay?"

"Fine," I said. "That's all I wanted in the first place."

"Okay. When Rachel came here to visit me, she told me that she . . . that she had feelings for Dex."

"I knew it!" I said, pointing at him.

"Are you going to listen or not?"

I swallowed hard and nodded.

"And she had been having those feelings for some time, but not that long a time."

"How long?"

"A few weeks . . . maybe a few months."

"A few *months*?" I shouted.

He gave me a look of warning, as if he were poised to exit the conversation.

"Sorry. Go on."

"I don't have much else to say."

"When did they first hook up?" I asked, petrified of the answer, but needing to know just how big a fool I had been.

He paused and then said that he didn't know.

"I can tell you're lying," I said. "I know you know!"

"What I do know is this," Ethan said, dodging the question. "Rachel didn't want to feel the way she did. She was in agony over the whole thing. She had every intention of going back to New York after her visit here and being your maid of honor. She was prepared to move on, force herself to get over Dex, and be your friend. Which is more than most people would do in her shoes."

My heart pounded in my ears. I was fixated on one thing. One fact. "Give me a date, Ethan. When did they first hook up?"

He crossed his arms and exhaled loudly.

"Was it before or after Rachel's birthday?" I asked. I honestly don't know what made me pick that date. Perhaps because Rachel's birthday is in late May, always coinciding with the start of summer. I could have just as easily said Memorial Day. But I didn't. I said, "Rachel's birthday," and by the look on Ethan's face, I knew I had hit the jackpot. My mind raced back to the night, how I had thrown a surprise party for her. Suddenly, I remembered with horror how Dex hadn't come home until nearly seven in the morning. How he had said he was with Marcus. And how Marcus had backed him up. They had *all* lied to me! My fiancé had spent the night with my best friend! Months before I had ever cheated on him!

Suddenly everything came into sharp focus: Dexter's later-than-usual nights working, how Rachel had dragged her feet during my wedding plans, and the July Fourth weekend! My God, Rachel and Dex had both stayed home from the Hamptons! They had been together that entire weekend! It was too horrible to be true, but I was certain that it was true.

I laid it all out for Ethan who didn't deny a thing. He just looked at me, without a trace of compassion or remorse.

"How could you, Ethan? How could you?" I sobbed.

"How could I what?"

"How could you be friends with her? How could you take me out with those people who knew the whole story? You made me look like a fool! All of you were probably laughing behind my back!"

"Nobody was laughing behind your back."

"Yeah, right. That mad cow laughed up a storm."

"Phoebe was a bit rude. I'll admit that."

"And admit the rest! Admit that Rachel told all of you what she was doing to me."

He hesitated and then said, "Her relationship with Dex *did* come up. But obviously I didn't think you'd ever meet Martin and Phoebe. And besides, we weren't discussing the situation in a 'ha ha what a fool Darcy is' kind of way. It was more of a 'gosh, how bad it sucks to have feelings for your best friend's fiancé' sort of way."

"*Right.* She *really* suffered."

"Well, didn't you suffer when you started seeing Marcus? While you were still with Dex?"

"It's not the same thing, Ethan."

How was it that everyone had such difficulty grasping the obvious difference between cheating on one's fiancé and screwing over your very best girlfriend?

"This isn't about me and Dex. It's about me and Rachel. And I would never have done that to her," I continued, feeling shocked that my mousy friend had it in her.

He looked at me, folded his arms, and cocked his head with a knowing smile. *"Really?"*

"Never," I said, taking mental inventory of Rachel's utterly unappealing ex-boyfriends. Her law school boyfriend and most significant ex, Nate, had a unibrow, sloping shoulders, and an effeminate voice.

"If you say so," Ethan said skeptically.

"What is that supposed to mean? I have never, *ever* tried to steal one of Rachel's boyfriends."

He smiled an oblique, private smile. I knew what he was driving at: I had hooked up with Marcus even though Rachel was interested in him.

"Oh, give me a freaking break, Ethan. Marcus was *not* Rachel's boyfriend! They had kissed, like, one time. It was never going to go anywhere."

"I wasn't thinking of Marcus."

"So then what *were* you thinking of?"

"Well . . . I just think that you would do the same thing to Rachel if the circumstances presented themselves. If you had fallen in love with one of her boyfriends, nothing would have stopped you from going after him. Not Rachel's feelings, not the stigma of taking your best friend's man. Nothing."

"No," I said firmly. "That's not true."

Ethan continued. He was on a roll now, leaning forward on the couch, thrusting his index finger at me as he talked. "I think you have a long, *long* history of going after exactly what you want, Darcy. Whatever that is. Come hell or high water. Until now, Rachel has always played second fiddle to you. And you shamelessly let her do the whole lady-in-waiting routine. All through high school she was at your beck and call, letting you show off. You liked it that way. And now that it is all over, you can't handle it."

"That's just . . . not true!" I sputtered, feeling my face burn. "You're being so unfair!"

Ethan ignored me and kept going, now pacing in front of his faux fireplace. "You were the star of the show in high school. The star of the show in college. The star of the show in Manhattan. And Rachel let you shine. Now you can't step back and be happy for her."

"Be happy for her for *stealing* my fiancé? You've got to be kidding me!"

"Darce—*you* did the same thing. It might be a different story if you were deeply in love with Dex, if you hadn't cheated on him also."

"But they did it first!"

"That is beside the point," he said.

"How can you say that?"

"Because. Because, Darcy, you never examine your own behavior. You just look to blame everyone else."

He then proceeded to bring up this ancient history from high school. Like why I had applied to Notre Dame when I knew that it was Rachel's dream to go there, and how crushed she was when I got in and she didn't.

"I didn't know she owned Notre Dame!"

"It was her dream. Not yours."

"So let me get this straight, she can go after my fiancé, but I don't have the right to apply to a stupid college?"

He ignored my question and said, "While we're on this topic, Darcy, why don't you tell me one thing . . . Did you *really* get in there?"

"Did I get in where?" I asked.

"Were you or were you not accepted at Notre Dame University?"

"Yes. I was," I said, almost believing the lie I had told all of my friends so many years ago. Notre Dame had been Rachel's first choice, but I had applied, too, thinking how great it would be if we could be roommates. I remember getting that rejection letter, feeling like a failure. So I told a harmless fib to my friends, and then covered by saying that I was going to Indiana anyway.

He shook his head. "I don't believe you," he said. "You did *not* get into Notre Dame."

I started to sweat. How did he know? Had he seen my letter? Had he hacked into the Notre Dame admissions office's computer system?

"Why is my choice of colleges relevant here?"

"I'll tell you why it's relevant, Darcy. I'll tell you exactly why. You have always competed with Rachel. From way back in the day until now. Everything has always been a contest with you. And part of what's eating you up inside is that Dex picked Rachel. He picked her over you."

I tried to speak but he kept going, his words cruel, stark, and loud. "Dex wanted to be with her and not you. Never mind that you didn't want to be with him either. Never mind that you cheated on him too. Never mind that clearly you and he weren't at all right for each other and you both saved yourselves a divorce by calling it quits. You can only focus on one thing: the fact that Rachel somehow beat you. And it kills you, Darce. I'm telling you, as your friend, that you need to let it go and move on," he finished in his debate-team tone.

I shook my head. I told him that he was wrong. I told him that nobody, nobody in my position, could be happy for Rachel. I felt myself getting shrill, desperate to make him see things my way, just as I had tried to do with Marcus.

"It's like this, Ethan . . . even if they hadn't done a thing behind my back, even if this relationship had begun *after* we broke up, it would still be . . . just *wrong*. You just don't go there with a friend's ex. Period. How is it that men have trouble seeing that? It's a basic life principle."

"She *loves* him, Darce. *That* is a basic life principle."

"Would you stop rubbing it in! I don't want to hear the word *love* again. Whether they *love* each other is totally beside the point. . . . You don't understand *anything* about friendship."

"Darcy. No offense—and I'm not saying this to be mean, because I care about you, which is why you're here right now for this purported *visit*," he said, making quotation marks in the air as he said the word *visit*. "But—"

"But *what*?" I asked pitifully, afraid of what he would say next.

"But I think *you're* the one who doesn't understand friendship," he said, speaking fast and furiously. "Not at all. Which is why you're sitting here essentially friend-less. At war with Rachel. At war with Claire. At war with the father of your child. At war with your *own mother,* who, as far as you know, has no clue where you are! And now you're mad at me too."

"It's not my fault that you all betrayed me."

"You need to take a long, hard look in the mirror, Darce. You need to realize that there are consequences to your basically shallow existence."

"I'm *not* shallow," I said, only half-believing it.

"You *are* shallow. You're utterly selfish and misguided, with totally screwed-up values."

He had gone too far. I might be a bit on the shallow side, but the rest of his accusations were ridiculous. "What the hell is that supposed to mean? Misguided?"

"It means that you're, what, five months pregnant now? And as far as I can tell, you're doing nothing to prepare for this child. Nothing. You come to London for this so-called visit, but I see no signs of you returning to New York—and meanwhile, you have made no effort to seek any prenatal care here in London. On top of that, you don't eat particularly well, probably in an effort to stay thin at the expense of your baby's growth. You had two glasses of wine tonight. And instead of saving for the child you have to raise alone, you are throwing money to the wind on posi-tively frivolous purchases. It's simply staggering to watch how utterly irresponsible and totally self-absorbed you're being."

I sat there, completely speechless. I mean, what do you say when someone tells you, essentially, that you're a shit friend, a horrible, irresponsible mother-to-be, and an empty, self-absorbed woman? Unless I counted some of the accusations I'd received from scorned lovers (which don't have much credibility), this was an unprecedented attack. He had said so many mean things, come at me from so many angles, that I was unsure how to defend myself. "I *am* taking prenatal vitamins," I said meekly.

Ethan looked at me as if to say, *If that's the best you can do here, I rest my case.* Then he announced that he was going to bed. His expression told me not to follow him, that he did not want me in his room.

But just to be sure, after I sat in the living room for a long while, licking my wounds and replaying his speech, I decided to go down the hall and check his door. Not that I would have opened it on a bet—I had some pride—I just had to know whether he had boxed me out for real. Did he regret his harsh words? Had he softened his opinion of me as his beer-buzz dissipated? I put my hand around the glass doorknob and turned. It didn't budge. Ethan had shut me out. There was something about that door, cold and unyielding, that made me feel angry and sad and determined all at once.

twenty-one

The next morning I awoke on my air mattress and felt my baby kick for the first time. There had been other times when I thought I felt her— only to realize that it was likely just indigestion, hunger pangs, or nerves. But there was no confusing that odd, unmistakable sensation of tiny feet moving inside me, churning up against my organs and bones. I put my hand on the spot, right under my rib cage, waiting to feel her again. Sure enough, there was another small but distinct nudge and twitch. I know it sounds crazy, especially considering that my stomach was quickly becoming the size of a basketball, but I think it took that flutter of baby feet for my pregnancy to move beyond the theoretical and feel real. I had a baby inside me, a little person who was going to be born in a few short months. I was going to be a mother. In a way, I already was.

I curled up in a fetal position and squeezed my eyes shut as I was bombarded by a riot of emotions. First I felt a burst of pure joy. It was an indescribable happiness, a kind that I'd never experienced before, a kind that can't be found by purchasing a Gucci bag or a pair of Manolo Blahniks. A smile spread across my face, and I almost laughed out loud.

But my happiness quickly commingled with an unsettling melancholy as I realized that I had no one to share my huge milestone with. I couldn't call my baby's father or her grandmother. I wasn't in the mood to talk to Ethan after all the mean things he had said to me. And most important, I couldn't call Rachel. For the first time since I found Dex in her closet, I really missed her. I still had Annalise, but she just wasn't the same. I thought of all the times in the past when I'd had good news, bad news, in-between news. How I could barely digest it before I was running next door or speed-dialing Rachel's number. When we were kids in Indiana, Annalise was always the runner-up, always the afterthought, always the second to know. With Rachel out of the picture, you'd think that Annalise would just replace her. But I was beginning to see that it didn't work like that. Rachel wasn't replaceable. Claire hadn't replaced her. Annalise couldn't either. I wondered why that was. After all, I knew Annalise would say all the right things, be as nice as she could be. But she would never be able to quench that deep-seated need to share.

As I turned over on my mattress to face the window, I heard Ethan's words: the part about me being a bad friend, the part about me being selfish and self-centered and shallow. A warm shame spread over me as I acknowledged that there was a ring of truth to his accusations. I looked at the facts: I had no doctor, no income, no close girlfriends, no contact with my family. I was on the verge of depleting all my savings, and all I had to show for myself was a closet full of gorgeous clothing, most of which no longer fit. I had moved to London to find change, but

I hadn't really changed at all. My life was stagnating. I needed to do more. For myself and for my baby.

I stared out my barred window into the dreary London morning, and vowed to make the day I first felt my baby kick a turning point in my life. I would prove to Ethan that I was not the person he had described the evening before. I got to my feet (which was becoming more difficult to do, particularly from a horizontal position on a soft air mattress) and found a pad of paper in the bottom of one of my suitcases. I ripped out a page and wrote: "Steps to Becoming a Better Darcy." I thought for a second, replaying Ethan's speech. Then I wrote:

1. Go to an ob-gyn in London and prepare for motherhood!
2. Be more healthy, i.e., eat better, no caffeine or alcohol
3. Find some new girlfriends (no competing with them!)
4. Let my family know that I'm in London and that I'm okay
5. Get a job (preferably a "do-gooding" job)
6. Stop buying clothes (and shoes, etc.) and start saving money!

Then, because something still seemed to be missing, I threw in a catchall:

7. Refine my character (i.e., be more thoughtful, less selfish, etc.)

As I reread my list, I found myself wondering what Ethan would say if he saw it. Would he praise my effort or would he scoff, "Don't be so naïve, Darcy. You can't just make a list and fix yourself overnight! It doesn't work like that."

Why did I care so much about what Ethan thought anyway? Part of me wanted to hate him. Hate him for siding with Rachel. Hate him for lying to me. Hate him for the awful things he had said about me. But I couldn't hate him. And in a bizarre, surprising way, all I wanted to do was see him, or at the very least set about changing his opinion of me.

I rocked once to gain momentum before standing again. Then I made my way down the hall to Ethan's room. Upon discovering that he had already left for the day, I went to the kitchen and whipped up a healthy egg-white omelet. Then I consulted my list and decided to clean his flat. I dusted and vacuumed, scrubbed the toilet, took out the trash, did two loads of laundry in his ridiculously small washer/ dryer unit (the Brits have miserable, third-world appliances), carefully stacked his magazines and newspapers, and soaped down the kitchen floors.

After the place was spotless, I wrote my mother a quick note, telling her that I was staying with Ethan in London. "I know we're not happy with each other right now," I wrote, "but I still don't want you and Daddy to worry about me. I'm doing fine." Then I wrote Ethan's phone number in a PS just in case she wanted to call me. I sealed and stamped my letter, showered, and headed out in the London drizzle, wandering up Kensington Church Street to Notting Hill. I resisted the urge to stop in a single store, gaining strength from my list, which was folded in neat thirds and tucked into my coat pocket. I even stopped in a charity thrift shop to ask for a job. No positions were available, but I felt proud of myself for trying.

On my way home, I ducked inside a coffee shop for a short rest, ordered a decaffeinated latte, and hunkered down in a big overstuffed armchair. On the couch next to me sat two women—a blonde and a brunette—who looked about my age. The blonde was balancing a baby on one knee as she struggled to eat a brownie with her free hand. Both girls wore tiny diamonds on their left ring fingers, and I recalled that Ethan had mentioned that the Brits are less ostentatious about engagement rings than Americans. Maybe that sort of thing was emblematic of what Ethan liked about London. The Brits' understated quality was the opposite of what he said I was—more or less a shameless show-off.

From the corner of my eye, I continued to study the women. The blonde had a weak chin but good highlights; the brunette wore gripping velour sweats but was holding an enviable Prada bag. I felt a pang of worry that I was being shallow, but reassured myself that it was okay to be observant; I just shouldn't draw conclusions about the women as people. I thought of how many times I had judged people by their footwear, and vowed that I would never do so again. After all, wearing a square-toed shoe in a pointy-toed season was not a crime. To prove the point to myself, I resisted looking down at their feet. I could feel myself turning into a more solid person already, and my spirits soared.

As I sipped my coffee and flipped through *Hello* magazine, I listened to the women talk, noting that their conversation sounded much more interesting in their British accents. The theme of their chat was marital woes—both had issues with their husbands. The blonde said that having a baby makes everything worse. The brunette complained that since she and her husband started trying to conceive, sex had become a chore. Every few seconds, I turned the pages of my magazine, which was filled with Hollywood stars, as well as people I had never seen before, presumably British television actors. And more photos of Posh and Becks.

The blonde sighed as she repositioned her squirming baby. "At least you're having sex," she said to her friend, as she reached down and pulled a pacifier out of a side pocket in her stroller and popped it into the baby's mouth. The baby sucked vigorously for several seconds before letting the pacifier drop to the ground. An apparent subscriber to the three-second rule, the blonde picked it up, swiped it across her sleeve, and reinserted it in her child's mouth.

"How long has it been?" the brunette asked, in a candid way that told me these two were not new or casual acquaintances. It made me ache for Rachel, for the way things used to be.

"I couldn't even say," the blonde answered. "Ages."

The brunette made a sympathetic clucking noise as she wrapped her tea bag around a plastic stirrer and squeezed with her thumb and index finger.

I closed my magazine and made eye contact with the blonde. She smiled at me, giving me an opening.

"She's really cute," I said, gazing at her baby and then realizing with panic that the baby could be a boy. It was impossible to tell. Yellow outfit, bald head, no gender-based accoutrement.

"Thank you," the blonde said.

Good. I guessed right. "What's her name?"

"Natalie."

"Hi, Natalie," I said in a high, singsongy voice. Natalie ignored me, kept straining to grasp her mother's brownie. "How old is she?"

"Twenty-two weeks." The blonde smiled as she jiggled her up and down on one knee.

"So . . . that's what? Five months?"

She laughed. "Yeah, right. Sorry. I remember before I had Natalie I wondered why mums gave their child's age in weeks. I guess it's an extension of the pregnancy."

I nodded as I noticed the brunette giving me a curious once-over as if to say, "What is your deal, American girl, sitting here alone on a weekday?"

"Yeah, I know what you mean. I'm eighteen weeks along myself—"

"Pregnant?" both women squealed at once as if I had

just told them that I was dating Prince William. It felt great to finally have a little enthusiasm over my news.

"Yes," I said, moving aside my coat and rubbing my stomach with my ringless left hand. "In fact, I just felt a kick for the first time this morning."

It struck me as a bit sad that I was first sharing such monumental news with strangers, but I told myself that they were potential new friends. Perhaps they would even become lifelong, to-the-grave mates.

"Congrats!" the blonde squealed.

"You look amazing for eighteen weeks!" the brunette said.

I smiled with what felt like sincere modesty. "Thank you."

"Boy or girl?" the brunette asked.

"I don't know yet for sure, but I'm fairly certain that it's a girl."

"I was too," the blonde said, rubbing Natalie's fuzzy head. "I just knew she was a girl."

"Did you find out ahead of time?"

"No, I wanted to be surprised," she said. "My husband knew, though."

I raised my eyebrows. "He knew and you didn't?"

She nodded. "Our doctor showed him the relevant anatomy on the sonogram while I closed my eyes. My husband swore that he wouldn't tell another soul. Not even our mums, who were positively dying to know."

"I can't believe he kept it a secret! That's amazing," I said.

"Her husband is great that way," the brunette said.

"Hmm." The blonde nodded. I had begun to notice that the Brits make that *hmm* sound often, in lieu of saying *yes* or *uh-huh* or *yeah*. She continued, "Never one slip with the pronouns. He was always very careful to say 'he or she' or just 'the baby.'"

"What about baby names? Wasn't it obvious when you'd discuss names?"

"Not at all. He covered both equally. . . . In fact, he pushed Gavin so hard that if anything, I thought we were having a boy."

"Wow. Your husband sounds like a great guy," I said.

She turned to look at her friend and they both burst into laughter. "We were just tearing him to shreds. He's being a bit of a prat these days."

I wasn't sure what a *prat* was, but I nodded empathetically and said, "I know how that is!"

A few seconds of silence passed and I could tell that the girls were again wondering about my situation.

"I'm Darcy, by the way," I said, with what I hoped was, a disarming, "I won't compete with you" smile.

"I'm Charlotte," the blonde said.

"And I'm Meg," the brunette said.

"It's so great to meet you both. I've been dying to have some female interaction since moving here," I said. It was the truth, although I don't think I consciously realized it until that moment.

"When did you move to London?" Meg asked.

"About a month ago."

"Did you move here alone?" she asked. It was as close as she could come to inquiring about the father of my child.

"Yes, I'm going it alone," I said.

Meg and Charlotte both stared at me, with what I detected as admiration. I gave them a warm, open smile, tacit permission to inquire further, which they did, tentatively. I answered each of their questions, only embellishing occasionally. For example, I told them that I caught Rachel in bed with Dex—and I left out Marcus altogether, thereby implying that Dex was the father. It just seemed easier that way, and frankly, what was the difference at this point? Both men were out of the picture. My audience of two was riveted. Charlotte even ignored Natalie, who was gumming the corner of an *Evening Standard*. I continued my tale, telling them I had quit my job, and come to London to live with my childhood friend Ethan. "He's straight, but we're just friends," I told them. A gay friend might be more interesting, and certainly more entertaining, but there was something compelling about an aboveboard, straight male–female friendship. Besides, it gave me more credibility as a nice girl. I could hear them saying later, "She's beautiful, but she doesn't go around stalking every available man."

Charlotte asked if I had any interest in Ethan. I shook my head vigorously. "Absolutely not . . . We're strictly friends. Although we did go out in the fifth grade!"

They laughed.

"So I'm entirely single . . . if you know anyone?" I said, fleetingly worrying that finding a man shouldn't be important to me. I dismissed the concern; a boyfriend needn't detract from my other, loftier goals.

Meg and Charlotte exchanged a thoughtful glance as if doing a mental inventory of all their male acquaintances.

"Simon?" Charlotte posited to Meg.

Meg made a face.

"You don't like Simon?" Charlotte asked her.

"I like Si well enough . . ." Meg said with a shrug.

I resisted the temptation to inquire about Simon's looks, but Meg seemed to read my mind because she giggled and said, "I doubt that Darcy is attracted to gingers!"

"Meg!" Charlotte said, reminding me of Rachel. Rachel must have said "Darcy!" in that same tone close to a million times. "Besides, I'd say Si is more of a strawberry blonde."

"He's a ginger and you know it!" Meg said, sipping her tea.

"What's a ginger?" I asked.

"You know, orange hair? I think you call it a 'red-head'?" Meg said.

I laughed. "Oh. Right."

"So? Do you like gingers?" Charlotte asked.

"Probably not my favorite," I said diplomatically, rationalizing that chemistry is beyond one's control. And for a relationship to work, the chemistry has to be there.

"I suppose gingers aren't sought after on either side of the pond," Meg opined.

Charlotte looked disappointed, so I said, "But there are exceptions. Look at cute little Prince Harry. I like his devilish little smile. It depends entirely on personality."

I couldn't help thinking of Marcus. It had been a misguided (to use Ethan's word) decision to start a relationship with him, a decision based largely on intrigue, lust, and competition with Rachel. But at least I wasn't driven by appearances. Marcus was far from perfect looking. So I knew I had it in me to look beyond the mere physical.

Charlotte smiled at me. "Precisely," she said, nodding. Then she turned to Meg. "Why don't you invite Darcy to your party? Isn't Si coming?"

"What a fab idea! You must come, Darcy. I'm having a few friends over this Saturday night. Won't you join us?" Meg asked.

"I'd love to," I said, thinking how satisfying it would be to tell Ethan I had been invited to a party *by women*. I took a mental inventory of my list. In just one short day, I had ticked off several items already. I had helped Ethan (by cleaning his apartment), I was being healthy (by not ordering a caffeinated beverage), and I had made a couple of new friends. I still needed to find a job and a doctor, so after a few more minutes of polite conversation, I asked Meg and Charlotte for a recommendation on both fronts.

"Oh, I have the perfect chap for you. Mr. Moore is his name," Charlotte said, consulting her address book and jotting down his number on the back of one of her own calling cards. "Here you go. Give him a ring. He's really lovely."

"How come he goes by 'mister' and not 'doctor'?" I asked, feeling a bit skeptical about the British health care system.

Meg explained that in England only nonoperating physicians are called doctors—something that goes back to medieval times, when all surgeons were butchers and therefore mere misters.

"As for the job," Charlotte said, "what is it that you did in New York?"

"I worked in public relations. . . . But I'm looking for something different here. Something that would help the poor, old, or sick," I said earnestly.

"That is *so* nice," Charlotte and Meg said in unison.

I smiled.

Meg told me that there was a nursing home right around the corner. She jotted down some directions on a napkin, and then wrote her own address and phone number on the other side. "Do stop by on Saturday," she said. "We'd love to see you. And so would Si." She winked.

I smiled, took my last sip of coffee, and said good-bye to my new friends.

That evening, when Ethan returned home, I was waiting for him with a homemade Greek salad, a glass of red wine, and softly playing classical music.

"Welcome home!" I said, smiling nervously as I handed him his glass.

He took it from me tentatively, sipped, and then looked around his apartment. "It looks great in here. Smells good too. Did you clean?"

I nodded. "Uh-huh. I scoured the place. I even cleaned

your room," I said, and then couldn't resist adding, "Still think I'm a lousy friend?"

He took another sip and sat on his couch. "I didn't say that exactly."

I sat next to him. "Yes you did."

He gave me a half-smile. "You can be a good friend when you try, Darce. You tried today. Thank you."

The old me would have held out for an over-the-top apology coupled with a complete retraction and a small gift. But somehow Ethan's simple "thank you" was enough for me. I just wanted to make up and move on.

"So guess what happened this morning?" I said, bursting to share my news with him. Before he could guess, I blurted out, "I felt my baby kick!"

"Wow," Ethan said. "That was the first time you felt it?"

"Yeah. But I haven't felt her since. Should I be worried?"

Ethan shook his head. "No. I remember when Brandi was pregnant . . . she would feel a kick one day and then nothing for several days. The doctor told her that when you're active, the baby is less likely to move around, because you're essentially lulling it to sleep," he said with a somewhat pained expression, as if it still hurt to think of Brandi's betrayal.

"Does it make you sad to think about her?" I asked.

He kicked off his wet Pumas, peeled off his socks, and propped his feet up on the coffee table. "I'm not sad about Brandi, but sometimes I am sad when I think about Milo."

"Milo? Was that the guy Brandi cheated on you with?"

"No. Milo's the baby."

"Oh," I said sheepishly, knowing that I should have remembered that detail. I looked at Ethan, wondering what empathetic words Rachel would offer. She always had a way of saying the right thing, making someone feel better.

I couldn't think of anything good so I just waited for Ethan to continue.

"For nine months, I thought I was going to be a father. I went to every doctor's appointment and fell in love with those ultrasound pictures . . . I even picked the name Milo." He shook his head. "Then we had the baby, and I realized he wasn't mine."

"When did you know for sure that he wasn't yours?"

"As soon as he was born. I mean, he was dark-skinned with black eyes and all this crazy black hair sticking up everywhere. I kept thinking of my own baby pictures. Bald and pink. Brandi's a blue-eyed blonde too. It didn't take a genius to figure out what was going on."

"So what did you do?"

"For the first few days, I think I was in shock. I pretended that it wasn't true, that it was just a fluke genetic thing. . . . All the while, in the back of my mind, I remembered that 'big b, little b' chart from high-school biology. . . . Two blue-eyed parents just couldn't make a Milo."

I touched his arm lightly. "That must have been so hard."

"It was awful. I mean, I loved that little boy. Enough so that I almost stayed with her. In the end . . . well . . . you know the rest." His voice cracked. "I left. It felt as though someone had died."

I remembered Rachel telling me about Ethan's divorce and the baby that wasn't his. At the time, I think I had been preoccupied with some crisis of my own and hadn't been particularly empathetic to his pain.

"You did the right thing," I said now, taking his hand in mine.

He didn't pull away. "Yeah. I guess I did."

"Do you think I did the right thing? Keeping my baby?"

"Absolutely."

"Even though you think I'm being a bad mother so far?" I asked, resisting the urge to tell him about my list. I wanted to make more progress before confiding in him.

"You'll get it together," Ethan said, squeezing my hand. "I have faith in you."

I looked at him, and felt the same way I did on Thanksgiving, sitting on our bench in Holland Park. I wanted to kiss him. But of course I didn't. I wondered why I resisted, when in the past I had always followed my impulses with not much thought of the consequences. Maybe because it didn't feel like a game with Ethan, the way it had with Marcus and so many guys before him. Maybe because I had more to lose. Blurring the line between friendship and attraction was a surefire way to lose a friend. And losing one good friend was enough this year.

Later that night, after Ethan and I watched the news, he turned to me and said, "C'mon, Darce. Let's hit the hay."

"The hay in your room?" I asked hopefully.

Ethan laughed. "Yeah. In my room."

"So you missed me last night?" I asked.

He laughed again. "I wouldn't go *that* far."

But I could tell by his expression that he *had* missed me. I could also tell that he was a little bit sorry for our fight, even though much of what he had said about me was true. Ethan liked me in spite of my flaws, and as I fell asleep next to him, I thought of how much more he was going to like the new and improved Darcy.

twenty-two

The next morning, prodded by another series of kicks from my baby, I decided that I would go apply for a job at the nursing home Meg and Charlotte had told me about. Ethan had already left for the day, so I used his computer to type up my résumé and a quick cover letter, which articulately explained that my success in the world of public relations had everything to do with my outgoing personality, and that certainly this quality would translate well in the group bingo setting. After I spell-checked the letter, opting for the British spelling of the words *colourful* and *organised*, I showered, dressed, and headed out into the London chill.

When I arrived at the nursing home, I was blasted with the distinct and depressing odor of old people and institutional food, and felt my first wave of morning sickness since my first trimester had ended. I found a mint in my purse and drew a deep breath through my mouth as I studied two little old ladies in matching floral smocks parked in wheelchairs in the lobby. Watching them laugh and chat together made me think of Rachel and how we used to say that when we were old and widowed we wanted to be put in a nursing home together. I remembered her saying that I would still be a guy magnet well into my nineties and could help her get dates with the cutest old men in the home. I guess she decided to play that one out sixty years early, I thought, as a gnomelike man, whom I'd assumed was a resident, came to the door and introduced himself as the manager.

"I'm Darcy Rhone," I said, shaking his hand.

"Bernard Dobbs," he said. "How may I help you?"

"The question is, Mr. Dobbs, how can *I* help *you*? You see, I have come today to find a position at this fine institution," I said, redecorating the shabby, poorly lit lobby in my mind.

"What sort of experience do you have?" he asked.

"I have a background in public relations," I said, handing him my résumé. "Which is a very interactive, people-driven business." Then I paraphrased my cover letter, concluding with, "Most importantly, I just want to help spread cheer to the elderly folk in your fine country."

Mr. Dobbs looked at me skeptically and asked if I had a work permit.

"Um . . . no," I said. "But I'm sure 'wink, wink, nudge, nudge' we could deal with that problem, couldn't we?"

He gave me a blank stare and then asked if I had ever worked in a nursing home. I considered lying. After all, I seriously doubted that he would place an international call to check my references. But I made a split-second determination that lying was not in keeping with the new Darcy, and that deceit wasn't necessary to get a job. So I told him no, I hadn't, and then added, "But believe me, Mr. Dobbs, I can handle anything here. My job in *Manhattan* was quite challenging. I worked long hours and was very successful."

"Hmm. Well. I'm so sorry, Dicey," he said, without sounding the slightest bit apologetic.

"It's Darcy," I said.

"Yes. Well. I'm sorry, Darcy. We can't have just *any-one* working with our residents. You must be qualified." He handed me back my résumé.

Just anyone? Was he for real? I pictured my future sister-in-law wiping up old-person drool as she hummed "Oh, Susanna." Her job hardly required much skill.

"I understand where you're coming from, Mr. Dobbs . . . but what experience do you really need to relate well to others? I mean, you either have that or you don't. And I have that in spades," I gushed, noticing a woman with a horrifying case of osteoporosis, inching her way down the hallway toward us. She craned her neck sideways and looked at me. I smiled at her and uttered a high, cheery "Good morning" just to prove my point.

As I waited for her to smile back at me, I imagined that her name was Gert and that she and I would forge a beautiful friendship, like the one in *Tuesdays with Morrie,* one of Dexter's favorite books, one of many that I had never found time to read. Gert would confide in me, tell me all about her childhood, her wartime remembrances, her husband, whom she had sadly outlived by several decades. Then, one night, she would pass quietly in the night, while I held her hand. Later, I would learn that she had bequeathed to me all of her worldly possessions, including her favorite emerald brooch worth tens of thousands of pounds. At her funeral, I would wear the pin over my heart and eulogize her to a small but intimate gathering. *Gertrude was a special woman. I first met her one wintery day . . .*

I smiled at Gert once more as she approached us. She muttered something back, her ill-fitting dentures wobbling slightly.

"Come again?" I asked her, to show Mr. Dobbs that not only was I kind and friendly, but that I also had a never-ending supply of patience.

"Go away and don't come back," she grumbled more clearly.

I smiled brightly, pretending not to understand her. Then I returned my gaze to Mr. Dobbs. "Well, then. As I was saying, I think you'll see upon careful review that I'm really quite qualified for any position you might have for me."

"I'm afraid I'm not interested," Mr. Dobbs said.

As Gert passed us, her eyes danced triumphantly. I was tempted to tell her and Mr. Dobbs off. Something along the lines of "Get a life," which I thought was particularly apropos for Gert, who appeared not to have many days left in her. Instead I politely thanked Mr. Dobbs for his time and turned to go.

Back outside, I embraced the cold day, clearing my nose of the sour nursing home stench. "Well. Back to the drawing board," I said aloud to myself as I headed for the High Street to buy a newspaper. I would check the classifieds and regroup over breakfast at the Muffin Man. I wouldn't let Mr. Dobbs or Gert get me down.

When I arrived at the tea house, I pushed open the door and said hello to the Polish waitress who had served Ethan and me on Thanksgiving. She gave me a perfunctory smile and told me I could sit anywhere. I chose a small table by the window, sitting on one chair and setting my purse, newspaper, and leather binder on the other. Then I consulted the sticky laminated menu and ordered herbal tea, scrambled eggs, and a scone.

As I waited for my food, I glanced around the flowery room decorated with Monet prints, my eyes resting on a petite girl sipping coffee at a table near mine. She had incredibly wide-set eyes, an auburn bob, and porcelain skin. She wore a wide-brimmed canary-yellow hat. She reminded me of Madeline, the character in the children's books, which I used to read with Rachel twenty-five years ago. When the girl's mobile phone rang, she answered it, speaking in a husky voice with a French accent. The French part fit the Madeline image, the husky part did not, as she seemed too diminutive to have such a deep voice. I strained to hear what she was saying—something about how she shouldn't complain about the London weather because it is even colder and rainier in Paris. After a few more minutes of chatter about Paris, she said, "I'll see you soon, *mon petit chou*." Then she laughed affectionately, snapped her phone shut, and stared dreamily out the window in a way that made me think that she had just conversed with a new lover. I tried to remember what *chou* meant in French. Was it a puppy? No, I was pretty sure that dog was *chien*.

I glanced around the Muffin Man again, hoping to find my Alistair, my own *chou*. But there were no solo male diners, handsome or otherwise. Only Madeline and an American couple consulting a Fodor's guidebook on Great Britain. The two were sporting matching, bulging purple fanny packs and bright white Reeboks. I couldn't help wondering why so many Americans (other than New Yorkers) have such a distinct lack of fashion sense, but the new Darcy didn't hold it against them.

After my waitress brought my breakfast, I studied the tea strainer and peered into the silver pot at the floating tea particles, trying to remember how Ethan had prepared it for us. To a coffee drinker, it all seemed pretty complicated. Then, right as I was wishing he were here with me to pour my cup of tea and listen to my Mr. Dobbs tale, in he strolled, looking adorable in a red cap and a brightly colored striped sweater. His cheeks were pink, as they always were in the cold—which made his eyes look even bluer.

"Ethan!" I spoke in a normal voice, but it registered loud in the small, quiet room. "Hey, there!"

I caught Madeline giving me a look, perhaps disapproving of my outburst. I fleetingly regretted being the loud American in the room.

"Hey, Darce," Ethan said, as he approached my table. "How did it go at the nursing home?" He must have returned to the flat, because I had left him a note about my job-hunting mission.

"Not so well. But I bought a paper to check the classifieds. Have a seat," I said, moving my purse and binder to clear a chair for him. "I'm so glad you're here. I was just thinking about you. How do you work this little contraption again?" I asked, motioning toward the tea strainer. Without sitting down, he leaned over my table, efficiently placed the strainer over my cup with one hand, and poured from the silver pot with the other.

"Have a seat," I said again.

He cleared his throat, looking uncomfortable. "Um . . . actually, I'm meeting a friend here."

"Oh . . . who?" I asked, worried that Phoebe was on her way.

"She's right over there." Ethan gestured toward Madeline and then, as she looked up at him, he winked at her—not in the smooth, sleazy way that some guys wink—more the cute, friendly sort of wink. Like Santa Claus if he were thin and young.

Madeline gave Ethan a pinky wave as she sipped her cappuccino from a glass mug. She then flashed him a small, private smile. I combined her smile with her *mon petit chou,* digesting the implications. . . . *Ethan has a girlfriend. And she's not only attractive, but she's French to boot!*

Ethan smiled back at Madeline and then looked down at me. "You're welcome to join us, Darce."

But I could tell he didn't mean it. "That's okay. You go ahead," I said quickly, feeling embarrassed for assuming he was ever-available for me.

"Are you sure?" He gave me a furtive, borderline sympathetic look.

"Yeah. Yeah. I have to run in a sec anyway. Check out the leads in my paper. You go on . . . really," I said.

"All right, then. I'll see you a little later, okay?"

"Yup. Sounds good," I said breezily.

As I watched Ethan amble toward Madeline's table, I felt strangely territorial. Almost jealous. The emotion caught me off guard. I mean, why should I care if Ethan had a girlfriend? I certainly wasn't interested in him. Sure, I had thought about kissing him, but that didn't mean I was in love with him or anything crazy like that. Perhaps seeing him with someone just made me long for a companion of my own. Perhaps I was worried about my standing in his flat. My rights to his comfortable bed.

From the corner of my eye, I saw Madeline stand and kiss her *chou* on one cheek and then the other. I know it is a European practice, but it still looked pretentious, and I vowed never to dole out the double kiss again. Ethan pulled off his cap, exposing his tousled curls. Then he sat and angled his chair toward her. Their knees touched.

I looked away and ate quickly, feeling queasy and hurt that Ethan hadn't told me about his relationship. I wondered what exactly was going on between them. Was he always off meeting her under the guise of finishing his book? Were they making mad love back at her place as I waited for him to come home every night? Why had he not told me about her? As I stood to pay my bill, I debated whether to say good-bye on my way out. On the one hand, I was curious to meet this girl and glean some insight into their fledgling (or was it established?) relationship. At the same time, I felt awkward, like I'd rather just sidle out the door unnoticed. It wasn't like me to be anything other than gregarious, and I wondered again why Ethan's having a girlfriend could affect me in this way.

As I stood by the cash register, a few yards from the lovebirds' table, I could hear Madeline's throaty French accent followed by Ethan's happy chortle. I presented my bill to the waitress along with a ten-pound note. She gave me my change, which I dropped into a little dish for tips. Then, just as I was heading out the door, I heard Ethan call out, "Hey, Darce. C'mere for a sec."

I turned around, pretending to be momentarily disoriented, as if I had forgotten altogether that he was there with a woman. Then I smiled warmly and took the few steps over to their table.

"Hey, there," I said casually.

"This is Sondrine," Ethan said. "Sondrine, this is Darcy."

Sondrine? What kind of name was that? I examined her closely. Her skin was poreless, and she had perfectly arched eyebrows. I hadn't had my own brows done since I had left New York.

"Nice to meet you, Sondrine," I said, catching myself in the pregnant-girl stance: knees locked, hands resting on my stomach. I dropped my arms to my sides, assuming a more attractive pose.

"And you," Sondrine purred in a phone-sex voice.

We exchanged a few more pleasantries, and then, just in case Ethan had downplayed my importance in his life—or failed to mention me altogether—I told him that I'd see him back home. I checked Sondrine's face for a flash of surprise or insecurity, but saw neither. Just pleasant indifference. As I departed the Muffin Man and rounded the corner back to Ethan's flat, I felt inexplicably wistful, almost sad. I felt my baby kick again, and I confided in her, whispering, "Ethan has a girlfriend. And I don't know why that upsets me."

* * *

I didn't see Ethan until much later that night when he finally returned to the flat, sans Sondrine. I was sprawled on his couch, half-asleep, waiting for him with a pit in my stomach as I listened to a Norah Jones CD.

"What time is it?" I asked.

"Tenish," he said, standing over me. "Have you eaten?"

"Yes," I said. "You?"

He nodded.

"Where've you been?" I asked, feeling like a suspicious wife who just found a smear of pink lipstick on her husband's starched white shirt.

"Writing."

"*Sure* you were," I said, trying to sound nonchalant and playful.

"What's that supposed to mean?" he asked, motioning for me to move over and clear a space for him.

I lifted my legs long enough for him to sit and then rested my feet on his thighs. "It means, were you *really* writing or were you hanging out with Sondrine?" I asked the question in the singsongy way that kids say, *"Ethan and Sondrine sitting in a tree, K-I-S-S-I-N-G!"*

"I really was writing," he said innocently. Then he tried to change the subject by asking what I did with my day.

"I looked for a job. Called some places. Surfed the Net."

"And?"

"All to no avail," I said. "Very frustrating . . . So what's the deal with Son-*drine*?" I pronounced her name as un-Frenchy as possible, making the word sound clunky and unattractive.

"She's cool. Fun to hang out with."

"Don't play dumb with me, Ethan."

He gave me a quizzical look.

"Is she your girlfriend or what?"

He yawned and stretched. "No, she's not my girlfriend."

"But you're her *petit chou*." I grinned.

"What?"

"I heard her on the phone talking to you right before you showed up at the Muffin Man. She called you her *petit chou*."

"You're too much," Ethan said, smiling.

"By the way, are you aware that a *chou* is a cabbage?" I asked, rolling my eyes. I had looked the word up on the Internet as soon as I had returned to the flat, and could not believe that she was using such a dumb pet name.

Ethan shrugged. "I had no idea. I took Spanish. Remember?"

"Too bad for you."

"Why?"

"Because your girlfriend's French, that's why."

"She's not my girlfriend, Darce," Ethan said unconvincingly. "We've just gone out a couple of times."

"When was that?"

"Once last week . . . and then today."

"Was last week a dinner date?" I asked, trying to remember which nights Ethan had stayed out late.

"No. We met for lunch."

"Where?"

"At a bistro in Notting Hill."

"Did you go dutch?"

"No. I paid. . . . Is your inquisition almost over?"

"I guess so. I just don't get why you didn't tell me about her."

He shrugged. "I don't know why I didn't mention her. It's really not a big deal," he said, as he kneaded my left heel and then my right. I couldn't remember the last time someone had given me a foot massage. It felt better than an orgasm. I told Ethan this. He gave me a proud smile that I translated as: "You've never had an orgasm with me." An image of Ethan and Sondrine, naked and sweaty, popped into my head. I pictured them postcoitus, sharing a cigarette. She had to be a smoker with that raspy voice.

"So tell me about her," I probed.

"There's not much to tell . . . I met her at the Tate Gallery. We were both there to see this exhibit," he said as he made a fist and rolled it along my arches.

"So what, did you meet in front of a painting?" I asked, thinking of my own trip to the National Gallery with Ethan and wondering why he hadn't invited me to the Tate.

"No. We met in the café at the museum. She was behind me in line. I got the last free table. She asked if she could join me," he said. I could hear the story being retold later, whenever anyone asked how they had met. I could see Sondrine linking her arm through his, concluding the tale with a coy, "He got the last Caesar salad *and* the last table!"

"What a sweet story," I said.

He ignored my sarcasm. "And then we walked around the museum together afterward."

The whole thing was a little too close to my Alistair fantasy for comfort. I swallowed, trying to identify the knotted feeling in my chest. It felt like envy and worry and loneliness all blended together.

I formulated a dozen more questions but decided against asking any of them. I had heard enough. Instead we just listened to Norah Jones. Ethan's eyes were closed, his hands still on my feet when he finally spoke. "You looked really pregnant in the Muffin Man today," he said.

"You mean fat?" I asked, thinking of Sondrine's delicate bird wrists. I was downright sturdy next to her.

"Not *fat. Pregnant.*"

"Pregnant and fat," I said.

He shook his head, opened his eyes, and gave me a funny look. "No. Pregnant and *radiant*."

I felt all tingly and knew that I was beaming. I thanked him, feeling shy.

Ethan kept looking at me with concentration, the way you study someone when you're trying to place them, remember their name. He finally said, "You really do have that glow."

"Thank you," I said again. Our eyes locked for a second, and then we both looked away at the same time.

There was no more conversation for a long time after that. Then Ethan suddenly turned to me and said, "Darce, I was wondering . . . why did you go to the nursing home today?"

"I told you—to get a job," I said.

"I know. But why a nursing home when you have a public relations background?"

"Because I want to help people. Be more compassionate and stuff."

Ethan chuckled and shook his head. "You're such a little extremist, aren't you?"

"What do you mean? *You're* the one who said I needed to change. Be a less shallow person and all that," I said, realizing how very much I wanted him to recognize the effort I was making.

"You don't have to change *everything* about yourself, Darce. And you certainly don't need to go working in a nursing home to be a good person."

"Well, it's a good thing. Because I didn't get hired." I smiled. "And to be perfectly honest, I don't particularly want to work with old people."

"Yeah. You don't have to be a martyr. Just find an enjoyable job and make a little loot. If you can add some value to the world in the process, all the better. But you have to be yourself."

"Be myself, huh?" I said with a smirk.

"Yeah," he said, grinning as he stood and walked toward his bedroom. "It ain't *all* bad."

I stood to follow him and then hesitated. I knew nothing had changed overnight, but there was something about seeing Ethan with a girl that made sleeping in bed with him feel strange, somehow wrong. I reassured myself that despite an occasional, fleeting attraction on my part, we were strictly friends. And friends could share beds. I used to have sleepovers with Rachel all the time.

Still, just to be sure, I waited for Ethan to turn around and say, "Are you coming?" before bounding (as much as a pregnant girl can bound) down the hall after him.

I didn't know how much longer I had before Sondrine would make her presence known in the flat, but I was going to savor every minute of it.

twenty-three

The next morning I called Mr. Moore, the doctor Meg and Charlotte had recommended. As it turned out, he had a cancellation in his morning schedule, so I took the Circle Line to Great Portland Street and followed my *A to Zed* to his office on Harley Street, a block of beautiful, old town houses, most of which appeared to have been converted to medical offices.

I opened the heavy red door to Mr. Moore's practice and walked into a marble foyer, where a receptionist handed me a form to fill out and pointed to a waiting room with a fireplace. Moments later, a plump, grandmotherly woman who introduced herself as Beatrix, Mr. Moore's midwife, collected me in the waiting room and led me up a winding, grand staircase to another room that looked as if it should have been roped off in a museum.

Beatrix introduced me to my doctor as he rose behind his mahogany desk, stepped around it, and gracefully extended his hand. I shook it and studied his face. With high cheekbones, wide-set brown eyes, and an interesting Roman nose, he was quite handsome. And he was elegantly dressed in a sharp navy suit and a green tie. He nodded toward a wing chair in front of his desk, inviting me to have a seat.

We both sat down, and for some reason I blurted out, "I expected a white coat."

He gave me a hint of a smile and said, "White is not my color." His refined accent seemed to transform the friendly quip into a line right out of a Shakespeare play.

Beatrix murmured that she'd be back shortly, and Mr. Moore asked me polite, getting-to-know-you questions: stuff about where I was from, when I had arrived in England, and when I was due. I answered his questions, telling him matter-of-factly that I had become pregnant unexpectedly, broken up with my boyfriend, and moved to London to start over. I also told him that I was due on May second, and that I had not been to the doctor in several weeks.

"Have you had an ultrasound?" he asked.

I was embarrassed to report no, remembering that I had blown off my ten-week ultrasound appointment in New York.

"Well, we'll do an ultrasound today and check on everything," Mr. Moore said, making a note on my chart.

"Will you be able to tell the gender?"

"I will . . . assuming your baby is cooperative."

"Really? Today?"

"Hmmm," he said, nodding.

My heart pounded with excitement and a dash of fear. I was about to see my daughter for the first time. I suddenly wished that Ethan were with me.

"Let's get started then," Mr. Moore said. "Shall we?"

I nodded.

"Just go right behind that screen, get undressed from the waist down, and pop onto the table. I'll return with Beatrix in a moment."

I nodded again and went to undress. As I slid off my skirt, I regretted not getting a bikini wax before my appointment. I was going to make a poor first impression on the impeccably groomed Mr. Moore. But as I got up on the table and tucked the paper cover neatly around me, I reassured myself that surely he had seen much worse. Minutes later, Mr. Moore returned with Beatrix, knocking on the partition that separated the examination room from his parlor.

"All set?" he asked.

"All set," I said.

Mr. Moore smiled as he perched on a small stool beside me while Beatrix hovered primly in the background.

"All right then, Darcy," Mr. Moore said. "Please slide down for me and place your feet in the stirrups. I am going to have a peek at your cervix. You'll feel a little pressure."

He put on latex gloves and checked my cervix with two fingers. I winced as he murmured, "Your cervix is closed and long. Wonderful." Then he removed his gloves, deposited them into a small waste can, slid my paper covering down, and squeezed a blob of gel onto my stomach. "I apologize if this feels a bit cold."

"No problem," I said, grateful for his sensitivity.

He slid the ultrasound probe over my stomach as a murky black-and-white image appeared on the screen. At first it looked like nothing but an ink blot, the kind that a psychiatrist uses, but then I made out a head and a hand.

"Omigod!" I shouted. "She's sucking her little thumb, isn't she?"

"Hmmm," Mr. Moore said, as Beatrix smiled.

I got all choked up as I told them that I had never seen anything so miraculous. "She's perfect," I said. "Isn't she absolutely perfect?"

Mr. Moore agreed. "Beautiful. Beautiful," he murmured.

He then squinted at the screen and carefully inched the probe along my stomach. The image disappeared for a second, then reappeared.

"What?" I asked. "What do you see? She *is* a girl, right?"

"Just give me a moment . . . I need to have a closer look. Then I'll take some measurements."

"What do you need to measure?" I asked.

"The head, abdomen, and femur. Then we'll look at the various structures. The brain, chambers of the heart, and so forth."

It suddenly occurred to me that something *could* be wrong with my daughter. Why had I not considered this before? I regretted all of the wine I had sipped, the coffees that I wasn't able to resist in the morning. What if I had done something to harm her? I anxiously watched the screen and Mr. Moore's face for clues. He calmly examined different parts of my baby, reading out numbers as Beatrix took notes on my chart. "Is that normal?" I asked at every turn.

"Yes. Yes. It's all terribly, beautifully normal."

At that moment, *normal* was the most wonderful word in the English language. My daughter didn't have to be a beauty like me. She didn't have to be extraordinary in any way. I just wanted her to be healthy.

"So. Are you ready to hear the big news?" Mr. Moore asked me.

"Oh, I know it's a girl," I said. "I've never had a moment's doubt, but I'm dying for confirmation so I can start buying pink things."

Mr. Moore made a clucking sound, and said, "Ahhh. Well, now. I should warn you that pink might not be the best choice."

"What?" I asked, straining to make out the image on the screen. "It's *not* a girl?"

"No. You are *not* having a girl," he said, turning to me with the proud smile of a man who assumes that a boy is always the preferred gender.

"It's a *boy*? Are you sure?"

"Yes. I'm sure. You're having a boy . . ." he said, pointing to the screen with his right index finger, the other hand still holding the probe against my stomach. "And *another* boy."

He turned away from the screen and beamed down at me, waiting for a reaction.

My mind churned wildly, landing on a once common word now infused with a crazy, new meaning: *twin*. I managed to spit out a question. "Two babies?"

"Yes, Darcy. You're pregnant with twin boys." Mr. Moore's smile grew wider. "Congratulations!"

"There must be some mistake. Look again," I said. He had to be wrong. Twins didn't run in my family. I hadn't taken any fertility drugs. I didn't *want* twins. And certainly not twin *boys*!

Mr. Moore and Beatrix exchanged a knowing glance and then chuckled their restrained English chuckles. That's when I thought maybe they were just pulling my chain. Playing some cruel little trick on me. Tell the unmarried Yank she's having twins. Good one. Ethan had told me that the sense of humor is different in England.

"You're kidding, right?" I asked, completely stunned.

"No," Mr. Moore said. "I'm quite serious. You are having two boys. Congratulations, Darcy."

I sat upright, my paper cover slipping off me and floating to the floor. "But I wanted a girl. *One* girl. Not *two boys*," I said, not caring that I was completely exposed from the waist down.

"Well. These things can't be ordered up like a mince pie," Mr. Moore said wryly, as he stooped to retrieve my covering and handed it to me.

I glared at him. In no way did I appreciate his analogy or his apparent amusement.

"Are you ever wrong about these things?" I asked desperately. "I've heard of that happening. I mean, have you ever made a mistake?"

Mr. Moore said he was quite sure I was having twins. Then he explained that occasionally girls are mistaken for boys, but rarely does it happen the other way.

"So you're *positive*?"

With the patience of Annie Sullivan teaching Helen Keller the alphabet, he pointed to the floating images on the screen. Two heartbeats. Two heads. And two penises.

I started to cry, as my visions of sugar and spice and all things pink and nice evaporated, replaced by horrid remembrances of my little brother, Jeremy. His lips vibrating together as he made endless, monotonous bulldozer sounds. I was about to have that times two. It was inconceivable.

Sensing my mounting despair, Mr. Moore switched into sympathetic mode, explaining that the news of twins is often met with something less than enthusiasm.

I fought back tears. "That is a gross understatement."

"It will just take some getting used to," he said.

"Two boys?" I asked again.

"Two boys," he said. "Identical twins."

"How in the world did this happen?"

Mr. Moore took the question literally because he gave me a quick biology lesson, pointing to the screen and explaining that my babies appeared to be sharing one placenta, but two sacs. "Or diamnionic monochorionic twins," he said. "Which means your fertilized egg divided between four and seven days postconception."

"Shhhit," I whispered.

He pushed a button, explaining that he was taking an ultrasound picture for me. He then moved the probe, snapped again. He handed me the two photographs, one labeled Baby A and the other Baby B. I reluctantly took them from him. Mr. Moore asked if I would like to get dressed and share a soothing cup of mint tea with Beatrix, who inched her way toward the table and smiled down at me.

"No. No, thank you. I have to go," I said, standing and dressing as quickly as I could.

Mr. Moore tried to coax me back on the table for further discussion, but I had to get out of there, irrationally believing that his office and its imposing Victorian formality had transformed my girl baby into a boy baby and then multiplied her by two. If I escaped, maybe it would all fix itself. I would go seek a second opinion. Surely there was a good American physician in London. One who had the title *doctor,* for heaven's sake.

"I'm sorry, Mr. Moore," I stammered. "But I have to go."

Mr. Moore and Beatrix watched as I finished dressing, collected my purse, and said, as I headed out the door, that he should bill me for the visit, and thank you very much. Then I made my way back to Harley Street, where I felt numbed by Mr. Moore's news and the biting London drizzle.

I walked all over town in a daze, the word *twins* drumming in my skull. I walked down to Bond Street, then over to Marble Arch, then across to Knightsbridge. I walked until my lower back ached and my hands and toes grew numb. I did not stop in a single store, no matter how tempting the window display. I didn't stop at all except for a few minutes at a Starbucks during the worst of the rain. I thought the familiar burnt-orange-and-purple décor would offer me some sort of solace. It didn't. Nor did the hot chocolate and bagel I hungrily swallowed. The thought of having one baby was intimidating. Now I was full-on scared. How would I be able to take care of twins—or even tell them apart? It felt surreal.

Around three o'clock, just as it was getting dark, I arrived home, frozen and exhausted.

"Darcy? Is that you?" I heard Ethan call from his bedroom.

"Yeah," I yelled back as I took off my jacket and kicked off my boots.

"Come on back!"

I walked down the hall and opened Ethan's door. He was stretched out on his bed with an open book resting on his chest. The lamp next to his bed cast a warm, soft glow on his blond hair, creating a halo effect.

"Can I sit down? I'm kind of wet," I said.

"Of course you can."

I sat cross-legged at the foot of his bed, rubbed the soles of my feet, and shivered.

"Did you get caught in the rain?" he asked.

"Yeah. Sort of. I've been walking in it all day," I said pitifully. "I left my umbrella at home."

"Not a good thing to leave behind in London."

"So. You'll never believe what happened to me today . . ."

"Were you mugged?" he asked, drumming his fingers on the spine of his book.

"No. Worse."

Ethan snickered. "Worse than someone stealing your Gucci bag?"

"This isn't funny, Ethan." My voice trembled.

His smile disappeared as he closed his book and tossed it on the bed next to him. "What happened?"

"I went to the doctor this morning . . ."

He sat up, a concerned look on his face. "Is everything okay with the baby?"

I uncrossed my legs and brought them up to my chest, resting my chin on my knees. "Everything is fine . . . with the ba-*bies.*"

Ethan's eyes widened. "Babies?"

I nodded.

"Twins?"

"Yes. Twins. Identical twin *boys*."

Ethan stared at me for a few seconds. "Are you kidding?"

"Do I look amused?"

The corners of his mouth twitched, as if he were trying not to laugh.

"It's not funny, Ethan. . . . And please don't tell me that I deserve this either. Because, believe me, I've already considered that I'm being punished. Maybe I was engaging in some frivolous behavior in Manhattan. Maybe shopping too much," I said. "Or railing on someone's appearance. Or having sex with Marcus behind Dexter's back. . . . And God frowned down upon me and *whazzam* split my embryo . . . giving me identical twin boys." I started to cry. It was really sinking in. Twins. Twins. *Twins.*

"Darcy. Chill, hon. I wasn't going to say anything like that."

"Then why are you smiling?"

"I'm smiling because . . . I'm happy."

"Happy that I'm getting screwed?"

"No, Darce. I'm happy *for* you. If one baby is a blessing, then you have twice the good fortune. Two babies! It's a small miracle. Not a punishment." His words were convincing, his tone and expression even more so.

"Do you think?"

"I *know*. . . . It's wonderful."

"But how will I do it?"

"You just *will*."

"I don't know if I can."

"Of course you can . . . Now. Why don't you go take a hot shower, put on warm pajamas, and I'll make you some dinner."

"Thanks, Ethan," I said, feeling soothed even before I

got out of my damp clothes. Ethan's nurturing quality was one of the things I liked most about him. He had this in common with Rachel. I thought of how Rachel used to bring pistachios over to my house whenever I needed some good cheering up. She knew pistachios were my favorite treat, but the best part was how she always assumed the role of the nut cracker, handing me filet after filet. I remember thinking they were that much tastier without the interruption and aggravation of peeling. Ethan's offer to make me dinner reminded me of those pistachio days.

"Just get in the shower and start thinking of boy names. Wayne and Dwayne might be just the ticket. What do you say?"

I giggled. "Wayne and Dwayne Rhone . . . I like it."

Later that night, after Ethan and I had eaten his homemade beef stew for dinner and spent much time admiring my boys' sweet, matching profiles in their ultrasound photos, we went to bed.

"How come you never spend the night with Sondrine?" I asked as I slid under the covers.

Ethan switched off the light, got in bed next to me, and said, "It's not that serious yet."

The *yet* gave me a small pang, but I just said, "Oh," and dropped the subject.

After a long silence, Ethan whispered, "Congratulations again, Darce. Twin boys. Awesome."

"Thank you, Ethan," I said, as I felt a kick from one of my little guys.

"Are you feeling a bit better about it?"

"A tiny bit maybe," I said. I wasn't yet thrilled with the news, but at least I no longer viewed it as a curse or a punishment. "Thank you for acting happy about it."

"I *am* happy about it."

I smiled to myself and slid my leg across the cool sheets, finding Ethan's chilly foot. "Love you, Ethan." I held my breath, worried that despite dropping the *I* in *I love you* (which always makes the sentiment seem safe and platonic), I had still said too much. I didn't want to give him the impression that I wanted more than his friendship.

"Love you too, Darce," Ethan said, wiggling his toes against mine.

I smiled in the dark, letting go of my worries, and falling into a very deep and peaceful sleep.

twenty-four

The next morning I awoke in a fresh panic. How in the world was I ever going to manage twins? Would Ethan let us live with him? Would two cribs even fit in my tiny room? What if I couldn't find a job? I had less than two thousand dollars left in my account— barely enough to cover my hospital bills, let alone baby supplies, food, rent. I told myself to calm down, stay focused on my list, and take things one day at a time.

So for the rest of the week, I was all about the job hunt. I kept an open mind, diligently seeking any kind of work: high-minded jobs, jobs in PR, even menial jobs. I checked the papers, made phone calls, hit the pavement. Nothing turned up—except some disappointing findings regarding the difficulty of securing a work permit. Even worse, I learned that all female employees in England are entitled to twenty-six weeks' maternity leave. Not exactly promising news. Who would hire me so far along in my pregnancy, knowing they'd have to let me go for six months? I began to worry that I was going to have to return to New

York. To my old job and my old life. It was the last thing I wanted to do.

By Saturday evening, I was totally drained and disheartened and ready to let my hair down at Meg's party, stop worrying for one night. I took my time getting ready, trying on several maternity outfits that I had purchased at H&M (which didn't count as frivolous shopping as my regular wardrobe no longer fit) before settling on a simple black dress. I stood in front of the mirror, admiring the way it hugged my stomach and hips, showcasing my bump. I added a touch of mascara and gloss, deciding not to hide my glow of pregnancy behind a veil of heavy makeup. Then I slid on a pair of simple black heels and my diamond studs from Dex. The result, if I do say so myself, was understated elegance.

Ethan returned home just as I was heading out the door.

He whistled as he rested his open palm on my stomach and then patted. "You look great. Where are you off to?"

I reminded him that I had been invited to a dinner party. "Remember? The girls I met at the coffee shop last week?"

"Oh, yeah. The English girls," he said. "I'm impressed that you got the invite. Most Americans don't get invited into a Brit's home until their going-away party." It wasn't his first comment on the closed nature of British society, one of the few things he did not like about the country.

"I am very excited about it," I said. "I hope it feels like a night out with Bridget Jones."

"You mean a bunch of neurotic women chain-smoking, talking about losing weight and shagging their bosses?"

"Something like that," I said, laughing. "So what are you up to tonight?"

"Didn't I tell you? . . . I'm going to dinner with Sondrine." I felt a stab of envy as he gave me a sheepish look. He knew full well that he hadn't mentioned his date with

her. In fact, he hadn't mentioned her at all since the day I
met her at the Muffin Man.

"No. You didn't tell me." I nodded toward the plastic
bag he was holding from Oddbins, a wine shop near us.
"And apparently you have plans for after dinner too?"

He said maybe, he'd see how dinner went.

"Well, have fun. I'm off," I said, telling myself not to
dwell on his relationship.

As I headed out the door, Ethan asked if I planned on
taking a cab.

"No. The tube," I said, holding up my tube pass. "I'm
very frugal these days— in case you hadn't noticed."

"It's too late for you to take the tube alone."

"I thought you said the tube was safe at night?" I asked.

"It is. But . . . I don't know. You're pregnant. Here you
go." He opened his wallet, pulled out a few bills, and tried
to hand them to me.

"Ethan, I don't need your money. I'm operating perfectly well within the confines of my budget," I said, even
though one of my credit cards had been declined at Marks
& Spencer that morning when I tried to buy a new bra to
support my burgeoning, pregnant-girl D cups.

He slipped the money back in his wallet and said,
"Okay . . . but please take a cab."

"I will," I said, feeling touched that he was being so
protective. "You be careful too." I winked.

He gave me a puzzled look.

"Wear a condom."

He rolled his eyes and gave me a dismissive wave, which
I translated to mean: "Don't be crazy. I'm not sleeping with
her anytime soon." Then he kissed me good-bye on the
cheek and I caught a whiff of his cologne. The scent was
nice, and it made me feel strangely melancholy. I reminded
myself that Simon the Ginger was waiting for me at an English dinner party in Mayfair.

But as I sat in the back of the cab on my way to Meg's flat, psyching myself up for the evening ahead, I couldn't get rid of the pit in my stomach. It wasn't just my seeming jealousy over Sondrine and Ethan's date, or my overarching worry about mothering twins. I was also just plain nervous for the party. Anxiety was not an emotion I could ever remember feeling when I went out in New York, and I wondered why tonight felt so different. Maybe it was because I no longer had a boyfriend or fiancé. I suddenly recognized that there was a safety in having someone, as well as a lack of pressure to shine. Ironically, this had cultivated a certain free-spiritedness that had, in turn, allowed me to be the life of the party and hoard the affection of *additional* men.

But I was no longer attached to someone and no longer in my comfort zone of Manhattan and the Hamptons, where I knew exactly what to expect at any bar, club, party, or gathering. Where I knew that no matter what the venue, I could have a few drinks and I would not only be the most beautiful woman in the room (except for the one time that I happened to be at Lotus when Giselc Bundchen walked in), but usually the most scintillating too.

But that had all changed. I didn't have a boyfriend, a perfect figure, or alcohol-induced outrageousness to fall back on. So I was more than a little apprehensive as we pulled up to Meg's town house. I got out of the cab and paid the driver through the front window (a practice I preferred to the New York way of passing bills over the seat). Then I took a deep breath, walked up to the door, and rang the buzzer.

"Hello, darling! So nice to see you again," Meg said as she answered the door. She gave me a kiss on the cheek as I noticed with minor relief that she was also wearing a black dress. At the very least, I had dressed appropriately.

"Great to see you too! Thanks so much for having me," I said, feeling myself relax.

Meg smiled and introduced me to her husband, Yossi, a rail-thin, dark-skinned guy with an unusual accent (I later learned he was Israeli but went to school in Paris). He took my coat and offered me a drink. "A glass of champagne perhaps?"

I rested my hand on my stomach and politely declined.

"How about a Perrier?" he asked.

"That would be lovely," I said, as Meg led me into her living room which looked like a spread in a magazine. The ceilings were higher than any I had seen in a private residence—they must have been at least sixteen feet high. The walls were painted a dark, romantic red. A fire was flickering in the fireplace, casting a soft light on the jewel-toned Oriental rug and dark, antique furniture. Faded hardcover books filled the shelves that lined one entire floor-to-ceiling wall of the room. There was something about all of those books that intimidated me, as if I might be quizzed on literature later.

The guests, too, were somehow intimidating. They did not resemble my homogeneous New York crowd. Instead, the dozen or so people in the room seemed so culturally and racially diverse that they looked like a Benetton ad. As Yossi returned with my sparkling water in a crystal goblet, Meg asked if I had had any luck in finding a job.

"No luck so far," I said. "But I did make it to the doctor."

"Did you find out the gender?" she asked eagerly.

"Yes," I said, realizing that I had forgotten to prepare for the question.

"A girl?"

"No. A boy," I said, making the split-second decision not to tell her about the twins just yet. Being single and expecting one baby seemed acceptable, maybe even au courant, but there was something about being single and having twins that seemed sort of embarrassing, almost low-rent, and certainly not the kind of news you want to broadcast at an elegant dinner party.

"Oh! A *boy!* How delightful!" Meg said. "Congratulations!"

I smiled, feeling vaguely guilty for not telling Meg the full story. But by then, she was leading me around the room, introducing me to the other guests. There was Henrik, a Swede, and Cecilia, his French wife, both cellists. Tumi, a jewelry designer from Cameroon. Beata, a handsome woman who was born in Prague, raised in Scotland, and now spent much of her time working in Africa with AIDS patients. Uli, a strapping German who worked with Yossi in banking. An older Arab man whose name was so full of odd consonants that I didn't catch it even after he repeated it twice. A handful of Brits, including Charlotte and her husband, John. And Simon the Ginger, who had a zillion freckles to go with the shockingly red hair. To my relief, he ignored me in favor of Beata, who, incidentally, was also a redhead (which always raises the interesting question of whether redheads pursue other redheads in a narcissistic way, or simply because they have no other choice, as nonredheads aren't interested).

In any event, I was the odd woman out. The only person at the mini UN convention who had nothing to contribute to the geopolitical conversation. I had no clue whether Asia was a market bubble or still a buy. No opinion on how the threat of terrorism and various elections were going to cause stock prices to tumble. Or whether the slump in luxury travel was nearly over. I knew nothing about the conflict in the Sudan that had caused a hundred thousand refugees to cross the border into Chad. Or the conversion of the pound to the euro. Or France's chances at the next World Cup. Ditto for rugby (something about the Five Nations?) and *Breakfast with Frost* (whatever that is). Nor did I realize that Tony Blair's "shameless love affair with America" was so offensive to the rest of the world.

I kept waiting for someone to bring up the royal family, the one topic that I knew a thing or two about. But when the royals were finally raised, it wasn't to comment on Fergie's yo-yo dieting, the conspiracy theory surrounding Di's death, William's latest love interest, or Charles and Camilla. Instead, they chatted about whether England should continue to have a monarchy at all. Which I didn't even know was up for debate.

After at least two hours of cocktails for everyone but me, we were all seated to a Moroccan feast, where people continued to drink heavily. In fact, the sheer amount of alcohol consumed was the only real similarity between my old world and this one. But unlike New York, where the more you drank, the more stupid you became, these people just got smarter. Not even Dex and Rachel talked about this heavy stuff when they were drunk. I found my mind drifting, wondering what Ethan was doing with Sondrine.

Then, toward the end of dinner, a very late guest arrived. I was sitting with my back to the dining room entryway when Meg looked up and said, "Why, hello there, Geoffrey, darling. Fashionably late again, are we?" At which point I heard Geoffrey apologize, explaining that he had been paged for an emergency C-section. That's when I turned around and found my one and only Mr. Moore looking incredibly handsome in a tweed sport coat, a cashmere turtleneck, and gray twill pants.

I watched as my doctor greeted his friends, shaking hands with the men and bending down to kiss the women. Then, his eyes rested on me. He gave me a funny look, and after a few beats, he smiled with recognition. "Darcy, right?"

Charlotte and Meg exchanged a look, as if remembering the connection.

"Oh, right! I forgot you two would have met," Meg said. "Darcy told us the fantastic, exciting news!" She was, of course, referring to my *one* boy.

Mr. Moore looked at me, as I realized with horror what was about to transpire. I tried to preempt it by saying, "Yes, he told me I was having *a* boy," but before I could, Mr. Moore blurted out, "Yes. Twins! Marvelous, isn't it?"

For the first time all evening, a hush fell over the room. Everyone looked at me. For someone who had spent three decades basking in attention, I should have been savoring the moment, but instead I was mortified as I confessed, "Um . . . I'm actually pregnant with twins."

"Twins!" came the collective roar at the table.

"Oh, my," Geoffrey said, looking horrified as he took the empty seat next to me. "Meg said 'fantastic news.' I just assumed . . . I'm truly sorry."

"No problem," I said quietly, but wanted to melt away as Meg stood and made a toast: "To our new American friend and her *two* babies! Congratulations, Darcy!"

So I was not only the dumb American, but an unwed, lying mother of two. I gave the group a large, fake smile and then mumbled with all the grace and dignity that I could muster, "Mr. Moore—Geoffrey—did give me a bit of a jolt last week when he told me I'm having two boys . . . I suppose I haven't fully digested it yet . . ."

Then I waited for the group to turn to other matters—which took a surprisingly long time considering their interest in much loftier topics. But when they finally did, my discomfort did not subside. I said very little. Just focused on eating my foreign, too flavorful food. Geoffrey, too, seemed just as uncomfortable and spent most of the evening avoiding me. When he did address me, it was in a formal and awkward manner, to ask things such as, "Are you enjoying your lamb shank tagine and apricot couscous?"

So I was very surprised when, at the end of the evening, as everyone was thanking Meg and Yossi and putting on their coats to leave, Geoffrey offered to drive me home. I accepted, assuming that he was trying to make amends. Clearly this was his way of apologizing for outing me. But the way he rested his hand gently on my back on our walk to his car suggested the possibility of something more. And despite the awkward fact that he had had his fingers in my vagina, I couldn't help feeling a flutter of excitement as he opened the door to his hunter-green Jaguar. After all, he *was* the most eligible man I had met in London. I told myself that I could always find a new doctor.

I lowered myself into the tan leather seat, catching Geoffrey glancing down at my ankles before he turned to walk around the car and slide in beside me. He started the engine and negotiated his way out of the tight parking spot as he said, "I feel just awful about tonight, Darcy. I am so sorry. That was incredibly unprofessional of me. I just assumed that you had told everyone. A terrible assumption indeed."

"No worries, Mr. Moore," I said, testing the waters. If he let the *Mr. Moore* stand, then he still saw me only as a patient he had wronged. And I would know that my ride was strictly a pity lift.

But instead he said, "Geoffrey. Please call me Geoffrey." He looked at me with his almond-shaped brown eyes rimmed with thick, dark lashes.

"Geoffrey," I said in a slightly flirtatious tone. "You are forgiven."

He looked over at me, nodded, and grinned. Then, after he had driven the equivalent of three New York City blocks, he asked, "So how are you feeling about . . . ev-erything?"

"I'm getting used to the idea. Maybe I'm even a tiny bit excited."

"Well, I think little boys are positively marvelous," he said earnestly. "I have one. He's called Max."

"Oh, really? How old is he?" I asked, wondering if Geoffrey also had a wife.

"He just turned four. They grow so quickly," Geoffrey said. "One second you're changing nappies. And the very next, you're watching them go off to school, too proud to even hold your hand." He laughed and then worked in somewhat awkwardly that he was "no longer with Max's mum."

I looked out my window, smiling to myself, knowing now that Geoffrey was *definitely* interested. And I couldn't help feeling smug. I still had it—pregnant with twins and all.

When we arrived at Ethan's flat, I asked Geoffrey if he'd like to come inside for a drink and talk some more.

He hesitated and said, "I would like that very much."

So a few minutes later, after discovering that Ethan was not yet home, I struck a provocative pose on the couch and engaged Geoffrey in pleasant conversation. We talked about New York and London. My job search. His profes-sion. Identical twins. Parenthood. Then we segued into more personal matters. We discussed Max's mother and their amicable split. We covered Marcus. Even an abridged version of Rachel and Dex. Geoffrey was a bit stiff, but still easy to talk to. And very easy on the eyes.

Then, right around midnight, he asked if I wouldn't mind enlisting his partner, Mr. Smith, as my new doctor. I smiled and said I had been thinking the very same thing.

"Well, then . . . now that we have cleared up that little

conflict, might I kiss you?" he asked, leaning in closer to me.

I said that he could. So he did. And it was nice. His lips were soft. His breath sweet. His hands gentle. All the boxes were checked. His name might as well have been Alistair.

Yet right in the heat of the first real kiss I'd had in months, with Geoffrey, a British doctor, dallying about my newly acquired cleavage, my mind was elsewhere, fixed on Ethan and Sondrine. Was his face buried in her neck or some such spot? Was he falling for her? Was she equally overcome by his spicy, yet subtle, cologne?

twenty-five

Geoffrey called me before noon on the following day, proving that he was man enough not to subscribe to any silly waiting games. Or perhaps only American men make you wait. In any event, he told me that he enjoyed my company and would love to see me again. I found his candor immensely attractive, which in turn made me feel that I had matured.

I shared this observation with Ethan later that night as he stood at the stove making us fried eggs and bacon for dinner. We both loved breakfast foods any time of day. In fact, one of the few things that Ethan and I agreed on in high school was that going to IHOP after football games was a better choice than the infinitely more popular Taco Bell.

"Yeah," he said. "Sounds like you might be ready for a real, healthy relationship."

"As opposed to pursuing someone like Marcus?" I asked.

He nodded. "Marcus was all about rebellion." He flipped one egg with a spatula and then probed gently at the yolk of the other. "You subconsciously knew that Dex was wrong for you, so you cheated on him to escape your engagement."

I considered this statement, and told him I thought he was right. Then I said, "So what about you and Sondrine?"

Ethan had not returned home the night before, and I had spent a long, restless night checking the clock and wondering what was happening between them.

Ethan blushed while he kept his eyes on our eggs.

"So? How was last night?" I asked.

He turned down the gas flame with a flick of his wrist and said, "We had a nice time."

I decided to cut to the chase. "Did you sleep with her?"

His cheeks turned a shade pinker. Clearly he had. "None of your business," he said. "Now make the toast, please."

I stood from the table and put two slices of wheat bread in his toaster. "It is *sort of* my business."

He shook his head and asked, "How do you figure?"

"I'm your roommate . . . and your bedmate . . . I need to know if my status is in any way threatened," I asked, treading carefully.

"Your status?"

"My spot in your bed?" I said, in my "no duh" tone.

"You can stay in my bed," he said.

"I can? Why's that?" I asked, perhaps a tad hopeful that Ethan had determined that Sondrine wasn't the woman for him in the long term.

"Because I'm not going to throw a pregnant woman to the wolves. . . . I'll just stay at her place," he said quickly, as if he had already given much thought to the issue.

Maybe he had even decided that it was no longer appropriate for us to sleep next to each other. At least I still had my bed for the short term, but what if Ethan and Sondrine became more serious and moved in together?

What then? I felt anxious at the thought of it—and maybe even a little sad. I liked how close Ethan and I were, and didn't want that to change.

I decided that I had to prepare for the worst. If Ethan and Sondrine did become serious, I sure as hell wanted to be in a relationship too. From an emotional standpoint (I mean, who wants to be alone?), and as much as I hated to admit it, from a financial standpoint. I so wanted to add "be self-sufficient and independent" to my list, but in practical terms, how could I stay in London, jobless, with two children on the way?

So I threw myself into dating Geoffrey, catching myself fantasizing about a big wedding and the blissful life after with our three boys and a couple of Cavalier King Charles spaniels. I could hear myself saying, years later, every time I would tell the convoluted story of how we met: "See? Things happen for a reason. My life was hell and then it all fell neatly, magically into place."

I told Charlotte and Meg of my hopes for the future as we strolled through Hyde Park with Natalie one afternoon. They both seemed thrilled with the idea of Geoffrey and me being together. They sang his praises, calling him a "wonderful father," a "brilliant doctor," and the "rare, highly evolved man who is not scared off by a pregnant woman."

"And," said Charlotte, as she maneuvered Natalie's pram around a cluster of Japanese tourists snapping photos of the Peter Pan statue, "he's gorgeous and rich to boot!"

I laughed. "Yeah. And you wanted to set me up with a damn ginger!"

Meg laughed. "I don't know why we didn't think of Geoffrey in the first place. I guess because we were thinking of him as your doctor."

Charlotte agreed. "I know! But it's so *obvious* now. Clearly you're perfect together."

Meg nodded. "He adores you . . . and you even *look* amazing together."

I had a second of uneasiness. "You look amazing together" was the kind of thing people always said to Dex and me, and look how we turned out. But I pushed the comparison out of my head and said with a chuckle, "Yeah. Well. Now I just have to find out whether he's good in bed. If so, this whole thing is a done deal!"

So a few nights later, I set about finding out. Our evening began at the Ivy, one of the most popular restaurants in London. The head chef was a friend of Geoffrey's, so we had a tasting menu prepared especially for us, followed by a magnificent slice of flourless chocolate cake for dessert, and some very expensive port for Geoffrey.

While we waited for the bill, Elle MacPherson and her husband sauntered in for a late reservation. They sat one table over from us. I caught Geoffrey inspecting her, and then glancing back at me as if comparing us feature by feature. When I asked him what he was thinking, he said, "You truly are prettier than she. I much prefer your eyes."

I smiled, and told him that he was more handsome than Elle's husband too. *Handsome* was the right word for Geoffrey's looks. He reached across the table and put his hand on mine. "What do you say we go back to my place?"

I leaned seductively across the table and said, "I thought you'd never ask."

We left the Ivy and returned to Geoffrey's flat, my first visit to his place. I pictured him living in a traditional town house, like Meg's, but instead it was a sleek, minimalist loft decorated with interesting sculptures, monochromatic paintings, and contemporary furniture. I thought of Marcus's sloppy apartment, relishing the absence of video games, fish tanks, dirty sneakers, and beer cans.

"I love your flat. It's *exactly* my taste," I said.

He looked pleased with the compliment, but confessed that he had used a decorator. "She's quite good. I don't have the patience for it."

I glanced around again, noticing a little red table and chairs covered with crayons, scraps of paper, and a half-assembled puzzle of a cartoon character I didn't recognize. "Max's play area?" I asked.

He nodded. "Although his stuff usually spreads from his bedroom to every corner of the flat."

I smiled.

"Could I see a picture of him?"

He pointed to his mantel. On it was a photo of Max walking along a pebbled beach, squinting up in the sunlight. "He's two and a half in that photo. It was taken at my cottage at St. Mawe's."

"What a beautiful little boy. He looks a bit like you," I said, glancing from the photo back to Geoffrey.

"He actually looks more like his mum," Geoffrey said. "But he got my nose. Poor chap."

I laughed and told him that I loved his nose. "It has character," I said, reminding myself of Rachel. She always talked of the character in someone's face, saying that small, pretty noses on men turned her off. I sort of knew what she meant. I liked the strong statement that Geoffrey's nose made.

He put his arms around me and kissed my nose. "And I love yours."

The exchange was one of those very early precursors to *I love you*. You know—when a couple goes around saying that they love certain things about each other. *I love your eyes. I love spending time with you. I love the way you make me feel.* And then out of the blue—a straight-up *I love you*.

Geoffrey offered me a drink. "Juice? Water? Tea?"

"Nothing, thank you," I said, shifting a Tic Tac from one side of my mouth to the other.

I watched him stride over to his wet bar and pour himself a glass of bourbon. Then he turned on his stereo. African music that reminded me of the background singers in Paul Simon's *Graceland* filled his flat. We sat on his modern leather couch, he draped his arm around my shoulder, and we talked. As I listened to his charming accent, punctuated by the atmospheric clinking of ice in his rock-cut tumbler, I tried to figure out who he reminded me of. I finally decided that he was a mature Hugh Grant, a straight Rupert Everett, and an English Dex Thaler. He was exactly what I would have ordered off a menu: an absolute gentleman—no part guy or boy.

And as always, he waited just long enough before he kissed me, not delving in too quickly. We were half-reclined, but every few minutes, Geoffrey would stop the tide, straighten up, sip his bourbon, and sort of silently gather himself. Then he'd kiss me again. The last such session concluded with him standing and issuing a formal invitation to his bedroom. I obliged, thinking how much I wanted to have sex. I missed it a lot. It had been my longest drought in at least a decade, maybe ever. More important, I wanted to take things to another level with Geoffrey. I wanted to infuse intensity and intimacy into our somewhat formal relationship.

Moments later I got my wish. Geoffrey and I were standing by his bed, undressing each other slowly. We faced each other, alternating pieces of clothing like a game of strip poker where you can't decide if you want to be the one naked and vulnerable or the one in control. I wanted everything, all at once. But I was patient, letting the suspense build. Finally we were both naked. For the first time, I was with a guy and feeling self-conscious about my body, but Geoffrey quickly dispelled any lingering worry I had that my pregnancy would turn him off. He kneeled in front of me and kissed my navel. The sensual gesture made me feel lush and beautiful.

Then he took my hand and led me over to his bed. The transition was smooth, like a scene in a movie where everything flows just right. After some quality foreplay, the somewhat awkward production of a condom, and Geoffrey's reassurance that sex was perfectly safe during this stage of my pregnancy, he entered me from behind, which was practical given my stomach issues, but nonetheless quite nice. Geoffrey lasted a very long time. A very, *very* long time. In addition to his impressive staying power, he was definitely less reserved between the sheets. At some point I stopped observing and just let myself go.

Then, in the sweaty aftermath, while listening to an a cappella tribal chorus of *tu lu lus,* he curled his body around mine, kissed the nape of my neck, and said, "You're amazing."

I thanked him and returned the compliment. He *was* amazing.

We both fell asleep and repeated everything in the middle of the night and then again in the very early morning. After our third time together, I looked into his eyes and saw something. Saw a look I recognized. It took a moment to place it, but when I did, I was certain of what it was. It was addiction. Geoffrey was addicted to me. And this fact alone felt like a very significant triumph in a season of heavy losses.

A short time later, I met Geoffrey's son, Max. Geoffrey went to pick him up at his mother's house in Wimbledon while I waited in his flat, resisting the strong temptation to snoop through his drawers. In the past, I wouldn't have been able to stop myself, but in the past, I think I *wanted* to find some fodder for a fight. A photo of another woman, an old love letter, a condom that predated me. Something to rile me up, fuel my jealous instincts, get my competitive juices flowing. I wasn't sure whether my pregnancy had matured me, mellowed me, or simply sapped my strength. But in any event, I was enjoying the ease of my new, tranquil relationship. I wasn't interested in barriers, only smooth sailing and a happy ending.

When Geoffrey and Max returned, I stood to greet them, my face stretched out in a huge smile. Max was adorable—cute enough to be in a Gap ad in his little navy overalls and fire-engine-red turtleneck. I felt my first wave of excitement over having sons instead of daughters.

"Hi, Max," I said. "How are you?"

"Fine," he said, avoiding eye contact as he got down on his knees and rolled his toy truck along the hardwood floor. I noticed that he had blue eyes, but lashes as dark as Geoffrey's.

I tried again to engage Max, lowering myself to the floor, where I sat back on my heels. "It's so nice to meet you."

Geoffrey mouthed, "He's shy," before gently prompting Max, "Can you tell Darcy it's nice to meet her too?"

"Nice to meet you, Darcy," Max mumbled, giving me a suspicious glance.

I suddenly wished that I had more experience talking to children. I struggled for a second and then said, "That's a great truck—lorry—you have there." I lowered myself further, sitting cross-legged.

Max glanced at me again, slightly longer this time. He gripped the cab of his truck and pushed it a few inches toward me. "It has big tires. See?" he said, almost as if he were testing me.

"It sure does. Some really, *really* big tires."

Max didn't seem too impressed with my answer. I

tried to dig up any scrap of information I had stored in my memory on trucks. "My brother, Jeremy, had a red lorry just like this one," I finally said. "Only the steering wheel was on the other side!"

"On this side?" he asked, pointing to the passenger side.

"Exactly!" I said, resting my hands gently over his and trying to remember the throaty sounds that Jeremy used to annoy me with when he played with his trucks. I cleared my throat, hoping that I could get them right.

"Vroom," I started, realizing that such a noise belonged more to a sports car. I tried again. *"Grrrrrrrr. Grrrrrrrrrrrr,"* I growled, easing the front wheels over my right knee. I felt slightly foolish, like a man must feel when prompted by his daughter to play with a Ken doll.

Fortunately, Max seemed to approve of my sound effects. I saw the corners of his mouth twitch into the smallest of smiles. This gave me confidence. So I made more motor noises, followed by the sound of an engine idling. *"Buh. Buh. Buh. Buh."* That had been one of Jeremy's favorites.

"Do it again," Max squealed.

I did, forgetting that Geoffrey was watching, perhaps even critiquing me.

"Grrrrrrrrrrrrrr," I said more robustly, as the rear wheels completed the bouncy climb over my leg. Then, I slipped off my socks, balled them up, and stuffed them into the cab of the truck. "Here. Some . . . cargo for you to drive . . . to the factory in . . . Liverpool," I said. It all sounded feasible, and I felt relieved that boy games might be easier and more fun than I had once thought.

"The factory in Liverpool," Max repeated happily.

And from that moment on, Max and I were fast friends. He didn't stop saying my name in his adorable English accent, leading me around by the hand, showing me his toys, even insisting that I take a tour of his bedroom. I basked in his acceptance, feeling thrilled that Geoffrey and I had cleared the final hurdle.

Later that night, after Geoffrey put Max to bed, he rejoined me in the bedroom, all smiles. "Well. You did it! He loves you."

"He does?" I asked, wondering if his father loved me too.

"Yes," Geoffrey said, grinning.

"Does that make you happy?" I asked, snuggling up to him.

"Over the moon," Geoffrey said as he smoothed my hair away from my face. "A million miles over the moon."

twenty-six

Geoffrey invited me to go to the Maldives with him and Max for Christmas, even offering to buy me a plane ticket.

I hesitated before asking, "Where are the Maldives exactly?"

He gave me the sort of affectionate gaze Dex had given me in the beginning whenever I confessed ignorance. "In the Indian Ocean, darling," he said, stroking my hair. "Think white-sand beaches, crystal-clear water, palm trees swaying in the breeze."

As tempting as a vacation in the sun was and as eager as I was to push things even further along with our relationship, I politely declined the invite, telling him that I thought he should spend quality father-son time with Max. The truth was, I didn't want to leave Ethan all by himself in London. He didn't have the extra cash to fly home for the holidays, and Sondrine was going to Paris for the week, so I think he was counting on spending time with me. Part of me was even excited that it would just be the two of us. I figured it might be our last hurrah—and our last flurry of sleepovers—before things really took off for each of us on the romance front.

I think Ethan felt the same way because on Christmas Eve morning, he went to Sondrine's to say good-bye and returned home in high spirits, suggesting that we go buy a tree together. "Better late than never!" he chirped. So we put on our warmest clothes and strolled over to the nursery near his house. Of course, the best trees were long gone, so we had to settle for a small fir with mangled branches and several bald patches around the base. As we dragged the tree home, it lost even more needles.

But between Ethan's ornament collection and a few pairs of my most sparkly chandelier earrings, our little tree became more than respectable. Ethan said the transformation reminded him of the tree in *A Charlie Brown Christmas.* I agreed and told him that it was the prettiest one I had ever owned, even though I had always made Dex buy grand eight-footers for our New York apartment.

We dimmed the lights in the living room and then switched on the white tree lights, spending the longest time just gazing at the tree, listening to Harry Connick Jr. croon Christmas carols, and drinking hot apple cider. After a long, cozy stretch of silence, Ethan turned to me and asked me if I had come up with any baby names.

I told him that I had a short list, but nothing concrete. I rattled some of them off. "Trevor. Flynn. Jonas. What do you think?"

"Honestly?"

I nodded.

"Hmm . . . Well, let's see . . . a guy named Trevor got caught stealing clothes from the dryers in my dorm at Stanford. Flynn sounds like *phlegm,* and Jonas conjures whales . . ."

I laughed, and said that I'd have to go back to the drawing board.

"Don't change on account of me."

I shook my head. "Nope. I want you to love my names."

He smiled and then suggested that we exchange our presents.

"Okay," I said, clapping excitedly.

He got up from the couch, sat cross-legged on the floor next to the tree, and handed me a large box wrapped with silver paper. "You first," he said.

I sat down beside him and carefully sliced open the paper the way my grandmother always did, as if to save it for future use. Then I opened the white box and the turquoise tissue paper inside to find a beautiful gray cashmere sweater coat from Brora, a store I had passed many times on the King's Road.

"It's not technically a maternity sweater, but it's quite roomy, and the lady at the store said that lots of pregnant women buy them," he explained.

I stood up and tried it on over my sweats. It fit perfectly, with room to grow, and the cashmere was positively luxurious. "I love it, Ethan!"

"See? It's belted," Ethan said earnestly. "So you can just loosen the belt as you get bigger . . . I thought you could wear it when you bring the boys home from the hospital. It will look really nice in photos."

"I will definitely do that," I said, loving that Ethan cared about photos. He was one of the few guys I knew who bothered to put them in albums. I looked at him and asked if he'd be there to take those photos.

"I wouldn't want to step on Geoffrey's toes . . . but I'd like to be there. It's your call."

"Geoffrey understands our friendship," I said, not knowing whether that was exactly true, but hoping that it was the case. It was the only way our relationship would work.

Ethan smiled and said, "There's another gift under

there." He pointed to a white envelope. On it, he had written, "To Darcy, Baby A and Baby B." Inside was a small square of blue paper. I studied it, puzzled. "What is it?"

"It's a paint swatch," he said. "I want to paint your room that color. For the nursery. I was going to just surprise you and do it, but then I worried that blue was too obvious for you. Would you rather do something more . . . unexpected?"

"I *love* this shade of blue," I said, feeling all warm inside and thrilled that Ethan wanted me to stay with him even after the babies arrived. I had been wanting to broach the subject for weeks, and now I had my answer. I threw my arms around his neck and kissed his cheek.

Ethan went on to tell me that he had measured a crib at Peter Jones and had determined that two would fit along the long wall. And that we could put a pad on top of that bookshelf and use it as a changing table.

I grinned and told him it was an excellent plan. "Now open your gift!" I said, handing him his package.

He opened it with exuberance, tearing off the paper, tossing it aside, and holding up the leather messenger bag I had found to replace his tattered nylon one. My only splurge in weeks. I could tell he loved it, because he immediately went to his room and brought out his old bag, unloading his papers and folders and transferring them to his new one. He swung it over his shoulder, then adjusted the strap slightly. "It's awesome," he said. "I look like a real novelist now."

He had begun to make a lot of comments like this lately. I could tell he felt anxious about the progress—or lack of progress—he was making on his book.

"Still having writer's block?" I asked sympathetically.

"Yeah. I feel like Snoopy stuck on that one line: 'It was a dark and stormy night.'"

I laughed and reassured him that surely all great authors

struggled with occasional writer's block, and that I knew he'd make some good headway in the new year.

"Thanks, Darce. I appreciate that," he said sincerely.

Then we curled up under a big blanket on the couch and watched a video of *It's a Wonderful Life*. Right around the part where the uncle accidentally gives the envelope of money to Mr. Potter, Ethan hit the pause button and asked if he could fast-forward to the end. "I can't stand this part. It's too frustrating."

I agreed. As we watched the grim scenes blur forward, I couldn't help thinking about my own life—specifically the rift with my mother. She had not contacted me once since I had sent her the note from London. I firmly believed that the ball was in her court, but by the end of the movie, as we watched the happy family scene where George Bailey's youngest daughter says, "Every time a bell rings an angel gets his wings," I decided to let go of my pride and call home.

Ethan was supportive of the idea, so I nervously dialed up my home in Indy. As the phone rang, I almost hung up, but grabbed Ethan's hand instead. My mom answered after five or six rings.

"Hi, Mom," I said, feeling scared and small.

She said my name icily and then silence floated over the wires. My mother was a champion grudge holder. I thought of my own grudge against Rachel, figuring that you didn't get these things from strangers.

"Did I interrupt dinner?" I asked.

"Not really. We were just finishing. Jeremy and Lauren are here."

"Oh," I said. "How are their wedding plans coming?"

"Just fine."

I waited for her to ask how I was, whether I was still in London. When she didn't, I offered it up awkwardly. "I'm still here in London. . . . You got my note, right?"

She said that she already knew I was in London, even before receiving the note, as she had run into Annalise's mother at the mall. She added that it had been embarrassing to hear of my whereabouts from someone else, which I thought was a petty point to raise given the fact that I had written her a note, and that I had been the one to phone her first. But I didn't let this deter me from telling her how sorry I was for disappointing her. I told her that it was understandable how shocked she had been upon my news. That no mother would want her daughter to get pregnant so fast on the heels of a broken engagement to another man. I also told her that she was right about Marcus. "He was a big jerk, Mom. I'm not with him at all anymore. I see now that you just wanted what was best for me."

Ethan squeezed my hand and nodded, as if to say, "Keep going. You're doing great."

I swallowed, took a deep breath, and said, "So anyway, I had an ultrasound here in London . . . and I found out what I'm having."

"A girl?"

"No. Not a girl. I thought it would be a girl too. But it's not a girl."

"So a boy then? That's great," she said emotionlessly.

"Well, yes. But . . . it's actually . . . *two* boys. I'm having twins. Identical twin boys! Isn't that just the *most craziest* thing ever?"

In my mind, I could hear Rachel instructing me that it's either "the craziest" or "the most crazy"—not "the most craziest." But this seemed an appropriate time to break the grammar rule. To me, having twin boys *was* the *most craziest*. "Can you believe that, Mom?"

I braced myself for the worst, but it didn't hurt any less when I got just that. She did not congratulate me. She did not ask about names. She did not ask how I was feeling.

She did not say that she was happy for me. She only asked how in the world I was going to manage twins. Tears stung my eyes as I calmly reassured her that I intended to make things work in London. I told her that I was looking for a job and was sure something would turn up. I told her of our plans to fix up a nursery in Ethan's flat, smiling at him gratefully. I told her how much I loved London, rain and all. Then I wished her a merry Christmas and told her that I loved her. I told her to tell my dad and Jeremy, and even Lauren, that I loved them, and that I'd be sure to call again soon. She said she loved me, too, but she said so briskly, with no warmth at all.

When I hung up, I lowered my head into my hands and cried. Ethan stroked my hair and said softly, "You did good, Darce. You did the right thing by calling her. I'm proud of you."

"I shouldn't have called. She was *awful!*"

"Yes. You should have. . . . Don't let her get you down. You can only control your own actions. Not other people's reactions."

I blew my nose and said, "I can't help feeling this way. She's my *mother.*"

"Parents often let you down," he said. "You'll just have to do a better job being a mother to your boys. I know you will."

"How do you know that?"

"Because, Darce, you've shown your true colors lately."

I blew my nose again. "What do you mean by 'true colors'?"

"I mean . . . you are a good person." Ethan touched my arm gently. "A strong person. And you're going to make a wonderful mother."

Over the years, I had received endless compliments and ego-stroking words from countless men. *You're beautiful. You're sexy. You're incredible. I want you. Marry me.* But this sentiment from Ethan was the nicest thing I had ever heard from a man. I put my head on his shoulder, basking in it.

"I'm going to try, Ethan. I'm really going to try."

The next morning Ethan and I awoke and sleepily wished each other "Merry Christmas."

"What are we going to do today?" I asked him.

"We're gonna chef it up," Ethan answered joyously.

We had gone grocery-shopping two days earlier, and his small English refrigerator was packed to the gills with all of our ingredients.

"What else?"

"Cooking Christmas dinner will take most of the day," he said.

I asked if he wished we had waited to open our gifts. I knew that Christmas wasn't about presents, but there is always a bit of a letdown when that part of the holidays has passed. Although, for once, I had enjoyed giving more than receiving.

Ethan said he preferred opening gifts on Christmas Eve, and then said, "I could give you something else though . . ."

I looked at him, and I think my face registered surprise. Was it my imagination or was his tone suggestive? Was Ethan coming on to me? Before I could answer, he continued innocently, "How about a poem?"

"Oh. Yeah. Sure," I said, feeling relieved that I hadn't responded inappropriately and embarrassed myself. "What's the title of this poem?"

He thought for a second and then said, " 'Hot Mama.' "

I smiled and told him to go on, remembering his funny impromptu rhymes in high school. He cleared his throat and started rapping, inserting little rhythmic sputters and head bobbing along the way:

You're one hot mama in your sexy gown.
The cutest little preggers girl in town.
You envisioned buying girly toys.
But instead you're having two bouncing boys.
You took the news in stride and did not cry or
    pout.
'Cause you know what motherhood's really
    about.
And no one will make a finer mutha.
Your baby is lucky and so is his brutha!

We both cracked up. Then he threw one arm over me and hugged me just as one of my babies delivered a sharp kick.

Ethan's face lit up.

I laughed. "You felt that?"

"Yeah. Wow."

"He got you."

"He sure did," Ethan murmured. He rested his hand on my stomach and gently pushed.

One baby responded with an impressive jolt. Ethan chuckled. "That's wild. I still can't believe you have two babies in there!"

"Tell me about it," I said. "I feel like I'm running out of room. It's starting to get really tight."

"Does it hurt?"

"Sort of. It's just this weird pressure down there. And I'm starting to get this annoying back pain."

Ethan asked me if I wanted a massage.

"Are your back massages as good as your foot massages?"

"Better," he said.

"Hell yeah, then," I said, as I rolled onto my side.

Ethan rubbed his hands together. Then he slid my nightgown up, exposing my bare back and apple-green thong. I felt my heart race with the realization that Ethan was seeing me essentially naked for the first time. I held my breath as he pressed his warm palms against the middle of my back and slowly worked upward between my shoulder blades. Then he firmly massaged my shoulders. "Is this too hard?" he asked softly.

"Nooo. It's awesome," I moaned, feeling all the tightness and tension drain from my body. As he kept massaging, I couldn't stop imagining sex with Ethan. I tried to dismiss the thought, remind myself that it would ruin our friendship, to say nothing of what it would do to our respective relationships—relationships that were actually working. No matter what, I didn't want to be a cheater ever again. I wondered if any such thoughts were crossing Ethan's mind as his hands drifted down my back, his thumbs kneading my muscles along the way. He spent a lot of time in the small of my back and then went even lower to the top edge of my thong, just over my tailbone. His touch became gentler as his hands swept out over my hips. He lingered there and then stilled, signaling the end of the massage.

"There," he said, patting my hips twice.

I turned around to face him, feeling oddly breathless. "Thanks. That was awesome."

He didn't respond, just looked at me with those clear, blue eyes. He was feeling something too. I was almost sure of it. I think I even saw his chest rising and falling under his T-shirt, as if he, too, were short of breath.

Then, after a long, strange moment, just as I thought he was poised to utter something meaningful, maybe even kiss me, he took a deep breath, exhaled loudly, and said, "Well, what do you say we hit the kitchen?"

Ethan and I spent most of the day in our pajamas, preparing our Christmas dinner. I played the role of sous-chef, diligently taking his instructions. I chopped and peeled vegetables while Ethan focused on the turkey and fancier trimmings. Other than burning my finger in the goose fat when I removed the parsnips from the oven, everything went remarkably smoothly. Almost like a cooking show, Ethan bragged at one point.

Then, just as it was getting dark outside, I took a shower. Under the hot water, I allowed myself to revisit his massage that morning, marveling that Ethan could make me feel the way he had. I found myself speculating about what he had been thinking. When I got out of the shower, I even craned to check out my back in the mirror, feeling relieved to see that my ass was still rather small and— knock on wood—stretch-mark and cellulite-free. I felt a wave of guilt and confusion. Was I grateful to have a nice ass for Geoffrey's sake, Ethan's, or my own? As I changed into a fresh pair of sweats, I told myself that I was being crazy, likely even imagining the erotic component of the whole massage.

When I returned to the living room, I discovered that Ethan had moved the kitchen table in front of the tree, and set it with his best dishes and an ivory damask tablecloth.

"How pretty," I said, kissing his cheek and feeling relief that I felt nothing more than affection for a good friend.

He smiled, adjusted the volume on his classical music, and pulled out my chair for me. "Let's feast."

And what a feast it was. Restaurant-worthy, for sure. We had a smoked-salmon salad with mustard and dill dressing as a starter, followed by our main course: a roast turkey seasoned with pink peppercorns, sage, and lemon. Our side dishes were roasted potatoes, pan-fried brussels sprouts with chestnuts, orange-glazed carrots, spiced red cabbage with apples, and parsnips seasoned with sea salt. And for dessert we had a delightful strawberry macaroon tart that Ethan had picked up from Maison Blanc, a bakery on Kensington Church Street.

We ate and ate until we literally couldn't take another bite, applauding our efforts along the way. Afterward, we rolled our way over to the couch, where we cozied up under a blanket in our standard head-to-feet position and watched the candles burn down to their nubs. Just as we were nodding off to sleep, the phone rang and jarred us awake. I silently hoped that it wasn't Sondrine—or Geoffrey for that matter. They had both already called earlier in the day, and I saw no reason why further conversation was necessary.

"You wanna get that?" I asked Ethan.

"Not really," he mumbled, but he picked up the phone and said hello.

He shot me a furtive glance and then said, with a strained expression, "Hi, there, Rachel."

I sat numbly next to him as I listened to him wish her a merry Christmas. He gave me another concerned look. I smiled to indicate that I was just fine. Then I went back to his bedroom and curled up under the covers. I tried to put Rachel out of my mind, but clearly that was impossible. I wondered if she was calling from Indiana. Whether Dex had come home with her. Seconds later Ethan appeared in the doorway. His face was solemn.

"Is it Rachel?" I asked.

"Yeah."

"Are you off?"

"No, not yet . . . I just wanted to check on you . . ."

"I'm fine," I said, reburying my face in the covers.

"Okay . . . I also wanted to ask you . . . can I tell her about your twins? She's asking about you . . ."

"It's none of her business," I snapped. "I don't want her to know anything about my new life."

Ethan nodded. "I respect that. I won't tell her anything."

I thought for a beat and then peered up at him. "Oh, go ahead. It makes no difference to me."

"Are you sure?"

"Yeah. Whatever."

Ethan nodded, closed the door, and then returned to the living room. I suddenly felt overcome with grief and had to fight back tears. Why was I so upset? Hadn't I moved beyond Rachel's betrayal? I had a new boyfriend, new girlfriends, a new best friend in Ethan, and two babies on the way. And I was sure that I would find a job in the new year. I was doing fine. So why was I sad? I thought for a few minutes, dug down to a very deep place, and came up with an answer that I didn't like. I didn't want to admit it to myself, but I knew that it had something to do with missing Rachel.

Against my better judgment, I got out of bed, opened the door, and strained to hear Ethan's end of the conversation. He was talking in a low voice, but I heard some snippets. "Twins . . . Boys. Identical boys. Amazing . . . Believe it or not, yes . . . Really great . . . She's really changed . . . Like a different person . . . Yeah. Her doctor [laughter]. Yeah, she switched doctors, of course . . . Uh-huh, good for her, you know? . . . So what about you and Dex? . . . Sure, yeah. That makes sense . . ." Then came a long silence. And finally, a bone-chilling word: *Congratulations.*

I could only think of one thing he could be congratulating her on.

Holy shit! Dex and Rachel got engaged! How could they have gotten engaged so quickly? I wanted to hear more, but I forced myself to close the door and crawl back under the covers. Then I repeated over and over: *I don't care about Rachel and Dex. I've moved on.* By the time Ethan returned to his bedroom, I half-believed my pep talk and, miraculously, was able to resist asking any questions about his conversation. I could tell Ethan was amazed by my restraint. He rewarded me with a kiss on my forehead and a gentle gaze. Then he told me to stay in bed. "I'll clean up. You stay here and rest."

I nodded, feeling drained and weary. "Thanks, Ethan."

"Thank *you*, Darcy."

"For what?" I asked.

He thought for a second and then said, "For a very memorable Christmas."

I gave him a brave smile and waited for him to leave before weeping silently into my pillow.

twenty-seven

Ethan, Sondrine, Geoffrey, and I did the whole double-dating thing for the first time on New Year's Eve. Geoffrey made reservations for us at Gordon Ramsey, the posh, Michelin-starred restaurant at Sloane Square, which was the perfect venue for a special occasion. Throughout the meal, we all praised the New French cuisine. Geoffrey called it "sublime" and Sondrine referred to it as a "symphony of flavors." I thought they both sounded a bit pretentious, although it was a fair description of my pot-roasted belly of West Country pork with aubergine caviar, and of Ethan's roast Scottish gray-legged partridge with braised red cabbage—which I tasted more than once.

Unfortunately, the interpersonal dynamic did not live up to the food. I think the measure of success of any double date is how well the women get along, and Sondrine and I just did not jell. On the surface, everything was pleasant enough. She was extremely nice to me and very easy to talk to, but she came across as condescending. It was almost as if she thought I needed reassurance on every front. She must have said four times, "You hardly look pregnant at all," which was no longer the case. I actually looked quite pregnant, and was comfortable with my new shape. And every time her career as a curator came up, she'd turn to me and purr, "I'm sure something will turn up for you very, very soon!"

I also had the distinct sense that Ethan had told her what a sybarite I had been in my old life, as she incessantly questioned me on my favorite clubs, designers, wines, and hotels. Of course, I still enjoyed those topics, but I would have appreciated at least a passing mention of my unborn sons.

Ethan and Geoffrey's interaction, too, seemed strained beneath a friendly exterior. If I had to bet on it, I would have said that Ethan thought Geoffrey was overly reserved and colorless, and I think Geoffrey was just generally annoyed by my relationship with Ethan, and specifically our unconventional sleeping arrangement. It had been the root of our first argument the night before. Somehow it had come up that I had slept in Ethan's bed over the holidays, and Geoffrey had grown quiet, almost sullen. After I coaxed it out of him, he told me that he thought it was "more than a bit odd" to sleep in a bed with a male friend. I reassured him that my relationship with Ethan was 100 percent platonic, feeling relieved that I could say so honestly. But I could tell he still felt somewhat threatened. This was evident at dinner whenever I tasted Ethan's food. After my third bite, Geoffrey aggressively offered me a taste of his entrée, and when I declined, he seemed a bit miffed. As if it were my fault that I didn't like the sound of filet of monkfish wrapped in Parma ham.

But the four of us made it through dinner, and then to Annabel's, an exclusive club on Berkeley Square, where we were joined by a dozen or so of Geoffrey's upper-crust pals. Sondrine was in her element amid the elegant crowd, and she made a point to talk to an array of strangers, mostly men. I knew what she was doing, because I had done it myself many times; she was showing Ethan that she was desired by other men. At one point, when she was engrossed in conversation with a tuxedoed gentleman who looked like a young Frank Sinatra, I asked Ethan if he was at all bothered. He gave me a confused look and then said, "Why? Because she's talking to that guy?"

I nodded.

He glanced at Sondrine, his face a mask of indifference. "Nah. Not at all," he said with a shrug.

I couldn't help feeling pleased with his answer. I wanted him to be happy, just not head over heels in love, and it seemed clear that that wasn't the case.

Geoffrey, on the other hand, *did* seem smitten. He introduced me proudly to all of his friends. He repeatedly pulled me aside to ask how I was feeling and if he could get me anything. And just before midnight, with the crowd counting down the seconds to the new year, he gave me a passionate kiss, whirled me around a full turn, and shouted above the din, "Happy New Year, *darling!*"

"Happy New Year, Geoffrey!" I said, feeling flushed and happy to be ushering in a monumental year with my dapper English beau. But I couldn't help feeling distracted, wondering what Ethan and Sondrine were up to. I glanced around the room and spotted them lounging on a sofa, holding hands, while he ordered more drinks from a waiter. As I watched them together, I silently willed him to look over at me. When he finally did, I discreetly blew him a friendly kiss. He grinned and blew one back, and I suddenly had an overwhelming urge to be next to him, to exchange our first words of the new year. I wanted to thank him for everything, for being such a good friend when I needed one the most.

At that very second, Geoffrey whispered in my ear, "I'm falling in love with you, Darcy."

I felt goose bumps rise all over my arms. Geoffrey's words were the answer to all of my wishes. But as I tried to say the words back—that I was falling in love too—I caught another glimpse of Ethan, and I couldn't get them out of my throat.

Much later that night, after we had said good-bye to Ethan and Sondrine, I was in Geoffrey's bed making love to him. I sensed that he wasn't entirely in the moment.

"Are you worried about the babies?" I finally asked. "Are you sure this is still safe?"

"Yes. Perfectly safe," he breathed. "I just worry anyway."

Proving that this was the case, he told me he would rather just cuddle anyway. "If that's okay with you?"

I told him it was fine with me, but I was a bit worried too. Then after a long, silent stretch, he said the words outright. "I love you, Darcy." His breath was warm in my ear, and I could feel the little hairs on my neck standing at attention. This time, I whispered that I loved him too. Then, I silently listed all of the reasons: I loved him for his gentleness. I loved him for being an amazing catch yet still vulnerable enough to be insecure. But most of all, I loved him for loving me.

As the winter in London dragged on and my due date neared, Geoffrey doted on me more and more. It was as if he had consulted every article ever written on how to treat a pregnant woman. He took me to the most fabulous restaurants: Mirabelle, Assagi, and Petrus. He bought me lavish gifts—Jo Malone bath oils, a Valentino clutch, lingerie from Agent Provocateur—which he'd leave for me on his bed, pretending to be just as surprised as I when I'd emerge from the bathroom to discover them. He reassured me that I was only becoming more beautiful with every passing day, insisting that he could not see the zits (or "spots" as he called them) that were frequenting my nose and chin. All the while, he would talk of our future. He promised to take me to see the exotic places he had traveled: Botswana, Budapest, Bora Bora. He promised me a wonderful life and made me feel like a lucky woman. A saved woman.

Yet as I lay next to him every night, I couldn't shake the feeling that something was very wrong. That no matter how perfect my life was becoming, something was missing. I suspected that it had something to do with my dire financial situation. I had never had such money worries in my life. Even in college, and my early days in New York, before I found my bartending job, all I'd had to do was phone my father and he'd help me out, wire me a few hundred dollars or send me a fresh credit card. Obviously, calling my dad was out of the question this time, so I finally swallowed my pride and confessed my situation to Geoffrey. My voice cracked with shame as I told him how I had blown my savings on a new wardrobe.

"Don't worry about money, darling," he said. "I can take care of you."

"I don't want you to have to do that," I said, unable to make eye contact.

"But I *want* to."

"That is so nice. Thank you," I said, my face growing hot. I knew I had to accept his help, but it wasn't easy. I told him I missed having a job, feeling completely independent.

He reassured me that I'd find a wonderful career after the babies were born. "You're bright, talented, beautiful.

When the babies are six months old, you can begin your search again. I can put you in touch with so many people . . . And in the meantime, I'm here for you."

I smiled and thanked him again. I told myself that I wasn't using Geoffrey. I loved him, and if you love someone, you can't use them. Not really. Besides, I knew I would pay him back someday, somehow.

I went to sleep that night feeling tremendously relieved to have had the difficult conversation, relieved that I had a safety net when my last pound was spent. My peace of mind was short-lived, however, and the pit in my stomach returned full force just days later.

This time, I confessed my misgivings to Charlotte and Meg over tea at Charlotte's flat. We were sitting at her small kitchen table, watching Natalie ignore her vast array of toys in favor of pots and pans that she had scattered all over the kitchen. I kept picturing how much more chaos *two* Natalies could inflict. "I just don't know what's wrong with me. Something's just *plaguing* me."

Charlotte nodded. "You're just feeling general anxiety over childbirth and motherhood. The whole scary journey ahead. And it can't help watching this!" She pointed at Natalie, rolled her eyes, and laughed.

"That has to be it," Meg agreed. She had just recently announced the wonderful news that she, too, was pregnant. But she was still in her very early weeks, with her own set of worries about miscarrying. "There's always something to fret about," she said.

"Hmm," Charlotte agreed. "The responsibility that is barreling toward you is bound to make you feel a bit insecure."

"Maybe you guys are right," I said, telling them about my crazy nightmares about losing or misplacing one, sometimes both, of my babies. I also dreamed about SIDS, kidnappings, *Sophie's Choice,* deadly fires, cleft palates, and missing thumbs, but the losing-a-baby motif was the most common. In one dream, I actually shrugged and said to Ethan, "Oh, well. Still got one left. And this one looks just like the lost one anyway."

"It's totally normal to have those dreams," Charlotte said. "I know I did. They'll go away . . . Just throw your-self into preparing for motherhood. You'll feel more con-fident that way."

I took her advice over the next few weeks, calling her and Annalise often to ask for advice. I also read articles and books on parenting philosophies, breast-feeding, and scheduling. And I signed up for a birthing class, where I learned everything from how to breathe during labor to how to bathe my babies.

But despite all of the assurances given to me and all of my preparation for motherhood, I *still* felt unsettled. I honestly had no idea what it was, but my mind kept drift-ing to Ethan. I barely saw him at all anymore. Every time I went to his flat to pick up clothing, he was gone, either out working or at Sondrine's. Or worse, I'd hear her husky laughter emanating from his bedroom. I wasn't jealous, because I was very happy in my own relationship. It was more just a pang of missing the way things used to be. I suppose that's the way you always feel when a close friend develops a romantic relationship that threatens to impact your friendship—or at least the everyday nature of it. I vaguely remembered feeling the same way when Rachel spent all of her time with her law school boyfriend, Nate. I reassured myself that although things would change in the upcoming year, Ethan and I would always remain close. Much closer than we'd ever been before my move to Lon-don. We just had to make the effort to see each other. So after a week of not connecting, I phoned his mobile and arranged a dinner alone.

"You seem down," Ethan said over our Thai takeaway back at his flat.

"Maybe a little," I said. "I think it's all the changes on the horizon. Meg and Charlotte said it's normal to feel apprehensive."

He nodded as he transferred our dinner from Styrofoam containers onto plates. "Yeah. Your life *is* about to change dramatically." Then he thought for a second and said, "Maybe it's also your unresolved conflict with your mother?"

"No," I said, blowing on my Pad Thai. "And I don't think it's Rachel, either, in case that's what you're thinking." I looked at him, expecting him to say something more about her. He still had not told me—nor had I asked—about their conversation on Christmas Day. Which was fine by me. I didn't want the confirmation of her engagement to upset the delicate balance in my life. I looked up at him and said, "I don't know. I can't put my finger on exactly what I'm feeling. Something just isn't quite right."

He suggested that perhaps I needed to nest. "You're prepared mentally . . . but now you have to get there physically." He took a sip of beer. "I think we need to get the nursery set up. I was thinking that I'd paint this weekend."

I smiled, thrilled that he still wanted us, but then hesitated and said, "What about Geoffrey?"

"What about him?"

"Well, I think he might want me to move in with him," I said. "He's been talking about finding a bigger flat," I said nervously, as if I were somehow betraying Ethan by moving out. We had come a long way since my frantic phone calls from New York when I had to practically beg to stay with him for a few weeks.

Ethan jabbed at a green pepper with one chopstick. "Is

that what you want? To live with Geoffrey?" he asked in a judgmental tone.

"Why do you say it like that?"

"I'm not . . . I mean . . . I just didn't know you two were *that* serious," Ethan said. "It seems like it's really happening fast."

I felt myself getting defensive as I told him yes, we were getting quite serious and that Geoffrey was everything I was looking for.

"As long as you're happy," Ethan said. "That's all I want for you."

"I *am* happy."

Ethan looked pensive as he took a bite of brown rice. He chewed, swallowed, sipped his beer, and then said, "Well, I still think we should go ahead and paint your room . . . just in case."

"Just in case Geoffrey and I break up?"

"No. I didn't mean that. I just meant . . . well . . . just in case it takes longer than expected for you and Geoffrey to feel ready to live together. In any event, I want the boys to have a room here too."

"That is *so* sweet, Ethan. You're such a good friend," I said.

So that weekend, while Geoffrey was on call, Ethan painted the nursery walls blue, touched up the bookcase with a coat of fresh white paint, and assembled the spindle cribs I had charged a few weeks earlier. Meanwhile, Meg and Charlotte took me shopping for more supplies. I stuck to the essentials—nappies, wipes, bottles, bibs, onesies, a changing pad, and a double stroller—and charged the items on my last remaining credit card. But as I paid, Meg and Charlotte sneaked off and surprised me by purchasing some gorgeous and way too expensive blue toile crib bedding and a matching curtain for the small nursery window.

"We saw you admiring it," Meg said.

"Thank you, guys, *so* much," I said, accepting the gift. It was the kind of thing Rachel always did for me—generosity I had taken for granted in my selfish past.

"You're *so* welcome," they said, looking as happy as I felt.

I told them how lucky I felt to have such close friends in London.

Later that night, as Ethan and I put the finishing touches on the nursery, I thanked him again too.

He smiled and said, "You feel better now?"

"Yeah," I said. "I do."

He rested his arm on the edge of Baby A's crib. "See? It was nothing that a little shopping spree couldn't cure."

I laughed, and said that he was right. "Yeah. Nothing that a little blue toile couldn't fix."

But as I packed my bag for Geoffrey's, I had a strong suspicion that things weren't that simple.

twenty-eight

I had my epiphany on Valentine's Day.

It was my idea to go on another double date with Ethan and Sondrine. Although our first effort wasn't an overwhelming success, I wanted to give it another try. Geoffrey protested a bit, saying that he preferred to be alone with me. I told him that where I came from, Valentine's was a cheesy, amateur nonevent and therefore we had two options: blow it off altogether and order a pizza, or share the evening with another couple. I told him I wasn't going to be one of those silly couples sitting alone at a table, all dressed up and eagerly ordering off a jacked-up, prix-fixe menu, and that going to dinner with another couple would temper the whole cheese factor. He reluctantly saw my point and made reservations for four at Daphne's, an Italian restaurant in South Kensington.

On the evening of the fourteenth, Geoffrey and I drove to the restaurant, arriving right on time. Sondrine and Ethan showed up nearly thirty minutes late with that telltale "I just had sex" look about them: messy hair, flushed cheeks, flustered expressions and all. Of course, I couldn't resist rubbing it in to the always-punctual Ethan, asking, "What were you two up to that you couldn't get here on time?"

Sondrine smirked, looking exceedingly pleased with herself, and Ethan mumbled guiltily, "Bad traffic. I'm really sorry, guys."

I raised my eyebrows and said, "Uh-huh. *Sure* it was the traffic," while Geoffrey found the maître d' and told him our party was "finally present." On the way to our table we made small talk—which with two women always includes some obligatory compliments. I praised Sondrine's Chanel ballet flats, and she told me for the zillionth time how marvelous I looked. Then she touched my stomach without asking permission first (something I did *not* appreciate from anyone other than Ethan or Geoffrey) and said, in an exaggerated tone, "This is *so* exciting!" Her words did not sound sincere. Perhaps because I remembered issuing similar statements to Annalise during her pregnancy while thinking, *Better you than me, sister.*

"How much longer do you have?" Sondrine asked.

"Geoffrey says term for twins is about thirty-six or thirty-seven weeks, so I guess I have about six weeks to go."

Geoffrey looked up from the wine list and gazed adoringly at me. He found my hand under the table and laced his fingers with mine. "We can barely stand the suspense," he said.

I saw a tightening in Ethan's face—a look he gets when he's upset where his mouth sort of twitches. I wondered what he was thinking. Just in case he felt excluded by Geoffrey's *we,* I said to Sondrine, "Yeah. It's really starting to feel real now. Especially when Ethan and I set up the nursery last weekend. It's adorable. Have you seen it yet?"

"No," she said stiffly, glancing at Ethan. Now it was her turn to be annoyed. I guess I could empathize with her. If I were dating a guy, I wouldn't want his female friend and her twins aboard in the flat. So she did what I would have done—she elicited disapproval from Geoffrey, her ally apparent. "Have you seen the room yet?" she asked him.

The tactic worked, because Geoffrey's lips fell into a sharp line. Then he said, "No. I haven't seen it yet . . . I've been really busy at work . . . and looking at flats. I'm trying to find something with a bit more room for us."

Sondrine lit up. "You and Darcy are moving in together?"

Geoffrey moved our clasped hands to the top of the table and gave me a look, the English equivalent of "aw shucks," while I said, "Yeah. We're thinking about moving in together."

"More than thinking about it, darling. . . . We're actively pursuing it, aren't we?"

"Right," I said. "That's the plan."

An awkward silence befell the table where we all just sort of smiled at each other and then looked down at our menus with seeming concentration. A moment later the waiter appeared to take our orders. As it turned out, we all wanted the filet mignon, medium rare. Sondrine and Geoffrey seemed to think that ordering four identical steaks was some sort of breach of etiquette so they changed their orders at the last second, Sondrine opting for the sea bass and Geoffrey going for the rack of lamb.

Throughout dinner, we all made a great effort to keep the conversation lively, but as on New Year's Eve, there was an unmistakable tension, a lot of fake smiles. Bottom line, nobody was having a particularly good time, and I had the feeling that it would be our last double date.

Then, right before our desserts arrived, I excused my-

self, announcing that it was the longest I had held my pee
in nearly two weeks. To my dismay, Sondrine said that
she would join me. We weaved our way through the maze
of overdressed couples to the bathroom, where she tried
to make interstall small talk with me, saying something
about what a cute couple Geoffrey and I made. I couldn't
bring myself to reciprocate the comment, so I just thanked
her instead. That's when I turned to flush and saw a bright
red ribbon in the water below. For one brief second, I was
confused. Then it registered. I was bleeding. I panicked and
wiped. Another smear of blood appeared on the white
tissue.

The next few minutes were hazy, but I remember gasp-
ing so loudly that Sondrine asked if I was okay. I remember saying no, I wasn't okay. And I remember feeling my
heart thudding in my ears, as I crumbled onto the edge of
the cold, enamel toilet seat.

"What's wrong, Darcy?" Sondrine asked over the sound
of flushing, an automatic hand dryer, and happy female
chatter.

I managed to say, "I'm bleeding." Then I remember
just sitting there in my stall with my underwear down at
my ankles, holding my legs together, as if the babies would
fall out otherwise. All the while, I visualized the passages
I had skimmed over in my pregnancy books. I could see
the words on the page: phrases such as "placenta previa"
and "premature rupture of the membranes" and even the
horrifying acronym CLIMB, which stood for "Center for
Loss in Multiple Birth." I couldn't catch my breath, let
alone stand and leave the bathroom.

Some minutes later I heard more commotion as Sondrine announced that a man was entering the restroom.
Then I heard Geoffrey's voice outside the stall and the
sound of his knuckles rapping hard against the metal door.
Somehow I managed to stand, pull up my pants, and swing

open the door. I saw Sondrine hovering at Geoffrey's side, and a few other women standing near the sinks, mouths agape.

"Sweetheart, what is it?" he asked me.

"There's blood," I said, feeling faint at the sound of the word.

"How much blood?" he asked, his brow furrowed.

I turned and pointed downward. The strands of red were dissipating, turning the water a frightening pink hue.

Geoffrey glanced down and then spoke with measured calm. He told me that third-trimester bleeding, particularly with multiples, was not uncommon. He said that everything was going to be fine, but that I needed to go to the hospital.

"Right now?" I said.

"Yes. Ethan's getting my car now."

"So this is really bad, right?" I asked. "You're scared, aren't you?"

"No, I'm not scared, sweetheart," he said.

"Could I be losing my babies?"

"No."

"Are you sure?"

I knew he couldn't possibly be sure of such a thing, but felt grateful when he said yes anyway.

"If I delivered now, would they live?"

He told me that it wouldn't come to that, but that if I had to deliver the babies, I was far enough along that they would survive. "Everything's going to be just fine," he kept repeating as he put one arm around me, the other hand at my bent elbow, and guided me out of the bathroom, through the dining room, and past our four plates of beautiful desserts. At the front door, Geoffrey handed the maître d' his credit card and said, "We're having a small emergency. I'm very sorry. I'll send someone to collect my card later."

The drive to the hospital was a blur, but I remember catching glimpses of Ethan's pale, worried face in the rearview mirror. I also remember Geoffrey repeating that everything was going to be fine, just fine. And most of all, I remember thinking that if he turned out to be wrong, if things weren't fine in the end, I wouldn't be able to bear the grief.

When we arrived at the hospital, Geoffrey and I went immediately to a small room on the labor and delivery wing, where a nurse handed me a hospital gown and instructed me to change and wait for my doctor to arrive. Mr. Smith came in minutes later, consulting with Geoffrey for a moment before examining me. He felt inside me with a look of intense concentration. Geoffrey hovered by my side.

"What?" I asked. "What's happening?"

Mr. Smith told me that although I was slightly effaced, my cervix was still closed. Geoffrey looked relieved, but I asked Mr. Smith the question anyway, "Does that mean the babies are okay?"

"Yes. But we're going to hook you up to the fetal monitor just to be absolutely sure," he said, and then motioned toward the nurse. I shivered as she slid my hospital gown up and strapped three monitors around my stomach. She told me one monitor would measure contractions, and the other two would trace the babies' heartbeats. I held on to the cold bar next to my bed and kept asking her if she could hear them.

Geoffrey told me to be patient, that the babies were still small and that sometimes it takes a moment to locate them. I waited, still imagining the worst. Finally, a joyous galloping sound filled the room. Then another. Two heartbeats. Two *distinct* heartbeats.

"So they're both still living?" I asked, my voice trembling.

"Yes, darling." Geoffrey's face broke into a smile. "They're both fine."

In that moment of relief, something in my mind clicked, and I realized what had been troubling me in recent days. It was all so clear. Maybe a crisis will do that for you—make you see things that were there all along. Or maybe it was the connection I felt to my sons, hearing the *whooshing* sound of their movements and the thumping of their tiny hearts. Or maybe it was the sense of enormous gratitude I felt for the miracle of not only one but two lives inside of me. Whatever it was, I had my awakening at that moment, right there in my hospital room.

Just to be sure, I asked Geoffrey if he wouldn't mind getting Ethan for me.

"Certainly," he said. "I'll send him back while Mr. Smith and I have a chat." He leaned down and kissed my forehead before leaving the room with his partner.

A moment later, a still pale Ethan opened my door and walked hesitantly toward me. His eyes were watery, as if he had been crying or trying hard not to cry.

"Didn't Geoffrey tell you? Everything is fine."

"Yes. He told me." Ethan sat tentatively at the foot of my bed. He squeezed my foot through the sheets.

"Then why do you look so upset?"

"I don't know . . . You just had me so worried . . ." His voice trailed off.

I adjusted my bed to a more upright position and then lifted my arms to indicate that I wanted a hug. Ethan obliged, his cheek resting against mine as his arms encircled me. In that simple but soulful embrace, one simple truth was confirmed in my heart: I was in love with Ethan.

twenty-nine

Geoffrey barged back into the room in the middle of my transforming hug with Ethan. At least it seemed as if he were barging, given my mind-set, but more likely it was his usual dignified entry. In any event, I felt flustered and guilty. I told myself that for once, I had not cheated. I couldn't control my feelings, and Geoffrey couldn't read my mind. Neither could Ethan for that matter. By all appearances, I was only hugging a friend. Yet inside I was reeling.

I watched Ethan stand and walk over to the window, as if to give Geoffrey and me privacy. I wanted to yell out, "No. You stay here. *You* belong next to me." But instead I looked at Geoffrey, standing at the foot of the hospital bed with his erect posture, in his starched white shirt and perfect suit and tie. Despite our ordeal, he remained composed, unruffled, and steadfast. It was clear to me why I had been confused about loving him, why I had wanted so much to love him. On paper, he was perfect: handsome doctor, committed lover, seeming savior.

"What happens now?" I asked Geoffrey as I fiddled

nervously with the unraveling hem of my hospital gown. Of course, I meant what would happen in the next few minutes and hours, but to myself, I was also wondering about the long-term future. I had been fooled into falling in love with what was on paper once before. Dex had been all about the checked boxes, the fine fiancé résumé— good guy, chiseled cheekbones, careful grooming, fat bank account. And look how disastrously that relationship had ended. I vowed to myself not to make another seven-year mistake. Or even a seven-day mistake. I needed to break up with Geoffrey within a week.

My soon-to-be-ex-boyfriend informed me in a brisk, professional tone that Mr. Smith had decided, and he agreed, that as a precautionary measure, I was to be on bedrest until the babies arrived. He said that they didn't want any unnecessary pressure on my cervix. I had read that bedrest was common in twin pregnancies, but I still felt shaken by the news.

"So I have to stay in bed all day?" I asked.

Geoffrey said yes, except to use the bathroom or shower. He said that I had to avoid all stress, as stress can cause contractions.

"Can I get up to fix meals?" I asked.

"No, darling. I will hire someone to come in and cook and look after you while I'm at work." He thought for a second and said, "I know a wonderful Portuguese woman who helped after Max was born. You will love her."

Ethan turned to face us, his eyes flashing. "That won't be necessary, Geoffrey." His tone was emphatic and take-charge. Sexy even. He continued, "I'll write at home and take care of her."

I smiled, feeling touched, and also tremendously relieved. I didn't want to stay in Geoffrey's flat. I wanted to be home with Ethan. I wanted to be with him forever. I marveled at how such a monumental realization can unfold in an instant and change every single thing in your life. I loved Ethan. It was crazy, but there it was anyway. Even if he never loved me back, my feelings for him negated any possibility of a future with Geoffrey. I had never understood what people meant when they said they'd rather be alone if they couldn't be in the right relationship. Now I got it. I wanted Ethan or no one.

"You don't mind writing from home?" I asked him tentatively.

"Not at all."

"But I thought you said you couldn't think in your flat?" I asked him. "I don't want to infringe on your creative process."

Geoffrey, who seemed to sense what was happening, seized on this opening and said, "Yes. We don't want to impose on your writing."

I held my breath and felt my muscles tense as Ethan walked over to my bed and squeezed my shoulder. "Darcy and her babies are not an imposition."

"Darcy?" Geoffrey looked at me plaintively, his palms pressed together in front of his chest. "Is this arrangement okay with you?"

"Yeah," I said apologetically.

"It's settled then," Ethan said. "Let's go home."

It was after midnight when Ethan, Sondrine, and I spilled wearily onto the dark, narrow street outside the hospital and waited for Geoffrey to swing his Jaguar around from the short-term parking lot. He got out of the car, hurried around to the passenger side, and helped me into the front seat. Ethan and Sondrine sat in the back.

On the drive to Ethan's flat, Sondrine chirped about how she'd come over and cook for me, and Geoffrey thanked Ethan half a dozen times for his "generous spirit" and his "willingness to help in a pinch." I stared silently out my window, trying to process exactly what I was feeling. There was guilt over my impending breakup with Geoffrey. There was relief that my babies were okay. There was worry that I still had a long road ahead of me. Most of all, there was my love for Ethan, a love that reached down to my core and made me feel both queasy and exhilarated.

When we arrived home, Ethan awkwardly invited Geoffrey and Sondrine inside. Of course, they had no choice but to decline. I mean, what were we all going to do? Pile in Ethan's bed for a midnight snack of tea and biscuits? I heard Ethan whisper an apology to Sondrine. She murmured something back that I didn't quite catch—something about how she'd miss him—and then there was the sound of a quick kiss. Geoffrey followed suit, brushing his lips against mine and saying that he would call me in the morning. Then he said, "Drink as much water as you can because dehydration can trigger contractions. And stay in bed." By his expression, it was clear that he had not forgotten that there was only one proper bed in Ethan's flat.

Ethan and I got out of the car and stood on the curb as Sondrine took my spot in the front seat. Geoffrey promised Ethan through his half-open window that he'd get Sondrine home safely. Then she gave us a little wave and slammed her door. A second later, the disgruntled duo was gone. I turned to face Ethan, feeling strangely shy in front of the boy I had known since the fourth grade.

I waited a beat and then said, "Did they seem . . . a bit miffed?"

A smile tugged at the corners of Ethan's mouth. "A little. Yes . . ."

His expression made me erupt into nervous laughter. "They were totally pissed," I said.

"They sure were," he said, grinning.

As Ethan helped me up the front stairs to his flat, we both insisted that there was nothing funny about Geoffrey and Sondrine being upset. To reinforce the point, I apologized to Ethan for ruining his Valentine's Day. He told me not to be silly, that I hadn't ruined anything.

"Sondrine might disagree with that."

He shrugged as he unlocked his door. "Sondrine will get over it . . . They'll both get over it."

I thought about how Sondrine and Geoffrey had become the *they,* and, if only for the time leading up to my delivery, Ethan and I would be the *we*. I liked being a *we* with Ethan, I thought, as he led me down the hall to his room. When he switched on his light, I saw his unmade bed, as well as the foil condom wrapper on his nightstand. The predinner romp was confirmed. Ethan looked embarrassed as he asked if I wouldn't mind hanging out on the couch while he changed the sheets. Something about his pained expression made me want to throw my arms around him, kiss him, and tell him how much I loved him.

Instead, I went and sat on the couch, feeling jittery and excited about sleeping next to Ethan. My heart refused to slow even after I reminded myself that the giddy brand of anxiety was still stress and that Geoffrey had said that stress causes contractions. A few minutes later, Ethan appeared in his T-shirt and boxers. I couldn't help gazing down at his legs. They were the same as they'd always been, thin calves covered with fine, light hair, but now they held incredible appeal.

"All set," Ethan said. "Did you want to change into some pajamas?"

I told him that none of mine fit anymore. I had been sleeping naked with Geoffrey for the past several weeks, but I didn't offer this part up.

"Do you want to borrow some of mine?" Ethan asked.

I told him yes, even though I doubted they would fit either. Ethan was only slightly larger than my normal size. He produced a plaid flannel pair and said, "Here. Try these."

I took them from him and said that I'd change in the bathroom.

"Okay. Hurry. You should be in bed."

I nodded and said that I would be back in a jiffy. I went to the bathroom and took off my clothes and stood sideways in front of the mirror. My stomach was huge. So huge that I could no longer see my feet without bending forward. I prayed that I would get even bigger over the next few weeks. The bigger the better. I peed and held my breath as I inspected the toilet. Much to my relief, there was no more blood.

I quickly brushed my teeth, washed my face with cool water, and put on Ethan's soft, worn pajamas, pushing the elastic waistband below my stomach. They fit—barely. I inhaled a sleeve, hoping to smell Ethan's cologne, but only got a whiff of fabric softener.

When I returned to Ethan's room, he was turning down the sheets, hotel-style. "Climb in," he said as he plumped my pillow with his fist.

I slid under the covers and asked if he was coming to bed soon. He said yes, soon, after he brushed his teeth and did a few other things. I wondered if one of the things he had to do was phone Sondrine.

If he did call her, the conversation didn't last long, because a few minutes later, he was back in the room, flicking off his lamp and getting in bed next to me. I longed to touch him, debating whether to seek out his hand under the covers. Just as I decided that I'd better not, he leaned over and planted a quick kiss just to the left of my mouth. His breath smelled of Listerine and his mouth left a trace of wet on my skin. I touched the spot as he said, "I'm so glad your babies are okay, Darce. And I'm glad you're here."

"Me, too, Ethan. Thank you."

In the darkness of his room, I squeezed my eyes shut and made everything black. I pretended that Ethan and I were really together, a permanent *we,* on the verge of becoming a real family.

I awoke the next morning to the ringing phone. My first thought was, *I hope it's not Geoffrey.* My next thought was, *I still love Ethan.* So, my feelings weren't just an illusion rooted in near tragedy. I felt the mattress jostle as Ethan reached down to grab the phone. I could hear Sondrine's French accent on the other line. I think she must have asked where I was sleeping because Ethan answered, "Right here."

The controlling, jealous, break-of-dawn maneuver was something I would have pulled in my former life, and I silently vowed that no matter what the circumstances of my future relationships, I would never behave that way again. It was selfish and unattractive. Ethan reacted as I knew he would—with restrained annoyance. I pretended to be asleep as he got out of bed and whispered fiercely in the hall that she was being ridiculous.

"Were you not there witnessing the same ordeal last night?" he asked. "What do you think? Something is going on? . . . No. No! She's my *friend,* Sondrine. . . . She doesn't want to stay over there . . . I don't know—would you like to ask her?"

The conversation went on like that for some time, until he said he had to go. When he hung up, I opened one eye and saw him in the doorway, his hair messy, sticking up all over the place like a Native American headdress. I asked if everything was okay.

"Yeah," Ethan said, but he looked agitated as he crossed the room to his closet and pulled out a pair of jeans and a navy roll-neck sweater.

"Is Sondrine mad that I'm staying here?" I asked.

"No. She's cool with it," he lied. "How are you feeling?"

"Fine, but I have to go pee."

Ethan nodded, looking nervous. We both knew what I really had to do: check for blood. He sat on the edge of the bed and waited for me. A moment later I returned and gave him the good report.

"All clear," I said, giving him the thumbs-up signal.

He smiled and told me to get back in bed. I did.

"Now," Ethan said. "What can I get you for breakfast?"

I didn't want to be any more trouble than I already was, so I said instant oatmeal would be great, even though I was really craving eggs.

"Okay," he said. "I'll be right back."

After he left I flipped through my *When You're Expecting Twins* book, which I had conveniently left next to his bed several weeks earlier. I studied a graphic on weeks of gestation and head circumference, determining that my babies' heads were currently the size of lemons. If I reached my goal of thirty-six weeks, they would grow to the size of grapefruits. I told myself I could do it.

Moments later Ethan returned carrying a wooden tray. On it was a plate of scrambled eggs, sliced tomatoes, and wheat toast, all beautifully presented with a sprig of parsley. "I overrode your cereal order. You need protein." I sat up and straightened my knees as he placed the tray as close to me as my stomach would allow—which wasn't very close. He sat down next to me on the bed.

"Thank you," I said. "Where's your breakfast?"

"I'm not hungry," he said. "But I'll just keep you company."

I smiled and took a bite of my eggs.

"Do they need more salt or pepper?" he asked.

"No. They're perfect," I said. "Thank you."

As I took my first bite, I felt both babies move simultaneously. Baby A jabbing hard under my rib cage, Baby B swimming calmly below, creating his standard rippling sensation. Of course, it could have been one baby, waving an arm as he kicked. But I didn't think so. It felt like both of them in tandem. I was starting to believe I could actually distinguish their movements, and from this, I read things into their personalities. Baby A seemed more assertive. Fittingly, a Type A. He'd be my athlete, my go-getter. Baby B seemed mellow and easygoing. The tenderhearted artist. I imagined them together, spilling off the school bus, identical figures from a distance. One bouncing his basketball, the other swinging his trumpet case.

No matter what their interests, I just hoped that my sons would be good, happy boys who would always have the wisdom and courage to follow their hearts.

For the rest of the day, except for a five-minute shower interrupted by Ethan who kept knocking on the bathroom door and yelling at me to hurry up, I stayed horizontal. I napped, read my *Twins* book, and flipped through my accumulation of *Hello* magazines. Mostly, though, I just thought about Ethan, imagining what it would be like to share a slow, passionate kiss with him. To make love to him. To hear him introduce me as his girlfriend, and then his fiancée. I briefly questioned whether this wasn't just one of my challenges, if it wasn't about my needing to have every man love me.

But I knew, deep down, that it had nothing to do with any of that. For the first time in my life, I was truly in love. It wasn't about what Ethan could give me or how we would look together as we walked into a room. It was just about Ethan. Good, quirky, adorable, passionate, smart, witty Ethan. I was crazy about him, and so revved up with emotion that I had to resist calling him back to the bedroom

as he had insisted I could do anytime. Instead, I patiently
waited for him to take breaks from his writing and poke
his sweet towhead into the room to check on me. Sometimes he'd just say a quick hello or get me a water refill.
Other times he'd bring me plates of wholesome snacks:
cheese and crackers, sliced pears, olives, homemade pasta
salad, and peanut butter sandwiches cut in quarters. He'd
always talk to me while I ate. And once, in the late afternoon, when it was raining really hard outside, he climbed
under the covers and took a short nap with me. He fell
asleep first, which gave me the chance to study his face. I
loved everything about it. His curly, full lips, his long,
sandy eyelashes that grew straight down, his regal nose.
As I admired his features, his mouth twitched in his sleep,
his lone dimple making a flash appearance. In that second,
I knew what I really wanted for my boys. I wanted them
to have Ethan as their father.

thirty

Over the next week, I relished my cozy existence with Ethan while tolerating the seemingly incessant interruptions from Geoffrey. He phoned every few hours and visited daily on his way home from work. Sometimes he'd bring dinner, and I'd be forced to spend the evening with him instead of Ethan (who would promptly depart for Sondrine's). Other times I'd pretend to be sleeping, and he'd simply leave me a note on his personal stationery, which, incidentally, was adorned with an engraving of his family coat of arms. It was the sort of touch that would have been right up my alley in the Alistair-fantasizing days. But now I preferred Ethan's no-nonsense, ruled yellow notepads. Now I preferred everything about Ethan.

One afternoon during my thirty-first week, Geoffrey paid me a surprise visit during his lunch break. I had fallen asleep reading an *Us Weekly* that Annalise had so thoughtfully sent me from home along with a tin of her famous oatmeal raisin cookies and a bottle of antistretch-mark body oil. When I awoke, there was Geoffrey perched oddly in a straight-backed dining chair pulled up next to the bed. I could tell by his expression that he felt the way I did whenever I watched Ethan sleep, and I knew that it was time to end things.

"Hello, darling," he said as I stretched and sat up. His voice was low and nurturing. "How are you feeling?"

"Fine. Just tired and generally uncomfortable," I said.

"Did Mr. Smith stop by this afternoon?"

"Yeah," I said, smiling. "Love the house calls doctors make in this country."

"And?" Geoffrey asked. "What did he say?"

"He said everything still looks good."

He nodded. "Good. Any cramping or spotting or contractions since then?"

I shook my head.

"Good girl." He reached out and smoothed my hair back from my forehead. Then he gave me a tiny, mysterious smile and said, "I've got something for you." He handed me three real estate flyers featuring wondrous, spacious flats in posh neighborhoods. The stuff of my dreams upon my move to London. My eyes lingered on the descriptions: five bedrooms, terrace, park view, working fireplace. I forced myself to hand them back to him. I couldn't wait another moment, couldn't risk letting those brochures reel the old Darcy back in.

"You're not in the mood to have a look?" Geoffrey asked.

"I don't think it would be a good idea," I said.

"Is something wrong?"

He knew there was. People always know. I searched for the right words, compassionate words. But it is very hard to sugarcoat a breakup when you're in another man's bed wearing his plaid pajamas. So I just blurted it out, the verbal equivalent of ripping off a Band-Aid: "Geoffrey, I'm really sorry, but I think we need to break up."

He shuffled the flyers and glanced down at the one on top, showcasing a flat in Belgravia that looked exactly like the block where Gwyneth Paltrow and Chris Martin resided. I felt a pang thinking that if I stayed with Geoffrey, I could be one of Gwyneth's gal-pals. I pictured sharing her clothes, her linking arms with mine and saying, "What's mine is yours." We'd be photographed together in *Hello.* As a huge Coldplay fan, Ethan would benefit too. I saw my boys in a playgroup with young Apple. Maybe one of them would someday marry her. I'd plan the rehearsal dinner, Gwynnie would do the wedding. We'd phone each other daily, discussing flower arrangements, cake tastings, wine selections. I snapped back to reality. Not even the lure of Gwyneth was enough to change my mind about Geoffrey.

He finally spoke. "Is it Ethan?"

I felt caught off guard and nervous hearing Ethan's name. I wasn't sure how to answer, but I finally said, "I just don't have the right feelings for you. I thought I did . . . but . . . I'm not in love with you. I'm sorry."

The straightforward, dressed-down words sounded familiar, and I realized how close they were to Dexter's breakup speech with me. It suddenly occurred to me that no matter when his affair with Rachel had begun, she hadn't been the cause of our breakup. Dex and I had split because we weren't right for each other, and because of that fact, he had been able to fall in love with her. Had we been on solid ground, Dex wouldn't have cheated on me. The realization was somehow freeing, and it enabled me to let go of another sliver of resentment toward both of them. I'd think about it more later, but for now, I refocused on Geoffrey, waiting for him to respond.

"That's okay," he finally said with an elegant wave of his hand.

I must have looked confused by his nonchalance

because he clarified. "You're just in a very difficult situation right now. Being in bed like this is bound to confuse you. We can sort it out later—after the babies arrive. And in the meantime, I really want to take care of you. Just let me do it, darling."

Coming from most men the words would have sounded either condescending or pathetic—a last, desperate attempt to hold a relationship together at its seams. But from Geoffrey it was just a dignified, pragmatic, and sincere declaration. For one beat, I was sold. After all, he was my ticket to staying in London for the long term. But even more important, Geoffrey was my emotional security blanket. It is impossible to overstate the unique brand of vulnerability that comes with pregnancy, particularly the circumstances of my pregnancy—and Geoffrey assuaged much of my anxiety. He was a good person who took excellent care of me, and implicit in his every touch was the promise that he always would.

But I wasn't in love with him. It was that simple. The concept of being with a man strictly for love used to seem naïve and high-minded, the kind of thing I used to scoff at Rachel for saying, but now I subscribed to the notion too. So I forced myself to stay on track.

"That is really very sweet," I said, reaching out to take his hand. "And I cannot tell you how much I appreciate your kindness, everything you have done for me. But we have to break up. It just isn't right to stay together when my feelings aren't there . . ."

Then to reinforce the point, I told him that I would miss him, although I knew I'd miss the fringe benefits that came along with him a bit more than I'd actually miss him. I let go of his hand.

Geoffrey squinted. His eyes were sad but dry. He said, without a trace of bitterness, that he was very sorry to lose me, but that he understood. He swung his briefcase onto his lap, snapped it open, and tossed the glossy brochures inside. Then he stood and headed for the door.

"Can we still be friends?" I called after him, feeling slightly frantic after his easy surrender. I worried that the question emanated from the old Darcy, the needing-to-be-worshipped-at-any-cost Darcy. Maybe I just wanted to retain control over Geoffrey. But as he turned to look at me over his shoulder, saying that he would like that very much, I knew that my intentions were pure. I wanted to remain friends with Geoffrey because I liked him as a person. Not because I wanted a single thing from him.

Later that night as Ethan lay next to me reading an article in *National Geographic* on global warming, I told him that Geoffrey and I had broken up that afternoon. I told him everything except Geoffrey's question about him.

Ethan listened, eyebrows raised. "Wow. I didn't even know you two were on shaky ground," he said, but his tone gave him away. Like Geoffrey, he wasn't all that surprised.

I nodded. "Yeah. I just wasn't feeling it."

"Was he okay?"

"I guess so," I said.

"And you?" he asked.

I shrugged. "I don't know. I feel guilty after all he's done for me. And I guess a tiny bit sad too . . . But mostly I think it's a good thing, even though it means I'll have to move back to New York sooner than I'd like."

Ethan blinked. "What?"

"I said I feel guilty—"

"No. The part about moving back?"

"I don't have a job, Ethan. I'll probably have to go back to my old one after the babies are born. I just don't have the money to stay here."

"You can stay here for as long as you want," Ethan said.

"I can't do that. I've been enough of a burden . . . And it's not like you're rolling in it." I smiled.

"I *love* having you here, Darcy. I can't wait for those babies to get here. I'm unbelievably pumped. Don't let money constraints force your hand. We'll work it out. I have money saved."

I looked at his earnest face and had to swallow back the urge to confide my feelings. It wasn't that I was afraid of rejection. It was more that for once, my feelings were selfless, and I didn't think it was fair to Ethan to unload everything on him. He was already in a relationship. He didn't need the pressure of worrying about me and how hurting my feelings might impact my pregnancy.

So I just smiled and said, "Thank you, Ethan. We'll see what happens."

In my mind, though, I knew that my time in London, as well as my time with Ethan, was running out.

thirty-one

The next day I hit the thirty-two-week benchmark, significant according to my *Twins* book in that my children would be "unlikely to suffer long-term health consequences as a result of their premature births." This felt like an enormous hurdle, which seemed ironic considering that I had achieved the goal by doing absolutely nothing but hanging out in bed, reading magazines and snacking.

To celebrate the milestone, Ethan surprised me with a homemade chocolate cake, bringing it back to the bedroom on his wooden tray. The cake was decorated with thirty-two blue candles, one for each week of my pregnancy, which he lit while singing, off-key, "Happy birthday, Baby A and B!"

I laughed, made a wish, and blew out the candles in two tries (which he said counted as I was having two babies). Then he cut the cake and served us each a big slice. I had seconds and then thirds, praising his baking efforts, especially the icing. When we finished eating, he cleared our plates and the tray and returned with a big box wrapped in mint-green and white polka-dotted paper.

"You shouldn't have," I said, hoping that he hadn't spent too much on the baby gift.

He ceremoniously rested the box on my lap. "I didn't . . . It's from Rachel."

I stared down at the package. Sure enough, the present-wrapping was unmistakably Rachel: perfect and pretty, but restrained enough not to look professionally wrapped. I observed her neat corners, the short strips of tape all parallel to the edges of the box, and her full, symmetrical bow. For some reason, that package unearthed all kinds of good memories, moments shared with Rachel over the years.

Ethan shot me a furtive glance. "Are you upset? Should I not have given it to you? I debated it for some time . . ."

"No. It's fine," I said, my hand running across the wrapping paper. Rachel's hand had touched this box, I thought, and I was overcome with the most absurd sensation that I was connecting with someone from the dead.

"Are you going to open it?" he asked.

I nodded.

"She sent it a few weeks ago, but she wanted me to wait until closer to your due date. I thought today was good . . . because I'm not worried anymore. Your babies are going to be fine."

My heart pounded as I carefully untied the white bow, peeled back the paper, and opened the box to find two white receiving blankets trimmed with light blue silk. They were the softest, most sumptuous things I had ever touched. I remembered that Rachel had given Annalise a similar blanket at her baby shower, but mine were even nicer. After a long moment, I removed the card from the envelope. It was letter-pressed with two baby carriages. I

opened the card slowly and saw her familiar, neat cursive.
I could hear her voice as I read silently:

Dear Darcy,

First, I want to tell you how sorry I am for everything that has happened between us. I miss our friendship, and I regret that I cannot share in this very special time in your life. But despite the distance between us, I want you to know that I think of you often. Many times a day. I am so pleased to learn from Ethan that you are happy and well. And twins! It is so you to turn an already wonderful event into something doubly exciting! And, finally, I just want to wish you heartfelt congratulations as you embark upon motherhood. I hope someday to meet your sons. I know they will be beautiful, amazing little boys, just like their mother.

> *Best wishes and much love always,*
> *Rachel*

Still clutching the card, I leaned my head back on my pillow. For months now, I had been waiting to hear something from Rachel, but I didn't realize how *much* I wanted to hear from her until I read her card. I looked up at Ethan. His face was placid, patient.

"Huh. Imagine that," I said, filling the silence.

"What'd she say?" Ethan asked.

I downplayed my emotion by rolling my eyes. Then I twisted my hair up in a knot, secured it with an elastic band, and said nonchalantly, "Let's just say, she is trying to make a comeback." My words were cavalier, but the catch in my voice gave me away. And against my best efforts, I could feel myself softening. I tried to mask my feelings by flinging the card his way, Frisbee-style. "Here you go. Read it for yourself," I said.

His lips moved as he read silently. When he got to the end, he looked up at me and said, "It's really nice."

"Yeah. These blankets are pretty nice too," I said, stroking the silk border with my thumb. "I guess I no longer want her to go to hell." I laughed. "Just a dingy place in heaven."

Ethan smiled.

"Does this mean I have to call her?" I asked him.

Part of me wanted his response to be, "Yes, you must call her now," because I wanted an excuse to swallow my pride and give in. But Ethan just said, "You don't have to call. Just send her a thank-you note." He handed the card back to me.

I couldn't resist rereading it aloud, parsing every sentence for its meaning.

"She said she's 'sorry for what happened between us.' Not *what she did*."

"I think that's implied."

"So what does that mean exactly? That she'd take back what she did with Dex if she could?" I asked, redoing my bun.

"She probably just wishes she had handled things differently," Ethan said.

"Like how?" I asked.

"I don't know . . . like waiting until after you and Dex broke up to start seeing him?"

"Did she tell you that? Do you know that for a fact?"

"Not for a fact. No."

"Okay," I said, my eyes scanning the rest of the card. "Moving on here . . . 'Despite the distance between us,' " I read aloud. "Do you think she means emotional distance or geographic distance?"

"Probably both," Ethan said.

"She thinks of me *every* day? Do you think she's exaggerating?"

"No. I don't, actually," Ethan said. "Don't you think of her every day?"

The answer was yes, but I pretended not to hear the question as I rattled on. " 'Pleased to learn from Ethan?' " I said, remembering the bits of the conversation I had overheard on Christmas. "What exactly did you tell her?"

"Well, obviously I told her you were having twin boys. You said I could . . . and I just told her that you're doing well here. That you've made some friends. And I told her about Geoffrey too."

"Have you talked to her since Geoffrey and I broke up?"

"No."

I briefly considered asking him about Rachel's engagement, but I decided that I still wasn't ready to have it confirmed. I closed the card and tucked it back into the envelope.

"She can't honestly think that we could really be close friends again?" I asked, my voice trailing off.

"She knows you pretty well, Darce. I don't think she expects you to fold," he murmured. His tone was matter-of-fact, but his expression said, "I think you will fold." Or maybe, "I think you already have folded."

I put off writing Rachel's thank-you note for nearly two weeks because I couldn't decide on the content or tone. Should I forgive her outright? Tell her that I missed her, too, and that although I would never fully accept her relationship with Dex, I wanted to repair our friendship? Was that even the case?

One evening, on the Saturday night of my thirty-fourth week, something compelled me to get out of bed and retrieve a small leather album in the closet nursery, stuck down in a side pocket of one of my suitcases. I had put together the album several summers before and had packed it at the last moment. I brought it back to bed and flipped through it, skipping past the photos of Claire and Dex and various other friends, and finding one of Rachel and me taken in the Hamptons right after she and Dex had graduated from law school. I studied our carefree poses, our broad smiles, our arms draped casually around each other as we stood by the water's edge in our bikinis. I could practically smell the salty air, feel the ocean breeze and the sand shifting under my feet. I could even hear her laughter. I wondered why beach photos taken of lost loved ones always seemed so much more poignant than other photos.

As I looked at that picture of us, I thought about everything that had happened between Dex and Rachel and me, deciding again that the cracks in our relationships had been a breeding ground for deceit. Dex and I had cheated on each other because we weren't right together in the first place. Rachel betrayed me because our friendship was a flawed one. I lied to her about Marcus because of the same negative undercurrent—the unspoken competition that can corrupt even the best of friendships. That had ruined ours.

As much as I wanted to hold them responsible, I knew that I was not blameless. We were all accountable. We had all lied and cheated. But despite everything, I knew we were still good people. We all deserved a second chance, a chance to be happy. I considered the expression "Once a cheater, always a cheater," and I dismissed it as a fallacy. People generally didn't cheat in good relationships, and I couldn't imagine Dex and Rachel cheating on each other. I also knew that if I were ever with Ethan, I would never cheat on him. I would be truc to him, no matter what, always.

And at that moment, there on the doorstep of forgiveness, I went into labor. It started out as an intense cramping in my lower abdomen, and when I got up to pee, fluid ran down my leg. My water had broken. I felt a strange sense of calm as I phoned Mr. Smith and reported my symptoms. He confirmed that I, indeed, was in labor, and he instructed me to come to the hospital as soon as possible. He said he would meet me there.

Ethan was at a sports bar in Piccadilly watching Stanford play in the NCAA basketball tournament. I hated to interrupt the game—he took March Madness very seriously—but he had made me promise to call for "the smallest of reasons," and I figured that my water breaking qualified. He answered on the first ring, shouting into the phone with bar noise in the background. "Darcy? Are you okay?"

"I'm fine . . . Is Stanford winning?"

"They haven't tipped off yet," he said. "I'm watching Wake Forest now. They're looking pretty solid—which is good because I have them going to the Final Four in my pool." I pictured him perched on a barstool gripping the yellow highlighter he used to mark up his brackets torn from *USA Today*.

"When does your game start?" I asked, debating whether I should wait until the game was over to have him meet me at the hospital.

"Soon. Why? Are you okay?"

I hesitated and then said, "I'm really sorry, Ethan. I know how much you look forward to this tournament and Stanford playing and everything . . . but my water broke. Do you think you could come home and take me to the hospital?"

"Oh, Christ! Don't move!" he shouted into the phone. "I'll be right there!"

Ten minutes later he burst through the door and streaked

down the hall toward the bedroom, yelling, "Cab's waiting outside! Cab's waiting outside!"

"I'm right here," I called out to him from the living room. My small duffel, which I had packed weeks earlier, was resting at my feet.

He ran into the living room, kissed my cheek, and breathlessly asked how I was.

"I'm fine," I said, feeling relieved to see him. "Would you mind tying my shoes? I can't reach."

"Oh, God. I'm so sorry I wasn't here," he said as he stooped down to tie my Nikes. His hands were shaking.

"Where's your jacket?" I asked, noticing that he had come home wearing only his lucky Stanford T-shirt. "It has to be freezing outside."

"I left it at the bar."

"Oh, Ethan, I'm sorry," I said. "And I'm really sorry about interrupting your game too."

He told me not to be silly, he'd get the jacket later, and the game wasn't important. As he bent down to pick up my bag, I noticed a clear patch adhered to his arm, peeking out from under his T-shirt.

"You've quit smoking?" I asked, realizing that I hadn't seen him with a cigarette in ages or, for that matter, detected any telltale tobacco odor on his clothing.

"Yeah. Can't have smoke around you or the babies." He nervously rubbed his patch as if to give himself a needed boost of nicotine.

I thanked him, feeling moved by his effort.

"Don't mention it. I needed to quit anyway. Now let's go!" He pulled me to my feet and shouted, "Schnell! Schnell!" which I figured meant "hurry" in another language, maybe German. He helped me to the door, where he grabbed his only other jacket, a bright yellow raincoat. Then he inhaled sharply, rubbed his hands together, and said, "Well. This is it."

During our cab ride to the hospital, Ethan helped me with my breathing exercises, which was amusing because he seemed to need more help breathing than I did. We determined that my contractions were six minutes apart and lasting about thirty seconds each.

"How bad does it hurt?" Ethan asked every time I winced. "On a scale of one to ten?"

My pain threshold was normally quite low, and I'd been known to bawl even during the removal of a splinter, so the pain actually felt like an eleven. But I told him a four because I wanted him to be proud of my strength. I also told him I wasn't scared—which is really saying something coming from a former pessimistic drama queen. But it was the truth—I *wasn't* scared. I just knew everything was going to be all right with my babies. I had made it to thirty-four and a half weeks. And I had Ethan with me. What more could I ask for? I felt like the luckiest woman in the world. I was ready to meet my sons.

We checked in at the hospital, and Ethan pushed my wheelchair to our assigned birthing room. He then helped me undress and change into my hospital gown. He blushed as I stood naked in front of him, and for a second I was embarrassed too.

"You ain't seen nothing yet," I said to ease the awkwardness. I laughed. "There is no modesty from here on out . . . And I sure hope you're not squeamish."

He smiled, held my hand, and said he could handle it. Then he helped me recline in bed. I felt relieved to stretch out—and overcome with a profound sense of fatigue. All I wanted to do was sleep, but the pain was too intense for napping. About five minutes later, Mr. Smith and his midwife arrived. She started my IV while he checked my cervix and informed me that I was nearly five centimeters dilated.

Shortly after that, an anesthesiologist brought my

epidural. I'd never been so excited to see a needle, anticipating a marvelous high, something akin to laughing gas
at the dentist. Instead of a tingly, floating sensation, however, the epidural only caused the absence of pain. But on
the heels of my vicious contractions, the absence of pain
felt downright euphoric.

Everything happened very quickly after that. I remember Ethan holding one leg, under my knee, my midwife
gripping the other, while Mr. Smith coached me to bear
down and push. I did—as hard as I could. Again and again.
I remember panting and sweating like mad, and making all
kinds of ugly faces and guttural cries. After a very long
time, my doctor announced that the first baby was crown-
ing. I sat up, straining to see, catching a glimpse of dark,
matted hair, then shoulders, torso, and two skinny legs.

"It's a boy," Mr. Smith confirmed.

Then I heard my son's first plaintive note in the world.
His voice was hoarse, as if he had been crying in the
womb for hours. My arms ached to hold him. "I want to
see him," I said through sobs.

"Just one moment," my doctor said. "We have to cut
the cord. . . . Ethan, do you want to do the honors?"

"May I?" Ethan asked me.

I nodded and cried harder. "Of course you can."

Ethan took the big metal scissors from my midwife
and carefully snipped the cord. Then my doctor tied it
and briefly examined my baby before bundling him in a
blanket and resting him on my chest. I shifted his head
over my heart, and he instantly quieted while I continued
to sob. I gazed down at his angelic face, taking in every
detail. The curve of his cheeks, his tiny but still full lips,
the dimple in his left cheek. Strangely enough, he looked
an awful lot like Ethan.

"He's perfect. Isn't he perfect?" I asked everyone and
no one.

Ethan rested his hand gently on my shoulder and said, "Yes. He *is* perfect."

I consciously savored the moment, deciding that everything I had ever read, seen, and heard about childbirth paled in comparison to what I was actually feeling.

"What's his name?" Ethan asked.

I studied my son's face, searching for the answer. My earlier flamboyant choices—names like Romeo and Enzo—seemed ridiculous and utterly wrong. His name suddenly came to me. "John," I said. "His name is John." I was certain that he would live up to the straightforward but strong name. He was going to make a wonderful John.

That's when Mr. Smith reminded me that I had more work to do, and my midwife scooped up John and handed him to a nurse. I tried to keep my eyes on my firstborn, but a fresh wave of pain enveloped me. I closed my eyes and moaned. The epidural seemed to be wearing off. I begged for another dose. My doctor told me no, offering some explanation I couldn't begin to focus on. Ethan kept repeating that I could do it.

Several minutes of agony later, I heard another wail. John's brother was born seconds after midnight. Identical twins with their own, separate birthdays. Although I knew the babies were identical, I was no less eager to see my second born. Ethan cut the umbilical cord, and my midwife swaddled the baby and handed him to me. Through more tears, I instantly surmised that this baby shared his brother's features, but his were slightly more defined. He was also a bit smaller, with slightly more hair. He wore a determined expression that struck me as amusing on such a tiny, new baby. Again, his name just came to me.

"You are Thomas," I whispered down at him. He opened one eye and peeped at me with apparent approval.

"May I hold them both together?" I asked my doctor.

He nodded and brought John back to my chest.

Ethan asked me if I had settled on middle names. I thought of Ethan's middle name, Noel, and decided that each of my sons should have a part of the best man I knew.

"Yes," I said. "Their names are John Noel and Thomas Ethan."

Ethan took a breath, blinking back tears. "I'm so . . . *honored*," he said, looking both surprised and touched. Then he leaned down to embrace us. "I love you, Darcy," he whispered in my ear. "I love all three of you."

thirty-two

FOR the next twenty-four hours, I had no sense of day or night. It was just a blur of time with John and Thomas. Ethan never left my side, unless on a specific mission for peanut butter crackers from the vending machine, painkillers from the nurses, or booties from the gift shop in the lobby of the hospital. He slept on a cot next to my bed, helped me to the bathroom, and snapped roll after roll of black-and-white film.

Ethan also saw to it that I phoned my mother. When I balked, saying I was too exhausted and hormonal to deal with her, he dialed my home number on his mobile and said, "Here. You'll regret it if you don't do this."

I took his phone just as my mother answered.

"Hi, Mom. It's me," I said, feeling defeated before the conversation even began.

"Hello, Darcy." Her voice was as formal and stiff as it had been on Christmas Eve.

I refused to be hurt and instead swiftly delivered my news. "I had my babies, Mom." Before she could respond,

I covered the basics, giving her their full names, as well as their weights, lengths, and times of birth.

Then I said, "Can you believe it, Mom? Twins born on separate days?" I looked down at John, sleeping on my chest, and then over at Thomas, whom Ethan was holding.

My mother asked me to repeat everything so she could write it down. I did, and then she said, "Congratulations, honey." A softness crept into her voice.

"Thanks, Mom," I said, as Ethan prompted me to share the smaller, but in many ways more important, details. "Tell her how John cries more than Thomas and has a birthmark in the shape of Italy on his knee. Tell her how Thomas peeps at you with one eye," he whispered.

I followed his lead, and although it could have gone either way, my mother chose to be satisfying, nearly joyful.

"I can't stand the thought of you being alone," my mother said in a nurturing and repentant tone.

"Thank you, Mom. That means so much to me. . . . But I'm not alone. I'm with Ethan," I said, not to be contrary, but because I wanted her to understand Ethan's importance in my life.

Ethan smiled as he repositioned Thomas in his arms and then kissed the top of his fuzzy head.

"Still. There is no substitute for a mother," she said firmly.

"I know, Mom," I said, feeling moved by the truth of her statement.

"So I'll come visit as soon as I can . . . In early June. As soon as we get through Jeremy and Lauren's wedding."

"Okay, Mom," I said. "That would be *really* great. Thank you."

"And Darcy?"

"Yeah?"

"I'm *so* proud of you."

I basked in her words. "Thanks, Mom."

"I love you, honey," she continued, her voice cracking.

"I love you too, Mom. And tell Dad and Jeremy and Lauren I love them. I'm really sorry I won't be able to come to their wedding."

"Jeremy understands," she said. "We all do."

As we said good-bye, I found myself pondering what Thomas and John's birth meant in the larger scheme of things, in the fabric of our family. I had created a new generation. The responsibility of it was awesome. My eyes filled with tears for what felt like the hundredth time since I had arrived at the hospital.

"This postpartum thing is no joke," I said to Ethan as I wiped my eyes with the sleeve of my nightgown.

Ethan brought Thomas over to me, and the four of us crowded into bed together. "Is she coming to visit us?" he asked.

The *us* was not lost on me. I smiled and said, "Yeah. After Jeremy's wedding."

"How do you feel about seeing her?" he asked.

"I can't wait, actually," I said, surprised by how much I wanted to share John and Thomas with her.

Ethan nodded and then glanced at me sideways. "Any other calls you want to make?"

I could tell that he was thinking of Rachel so I said her name as a question, the two syllables lingering in the room, sounding both comforting and menacing at once.

"Well?" he asked. "What do you think?"

"As a matter of fact, I think I *will* call her," I said resolutely. "And then Annalise. And then Meg and Charlotte."

It was the right order.

"Are you sure you want to talk to Rachel?" he asked.

I nodded. I couldn't put it into words, but in some inexplicable way, I felt compelled to forge an official truce with

my ex–best friend. No matter what had happened in the
past, or what the future held for us, I wanted Rachel to hear
the news of Thomas and John's birth from me. So I dialed her number on Ethan's mobile before I could change
my mind. As I listened to her phone ring, I couldn't decide whether I wanted her to answer or for her machine
to pick up.

I got the one thing I hadn't banked on.

"*Hell*-o," Dex said cheerily.

I panicked, gave Ethan a wide-eyed look of horror, and
frantically mouthed, "Dex!"

He grimaced empathetically and then made a moti-
vating fist in the air and whispered, "Go on. Do it. Ask to
speak to Rachel."

So I did, gathering strength by glancing down at John,
who was making a soft, sucking noise in his sleep. Dex
was ancient history. Literally two lifetimes ago.

I took a deep breath and said, "Hi, Dex. It's Darcy. Is
Rachel there?"

"Hello, Darcy," Dex said formally. Then he paused as
if he were some kind of gatekeeper, suspecting trouble
from abroad. "Rachel's right here," he finally said.

There was another long pause, and a rustling on the
line. I pictured him covering the phone and coaching her,
saying something like, "Don't let her suck you into a conflict."

I thought back to the last time I had seen Dex, in our
old apartment, and felt ashamed of the stunt I had tried to
pull. I guess my reputation was deserved, and I couldn't
blame him for being wary of me now.

"Hi, Darcy," Rachel said timidly, her voice crackling
over the distance. It was a voice I had heard nearly every
day for twenty-five years, and I felt amazed at how it
could now sound both familiar and utterly foreign.

"Hi, Rachel . . . I had something—I wanted to tell you

something," I babbled as my heart raced. "I had my babies last night. Two boys."

"Congratulations, Darcy," she said. Her voice was warm and sincere. "I'm *so* happy for you."

"Thank you," I said.

"What are their names?" she asked tentatively.

"John Noel and Thomas Ethan."

"I *love* those names," she said, and then hesitated. "After Ethan?"

"Yeah," I said, wondering if Ethan had told her how close we had become. If he hadn't, she was likely thinking that I was trying to infringe on her turf as Ethan's close female friend. It wasn't beyond the pale of my old tricks, and I felt another flicker of embarrassment over the person I used to be. Still, I resisted the urge to explain why the names were appropriate, and instead, rattled off the other birth statistics.

"How do you feel?" she asked softly.

I could feel myself relaxing as I said, "I'm fine. It wasn't a bad delivery . . . I'm just *really* tired now, but from what I hear, it only gets worse."

I laughed, but Rachel stayed serious. She asked if my mother was coming to help.

"Uh-huh. I just talked to her," I said. "You are only the second person I've called."

I wanted her to know the order. I wanted it to count as my between-the-lines apology. I didn't feel up to a full-blown examination of our friendship, but I wanted her to know that I was sorry about what had happened between us.

After a long pause, she said, "I'm *really* glad you called, Darcy. I've been thinking of you so much lately, wondering how you are."

"Yeah. I got your note. And the blankets," I said. "They're really special. I love them. Thank you."

"You're so welcome," she said.

"So how are you?" I asked, realizing that I wasn't ready to let her go just yet. I wanted more of her.

"Fine. I'm fine," she said somewhat hesitantly.

"What has been going on in your life?" I asked, referring to Dex, but also everything else.

"Well . . . I paid off my loans finally, and quit my job. I do legal work for an AIDS foundation in Brooklyn now."

"That's great," I said. "I know you must be much happier."

"Yeah. I like it a lot," she said. "It's so nice not to worry about billable hours. . . . And the commute's not too bad."

I could tell she was avoiding any mention of Dex, so after another few seconds of silence, I said, "So you and Dex are doing well?"

I wanted to show her I was fine with the status quo. And although it still felt funny to think of them together, I really *was* remarkably okay with things. How could I begrudge anyone happiness when I felt so fulfilled and contented?

She made an *umm* sound, hesitated, and then said, "Didn't Ethan tell you?"

"About your engagement?" I guessed.

"Um . . . well, actually . . . Dex and I are . . . married," Rachel said softly. "We got married yesterday."

"Wow," I said. "I didn't know."

I waited for a wave of jealousy or bitterness to hit me. Or at least a healthy dose of wistfulness. Instead, I felt the way I do when I read about a celebrity wedding in *People*. Interested in the details, but not wholly invested in it.

"Congratulations," I said, understanding why Dex sounded wary of my call. The timing was definitely suspect.

"Thank you, Darcy," she said. "I know . . . this is all so bizarre, isn't it?" Her tone was apologetic.

Was she sorry for marrying Dex? For not inviting me? For everything?

I let her off the hook, and said, "It's fine, Rachel. Truly. I'm happy for you."

"Thank you, Darcy."

My mind filled with questions. I considered censoring them, but then thought, why not ask?

"Where was your ceremony?" I asked first.

"Here in the city. At the Methodist church on Sixtieth and Park."

"And your reception?"

"We had it at The Inn at Irving Place," she said. "It was very small."

"Was Annalise there?"

"Yeah. Just a few friends and our families . . . I wanted you to be there, but . . ." Her voice trailed off. "I knew you wouldn't come. *Couldn't* come, I mean."

I laughed. "Yeah. That would have been sort of weird, huh?"

"Yeah. I guess so," she said wanly.

"So where are you guys living now?" I asked.

She told me they had bought an apartment in Gramercy—which had always been Rachel's favorite neighborhood in the city.

"That's awesome. . . . And are you going on a honeymoon?" I asked, thinking of their trip to Hawaii, but refusing to succumb to negative emotion.

"Yeah . . . We leave for Italy tonight," she said.

"Oh. That's great. I'm glad I caught you."

"Yeah. Me too," she said.

"So I hope you have a good time in Italy. Give Dex my best too. Okay?"

She said that she would do that. Then we congratu-
lated each other again, and said good-bye. I hung up and
looked at Ethan through fresh tears. The kind that come
after you've survived an ordeal.

"I was going to tell you," Ethan said. "But with your
preterm labor, I didn't want to upset you, and yesterday
wasn't the day for it. . . . Besides, I thought Rachel should
tell you herself."

"It's fine," I said. "I'm surprisingly fine with it . . . I
guess you were invited?"

He nodded. "Yeah. But I never planned on going."

"Why not?"

"You think I would have left you?"

"You could have."

He shook his head emphatically. "No way."

"You're closer to her," I said, perhaps to gauge his
feelings for me, but also because I felt guilty that he had
missed one of his best friend's weddings because of me.

"I'm closer to *you*," he said earnestly.

I smiled, feeling no sense of victory over Rachel, just
an incredible closeness to Ethan. I wondered if he felt the
way I did—or whether it was only love for a friend.

"And just look what I would have missed," Ethan said,
gazing down at John and Thomas.

I thought about the two events—the birth of my babies
and Rachel's wedding—transpiring virtually simultaneously, on opposite sides of the Atlantic.

"Can you believe it all happened on the very same
day?" I asked him.

Ethan shook his head. "Frankly, no. I cannot."

"Guess I'm never going to forget their anniversary."

Ethan put his arm around me and let me cry some
more.

* * *

On the day of our discharge from the hospital, Geoffrey stopped by to visit us during his rounds. He shook Ethan's hand, kissed me on the cheek, and admired my sons.

"What a nice guy," Ethan said after Geoffrey had left the room.

"Yeah, he could win the ex-boyfriend-of-the-year award," I said, thinking that as nice as Geoffrey was, I was still certain that I had done the right thing in breaking up with him. The fact that our relationship had weathered the transition to friendship so seamlessly was just further confirmation.

I put on the sweater that Ethan had given me for Christmas as he reswaddled John and Thomas in Rachel's blankets, handing me both bundles, one in each arm. Then Ethan finished packing our belongings, which had spread to every corner of the room.

"I don't want to go," I said.

"Why not?" he asked.

I tried to explain my feeling of wanting to stay in the hospital forever, with a fleet of nurses and doctors catering to me and my children. I felt envious of the women just going into labor, and told Ethan that I'd take the pain all over again for a few more nights at the inn.

Ethan reassured me that I had nothing to worry about. "We'll be fine," he said. "You'll see."

It was that *we* that held me together through those first crazy days and weeks at home. It got me through the fear that my babies would suddenly stop breathing, the frustration with breast-feeding, my insecurity during bath time, and all the other mundane but seemingly insurmountable tasks. Most of all, it got me through the agony of the sleepless nights. You hear parents of *one* newborn talk about how grueling the lack of sleep is, but experiencing the endless cycle of waking-feeding-changing with twins is simply not to be believed. Let's just say I understood why sleep deprivation is the number-one form of torture for political prisoners.

Our days weren't much easier. Laundry and dishes and bills accumulated at an alarming rate. Food disappeared even more quickly, and we often resorted to opening dusty canned goods rather than schlepping our delirious selves the few blocks to the grocery store. There were many days when we didn't even change out of our pajamas or brush our teeth before late afternoon. And I certainly didn't have the energy to put on makeup or blow-dry my hair or even look in the mirror except in passing, catching horrific glimpses of my matted hair, sunken eyes, and a lingering fifteen pounds, mostly around my middle.

In short, it wasn't exactly a breeding ground for romance, but there it was anyway, blooming between Ethan and me, evident in every small act of kindness. It was love as a verb, as Rachel used to say. Love that made me more patient, more loyal, and stronger. Love that made me feel more complete than I had ever felt in my glamorous, Jimmy Choo–filled past.

Yet on the surface, Ethan and I remained "just friends." They were two words that haunted me, especially when Ethan went off, every few days, to spend time with Sondrine. She was still his girlfriend. I was just his friend. Sure, we were friends who exchanged soulful glances, friends who slept in a bed filled with sexual tension, friends who found any excuse to touch, but I worried that we'd never take that perilous leap of faith toward becoming a real couple, a permanent team. I had nightmares of a tragic ending: Ethan marrying Sondrine while I returned to New York with Thomas and John. I would awaken, sweating and teary, tasting the grief and heartbreak I'd face if I had to spend the rest of my life wondering just how incredible we could have been together, if only one of us had stepped up and taken the chance.

Then, one afternoon in late April, as Ethan and I took the boys out for our daily walk around Holland Park, he solemnly reported that the night before, over oysters at Bibendum, he had ended things with Sondrine. I felt a rush of excitement and opportunity. I also sensed uneasiness between us. Our last obstacle was gone, but now what?

I let out a nervous laugh and said in a teasing tone, "Kind of weird to dump someone over oysters, isn't it?"

"Well," Ethan said, his eyes focused on the path ahead of us. "I'm not always the slickest guy . . . as you well know."

His "as you well know" seemed loaded with meaning and made me even more anxious. So I stumbled on, rambling about how I thought you weren't supposed to eat oysters in months containing the letter *r*.

"We had rock oysters—fins de clair—which you can eat year-round. But thanks so much for your concern," he said, yawning with feigned nonchalance.

"Anytime," I said, as we strolled around the top of the Cricket Lawn. A long minute passed, the silence between us thickening.

"How do you feel?" I finally asked, choosing my words carefully. "About the breakup?"

Ethan glanced at me with raised brows. "It was a long time coming. I think I was just too sleep-deprived to get around to it sooner, you know?"

I nodded. I knew.

"I just didn't feel that close to her," he continued. "After this long, I should have felt closer to her. Or at least had the sense that I knew her . . . I mean, I knew her taste in music, art, food, travel, literature. But I still didn't know *her*. Or maybe I just didn't want to know her badly enough."

I nodded again, noticing that we were both walking at a faster clip and avoiding eye contact.

"There was other stuff too," he chattered nervously. He stopped pushing the pram long enough to reach down and adjust John's cap, which had slipped down over his eyes, and then said, "She was so relentlessly anti-American. I'm the first guy to step up and criticize our government. But it raised my hackles when she did it. I found myself constantly grinding my teeth to keep from saying, 'Your ass'd be speaking German if it weren't for us.'"

I smiled, pretending to be distracted by a nearby three-on-three football game.

"And then there's her scent . . . ," he said.

"What? She doesn't bathe enough?"

He shook his head. "No. She's perfectly clean. And she wears nice perfume and all of that. But there's something about her actual, *natural* scent. The way her skin smells. I just didn't like it. . . . So you know, it's hard to fix that one."

"Do I have a scent? When I'm not wearing perfume?" I asked, suddenly worried that Ethan didn't like mine either, and that I was only imagining our physical, chemical connection.

Ethan glanced at me, blushing scarlet. "Yeah. You do have a scent," he said slowly.

"And?" I asked, my heart pounding.

He stopped walking, turned to face me, and stared into my eyes. "You have an almost citrusy scent. Sweet, but not too sweet."

His expression removed my last trace of doubt. I was sure now—Ethan loved me as much as I loved him. I smiled, feeling light-headed and breathless as he wrapped his hand around mine, his other still gripping the handle of the pram. We had held hands many times before, but this time was different. It was a precursor to something

more. Sure enough, Ethan pulled me against him. Then
he closed his eyes, buried his face in my neck, and inhaled.

"Yeah. You smell like an orange," he whispered. "An
orange in your stocking on Christmas morning."

An electrical charge passed through my body, and I
learned what it means to be weak in the knees. I closed
my eyes and put my arms around Ethan's shoulders, holding on tightly. Then, right in the middle of Holland Park,
amid footballers and dogs and babies, Ethan and I shared
our first real kiss. I'm not sure how long it lasted—ten
seconds or five minutes or something in between—but I
do know that everything in the world seemed to halt, except our hearts, thudding against each other. I remember
his warm hand slipping up under my jacket and shirt, his
long, slender fingers pressing into my back. I remember
thinking how much I wanted to feel all of his skin against
mine.

When we finally separated, Ethan said my name in a
way nobody had ever said it, his voice filled with equal
parts affection and desire. My eyes welled as I looked into
his. He was still Ethan, the scrawny kid on the playground
and my best friend. But he was also someone new.

"I think you know the real reason Sondrine and I broke
up," he said.

"Yeah. I think I do," I whispered.

I could feel myself beaming, bursting with anticipation
of what was to come. That afternoon and every day to follow. I hooked my hand over his elbow, as we turned the
pram around and headed toward home.

two years later

It is a brilliant summer day in London. I am waiting in Holland Park, wearing an ivory gown made of chiffon so soft I can't stop touching it. The dress comes to a *V* in the back, and the front is gathered over the bustline and accented with a shimmering of beads. The skirt is a loose A-line—romantic and simple—and it sways just right in the breeze. The woman at the Kensington bridal shop told me that the design was inspired by the Edwardian era—which sounded like something Ethan would love. It was the first dress I tried on, but when you know something is right, you just know.

As the string quartet begins to play, I peek around the corner of the Belvedere, into the gardens, and allow myself a glimpse of Ethan. We've only been apart twenty-four hours, but for us, it is a long stretch. Whether it is our separation, his Armani suit, or the emotion of the day, he has never looked more handsome. I feel a tightening in my chest, and take rapid, shallow breaths to keep from crying. I don't want to ruin my mascara so early in the day. For a moment, I wish I had my father to lean on or a bridesmaid to trail behind. But no, I made the right decision. I am walking solo on my wedding day, not out of spite or to make a statement, but rather as my own private symbol of how far I've come.

I take a deep breath and round the corner toward the gardens. Ethan is now in full view. I can see in his face that he thinks I look beautiful, and I can't wait to hear him put his feelings into words later. No one can express himself as he can. I keep my eyes locked with his. I am finally beside him.

"Hi," he whispers.

"Hi," I whisper back as the minister begins to speak.

The ceremony is short, despite the hours Ethan and I spent crafting our vows. We kept some parts traditional, discarded the rest, but every word is imbued with our own meaning. At the end, Ethan's eyes are damp and red-rimmed. He leans forward and brushes his lips against mine. I kiss my husband back, memorizing the moment, the feel of the sun on my skin, the scent of wildflowers in the arch around us, the sound of applause and snapping cameras and the jubilant notes of Beethoven's "Ode to Joy."

I feel buoyant as Ethan and I turn, hand in hand, and face our guests. I see my mother first, dabbing at her eyes with a lace handkerchief. My dad sits beside her, holding Thomas and John. My parents are thrilled that I found true love, and that I found it with a Stanford-educated novelist, whose book about finding love in unexpected places is an international bestseller. I doubt if my parents will ever change—they will always care a lot about money and material things and image, but I also know that part of our rift was caused by worry and concern for a child. I understand these emotions now.

As Ethan and I walk down the garden path, we smile at our other guests. I see my brother and Lauren, who is newly pregnant . . . Ethan's mother and father, who by all appearances were rekindling a romance at last night's rehearsal dinner . . . Annalise, Greg, and sweet, little Hannah, who is about to turn three . . . Martin and his new girlfriend, Lucy . . . Phoebe, whom I have grown to appreciate, and almost like after a few cocktails . . . Charlotte and John with Natalie . . . Meg, Yossi, and their son, Lucas . . . Geoffrey and Sondrine, who, much to Ethan's and my amusement, are recently engaged.

Then I spot them in the back row. Rachel and Dex with their baby daughter, Julia, a clone of her mother, but with Dexter's dark, wavy hair. She is wearing the pink smocked dress I sent for her first birthday. As I pass them, I point to the blue silk trim from Thomas and John's worn-out baby blankets, now a ribbon tied around my bouquet of white lilies. Rachel and I don't talk often, but I did tell her about my plan to use the ribbon as my "something blue." I could tell she was touched, pleased to play an indirect role in our day.

"You're gorgeous!" she mouths to me now.

Dex smiles at me, almost fondly, and I acknowledge him with a pleasant nod. It is hard to believe we were together for seven years. He now seems to be nothing more than an acquaintance with exceptionally good hair.

As we come to the end of the path, I turn back to face Ethan. Then we scoop up Thomas and John, who have broken free of my dad and chased after us.

"Are we married yet, Mummy?" they ask in the British accent they did not learn at home.

"Yes!" I laugh.

"Yes! We *are* married!" Ethan says.

At last.

I think back to that autumn day when Ethan proposed. We were on a weekend trip to Edinburgh, celebrating my new job as a fund-raiser for the Adopt-A-Minefield organization. After checking into our hotel, we decided to climb Arthur's Seat, a small mountain overlooking the ancient city. As we rested on the hillside and admired the sweeping views below, Ethan presented me with a tiny slip of paper so worn it felt like velvet. Upon closer examination, I could see that it was the note I had given him in the fifth grade. The "Will you go out with me?" note, its *yes* box checked with a red-colored pencil.

"Where in the *world* did you find this?" I said, feeling giddy that he had preserved the oldest piece of our history together.

"I found it in a box of old papers," he said, smiling. "I thought I had given it back to you, but I guess I never did?"

"No. You just told me yes at recess. Remember?"

"I guess so." Ethan nodded and then said, "Turn it over."

I did, and on the other side, I could see that he had written a question of his own.

Will you marry me?

I looked up, startled. Then I cried and said yes, *yes*! Ethan's hands trembled slightly as he removed a small box from his jacket pocket, opened it, and slid a sparkling cushion-cut diamond ring onto my finger.

"It doesn't take vows or genetics to be a family. We are one already," Ethan said. "But I want to make it *official*. I want to make it *forever*."

Then, always one to capture a moment on film, he extended his arm and snapped our engagement photo. I knew my hair was messy from the wind and that both of our noses were red and running from the cold, but I didn't care. I had learned to let those surface issues go, to value content over form. I knew that every time I'd look at that picture of us on the mountain in Scotland, I would see no imperfections, and would only think of Ethan's words. *I want to make it official. I want to make it forever.*

So on this joyful June day, below skies so blue they look airbrushed, we are just that: an official family, embarking on our forever.

Later, after we all have moved into the Belvedere for a champagne brunch, the toasts to Ethan and me begin. Some people joke about our fifth-grade romance. Others reference our hectic life as the parents of twins, marveling at how we do it all. Everyone says how happy they are for us.

Then, when I think that the last toast is over, Rachel stands tentatively and clears her throat. She seems nervous, but perhaps I just know how much she hates giving speeches.

"Nothing could make me prouder or happier than being here to witness the marriage of two such close friends," she starts, looking up from an index card and glancing around the room. "I have known Darcy and Ethan for what feels like forever, and so I know what fine people they are. I also know that they are *that* much better together." She pauses, her eyes meeting Ethan's, then mine. "I guess that's the power of true love and true friendship. . . . I guess that's what it's really all about." She raises her glass, smiles, and says, "So here's to Ethan and Darcy, true love and true friendship."

As everyone applauds and sips champagne, I smile back at Rachel, thinking that she got it just right. Love and friendship. They are what make us who we are, and what can change us, if we let them.

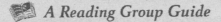 **A Reading Group Guide**

1. Many readers of *Something Borrowed* expressed doubts at being able to read and enjoy a book written from Darcy's point of view. Were you reluctant to read her story? Did your feelings about her ever change? If so, at what point in the story?

2. What do you view as Darcy's greatest weakness? Could this also be considered her greatest strength? If so, how?

3. What do you think caused Darcy's breakup with Marcus? Do you think Marcus was more or less responsible for it than Darcy was?

4. In many ways this is a story about personal growth and transformation. Do you think people can fundamentally change? How difficult did it seem for Darcy to change? What role did Ethan play in those changes? What role did her pregnancy play?

5. What do you think would have become of Darcy if she had not become pregnant? If she hadn't gone to London? What would some of the key differences be living in London as opposed to New York? Do you think some of these differences helped Darcy evolve?

6. How do you think Darcy's relationship with her mother plays a role in the person she is?

7. In what ways are Dex, Marcus, and Ethan different? In what ways are they similar? Do you think their similarities are true of men in general?

8. Where do you see Darcy and Rachel in five years? Ten?

9. If you were Darcy, would you have been able to forgive Rachel? Would you have invited her to your wedding? Do you feel there is a line that can be crossed in friendship where forgiveness isn't possible?

10. What are your views regarding the closing sentences of the book: "Love and friendship. They are what make us who we are, and what can change us, if we let them."?

For more reading group suggestions, visit
www.readinggroupgold.com.

Enjoy a sneak peak into the novels of Emily Giffin,
and discover why millions of readers all over the world
have fallen in love with them . . .

something borrowed

Now available from St. Martin's Paperbacks

Emily Giffin's debut novel about young Manhattan
attorney Rachel White—always responsible, always
the "good girl." Until she does the unthinkable and
falls in love with her best friend's fiancé . . .

baby proof

Now available in trade paperback from St. Martin's Griffin

First comes love, then comes marriage. Then comes
. . . a baby carriage? *Baby Proof* is a thought-provok-
ing and endlessly entertaining novel that explores the
question of whether there is ever a deal-breaker when
it comes to true love.

love the one you're with

Now available in trade paperback from St. Martin's Griffin

Emily Giffin's powerful and emotionally compelling
novel in which one woman finds herself at the
crossroads of true love and real life, asking herself:
how can I truly love the one I'm with when I can't
forget the one who got away?

something borrowed

I was in the fifth grade the first time I thought about turning thirty. My best friend Darcy and I came across a perpetual calendar in the back of the phone book, where you could look up any date in the future, and by using this little grid determine what the day of the week would be. So we located our birthdays in the following year, mine in May and hers in September. I got Wednesday, a school night. She got a Friday. A small victory, but typical. Darcy was always the lucky one. Her skin tanned more quickly, her hair feathered more easily, and she didn't need braces. Her moonwalk was superior, as were her cartwheels and her front handsprings (I couldn't do a hand-spring at all). She had a better sticker collection. More Michael Jackson pins. Forenza sweaters in turquoise, red, *and* peach (my mother allowed me none—said they were too trendy and expensive). And a pair of fifty-dollar Guess jeans with zippers at the ankles (ditto). Darcy had double-pierced ears and a sibling—even if it was just a brother, it was better than being an only child as I was.

But at least I was a few months older and she would never quite catch up. That's when I decided to check out my thirtieth birthday—in a year so far away that it sounded like science fiction. It fell on a Sunday, which meant that my dashing husband and I would secure a responsible babysitter for our two (possibly three) children on that Saturday evening, dine at a fancy French restaurant with cloth napkins, and stay out past midnight, so technically we would be celebrating on my actual birthday. I would have just won a big case—somehow proven that an innocent man didn't do it. And my husband would toast me: "To Rachel, my beautiful wife, the mother of my children, and the finest lawyer in Indy." I shared my fantasy with Darcy as we discovered that her thirtieth birthday fell on a Monday. Bummer for her. I watched her purse her lips as she processed this information.

"You know, Rachel, who cares what day of the week we turn thirty?" she said, shrugging a smooth, olive shoulder. "We'll be old by then. Birthdays don't matter when you get that old."

I thought of my parents, who were in their thirties, and their lackluster approach to their own birthdays. My dad had just given my mom a toaster for her birthday because ours broke the week before. The new one toasted four slices at a time instead of just two. It wasn't much of a gift. But my mom had seemed pleased enough with her new appliance; nowhere did I detect the disappointment that I felt when my Christmas stash didn't quite meet expectations. So Darcy was probably right. Fun stuff like birthdays wouldn't matter as much by the time we reached thirty.

The next time I really thought about being thirty was our senior year in high school, when Darcy and I started watching the show *Thirtysomething* together. It wasn't one of our favorites—we preferred cheerful sitcoms like

Who's the Boss? and *Growing Pains*—but we watched it anyway. My big problem with *Thirtysomething* was the whiny characters and their depressing issues that they seemed to bring upon themselves. I remember thinking that they should grow up, suck it up. Stop pondering the meaning of life and start making grocery lists. That was back when I thought my teenage years were dragging and my twenties would surely last forever.

Then I reached my twenties. And the early twenties did seem to last forever. When I heard acquaintances a few years older lament the end of their youth, I felt smug, not yet in the danger zone myself. I had plenty of time. Until about age twenty-seven, when the days of being carded were long gone and I began to marvel at the sudden acceleration of years (reminding myself of my mother's annual monologue as she pulled out our Christmas decorations) and the accompanying lines and stray gray hairs. At twenty-nine the real dread set in, and I realized that in a lot of ways I might as well be thirty. But not quite. Because I could still say that I was in my twenties. I still had something in common with college seniors.

I realize thirty is just a number, that you're only as old as you feel and all of that. I also realize that in the grand scheme of things, thirty is still young. But it's not *that* young. It is past the most ripe, prime childbearing years, for example. It is too old to, say, start training for an Olympic medal. Even in the best die-of-old-age scenario, you are still about one-third of the way to the finish line. So I can't help feeling uneasy as I perch on an overstuffed maroon couch in a dark lounge on the Upper West Side at my surprise birthday party, organized by Darcy, who is still my best friend.

Tomorrow is the Sunday that I first contemplated as a fifth-grader playing with our phone book. After tonight my twenties will be over, a chapter closed forever. The feeling I have reminds me of New Year's Eve, when the countdown is coming and I'm not quite sure whether to grab my camera or just live in the moment. Usually I grab the camera and later regret it when the picture doesn't turn out. Then I feel enormously let down and think to myself that the night would have been more fun if it didn't mean quite so much, if I weren't forced to analyze where I've been and where I'm going.

Like New Year's Eve, tonight is an ending and a beginning. I don't like endings and beginnings. I would always prefer to churn about in the middle. The worst thing about this particular end (of my youth) and beginning (of middle age) is that for the first time in my life, I realize that I don't know where I'm going. My wants are simple: a job that I like and a guy whom I love. And on the eve of my thirtieth, I must face that I am 0 for 2.

First, I am an attorney at a large New York firm. By definition this means that I am miserable. Being a lawyer just isn't what it's cracked up to be—it's nothing like *L.A. Law,* the show that caused applications to law schools to skyrocket in the early nineties. I work excruciating hours for a mean-spirited, anal-retentive partner, doing mostly tedious tasks, and that sort of hatred for what you do for a living begins to chip away at you. So I have memorized the mantra of the law-firm associate: *I hate my job and will quit soon.* Just as soon as I pay off my loans. Just as soon as I make next year's bonus. Just as soon as I think of something else to do that will pay the rent. Or find someone who will pay it for me.

Which brings me to my second point: I am alone in a city of millions. I have plenty of friends, as proven by the solid turnout tonight. Friends to Rollerblade with. Friends to summer with in the Hamptons. Friends to meet on a Thursday night after work for a drink or two or three. And I have Darcy, my best friend from home, who is all of the above. But everybody knows that friends are not enough, although I often claim they are just to save face around my married and engaged girlfriends. I did not plan on being alone in my thirties, even my early thirties. I wanted a husband by now; I wanted to be a bride in my twenties. But I have learned that you can't just create your own timetable and will it to come true. So here I am on the brink of a new decade, realizing that being alone makes my thirties daunting, and being thirty makes me feel more alone.

The situation seems all the more dismal because my oldest and best friend has a glamorous PR job and is freshly engaged. Darcy is still the lucky one. I watch her now, telling a story to a group of us, including her fiancé. Dex and Darcy are an exquisite couple, lean and tall with matching dark hair and green eyes. They are among New York's beautiful people. The well-groomed couple registering for fine china and crystal on the sixth floor at Bloomingdale's. You hate their smugness but can't resist staring at them when you're on the same floor searching for a not-too-expensive gift for the umpteenth wedding you've been invited to without a date. You strain to glimpse her ring, and are instantly sorry you did. She catches you staring and gives you a disdainful once-over. You wish you hadn't worn your tennis shoes to Bloomingdale's. She is probably thinking that the footwear may be part of your problem. You buy your Waterford vase and get the hell out of there.

"So the lesson here is: if you ask for a Brazilian bikini wax, make sure you specify. Tell them to leave a landing strip or else you can wind up hairless, like a ten-year-old!" Darcy finishes her bawdy tale, and everybody laughs. Except Dex, who shakes his head, as if to say, what a piece of work my fiancée is.

"Okay. I'll be right back," Darcy suddenly says. "Tequila shots for one and all!"

As she moves away from the group toward the bar, I think back to all of the birthdays we have celebrated together, all of the benchmarks we reached together, benchmarks that I always reached first. I got my driver's license before she did, could drink legally before she could. Being older, if only by a few months, used to be a good thing. But now our fortunes have reversed. Darcy has an extra summer in her twenties—a perk of being born in the fall. Not that it matters as much for her: when you're engaged or married, turning thirty just isn't the same thing.

Darcy is now leaning over the bar, flirting with the twenty-something, aspiring actor/bartender whom she has already told me she would "totally do" if she were single. As if Darcy would ever be single. She said once in high school, "I don't break up, I trade up." She kept her word on that, and she always did the dumping. Throughout our teenage years, college, and every day of our twenties, she has been attached to someone. Often she has more than one guy hanging around, hoping.

It occurs to me that I could hook up with the bartender. I am totally unencumbered—haven't even been on a date in nearly two months. But it doesn't seem like something one should do at age thirty. One-night stands are for girls in their twenties. Not that I would know. I have followed an orderly, Goody Two-shoes path with no deviations. I got straight As in high school, went to college, graduated magna cum laude, took the LSAT, went straight to law school and to a big law firm after that. No backpacking in Europe, no crazy stories, no unhealthy, lustful relationships. No secrets. No intrigue. And now it seems too late for any of that. Because that stuff would just further delay my goal of finding a husband, settling down, having children and a happy home with grass and a garage and a toaster that toasts four slices at once.

So I feel unsettled about my future and somewhat

regretful about my past. I tell myself that there will be time to ponder tomorrow. Right now I will have fun. It is the sort of thing that a disciplined person can simply decide. And I am exceedingly disciplined—the kind of child who did her homework on Friday afternoons right after school, the kind of woman (as of tomorrow, I am no longer any part girl) who flosses every night and makes her bed every morning.

Darcy returns with the shots but Dex refuses his, so Darcy insists that I do two. Before I know it, the night starts to take on that blurry quality, when you cross over from being buzzed to drunk, losing track of time and the precise order of things. Apparently Darcy has reached that point even sooner because she is now dancing on the bar. Spinning and gyrating in a little red halter dress and three-inch heels.

"Stealing the show at your party," Hillary, my closest friend from work, says to me under her breath. "She's shameless."

I laugh. "Yeah. Par for the course."

Darcy lets out a yelp, claps her hands over her head, and beckons me with a come-hither expression that would appeal to any man who has ever fancied girl-on-girl action. "Rachel! Rachel! C'mere!"

Of course she knows that I will not join her. I have never danced on a bar. I wouldn't know what to do up there besides fall. I shake my head and smile, a polite refusal. We all wait for her next move, which is to swivel her hips in perfect time to the music, bend over slowly, and then whip her body upright again, her long hair spilling every which way. The limber maneuver reminds me of her perfect imitation of Tawny Kitaen in the Whitesnake video "Here I Go Again," how she used to roll around doing splits on the hood of her father's BMW, to the delight of the pubescent neighborhood boys. I glance at Dex, who in these moments can never quite decide whether to be amused or annoyed. To say that the man has patience is an understatement. Dex and I have this in common.

"Happy birthday, Rachel!" Darcy yells. "Let's all raise a glass to Rachel!"

Which everyone does. Without taking their eyes off her.

A minute later, Dex whisks her down from the bar, slings her over his shoulder, and deposits her on the floor next to me in one fluid motion. Clearly he has done this before. "All right," he announces. "I'm taking our little party-planner home."

Darcy plucks her drink off the bar and stamps her foot. "You're not the boss of me, Dex! Is he, Rachel?" As she asserts her independence, she stumbles and sloshes her martini all over Dex's shoe.

Dex grimaces. "You're wasted, Darce. This isn't fun for anyone but you."

"Okay. Okay. I'll go . . . I'm feeling kind of sick anyway," she says, looking queasy.

"Are you going to be okay?"

"I'll be fine. Don't you worry," she says, now playing the role of brave little sick girl.

I thank her for my party, tell her that it was a total surprise—which is a lie, because I knew Darcy would capitalize on my thirtieth to buy a new outfit, throw a big bash, and invite as many of her friends as my own. Still, it was nice of her to have the party, and I am glad that she did. She is the kind of friend who always makes things feel special. She hugs me hard and says she'd do anything for me, and what would she do without me, her maid of honor, the sister she never had. She is gushing, as she always does when she drinks too much.

Dex cuts her off. "Happy birthday, Rachel. We'll talk to you tomorrow." He gives me a kiss on the cheek.

"Thanks, Dex," I say. "Good night."

I watch him usher her outside, holding her elbow after she nearly trips on the curb. *Oh, to have such a caretaker.* To be able to drink with reckless abandon and know that there will be someone to get you home safely.

Sometime later Dex reappears in the bar. "Darcy lost her purse. She thinks she left it here. It's small, silver," he says. "Have you seen it?"

"She lost her new Chanel bag?" I shake my head and laugh because it is just like Darcy to lose things. Usually I keep track of them for her, but I went off duty on my birthday. Still, I help Dex search for the purse, finally spotting it under a bar stool.

As he turns to leave, Dex's friend Marcus, one of his groomsmen, convinces him to stay. "C'mon, man. Hang out for a minute."

So Dex calls Darcy at home and she slurs her consent, tells him to have fun without her. Although she is probably thinking that such a thing is not possible.

Gradually my friends peel away, saying their final happy birthdays. Dex and I outlast everyone, even Marcus. We sit at the bar making conversation with the actor/bartender who has an "Amy" tattoo and zero interest in an aging lawyer. It is after two when we decide that it's time to go. The night feels more like midsummer than spring, and the warm air infuses me with sudden hope: *This will be the summer I meet my guy.*

Dex hails me a cab, but as it pulls over he says, "How about one more bar? One more drink?"

"Fine," I say. "Why not?"

We both get in and he tells the cabbie to just drive, that he has to think about where next. We end up in Alphabet City at a bar on Seventh and Avenue B, aptly named 7B.

It is not an upbeat scene—7B is dingy and smoke-filled. I like it anyway—it's not sleek and it's not a dive striving to be cool because it's not sleek.

Dex points to a booth. "Have a seat. I'll be right with you." Then he turns around. "What can I get you?"

I tell him whatever he's having, and sit and wait for him in the booth. I watch him say something to a girl at the bar wearing army-green cargo pants and a tank top that says "Fallen Angel." She smiles and shakes her head. "Omaha" is playing in the background. It is one of those songs that seems melancholy and cheerful at the same time.

A moment later Dex slides in across from me, pushing a beer my way. "Newcastle," he says. Then he smiles, crinkly lines appearing around his eyes. "You like?"

I nod and smile.

From the corner of my eye, I see Fallen Angel turn on her bar stool and survey Dex, absorbing his chiseled features, wavy hair, full lips. Darcy complained once that Dex garners more stares and double takes than she does. Yet, unlike his female counterpart, Dex seems not to notice the attention. Fallen Angel now casts her eyes my way, likely wondering what Dex is doing with someone so average. I hope that she thinks we're a couple. Tonight nobody has to know that I am only a member of the wedding party.

Dex and I talk about our jobs and our Hamptons share that begins in another week and a lot of things. But Darcy does not come up and neither does their September wedding.

After we finish our beers we move over to the jukebox, fill it with dollar bills, searching for good songs. I push the code for "Thunder Road" twice because it is my favorite song. I tell him this.

"Yeah. Springsteen's at the top of my list, too. Ever seen him in concert?"

"Yeah," I say. "Twice. *Born in the U.S.A.* and *Tunnel of Love.*"

I almost tell him that I went with Darcy in high school, dragged her along even though she much preferred groups like Poison and Bon Jovi. But I don't bring this up. Because then he will remember to go home to her and I don't want to be alone in my dwindling moments of twentysomething-ness. Obviously I'd rather be with a boyfriend, but Dex is better than nothing.

It is last call at 7B. We get a couple more beers and return to our booth. Sometime later we are in a cab again, going north on First Avenue. "Two stops," Dex tells our cabbie, because we live on opposite sides of Central Park. Dex is holding Darcy's Chanel purse, which looks small and out of place in his large hands. I glance at the silver dial of his Rolex, a gift from Darcy. It is just shy of four o'clock.

We sit silently for a stretch of ten or fifteen blocks, both of us looking out of our respective side windows, until the cab hits a pothole and I find myself lurched into the middle of the backseat, my leg grazing his. Then suddenly, out of nowhere, Dex is kissing me. Or maybe I kiss him. Somehow we are kissing. My mind goes blank as I listen to the soft sound of our lips meeting again and again. At some point, Dex taps on the Plexiglas partition and tells the driver, between kisses, that it will just be one stop after all.

We arrive on the corner of Seventy-third and Third, near my apartment. Dex hands the driver a twenty and does not wait for change. We spill out of the taxi, kissing more on the sidewalk and then in front of Jose, my door-man. We kiss the whole way up in the elevator. I am pressed against the elevator wall, my hands on the back of his head. I am surprised by how soft his hair is.

I fumble with my key, turning it the wrong way in the lock as Dex keeps his arms around my waist, his lips on my neck and the side of my face. Finally the door is open, and we are kissing in the middle of my studio, standing upright, leaning on nothing but each other. We stumble over to my made bed, complete with tight hospital corners.

"Are you drunk?" His voice is a whisper in the dark.

"No," I say. Because you always say no when you're drunk. And even though I am, I have a lucid instant where I consider clearly what was missing in my twenties and what I wish to find in my thirties. It strikes me that, in a sense, I can have both on this momentous birthday night. Dex can be my secret, my last chance for a dark twenty-something chapter, and he can also be a prelude of sorts—a promise of someone like him to come. Darcy is in my mind, but she is being pushed to the back, overwhelmed by a force stronger than our friendship and my own conscience. Dex moves over me. My eyes are closed, then open, then closed again.

And then, somehow, I am having sex with my best friend's fiancé.

baby proof

It was subtle at first, as changes in relationships typically are, so it is hard to pinpoint the genesis. But, looking back, I think it all began when Ben and I went on a ski trip with Annie and Ray, the couple who had set us up on our first date. I had known Annie since our bingeing college days, so I noticed right away that she was sticking with Perrier. At first she claimed to be on antibiotics for a sinus infection, but the whole antibiotic excuse had never slowed her in the past so I dragged the truth out of her. She was eight weeks pregnant.

"Was it planned?" I blurted out, thinking surely it had been an accident. Annie adored her career as a documentary filmmaker and had a million different causes on the side. She had never expressed an interest in having children, and I couldn't fathom her making time for motherhood.

Annie and Ray clasped hands and nodded in unison.

"But I thought you didn't want kids," I said.

"We didn't want kids right *away,*" Annie said. "But we feel ready now. Although I guess you're never completely ready!" She laughed in a high-pitched, schoolgirlish way, her cheeks flushing pink.

"Hmm," I said.

Ben kicked me under the table and said, "Well, congratulations, guys! This is awesome news." Then he shot me a stern look and said, "Isn't that wonderful news, Claudia?"

"Yes. Wonderful," I said, but I couldn't help feeling betrayed. Ben and I were going to lose our favorite traveling companions, our only close friends who were as unfettered as we were by babies and all their endless accoutrements.

We finished dinner, our conversation dominated by talk of children and Westchester real estate.

Later, when Ben and I were alone in our room, he chastised me for being so transparently unsupportive. "You could have at least *pretended* to be happy for them," he said. "Instead of grilling them about birth control."

"I was just so shocked," I said. "Did you have any idea?"

Ben shook his head and with a fleeting expression of envy said, "No. But I think it's great."

"Don't tell me you want them now, too?" I asked him, mostly joking.

Ben answered quickly, but his words registered flat and false. "Of course not," he said. "Don't be ridiculous."

Over the next few months, things only got more troubling. Ben became all too interested in the progress of Annie's pregnancy. He admired the ultrasound photos, even taping one to our refrigerator. I told him that we were not a "tape things to the refrigerator" kind of family.

"Jeez, Claudia. Lighten up," Ben said, appearing agitated as he pulled down the murky black-and-white image and slapped it into a drawer. "You really should be happier for them. They're our *best* friends, for chrissake."

A short time after that, right before Annie and Ray had their baby, Ben and I planned a last-minute weekend getaway to the resort where we had been married. It was early January when the abrupt disappearance of Christmas decorations and tourists always makes Manhattan seem so naked and bleak, and Ben said he couldn't wait until early March for our tentatively planned trip to Belize. I remember tossing some shorts and a new red bikini into my leather duffel and remarking how nice it was to have spontaneity in our relationship, the freedom to fly off at a moment's notice.

Ben said, "Yes. There are some wonderful things about our life together."

This sentence struck me as melancholy—even ominous—but I didn't press him on it. I didn't even pressure him to talk when he was uncharacteristically taciturn on our flight down to the Caribbean.

I didn't really worry until later that night when we were settling into our room, unpacking our clothes and toiletries. I momentarily stopped to inspect the view of the sea outside our room, and as I turned back toward my suitcase, I caught a glimpse of Ben in the mirror. His mouth was curled into a remorseful frown. I panicked, remembering what my sister, Maura, once said about men who cheat. She is an expert on the topic as her husband, Scott, had been unfaithful with at least two women she knew of. "Look out if they're really mean or really nice. Like if they start giving you flowers and jewelry for no reason," she had said. "Or taking you away on a romantic getaway. It's the guilt. They're trying to make up for something." I tried to calm down, telling myself that I was being paranoid. Ben and I always took spontaneous trips together; we never needed a reason.

Still, I wanted to dispel the lingering images of Ben pressed against a sweaty bohemian lover, so I sat on the bed, kicked off my flip-flops, and said, "Ben. Talk to me. What's on your mind?" He swallowed hard and sat next to me. The bed bounced slightly under his weight and the motion made me feel even more nervous. "I don't know how to say this," Ben said, his voice cracking. "So I'll just come out with it."

I nodded, feeling queasy. "Go ahead."

"I think I might want kids after all."

I felt a rush of relief and even laughed out loud. "You scared me." I laughed again, louder, and then opened a Red Stripe from the minibar.

"I'm serious, Claudia."

"Where is all of this coming from? Annie and Ray?"

"Maybe. I don't know. It's just . . . it's just this *feeling* I have," Ben said, making a fist over his heart.

At least he hasn't cheated on me, I thought. A betrayal of that magnitude could never be erased or forgotten. His fleeting wish for a child would surely go away. But as Ben continued to spout off his list of reasons why a baby might be a good thing—stuff about showing children the world, doing things better than our parents had done—my relief gave way to something else. It was a sense of losing control. A sense that something was slipping away.

I tried to stay calm as I delivered a rather eloquent speech. I told him that all of that parenthood stuff wasn't who we were. I said that our relationship was built upon our unique twoness, the concept that three or more is a crowd. I pointed out that we couldn't have taken this last-minute trip. We'd be anchored to home all the time.

"But we'd have *other* things," Ben said. "And what if we really are missing out on something great? I've never heard a single person say they regret having a child."

"Would they admit it if they did?" I said.

"Maybe not," Ben said. "But the point is, I don't think they ever would."

"I *totally* disagree . . . I mean, why are there boarding schools? The mcre existence of boarding schools proves something, right?" I asked. I was partly kidding about the boarding schools, but Ben didn't laugh.

I sighed and then decided to change the subject altogether, focus on having fun. Show Ben what we'd be missing with children.

"Let's get changed and go to dinner," I said, turning up "One Love" on our portable CD player and thinking that there's nothing like a little Bob Marley to put you in a childfree, unencumbered state of mind.

But despite my best efforts to have a good time, the rest of our weekend passed with an increasing tension. Things felt forced between us, and Ben's mood went from quiet to lugubrious. On our third and final night on the island, we took a cab to Asolare, a restaurant with incredible views of Cruz Bay. We ate in virtual silence, commenting only on the sunset and our perfectly prepared lobster tail. Just as our waitress brought us our coffee and sorbet, I looked at Ben and said, "You know what? We had a *deal*."

As soon as the words came out, I knew how utterly ridiculous I sounded. Marriage is never a done deal. Not even when you have children together, although that certainly helps your case. And the irony of that seemed overwhelmingly sad.

Ben tugged on his earlobe and said, "I want to be a father."

"Fine. Fine," I said. "But do you want a baby more than you want to be my husband?"

He reached out and put one hand over mine. "I want *both*," he said as he squeezed my fingers.

"Well. You can't have both," I said, trying to keep the angry edge out of my voice.

I waited for him to say that of course he'd always pick me. That it was the only thing in the world he was really sure of. "So? Which is it?" I said.

It wasn't supposed to be a test, but it suddenly felt like

one. Ben stared down at his cappuccino for a long time. Then he moved his hand from mine and slowly stirred three cubes of sugar into his mug.

When he finally looked up at me, there was guilt and grief in his gray-green eyes, and I knew I had my answer.

love the one you're with

It happened exactly one hundred days after I married Andy, almost to the minute of our half-past-three-o'clock ceremony. I know this fact not so much because I was an overeager newlywed keen on observing trivial relationship landmarks, but because I have a mild case of OCD that compels me to keep track of things. Typically, I count insignificant things, like the steps from my apartment to the nearest subway (341 in comfortable shoes, a dozen more in heels); the comically high occurrence of the phrase "amazing connection" in any given episode of *The Bachelor* (always in the double digits); the guys I've kissed in my thirty-three years (nine). Or, as it was on that rainy, cold afternoon in January, the number of days I had been married before I saw him smack-dab in the middle of the crosswalk of Eleventh and Broadway.

From the outside, say if you were a cabdriver watching frantic jaywalkers scramble to cross the street in the final seconds before the light changed, it was only a mundane, urban snapshot: two seeming strangers, with little in common but their flimsy black umbrellas, passing in an intersection, making fleeting eye contact, and exchanging stiff but not unfriendly hellos before moving on their way.

But inside was a very different story. Inside, I was reeling, churning, breathless as I made it onto the safety of the curb and into a virtually empty diner near Union Square. *Like seeing a ghost,* I thought, one of those expressions I've heard a thousand times but never fully registered until that moment. I closed my umbrella and unzipped my coat, my heart still pounding. As I watched a waitress wipe down a table with hard, expert strokes, I wondered why I was so startled by the encounter when there was something that seemed utterly inevitable about the moment. Not in any grand, destined sense; just in the quiet, stubborn way that unfinished business has of imposing its will on the unwilling.

After what seemed like a long time, the waitress noticed me standing behind the Please Wait to Be Seated sign and said, "Oh. I didn't see you there. Should've taken that sign down after the lunch crowd. Go ahead and sit anywhere."

Her expression struck me as so oddly empathetic that I wondered if she were a moonlighting clairvoyant, and actually considered confiding in her. Instead, I slid into a red vinyl booth in the back corner of the restaurant and vowed never to speak of it. To share my feelings with a friend would constitute an act of disloyalty to my husband. To tell my older and very cynical sister, Suzanne, might unleash a storm of caustic remarks about marriage and monogamy. To write of it in my journal would elevate its importance, something I was determined not to do. And to tell Andy would be some combination of stupid, self-destructive, and hurtful. I was bothered by the lie of omission, a black mark on our fledgling marriage, but decided it was for the best.

"What can I get you?" the waitress, whose name tag read *Annie,* asked me. She had curly red hair and a smattering of freckles, and I thought, *The sun will come out tomorrow.*

I only wanted a coffee, but as a former waitress, remembered how deflating it was when people only ordered a beverage, even in a lull between meals, so I asked for a coffee and a poppy seed bagel with cream cheese.

"Sure thing," she said, giving me a pleasant nod.

I smiled and thanked her. Then, as she turned toward the kitchen, I exhaled and closed my eyes, focusing on one thing: how much I loved Andy. I loved everything about him, including the things that would have exasperated most girls. I found it endearing the way he had trouble remembering people's names (he routinely called my former boss Fred, instead of Frank) or the lyrics to even the most iconic songs ("Billie Jean is not my mother"). And I only shook my head and smiled when he gave the same bum in Bryant Park a dollar a day for nearly a year—a bum who was likely a Range Rover-driving con artist. I loved Andy's confidence and compassion. I loved his sunny personality that matched his boy-next-door, blond, blue-eyed good looks. I felt lucky to be with a man who, after six long years with me, still did the half-stand upon my return from the ladies' room and drew sloppy, asymmetrical hearts in the condensation of our bathroom mirror. Andy loved *me,* and I'm not ashamed to say that this topped my reasons of why we were together, of why I loved him back.

"Did you want your bagel toasted?" Annie shouted from behind the counter.

"Sure," I said, although I had no real preference.

I let my mind drift to the night of Andy's proposal in Vail, how he had pretended to drop his wallet so that he could, in what clearly had been a much-rehearsed maneuver, retrieve it and appear on bended knee. I remember sipping champagne, my ring sparkling in the firelight, as I thought, *This is it. This is the moment every girl dreams of. This is the moment I have been dreaming of and planning for and counting on.*

Annie brought my coffee, and I wrapped my hands around the hot, heavy mug. I raised it to my lips, took a long sip, and thought of our year-long engagement—a year of parties and showers and whirlwind wedding plans. Talk of tulle and tuxedos, of waltzes and white chocolate cake. All leading up to that magical night. I thought of our misty-eyed vows. Our first dance to "What a Wonderful World." The warm, witty toasts to us—speeches filled with clichés that were actually true in our case: *perfect for each other . . . true love . . . meant to be.*

I remembered our flight to Hawaii the following morning, how Andy and I had held hands in our first-class seats, laughing at all the small things that had gone awry on our big day: *What part of "blend into the background" didn't the videographer get? Could it have rained any harder on the way to the reception? Had we ever seen his brother, James, so wasted?* I thought of our sunset honeymoon strolls, the candlelit dinners, and one particularly vivid morning that Andy and I had spent lounging on a secluded, half-moon beach called Lumahai on the north shore of Kauai. With soft white sand and dramatic lava rocks protruding from turquoise water, it was the most breathtaking piece of earth I had ever seen. At one point, as I was admiring the view, Andy rested his Stephen Ambrose book on our oversized beach towel, took both of my hands in his, and kissed me. I kissed him back, memorizing the moment. The sound of the waves crashing, the feel of the cool sea breeze on my face, the scent of lemons mixed with our coconut suntan lotion. When we separated, I told Andy that I had never been so happy. It was the truth.

But the best part came after the wedding, after the honeymoon, after our practical gifts were unpacked in our tiny apartment in Murray Hill—and the impractical, fancy ones were relegated to our downtown storage unit. It came as we settled into our husband-and-wife routine. Casual, easy, and real. It came every morning, as we sipped our coffee and talked as we got ready for work. It came when his name popped into my inbox every few hours. It came at night as we shuffled through our delivery menus, contemplating what to have for dinner and proclaiming that one day soon we'd actually use our stove. It came with every foot massage, every kiss, every time we undressed together in the dark. I trained my mind on these details. All the details that comprised our first one hundred days together.

Yet by the time Annie brought my bagel, I was back in that intersection, my heart thudding again. I suddenly knew that in spite of how happy I was to be spending my life with Andy, I wouldn't soon forget that moment, that tightness in my throat as I saw his face again. Even though I desperately wanted to forget it. *Especially* because I wanted to.

I sheepishly glanced at my reflection in the mirrored wall beside my booth. I had no business worrying about my appearance, and even less business feeling triumphant upon the discovery that I was, against all odds on an afternoon of running errands in the rain, having an extraordinarily good hair day. I also had a rosy glow, but I told myself that it was only the cold that had flushed my cheeks. Nothing else.

And that's when my cell phone rang and I heard his voice. A voice I hadn't heard in eight years and sixteen days.

"Was that really you?" he asked me. His voice was even deeper than I remembered, but otherwise it was like stepping back in time. Like finishing a conversation only hours old.

"Yes," I said.

"So," he said. "You still have the same cell number."

Then, after a considerable silence, one I stubbornly refused to fill, he added, "I guess some things don't change."

"Yes," I said again.

Because as much as I didn't want to admit it, he was sure right about that.

DEBORAH FEINGOLD

EMILY GIFFIN is a graduate of Wake Forest University and the University of Virginia School of Law. After practicing litigation at a Manhattan firm for several years, she moved to London to write full time. The author of four other *New York Times* bestselling novels, *Something Borrowed, Baby Proof, Love the One You're With,* and *Heart of the Matter,* she now lives in Atlanta with her husband and three young children.

Visit www.emilygiffin.com.

ISBN 978-0-312-54807-0

FOLLOWING THE SMASH-HIT
SOMETHING BORROWED COMES A STORY
OF BETRAYAL, REDEMPTION, AND FORGIVENESS

Darcy Rhone has always been able to rely on a few things: her beauty and charm. Her fiancé Dex. Her lifelong best friend Rachel. She never needed anything else. Or so she thinks until Dex calls off their dream wedding and she uncovers the ultimate betrayal. Blaming everyone but herself, Darcy flees to London and attempts to recreate her glamorous life on a new continent. But to her dismay, she discovers that her tried-and-true tricks no longer apply—and that her luck has finally expired. It is only then that she can begin her journey toward redemption, forgiveness, and true love.

"Witty and compelling."
—CHARLOTTE OBSERVER

"Giffin's writing is ___ rm and engaging.
___ s cheering for Darcy as
sh ___ in this captivating tale."
—BOOKLIST, "STARRED REVIEW"

"Darcy is Scarlett O'Hara set in modern day."
—NEWARK STAR-LEDGER

ISBN 978-0-312-54807-0
50799

9 780312 548070

EAN

U.S. $7.99
CAN. $9.99